MW01436446

ALSO BY PATRICIA STEELE
Living with Cystic Fibrosis (article)
A Roundabout Passage to Venice
Mind the Gap in Zip It Socks
Tangled like Music
Cooking DRUNK
Goodbye Balloon

The Callinda Beauvais Mystery Series:
Shoot the Moon
Wine Vines and Picasso

BY PATRICIA RUIZ STEELE
Spanish Pearls Series:
The Girl Immigrant
Silván Leaves
Ruiz Legacies - work in progress

Special Author's Note: The inset photo of a man playing his guitar on the book cover is my brother, Richard Bettencourt. Years ago, he asked me to tole paint pink dogwood blossoms on the face of his favorite guitar and I obliged. Taking a short cut I'd learned in paint class, I placed the body of his guitar (without the arm of course) into my oven so the light inside would dry the paint between coats. And then in a rush to go shopping one day, I decided to broil hamburgers for my family and forgot the guitar was inside. A burst of flame, a damaged guitar and many tears later…even though it was sort of repaired, it was never the same. I am very lucky that Rick still loves me. It was apropos to include him and his beautiful guitar covered in another layer of pink dogwood blossoms (yes, he asked me to do it again) on my book since Picasso's guitar painting wasn't allowed and you know what? I love this one better.

WINE, VINES and PICASSO

A Callinda Beauvais Mystery, Book Two

Patricia Steele

Patricia Steele

A sequel to *Shoot the Moon*

Author's Note:

Thank you for taking time to read Wine, Vines and Picasso. This is a work of fiction. Names, characters, businesses, places, events and incidents are either the products of the author's imagination or used in a fictitious manner. Any resemblance to actual persons, living or dead, or actual events is purely coincidental. I salute the family of Pablo Ruiz Picasso, because I took some literary license with his history. He now has new friends, part ownership in a winery near Jerez and a mystery to enhance his noted artist's biography. If there are mistakes in the story, they are my mistakes totally. However, the life lessons and values are real. I learned them from many people who have graced my life. Some, I still miss every day. Others are still touching my life with a smile.

Plumeria Press
Printed in the United States of America

ISBN: 978-0-9890013-9-7
Copyright @ 2015 by Patricia Steele
All rights reserved.

Cover artwork created by Edna Harris at Candy Wrapper Creations
Artwork photographed by Charlene Rule

www.patriciabbsteele.com
www.facebook.com/patriciabbsteele.com
www.amazon.com/author/patriciasteele

ACKNOWLEDGEMENTS

I want to thank my new Spanish friend, José Luis Sanchez Mesa whose town, Algodonales, resides a bit within my pages. He is painstakingly reading/translating both The Girl Immigrant and Silván Leaves from English into Spanish for his personal reading. He also created a documentary regarding how the descendants of Spanish immigrants have been impacted by their ancestors leaving Spain to begin new lives in America. It was great fun creating a video for him explaining my Spanish family history.

I thank my Ruiz ancestors, from southern Spain in and around Málaga, who truly believe we have a distant relationship to Pablo Ruiz Picasso. The misty myth has been fruit for conversation over the years until my insatiable obsession with genealogy found that the myth had roots. Also, I want to thank my French adopted family in Provence, who lived in "the old mill house" in Pertuis, where most of this story takes place and my tiny bit of French conversation salutes them.

I want to thank my French "daughter", Chloe Guerber-Cahuzac for proofreading my French conversation and answering my many questions about the culture and language that I had forgotten over the years. And thanks to my friend, Aurore Frenot, who helped me "find" the universities where my characters studied wines near her home in Provence.

And beta reader's invaluable thought-provoking suggestions, I could not have tightened up my story.

Neyda Bettencourt
Linda Dixon Schmalz
Lucinda E. Clarke
Jeannette Rhodes

As always, I thank my husband, J.D., for allowing me the silence and solitude to write to my heart's content.

One

A woman's overwrought voice slapped into Callinda Beauvais like an old wound on a rainy day. "*Bon jour*, Callie. *Qu'est-ce que tu voudrais faire? Je voudrais un…..*" The answering machine clicked off. Callie stood motionless in the middle of the room. *Why would Cendrine ask me what she should do… without telling me the problem?* She hadn't spoken to the family since the last grape harvest at the vineyard in Provence. Her niece had sounded anxious; a faint thread of hysteria was in her voice.

Callie glanced at her watch. *Nearly six p.m. in Oregon means it's three a.m. in France. I'll call her tomorrow.* She sank into a chair and gazed into her garden where patio lights twinkled in the dark corners of her courtyard. The quiet slammed into her. Not even imagining the image of Nate Oleander's face seemed to lift her spirits.

The puzzling message had just added another complex layer to some budding doubts she had in her personal life. Although Nate had released her from a self-made cocoon of widow's grief, she knew she might love again, but would she? Setting her jaw, she vowed to make changes in her life. With a ripple of urgency, Callie tossed clothes into a tote and loaded her car just after lunch the next day. Less than an hour later, she passed Grand Ronde's Indian Casino as she drove west from Portland toward the Pacific Ocean. She had to stop running. François was gone. Her mother was gone. Her best friend, Livvy, was happy. *Now it's my turn. François would want me to live again, wouldn't he?* Her lips quivered slightly as her fingers wrapped around the wheel. The thought tore at her insides.

Three years had elapsed since she'd been to her beach house in Neotsu, Oregon. During that time, she'd lived on past memories, refusing to allow a man in her life. The only things left were the raw sores of an aching heart. Until she met Nate. Callie analyzed their friendship as she drove her Audi across the mountain pass along the curving forest highway. She needed to think and think some more. Suddenly, she slapped her hand against the steering wheel. *Damn. I forgot to call Cendrine before I left.*

Later, burdened with a bag of groceries and a tote slung over her shoulder, she wrestled open the side door. It was exactly as she'd left it. The maintenance people kept it beautiful, clean. After tossing her bag in the bedroom and some food in the fridge, she opened a bottle of Cabernet. She'd drink goodbye to the past, toast the present and enjoy undisturbed, quiet peace regardless of her decision about Nate.

Bright blue sky peeked out of faint clouds. Far off, a boat drew a wake on the lake and the sound of an airplane carried across the water. After yanking some logs and starter kindling off the pile near the huge stone fireplace, she had a bright fire crackling in minutes. With an audible sigh, she reached for her wineglass, plopped her body down into deep cushions, stared into the fire and sipped. She reached for the telephone, dialed Cendrine and then puzzled when there was no answer. Then she closed her eyes.

Two hours later, Callie was stretched out on her couch fast asleep; a fire burned low and the wine glass sat empty. Dreams skittered across her brain, eyelids fluttering, François and Nate were in the boat racing across the lake and then her mother pointed toward her. *What?* Callie kept asking. *What, Mom?* She tossed and turned, groaning.

Callie's heartbeat accelerated, rushing her awake, her breath quick like the brush of angel's wings. She sat up and massaged her temples. "Nate in François' boat?" she whispered into the darkened cottage. Tears slid silently down her cheeks. A kaleidoscope of emotions cascaded through her body. Within seconds, she was crying and she couldn't stop. She knew her mother was telling her to bury the past and open the door to the future. Whimpering like an injured puppy, she pulled herself into a ball and stared into the dying flames. *Mom was right; people are put in our path as signposts to point us in the right direction.* Returning to her cottage was allowing her to heal. She would call Nate as soon as she got home again.

***

In Portland the following morning, a warm glow flowed through Callie as she sat in her best friend's office at Larkspur Insurance. "Cendrine left another message. I should fly to Pertuis. I can help and just......."

"...........run away?" Olivia struggled with irritation.

"I don't need to run away, Livvy. We're trading phone calls and frankly, I'm worried."

"Well, take Nate with you…after my wedding." Olivia's diamond earrings glimmered as the sun shifted through her office window. Her green eyes stared at Callie with a question.

"No, François' ghost would be between us. Of course it would."

Olivia Phillips bit her lip and heaved a heavy sigh.

Callie grinned. "Nate and I had a long talk last night after I'd falsely accused him of…well. You know why. We spent time under the stars…"

"You mean, in your hot tub?" Olivia perked up.

"He is really a lovely man, Livvy. Now back to work," she teased without answering. With a small wave, she left the office.

***

At dawn the next day, the phone woke Callie from a deep sleep. Her eyelashes fluttered and she jerked awake with a gasp. Twisting both hands beneath her pillow, she nuzzled deeper into its folds. The phone jangled again. Callie's tousled head lifted off the pillow a few inches, a swath of chestnut and silver bangs covered one eye.

"François? François, are you awake?" An eerie silence met her question as December's morning sun streamed through the bedroom window. Empty space met her questing fingers. And then her eyes popped open and reality swooped down like a hammer. She heaved herself onto her back. "Of course, François can't answer the damn phone." She was sick with the struggle within her. *I'm a widow. Say it!*

Flipping the covers off her small, satin-clad body, she jerked the coverlet upward. Goose bumps rose on her arms; she swore she saw the indentation of François' head on the other pillow. Would she ever adapt to widowhood? The morning's slip confused her. *It's Cendrine's phone messages. They've taken my mind back to Provence and of course, to François.*

A niggle of alarm wormed its way through her mind when ringing split the air again. Making a mad dash for the phone, her niece's words crashed together like a racing freight train. Listening intently to the garbled story, Callie's chin sank to her chest. "Slowly, *ma chérie*. And please, in English. My French needs some practice….."

"Callie...I cannot tell *grand-mère* and *grand-père*. Olivier took money from the vineyard's account. I do not know why. I'm scared and I do not know what to do and he...has disappeared. Please come help me."

Pressing her hand to her forehead, Callie closed her eyes. "Yes, *chérie*, I will come. Ask your father to please wait. We will tell your grandparents together. My heart aches for you, but there must be a good reason why...?"

Just when Callie thought her world was leveling out, her family dropped a pebble in the pond. Raking fingers through her chestnut hair, she lifted silver bangs off her forehead with a flip of her wrist. Still being part of François Beauvais' family touched her deeply. They were always there for her. Now it was her turn.

Why would Olivier do this and where was he? Sighing heavily, she started coffee perking. As its aroma wafted toward her, a plane reservation was already confirmed. And her mind had already flown toward France.

And Nate? He'd helped keep the clasp closed on her heart's memory box. Squeezing her eyes shut, she sniffed and wiped away moist eyes. But, would he ever be part of her soul like François? Would he ever understand her closeness to her Provence family? *Is Nate's understanding as important to me as being a Beauvais when the family needs me?*

She shrugged away the questions and rummaged around inside her closet. Jerking out luggage, she tossed her clothing in haphazardly. Filled with a riot of questions, she remembered Cendrine's words; Embezzled, disappeared, Spaniard, wine label, señorita riding a cork. Her hands stilled as she folded another blouse. *Olivier embezzling Beauvais Vineyard funds? Never! There must be a good reason why he took so much money, but where is he?*

A hard knot tightened in her stomach and she slumped on her bed.

"Cendrine's husband would no more steal money from the family vineyard than I would!"

Two
One week earlier

"*Señor* Olivier Benoit?" The Spanish accent was strong, unfamiliar; heavy breathing came clearly across the phone line.

"Yes, this is Olivier Benoit. How can I help you?"

"We must meet. I have information from your father."

"My father is dead." Olivier's breath hitched.

"I know this. I will visit you tomorrow."

Before Olivier could respond, the man had hung up.

Olivier Grant Benoit didn't move for a moment. When he looked up from his laptop, he gazed toward the many rows of Grenache grapevines outside his mullioned window. He'd inched it open a few minutes earlier to enjoy the crisp breeze on his face. And he tried to imagine the promised smell of thyme and rosemary that spring would bring.

After talking on the phone with his great-grandfather Bruce, the day before, he'd gone to bed thinking of his Scottish family and his parents, Alexandre Sylvain Benoit and Maeve Mairi Campbell. And the story that often surfaced about the old wine bottles. GrandPapa was eighty-six years old and still sharp. He hadn't believed Pablo Picasso had shown Alexandre old bottles of brandy with a unique label years ago. Sure, Olivier knew there was some truth to it, but over time, he was sure it had grown out of proportion with the telling. Could this stranger be part of that story?

He stared at the miles of grapevines as thoughts raced through his head. He smiled widely. Between having a love of numbers and an obsession for grapes, he was in the perfect spot; an accountant and office manager for Beauvais Cellars. At forty years old, he had a loving wife, two beautiful children and another arriving in two months. He was a happy man...so content that it sometimes frightened him.

Olivier had seen Cendrine for the first time while sipping an espresso outside a bistro in Aix-en-Provence several years earlier. He'd been charmed.

As she spoke with the older man sitting next to her, he overheard the words grapes, finances and wine. His ears had perked up. He'd just finished a secondary course in Mathematics and Computer Science at the university in Aix and he'd been typing a resume on his laptop in front of him. When the older man raised his voice, telling Cendrine he was a winemaker, not an accountant, Olivier had snapped his laptop shut and introduced himself.

Within a week, he was the new accountant at Beauvais Cellars. He fell in love with the vineyard, their wines and Cendrine simultaneously. They were married the following year. He'd stolen as many moments as he could away from the company's books to follow his father-in-law, Andres Frenot, through the vines and into the winemaker's head.

Olivier was an only child. He knew his parents had met in Paris where his father studied. His mother was visiting her Scottish aunt, who owned a bistro near the university. It was a loving romance. After their marriage, they lived in France until Olivier was ten years old, visiting between Scotland and France if money and time allowed. He was very close to his Scottish grandparents, Ainsley Campbell and Mairi Baird Campbell. He especially loved his great grandfather, Bruce Alec Baird.

GrandPapa Bruce had a wild hank of red hair and blue-gray eyes that mirrored Olivier's reflection when they stood face to face. His great grandfather doted on him, even though there was another great grandchild who lived in Scotland. Olivier's unmarried aunt Aila Campbell died in childbirth giving birth to that son a year after Olivier's birth. Despite Conall Baird Carson being raised by the boy's father, the Baird family cultivated a relationship with him. Although he was Olivier's only cousin, he was far from his favorite. Olivier's face twisted every time he thought about Conall.

Olivier pondered the Spaniard's phone call, not wanting to return to his computer. He thought about the time he spent in Scotland during school holidays. His great grandfather had noticed his aptitude for numbers and paid Olivier's tuition to the University of Edinburgh where he earned his diploma in financials. After graduation, he hoped to educate himself about grapevines, hoping to one day make some wine.

Olivier scribbled on his pad and thought of his father, Alexandre, who was born near Beaurecueil. In his youth, Alexandre had loved the vines and volunteered to work in a vineyard near Mont Sainte-Victoire. There, he worked the soil and learned about ancestral cultivars, viniculture and viticulture. Alexandre had become friends with Pablo Ruiz Picasso, the self-exiled Spanish artist and sculptor, who had purchased and renovated the nearby Chateau of Vauvenargues. His father had also become friends with the artist's master gardener, Fernando.

Olivier pursed his lips as he tried to remember the stories his father told him during his life. The man on the phone sounded old, maybe as old as his father had been when he'd died six years earlier. He pulled a pencil off his desk and held it between his teeth. If this man was a friend of his late father's, maybe he was the Fernando in his father's stories? The man didn't give him much of a choice about meeting him. Tomorrow would give him some answers. Coupled with the conversation with GrandPapa the night before, he wondered if there was a connection between the old stories and this man.

When his father-in-law, Andres Frenot, brought in the mail a few moments later, Olivier dropped the pencil and looked at the man kindly.

"*La poste*, Olivier."

Olivier saw Andres smile tiredly before sitting on the carved chair near his son-in-law's desk. He remembered when Andres had first taught him to prune a head-trained vine just before the beginning of warmer weather while the ground was often still muddy from the winter snow and rain. The vintner had given him a pruning knife to trim back nearly all of the previous year's vine growth. When Andres saw Olivier's eyes dance with excitement at the prospect of working with the vines, they'd shared a warm connection ever since. He'd told Olivier over the years, that seeing his daughter, Cendrine, love a man who also loved the vines, gave him contentment.

"*Se il vous plaît venir dîner ce soir, Andres. Cendrine fait Bouillabaisse et Bernadette et François vous manquez.*" Please come to dinner tonight, Andres.

Cendrine is making *Bouillabaisse* and Bernadette and François miss you. Olivier stared hard at the old man.

"*Oui, bien*. Andres nodded, touched the rim of his hat and got up with a short grunt. His khaki pants were dirty, a sure sign he had been pinching off dead leaves, runners or pulling weeds. The man never stopped cultivating and babying the stock on every inch of the Beauvais property.

After he left, Olivier called Cendrine. She did not see a lot of her father and her heart noticed. He knew Andres loved his daughter and his grandchildren, but he was a veritable hermit, living and breathing for his vines.

Olivier tamped down questions about the Spaniard's mysterious phone call and pushed his uneasiness away. He had work to do and family folklore and a mysterious friend of his father's had to wait.

Cendrine smiled when she saw Olivier's photo light up the screen. She grabbed it before Bernadette's little fingers darted toward the cell phone. "*Bonjour?*"

"*Andres a accepté de venir dîner ce soir. Mettez le rosé au frais, ma chérie.*" Andres is coming to dinner. Chill your pink wine, sweetheart.

"*Le vin du rosé, haha. Vous voulez dire que le vin mousseux rosé, hein?*"

"Yes, I mean pink sparkling wine. I am corrected." He grinned.

Cendrine danced Bernadette around the room as her daughter squealed with delight, curls bouncing. Young François laughed to see his mother and sister dancing around the dining room table before he lifted another plastic animal into the fenced farmyard on the floor.

After Bernadette caught her balance, Cendrine turned toward the kitchen pots. While she pulled out ingredients to make her fish broth, the fennel and a bottle of pastis, she pushed two bottles of sparkling wine into the fridge. The baguette lay wrapped on the countertop. The clams, shrimp and halibut chilled beside her wine. She had already crushed the fresh breadcrumbs and garlic for the *rouille*, a sauce she would use with her special *bouillabaisse* recipe. The classical Provençal fish stew recipe was handed down from her mother. Her father loved it and tonight, Cendrine was determined to recreate whispery memories that were happy, not sad.

As she worked, her mind slipped back to the day when she was fifteen years old, the day her father changed. Her mother and brother had driven to the mountain town of Florac, a three hour drive through Arles and Nimes to investigate an internship for Gilles. Cendrine wrestled with the memory. She had been pruning the grapevines with her father that day, pretending she could prune faster than he could. Laughter had filled the air around them when an unfamiliar car tore up the curving driveway and slid to a stop. Two uniformed policemen got out and walked slowly toward them. Cendrine remembered how the hairs on her arms rose up and froze there. Her father held his breath. The car had slipped off an embankment in the rainstorm that morning. Both killed instantly. And with their deaths, she also lost the laughing father she had always known. She had been lovingly stranded with her grandparents and uncle François.

And then there was Callie. She smiled, washed her hands and carried the pot to the stove. Tonight, she would remember family times, smell the fish stew and close her eyes and feel her *Maman* beside her. She struggled against the promise of tears and turned abruptly toward her children.

Upstairs, Olivier showered and pulled a large box of papers from underneath the closet shelf. It held everything his father had left for him. It had been too difficult to read the contents when he died. Each time he flipped through the papers, his throat closed up and he slid the box back into its place without completing the task. Today, he must gather up his strength. He berated himself because his father had been dead for six years already.

His fingers touched the papers apprehensively before he dipped into the depths and pulled everything onto the bed. He heard Cendrine singing to the children and he smiled at the small pleasure. When he lifted a piece of paper that appeared crumpled and then smoothed afterward, his heartbeat sped up. It was a drawing that his father had talked about many times. It was in pen and ink, but Olivier knew the significance of the image. It did not show the mark of origin. Nor did it have the artist's initials. Could this be the artwork for the brandy label in the old stories? Could his father really have known the famous Picasso? Did he really see bottles of brandy in the estate's cellar with the label of this drawing? Olivier sighed loudly.

Inside the sheaf of papers was an old photograph of two chairs painted in red, yellow and green. On the back, his father had written "Pablo painted these to remember his native Spain and the forests of Vauvenargues and Mont Sainte-Victoire. Olivier dropped the photograph onto the pile of papers. Why had he waited so long to open this box? The children's giggles pulled his mind back and he pushed the box aside slowly.

Lying back on the bed, he closed his eyes and let the stories lead him toward his father's voice: "You see, Olivier, my obsession with grapevines and wine amused my friend, Pablo. He exiled himself from Spain because of their civil war and he chose to live in France. He often produced paintings of my nearby village, Vauvenargues. He told me he never painted Mont Sainte-Victoire, the mountain near our village, because Paul Cezanne, a native of Aix, already had. He said Cezanne painted the mountain and now he, Pablo Picasso, owned it. He painted two chairs almost as soon as he arrived in the colors of yellow and red for his native Catalonia and green for the forests of Vauvenargues and Mont Sainte-Victoire. Even though Pablo was born in Madrid, his family moved to Catalonia when he was young."

Olivier smiled as he imagined his father's voice. "Picasso purchased the Chateau of Vauvenargues in 1959 because he wanted a more isolated working place than his previous home, La Californie in Cannes. I was sad to see him leave Vauvenargues when he moved to Mougins in 1962. He died there when he was ninety two years old. He and Jacqueline are buried in the grounds of the chateau at Vauvenargues though, which is still the private property of the Picasso family."

"Pablo loved painting, Olivier, and his paintings covered the walls inside the chateau. They were wild, some of them. Others had blues and greens, boxes of black. The faces of the people Pablo painted were never smooth, but crooked everywhere. His wife, Jacqueline, I rarely saw. I know Pablo was sad to be estranged from his children, some from a previous marriage and another from a liaison."

"One day, during one of my visits, Pablo surprised me when he held up a miniature painting of me and Fernando, with the vineyard as a back drop. The small painting had none of Pablo's typical cubism where objects are broken apart and reassembled in an abstracted form. They highlighted composite geometric shapes and depicted them from multiple simultaneous viewpoints to create physics-defying, collage-like effects. To be honest, none of his paintings made me smile. But on the painting of me and Fernando, I saw the señorita riding a cork and her dark hair flowed behind her. When I asked Pablo about the label, he held his finger to his lips and smiled slyly before leading me into the dark cellar at the chateau. I did not know until much later that Fernando, who was his master gardener, already knew of the bottles. I learned, later, where the wine came from."

Alexandre had never seen the painting again. Despite being sworn to secrecy about the old bottles that Pablo showed to him, he had told his father-in-law, Bruce Baird. Fernando was surely sworn to secrecy as well. Olivier remembered asking his father if he had ever drank any of the mysterious wine. His father didn't answer.

Olivier lifted the drawing again and tried to visualize the label, colored on a bottle. The wine must be Spanish since a Spanish woman's image was splashed across the label. Was it Pablo Picasso's wine? If so, Fernando would know. Since both men were painted into the miniature, he was part of his father's story. And he was also probably already dead.

Olivier's eyelids popped open. It must have been Fernando on the phone. He sat up, swung his feet onto the floor and pushed everything back into the box. Before he had another coherent thought, François and Bernadette skipped into the room trying to beat one another to his side. Both gasping for breath, they said in unison, *"Grand-père est arrivé et le dîner est prêt, Papa."* Grandpa has arrived and time for your dinner, Papa. Olivier pulled the children to him and laughed, knowing they were repeating their mother's message word for word.

"Olivier?" Cendrine's voice followed her children up the stairs.

"J'arrive. I am coming.

The aroma from the kitchen was enticing and the soft murmur of conversation pulled him forward. Taking a tiny hand in each of his own, Olivier guided his children toward the dining room. For now, he would think nothing more about the strange phone call or the box of papers. Just knowing the wine label truly existed and that his father was friends with Pablo Picasso was more than his mind could assimilate. Fish stew, sparkling wine and an evening with his family was all he wanted.

Andres leaned his elbows on the table top and smiled at Olivier as he drew the children toward him. When they scrambled into their chairs, he inhaled the steaming stew and lifted his misted eyes to his daughter. "*Maman's?*"

"*Oui, Papa.*" Cendrine reached across the table and covered her father's callused hand with her own and they stared at one another. After withdrawing her hand, she placed it quickly over her heart and slid it down over her blooming baby.

Olivier watched Andres' face when Cendrine caressed her pregnant belly. He knew the old man wished for the hundredth time that his wife, Chloe, could have lived to see her daughter grow to womanhood, marry and give her grandchildren. Olivier was sure he was remembering Chloe caress her pregnant belly, the same way her daughter did during their meals. He had told Olivier this several times. He watched the old man, knowing those memories filled his mind. When he saw his soup spoon still for a moment, Olivier was sure of it.

As Andres sipped his daughter's fish stew, as he had many years ago from his wife's table, he smiled and nodded toward her. Olivier could see he had difficulty swallowing the lump in his throat but when he lifted his eyes to Cendrine across from him, the lump dissolved and a smile took its place. Olivier's breath held a moment because he saw something in the old man's face he'd never seen before. Was he finally going to share his life with this family? Olivier touched his wife's hand and motioned his head, so she could see the change on her father's face as he lifted his spoon again.

Three

The next morning, Cendrine gathered the children into the car for a visit with their *grand-mère* and *grand-père*. Bernadette and François ran from the car and up the steps like a shot, before Cendrine could shut her car door and follow.

"*Moi d'abord, moi d'abord.*" Me first, me first.

As Janine reached for the doorknob and swung open the heavy door, the small whirlwinds both surrounded her with their little arms, teasing and shoving each other, quieting quickly under their mother's stern glance. Her white hair was beautifully combed and a headband held the bangs off her face. She was a lovely woman. She had kind green eyes with gray specks that mirrored those of her granddaughter. Cendrine laughed and pulled their coats off in flight as they sped into the living room looking for their *grand-père*.

Her *grand-père*, Michel Beauvais, was the patriarch of Beauvais Cellars and a native of Pertuis, a small village north of Aix-en-Provence. Naturally, having grown up in such a prestigious French wine region as Provence, Michel found himself drawn to winemaking. This led to his enrollment at Suze-la-Rousse, in southeastern France situated in the heart of the Rhône Valley vineyards at the University of Wine. There, he had learned oenology, marketing and management for the wine industry. While there, he befriended classmate Janine Claudette Marseille. After graduation and joint internships at a very well known French Château, they didn't think twice about returning to Pertuis, marrying and establishing Beauvais Cellars. As the Second World War ended, they received a small financial boost from Michel's father, who owned a bastide outside Aix; they would create a new beginning. The next year, Chloe was born. François followed a few years afterward.

Janine and Michel Beauvais adored Chloe's daughter, Cendrine, their only living grandchild. When Cendrine became pregnant after her marriage to Olivier, they were delighted. When twins were born, they were thrilled; one baby for each of them.

When their daughter, Chloe, had died along with their grandson, Gilles, twenty years earlier, Cendrine had filled their world alongside their son, François. Without them, they surely could not have born the pain. He was their rock and when he decided to study transnational wine trade law to benefit Beauvais wine in California, how could they argue? But they did, of course.

When he brought his American fiancé home to meet the family within two months, they were not happy. They'd hoped he'd marry a French woman, stay nearby. However, when Callinda Larkin Augustine arrived with her quick smile, dimples and freckled face, they were enchanted. Despite François and the family calling her Callie, she remained Callinda to them.

After their son's marriage, they hoped the couple would live in France and they did for a time. When they purchased an old stone mill near the family vineyard in Pertuis, their hopes were fueled when renovations began. However, Callinda's mother lived in Oregon. Their love for their daughter-in-law grew; she taught them to speak English and they taught her French. With great determination, she stumbled through their French language and they fell in love with the American woman.

They watched young Cendrine learn to love Callinda as a surrogate mother and François treated her like his own child. The girl needed special attention after losing her mother and brother, especially since her father withdrew within himself and had become a gruff curmudgeon.

Losing François in the boating accident on the coast of Oregon three years earlier nearly killed the old couple. Again, it was Cendrine's love and support that helped them carry on. The twins were born shortly after his death and were like a breath of fresh air. Holding both babies took the numbness up a level and being part of their little lives twice a week kept notching it upward. Now, with a new little one on the way, they hoped to live long enough to enjoy them all just a while longer. At eighty-five years old, they lived for every moment and thanked life for the joys they brought to two old people.

"*Salut, mon poussin.*"(hello, my chick) Her grandmother gave her the customary cheek kisses and opened her arms to the children.

"Good news! Papa came to dinner last night and I think he was very happy to be there. There was something. A change or thoughts that moved him from being grumpy to something better…"

Janine clapped her hands and reached for Cendrine for a big hug. "It is certainly time, little one. I have made *brioche* to enjoy with our *café au lait*. Come, sit. Tell me how you and little missy are feeling."

Cendrine gave her grandfather a quick hug while the twins sat on his footstool mesmerized by a basket of toys they knew waited by his chair. "You know, Olivier thinks this is a boy, not a missy."

"*Non. Une fille,*" No, a girl. Janine answered with confidence.

"I came to tell you about the new brochures we just received. Olivier ordered two hundred and they will soon be sitting in the bistros, the boulangerie (bakery) and fromage (cheese) shops from Pertuis to Aix to Marseille. He has a wine distributor in Paris, who……." She saw her grandmother's face pale and knew she was thinking of her uncle François. She reached over to squeeze her grandmother's fingers and caressed the hand that gripped her own.

"Go on, *chérie.*" Janine lifted her hand to reposition her headband.

"Remember when I learned about sparkling wine at Champagne Batisse Grandin near Paris?"

"Yes, of course."

"Well, I just received a letter from my friend who interned with me. Antoine moved to Scotland. He exchanged grapes for malted grain and he's learning to make whiskey at Ambrose MacDonald Distillers, Ltd. He said Mr. MacDonald was friends with the famous William Grant & Sons Distillers, the maker of Glenfiddich whiskey in Scotland."

Janine listened and glanced over at her husband, who was also interested, but puzzled. "And?" They both asked.

"He learned the recipe for a special emulsion brew before he left the Champagne winery. He couldn't tell me before he left, but now that he works at the distillery…."

Janine and Michel listened shrewdly. Cendrine's hands flew around her face as she continued, "Before he left Paris, he overheard the winemaker mention a new label…"

Her grandparents smiled at her ebullient enthusiasm.

"…And since Chardonnay brings elegance to sparkling wines, the pinks are made from black-skinned grapes." Cendrine took a breath as her excitement tried to keep up with her words and Antoine's letter.

"We know this, *chérie*." Michel's eyebrows furrowed. The children began to scramble around on the floor. François squealed loudly when his sister tipped the basket and his great grandfather popped his bottom. Bernadette laughed, but put her head down quickly when she got a look.

Cendrine scolded them before continuing, "Of course, since sparkling pink wines were always my favorites, Antoine remembered that I never shut up about it. Of course, I love all our wines but…I digress. Antoine and I learned how rosé is made either by adding red wine to a white blend or by fermenting the juice in contact with the skins. They all come with varying degrees of sweetness, due to the addition of a dosage. He said they recently changed the ratio and will soon release a brand new rosé with their next bottling. I can do it too!" Her face glowed.

Michel chuckled, but listened while he gave his wife a wink.

Cendrine inhaled quickly, pushing her golden brown hair behind one ear. "We learned the timing difference when bottles are turned upside down and about the disgorgement stage in sparkling wine production, where the lees our wine is aged in are removed from the bottle necks like the *methode traditionelle*. I think you've seen Papa immerse our inverted bottles into a freezing solution so our lees solidify into a single frozen pellet. When the seal is removed from the bottle, this pellet is ejected, propelled by the pressurized carbon dioxide created by the primary fermentation. The space created in the bottle by the ejected lees is then filled with a mixture of wine and sugars and freezing them. When the neck of the bottle begins to freeze upward, they measure the iced area to formulate the……" Cendrine's voice took on the cadence of a fast-moving train, her hands spinning in tandem with its wheels.

"It sounds like a soap opera, *chérie*. You know, we have not been involved in your sparkling wines. What exactly is Antoine telling you? This is the same formula you learned during your studies, *oui*?"

"He's telling me there is a new, darker pink sparkling wine. I want to create a new label." She paused a moment "And call it *Chloe Rosé*." She waited to see her grandparent's faces and she was not disappointed when their smiles grew wide.

"You will stop our current label or add another? How will this new label impact our vineyard budget?" Michel's voice rose.

"Two labels. We can split the grapes so it will not cost us more money. I want ours to stand above the others. Spain has *Cava*, Italy's bubbles are *Prosécco* and *Moscato d'Asti*, and French sparkling wines from everywhere outside of Champagne are referred to as *Cremant*. Our current label ratio is 3-1 but this new rosé is 5-1. I am very excited but, I want your approval. Our Chardonnay harvest will be bigger and better than last year, so we have many grapes on the vine. Papa tells me it is our best year after the freezing problem a few years ago." She pushed her hands between her knees and held them rigid as she eyed her grandparents and held her breath.

They studied her. "You are little excited, *non*?"

Everyone laughed and the children stopped to follow the conversation a moment before dipping their hands into the toy basket again.

"The name of the new rosé is very emotional, of course, since you are naming it after your mother. The vineyard was actually more hers and Olivier's, to do with as they wished, than theirs. They were, however, pleased to be involved in the decision.

Michel responded softly, "Cendrine, nearly 60% of our production is red wine, 35% rosé and 5% white. If we continue growing Beaujolais, Grenache, and Chardonnay, how will the percentages change when you add a darker pink sparkling wine? We are under strict guidelines in order to label our wines *Côtes de Provence*. Since Provence produces nearly 80% of the rosé, we must take care with our numbers, especially if we want to continue producing and releasing white *nouveau* wine in December following the harvest. That's only two weeks after the release of our Beaujolais Nouveau. The bottling will soon begin, Andres told me yesterday."

"Yes, I know that, *grand-père*, but……"

"…And do not forget the AOC requirement is at least 20% of our wine must be blended from wine produced by the *saignee* method of maceration, so we must press the wine after 12-24 hours of skin contact. If you use Antoine's new formula to create this darker rosé, can you keep the AOC label? Remember how François watched the codes with his law firm?"

Cendrine nodded, but appeared crestfallen and bit her lip.

"What does your father think of the newer pink?" Janine quietly interjected; knowing how close Cendrine had been to her uncle and their many conversations regarding wine law and winemaking.

"I just received Antoine's letter. I haven't discussed it with Papa yet. I saw an unfamiliar car in front of Olivier's office this morning, so I didn't stop. I will talk to him when I go home. Kind of strange and exciting, don't you think?" Cendrine caressed her belly as her eyes darted to a tiny hummingbird sipping from a bright feeder hung on a shepherd's hook outside the window.

"And this new label will follow the same grape rules we have always used practicing *lutte raisonée*, no herbicides?" Michel was bent on connecting all the dots and his knowledge of wine, grapes and ethics remained clear, even though he was approaching ninety years old.

"*Oui*, other treatments are used only if absolutely necessary, *grand-père*." Cendrine took a deep breath. She and her grandfather stared at one another. Her passion for the grape and winemaking always made him smile since he had loved the industry since the First World War ended. He'd studied winemaking at Suze la Rousse. When he'd found a young woman equally immersed in grape growing, varietals, blending and fermentation, he had married her. Cendrine grinned because she knew her grandfather was seeing that same young woman again as her own excitement bubbled over.

"Let's cut the *brioche* and drink some coffee, shall we? I could see you had something on your mind, so I didn't want to rush you," Janine murmured as she led Cendrine over to her large farm table. The twins rushed up to the table and pulled the heavy chairs away to climb up to join them...and all this wine talk makes me hungry."

Janine motioned to Michel and he shook his head. He hadn't been feeling well and she didn't push him.

Cendrine fished a piece of pastry from the plate and cut it into small pieces for her children before slipping a large piece into her mouth. "Mmmmmm...so good. *Merci*."

The morning sunshine slipped through the windows and bathed her granddaughter's face in a golden light. Janine caught her breath. Cendrine looked up quickly. She knew she resembled her mother, Chloe. She also knew her grandmother was thinking of her. Losing her only daughter was hard and one would think twenty years afterward, the loss would lessen but Cendrine knew it did not. She missed her mother every single day and knew her grandparents did also.

Now, Chloe seemed to whisper through Cendrine and her grandchildren. Chewing her pastry slowly, Janine sipped her coffee and studied Cendrine. "What are you going to name our little missy, Cendrine?"

Her granddaughter laughed aloud. "Olivier is sure it's a boy...this time. I told you....."

Janine caught Michel's eye and his chuckle could be heard from the other room. Neither cared the gender as long as the child was healthy, but they enjoyed hearing laughter in the big, old homestead, so they invented conversations just to make it happen.

François pulled at his great grandmother's apron and she leaned toward him. "*Maman dit que nous allons avoir un nouveau petit frère.*" Mama says we will have a new baby brother.

Bernadette's bright curls bobbed in agreement as the room erupted in more laughter. The children had been well brainwashed.

The *brioche* was gone and the coffee had turned cold; Cendrine knew it was time to leave and let her grandparents rest. Always careful of their health, she noticed that her grandfather hadn't moved from his chair, nor had he wanted any pastry. She glanced at the table beside his chair and found no cup of coffee, which was unusual. She kissed his forehead and turned to her grandmother, who met her eyes with a nod. Her brow creased as she bundled coats on the children and guided them to the car.

Once inside the car with the children belted into car seats, Cendrine took a deep, steadying breath. "They're over eighty five and I should expect it but I don't have to like it," she whispered as the put her Peugeot in gear.

Earlier that morning, Olivier lifted his head at the tapping on his office door. Rousing from his gaze with a jerk, he gripped his fingers around his coffee cup. His mind had raced in tandem between excitement and anxiety, waiting for the Spaniard to arrive. He hadn't given him a time, so Olivier remained in his office all morning, hoping he'd soon arrive to put him out of his misery. He glanced out the window to watch Andres wander through the vineyard toward the warehouse, which was now teeming with workers. The new bottling had just begun again.

When Olivier opened the door, an old man wrapped in a dark coat shuffled into the room, his eyes round with apprehension and more. He removed his heavy cloth hat and stuffed it into his pocket. His manner was gentle, but his eyes were anxious. His right hand shot out toward Olivier.

"You are Olivier?" The man pronounced his name the French way making it sound like *o-liv-e-A*.

"Yes, I am Olivier. You were a friend of my father's, Alexandre Benoit?" He pulled out the chair next to his desk and watched the old man slide into the seat, looking weary and just a little frightened.

"*Si.* Your father was my very good friend. I have something for you." The old man's face was leathery, dark. His thick, white mustache grew above his lip profusely and his dark eyes were large, sunken in his face.

"I think you must have been the gardener for Pablo Picasso. Am I right? Do you know about a wine label showing a Spanish woman riding a cork? My father told me about this, but I do not know if it is true." Olivier's words fell over one another.

The man studied Olivier quietly before he nodded. And then he began to talk. "Yes, I am Fernando. *Señor* Picasso had a wine cellar deep beneath the chateau where he stored old bottles of brandy wine. Your father and I promised never to tell of it. But I am here now because someone has been following me in Málaga. I fear it is about those bottles."

"Why? If you told no one, why would you think they are following you because of the old bottles? Are the old bottles still hidden in the chateau's wine cellar after all this time? Who made this wine? Was the wine from Pablo Picasso's vineyard by the estate? And the label. What about the label?" Olivier's voice raised an octave as he peppered the old man with questions.

Fernando Sanchez Ortega stared at the young man and then he chuckled. "Yes, you are definitely Alexandre's son. You remind me of my friend, very much. He was always full of questions. I will try to answer but please let me tell the story first, agreed?"

Olivier nodded, apologizing with a look.

Fernando sat on the edge of his chair. Hesitating a moment, he hoisted a satchel onto his lap and lifted the leather flap. His hand dove inside and withdrew a colored photograph. "This is the man who has been following me."

Olivier stared at the photograph but it was too blurry to recognize the man behind the wheel of a car on the busy city street.

"I believe this might be the same young man who questioned me about the old bottles twenty years ago. I pretended ignorance. He did not tell me his name and I do not know how he knew about the wine. I lived in Málaga at the time. He was a young man about twenty years old. He had an accent, not Spanish, not French. When he left, I asked myself what he could know of the bottles. But I never saw him again."

"And you think the same man is following you now? What the hell does he think you know now that you didn't know then? And why would he wait twenty years to find you again? Who could it be and how could he know about the bottles?" He tapped his fingers on his desk. "And how did this mystery man know who you were and where you lived in the first place?"

Fernando pulled on the ends of his white mustache before answering. "Yes, I know the label with the señorita riding the cork you mention. It is important, I think," he whispered. "I've thought of the image many times because it was so important to *Señor* Picasso. I've lived with it too many years already. It is difficult discussing the secret aloud now and I am surprised how good it feels to give the image and story to you."

"It is real then."

Fernando nodded.

"Who took this photo?" Olivier punched the photograph.

"My daughter has seen the man several times and this last time, she had her cell phone in her hand. She photographed him while he was driving away in a blue Citroen. She was afraid and told me to find you. We both think it is about *Señor* Picasso's lost wine." His eyes clouded over and he rubbed his hand over his lined face in exasperation.

"Lost wine?" Olivier sat up straighter.

"Yes, the wine with the *señorita's* label, *Sueño España*."

Olivier exhaled loudly. "*Sueño España*. Spanish Dream? What do you know of it? My great grandfather and I heard my father's stories. GrandPapa didn't believe it. He doubted Pablo Picasso would have befriended a local peasant or shown him this mysterious wine."

Fernando grunted, dug into his satchel again and handed Olivier a small oil painting. It showed Fernando as a young man standing beside a young Alexandre, Olivier's father. The bottle on the table beside the men revealed a Spanish woman riding a cork with her black hair streaming behind her.

Olivier was stunned. He'd heard the story and had not believed it was true. He held the painting in both hands and then turned to stare at the old gardener. His hands shook. It was his father and Fernando. The mountain was behind them, the bottle beside them. It was the same portrait his father had told him about many years earlier.

"You see, *Señor* Picasso had many bottles in the old estate. We three drank one only; your father and I agreed it was very smooth brandy wine." He reached his fingers to his lips and kissed them. "Very good."

Olivier couldn't take his eyes off the painting. "Did Picasso paint this miniature?" Olivier was confused and tried to go slowly, but his mouth was far ahead of his brain. "It is so different from his others."

"I painted it. He told me this painting was too *simpatico*, smooth, friendly… and his paintings were more Picasso. *Señor* Picasso painted in pieces, trying to remake nature similar to Paul Cezanne's art. He told me that he believed Cezanne was the father of cubism and that is how his paintings looked, not like this one. I paint…… different."

Olivier's heart thumped through his shirt and he wondered if the Spaniard could hear it from his chair. "You painted it. It is a very good likeness of my father. The colors are beautiful…you are a gardener who is also a very good artist? And the label?" His eyes lifted from the painting to the man beside him.

"*Sí, señor*, when I was very young, I went to France to become a great painter and chose grapevines and dirt instead." Fernando shook his head with the memory. "When Pablo Picasso saw this painting, he laughed and told us the señorita would ride her cork until she was ready to get off."

"What? What does that mean?" Olivier's struggle between myth and reality made his head hurt.

"I do not know, but *Señor* Picasso was angry when he saw me sketching a drawing of the label onto paper a few days later and grabbed it to toss away. I did not draw it again." Fernando grimaced at the memory.

Olivier stared at him, knowing where the drawing now resided.

"This brandy was very special to *Señor* Picasso because his friend produced it shortly after the Spanish Civil War. He'd already left Spain, because he was very angry with Spanish politics. He did not want Francisco Franco to steal the brandy from his friend. *Señor* Picasso knew it was very, very good brandy. And he was very, very angry."

"I am familiar with wines in Provence, but I know nothing about brandy except you drink it in small glasses, sipping it slowly."

Fernando laughed a bit, his voice still shaky. "The Spanish winemaker used grapes and distilled it three times to mellow it. Storing brandy is sometimes a problem. If it has a cork, it must be laid on its side to keep the cork wet. If stored standing up, the cork dries up and the alcohol evaporates, then the water will be next. These old bottles had wax seals over the corks and the brandy level was perfect. So, the brandy sat up high on the neck of the bottle. *Señor* Picasso was always very careful to keep the bottles tilted so these corks remained wet."

Olivier stared at the old man. "Do you know where the bottles are now? You said they were lost. Could the brandy still be drinkable?"

"The bottles were moved from the chateau when *Señor* Picasso left in 1962. Brandy can age many years to remain smooth. If it is preserved correctly, those bottles could sit for 200 years and taste good. However, if brandy has been exposed to extreme temperature changes, it is not drinkable and may smell like kerosene or rotten fruit when you open it. This brandy has been kept in a cool, dark place and it should taste the same as when *señor* Alonzo put it in the bottle. *Señor* Picasso said the brandy was produced shortly after the Second World War ended. So, in 1962, the brandy would be…" He paused, held his fingers to his head and wrinkled his brow before looking up at Olivier. "….almost twenty years old."

"And now…the bottles of brandy are about seventy years old. Do you know who moved them to this cool, dark place you mention?" Olivier sat on the corner of his desk and raised both hands toward the Spaniard.

"*Sí.*" He looked steadily at Olivier. "Me and your father. *Señor* Picasso told us where to hide them. He also told me never to tell anyone except you when you became an adult….and only if I trusted you with his secret. He also told me to wait until after Alexandre's death." Fernando reached up to scratch the side of his nose. "The Spanish culture was in *señor* Picasso's blood. He did not want flamenco guitar music to disappear."

"Flamenco guitar music?" He mused a moment. "What if you had died before my father?" Olivier's light complexion turned the color of strawberries and his eyes rounded in surprise. And then, he stood up and paced the small office before dropping back into his chair.

"My daughter had a letter for you in case I died first." The old man bunched up the satchel as if trying to decide what to say next.

"What am I supposed to do with this information? I don't know if I want to know where you hid those bottles." Olivier closed his eyes and shook his burnished head in exasperation. Wiping his brow with a shaking hand, he waited to hear more.

Fernando removed an envelope from his satchel and handed it to Olivier. "This letter is for you from my old friend, your father. I will return to Málaga now and live my life. It is not my problem anymore and I am happy to give this to you. If anyone asks me about the old bottles, I will again say nothing. The painting is yours, my young friend. *Vaya con Dios*."

Across the great expanse of gardens, Cendrine watched the old man shuffle out of Olivier's office just after she arrived home again. His gray hair curled over his collar; the car looked like a rental. She glanced at the outbuilding where Olivier's office sat and narrowed her eyes. Turning, she studied the man from the window a moment longer as a kernel of unease crawled up her spine before she dropped the curtain back into place.

***

Olivier's fingers tapped against his father's letter after the Spaniard drove away. He picked it up and turned it over, wondering why he didn't rip it open and read its contents. He remembered hearing his parents discuss Picasso and his father's younger life near the chateau. He also remembered how his father's voice softened when he discussed his friendship with both Pablo Picasso and Fernando Sanchez. The friendships had been important.

His mother, Maeve, often asked Alexandre to tell her stories about his time in the vineyards near Mont Sainte-Victoire; she wanted to hear how the vines were planted and plowed and how he worked the soil and learned about ancestral cultivars, viniculture and viticulture. In Scotland, vineyards were a novelty. In France, they were so abundant, she imagined herself running through the grapevines barefoot. She wanted to hear about the birds flapping through the vines and how Picasso chased them even though he was too old to be running through a vineyard. She'd been fascinated with the story of the bottles and never tired of listening to her husband describe the label showing the Spanish woman exultantly racing across the label.

Now, their son held an envelope in his hand that might hold some answers, too apprehensive to unseal it and read what his father had written. Olivier smiled as he reminisced, almost hearing the murmur of his parent's voices. His throat clogged. He wondered if the pain of losing them would ever diminish. He was always wary of bringing up his mother's name to his GrandPapa because his granddaughter's death still had the ability to make the old man cry.

Bruce Alec Baird picked up the phone on the first ring.

While gently caressing the painted face of his father in the portrait with his thumb, Olivier repeated part of the conversation he'd had with Fernando Sanchez. "GrandPapa, I had a very strange visitor today. I think you will be very interested to learn that the old stories Papa told us about the wine bottles in Pablo Picasso's cellar are true."

Silence met his surprising statement. "Th' auld bottles wi' th' hen ridin' th' cork.?" The old man's breathing quickened.

"Yes, that's what I am telling you." Olivier glanced out the window. Andres was walking through the vineyards across the grounds to his cottage at the end of the property. The wind had picked up and scarlet, shooting ribbons rose in the air to frighten the birds from the vines.

"Interestin' timin', son. My friend, William, was haur a few days ago askin' me if thaur was any truth tae those rumors."

"…..William Grant?"

"Och, no, it was his son. He tauld me his friend has some kind ay proof 'at yer faither stole them frae Picasso an' hid them fur his ain treasure. Ah jist laughed. But now…."

"….My father never stole anything. That's a lie. Did you tell him about those old wine bottles?" Olivier was livid.

"Calm doon, son. Ah hae ne'er repeated th' story tae anyone only discussed it wi' ye, Alexandre an' Maeve. Tae mah knowledge, nobody woods hae tauld authers inside th' family. This is preposterous an' e'en if they're still in existence, they must belong tae th' Picasso family anyway. An' anither thing, when William called, he said *we* nae *Ah*."

"Well, I'm stumped. Someone told William then, aye?"

"Aye and yer Spaniard said that the brandy IS still good?" Bruce Baird's voice turned warm.

Olivier smiled tiredly. "Yes, it is probably still good. Fernando told me that brandy acquires its taste from fermentation and oak barrel aging. After typical grape wine distillation, the unaged brandy is placed into oak barrels to age. Spanish brandies are aged using the *solera* system, an aging process that blends brandy over many years. *Solera* means literally *on the ground* in Spanish, and it refers to the lower level of the set of barrels used in the process; the liquid is transferred from barrel to barrel, right *on the ground*. After a period of aging, the mature brandy is mixed with distilled water to reduce alcohol concentration and bottled. Once bottled, the liquid only has contact with glass, which has no flavor for the brandy to absorb. Once opened, deterioration occurs, slows down by keeping it cool and stored in a bottle keeping the cork wet."

"Och, then, be in tooch, son, an' be cannie fur god's sake!"

"Yes, I will be careful, GrandPapa." Olivier's stomach rumbled as he replaced the receiver. He picked up the small painting again and studied the faces and the bottle before he scanned it and emailed it to himself to magnify. The painting was too small to see the AOC seal designating where the grapes were grown. He shrugged. French law did not mandate a seal until the 1950s, well after the Spanish Civil War. Since he knew the bottles originated in Spain and Picasso was already an exile, he wondered how he moved all the bottles to France at all. He obviously had inside help and it must have been a massive, secret network of people.

Olivier shook his head as a hundred thoughts rampaged through his brain. His ginger-colored hair fell over his collar, looking more red than usual as the sun burned through the window, leaving gold stripes of sunshine painted in their strands.

The phone rang, but he ignored it, letting it go to voicemail.

He had difficulty reconciling the laughing young men in the small painting with his father and the man who'd just left his office. He pulled the miniature painting toward him again and placed it near his father's letter, pushing it from side to side, fingering the edges.

When the delivery truck drove across the way toward the warehouse, he expected the invoice to be brought into his office. The men surrounding the truck to unload the contents appeared in a blur.

"Oh, hell. Now what do I do?" he said aloud. He tapped a hand on his chest and pressed it over his heart. The long envelope was gripped in the other. He wondered why he hadn't told his GrandPapa that the old Spaniard had given him more than just an oil painting and confirming the old family story that was no longer a myth.

Four

Cendrine whispered near his ear and her hands roamed over his chest, running her fingers through the curling red hair. "The children are still asleep, *chérie*...you do not have to plant the new vines too early, am I right? Papa can wait....."

Olivier smiled and rolled toward her, meeting her smile with one of his own. Reaching beneath the covers, he caressed her belly and bent his head to run his lips over the bulging baby bump just below her belly button. When she groaned and moved toward him, the sound of little footsteps sounded in the hall.

Then he groaned for an entirely different reason.

She grinned and kissed his nose. "Next time, *mon chérie*."

He groaned again as his children ran into the room, squealing before they jumped up on the bed.

The day had begun at the Beauvais Vineyard.

Today, his father-in-law, Andres Benoit, and the workers would plant white wine grapes and Olivier had promised to help. Provence, sitting within a classic Mediterranean climate, with the sea forming its southern border had mild winters followed by warm summers with little rainfall. Sunshine was abundant with the grapevines receiving more than 3,000 hours per year, twice the amount needed to ripen grapes. The sun could over-ripen grapes if vineyard owners were not cautious. The strong mistral wind could cool the grapes from the heat and dry the grapes after rain, providing some protection against rot and grape diseases, but it could also damage vines that were not securely trained and protected by hillsides. In areas where the wind was particularly strong, the ideal vineyards were on hillsides facing south towards the sea, with the hill providing some shelter from the mistral's strength. Though the soil across Provence is varied, their vineyard was mottled with deposits of limestone and shale and the grapes produced were very fine.

Two days passed before Olivier could no longer postpone reading his father's letter from the grave. His belly cramped with the anxiety of what lay inside. After he posted the wine orders, Andres walked in with the daily mail and invoices.

"*Merci*, Andres. The delivery was complete?"

Andres nodded, tipped his hat, and left to tackle another project.

Quickly thumbing through the stack of mail, Olivier tossed it all aside. With the monthly financials to complete, he didn't waste time on incidentals. However, one envelope stuck out from the others, brown and awkward, where he'd tossed the pile into the round tray. Curious, he inched it out and slit it open, thinking it might be a strange advertisement. He was wrong.

Inside the battered envelope, was a letter created with words cut from magazines. Although amateurishly prepared, it had his undiluted attention as the words sizzled into his brain.

> Olivier Benoit - I know your father stole Picasso's wine bottles and the French and Spanish governments would be interested to learn this. To keep this secret, I want 50000 euros. If you do not give me the money, I will take your beautiful, pregnant wife away when you least expect it. I am serious. You have 24 hours to drop the money into the bin at the corner of Benjamin Franklin and Zac St Martin at Le Village Provencal. NO POLICE!

Olivier started shaking so badly, he fell into his chair. He read the letter twice, willing the words to change. 50000 euros! Where would he get that much money? Who was this letter from? The brandy bottles again. Someone from his father's past? It really had nothing to do with him; his father was dead and if the government was given this information, what could they do to Olivier? But he knew the person who sent this letter could hurt Cendrine whether he was part of the old stories or not.

He took a deep breath and saw Andres walking across the green miles of vineyard, ever vigilant of the grapevines. He touched several vines and tampered with the wires, rearranging the canes to suit himself.

Olivier dazedly pulled his eyes away from the view. His eyes fell on his computer screen and stared at the Beauvais Vineyard's bank statement in front of him. His father was not a thief. Although his father was dead and Olivier wasn't involved, he also knew that twenty four hours was not long enough to gather that much money. If he paid the money with vineyard funds, he could replace it with his annual stipend, which would be deposited at month end. Nobody would know the difference. The wine accounts were up to date and orders would soon be invoiced; more money would be deposited. He slammed his fist onto his desk and watched the cup jump and crash to the floor. The man would NOT take Cendrine. *Ce n'est pas vrai.* He could not believe the nightmare brewing was because of some dusty old bottles of brandy.

He stared at the grapevines again before turning his thoughts to the grapes and the bundle of money they generated. He shook his head trying to clear his conscience. The vines at Beauvais Vineyards were finally beginning to fully produce after a freak hailstorm two summers ago wiped out the fall harvest. Andres told Olivier it took three years for new plants to mature to where they support a profitable harvest. Two years ago, the cordons had just made the mark. The ice decimated the plants. Their Grenache suffered some damage. The vineyard had contracted with growers throughout Provence. Everyone helped each other. Beauvais Vineyards faced the difficult decision of starting again from scratch, with no grapes for three more years, or tending the damaged vines in hopes they would recover. Andres said they should keep the vines and they did.

Thousands of dollars later, it was almost too much to bear emotionally to start over. Last year they were still fighting to come back. Not only was Andres the best winemaker, he was also the best vineyard manager the Beauvais Vineyards had had in many years. People were still buying wine. The vineyard's reputation was thriving and it was making money. And Olivier was in charge of the accounts. He could replenish the funds with his own money. Cendrine would never know and neither would her grandparents or her father. He watched Andres lean in toward the grapes and Olivier smiled as he noted the love the old man showered the vineyard with, every day on every acre.

His annual stipend was the only answer. Since GrandPapa was a silent partner in a whiskey distillery, he shared it with his family. Every year, Olivier received nearly 60000 euros, which they saved for the children's college funds. Since graduating from college and working at the vineyard, they had not needed the whiskey money. In fact, he had never spent any of the stipend funds since he'd married Cendrine five years earlier.

Twenty four hours wasn't long enough to cash their college funds.

Would he tell Cendrine about this threat? No.

Would he tell anyone? No.

GrandPapa, the grandparents, Andres? No.

He pushed both hands through his hair before he lifted his father's letter and slit it open. Three pages later, after his father's words and faraway voice had permeated through his head, the gloom multiplied. Olivier reached for a bottle of red wine. Twisting the cork from the bottle, he lifted it to his lips and drank with his eyes closed. And then he stared out the window for a long time.

Five

The next morning, Cendrine's head ticked off several ideas for her *Chloe Rosé*. Keeping pace with Champagne Batisse Grandin in Champagne-Ardenne made her brain tingle; her father agreed. Yes, they taught her the intricacies of sparkling wine making and yes, she was happy they did. But, Beauvais Cellars wasn't an ordinary winery; they produced several varietals. Andres produced the reds and whites. And Cendrine supervised the production of the rosé wine. Now, she would have two labels. Her golden brown hair swung across her shoulders as she rushed to finish the laundry after putting the children in front of their favorite video, Toy Story.

When Olivier had fervently suggested they go on a short holiday the evening before, he seemed nervous and angry when she stalled on his idea. She did not want to disappoint him, but she was determined to get the ball rolling, as Callie would say. She sighed. Maybe they could go away for just three days instead of his hopeful ten. She would finish the laundry and make her notes while Sheriff Woody fought Buzz Lightyear for a place in Andy's heart. Cendrine heard the voice of the happy cowboy chatting with the other toys as Andy played with the spaceman toy.

During these moments to herself, she took a deep breath and her mind mulled over the new wine project. She was surprised to see Olivier drive away from the office just before lunch. Her father had already taken in the mail. All of the grapes had been hand-harvested. In the winery, which essentially was a large warehouse, the area was teeming with workers, and..... Cendrine shook her head to focus on her new venture. He would probably mention the errand to her later. As the sounds of his car disappeared, she was already entrenched in Antoine's letter, scribbling in a spiral notebook.

***

Olivier arrived at the appointed corner as instructed and studied the dropbox waiting for his packet of money. His white knuckles clutched the steering wheel and he was sure he was going to vomit. Sweat dripped down his neck and found its way south. Quickly glancing around at other cars and passersby, he squeezed the packet of money between his fingers and then he reached for the door handle. How could he leave it in a drop box? A brace of wind tossed his red hair into his face as he looked around the area again, fearful of being watched. Was the son of a bitch watching him to make sure he followed his instructions? Glancing into the hotel's café near the dropbox, his eyes stared at the patrons, but he couldn't see through the darkened glass or the tables beyond.

The wind picked up as he scanned the area near the box before lifting its lid. Nonchalantly dropping the thick, sealed packet of euros as if it was a soiled diaper, his heart thudded when he heard it drop. He retraced his steps and moved his car to park a block away, intent on seeing and following the person who picked up his money.

Olivier sat there a long while, eyes never leaving the corner. He knew he didn't have a choice, did he? If he had, he would have taken another route. He had to keep Cendrine and their unborn baby safe. His eyes never wavered from the box, but his mind flew into the past during his interminable waiting. He loved Cendrine and their life together. Filling his head with her, he thought of their conversations. Her parents met while at universities in northern France. After their marriage, they lived in Pertuis, where Andres interned under the winemaker for the family vineyard, Beauvais Cellars. Chloe had always worked the vines with her parents and she passed her love of the grapevines and winemaking to her children, Cendrine and Gilles.

When Cendrine was fifteen, her mother and brother died in a car crash and their deaths shook the family. Olivier tapped the steering wheel and narrowed his eyes, waiting for someone to approach the box.

He thought of Chloe's brother, François, who became more than an uncle to Cendrine when her father's over protectiveness generated frustration for the young Cendrine. Cendrine's love of winemaking led her to the University at Montpellier SupAgro where she learned more about vines and wine. She always wanted to specialize in sparkling wines and was thrilled to be accepted for an internship in the Champagne region outside Paris where the world's most famous sparkling wine is created.

Olivier smiled as he recollected how animated Cendrine became when talking about her sparkling wine. Beauvais Cellars could not call their sparkling wine champagne; which was a point of much controversy and legal wrangling since it is a legally controlled and restricted name. But Cendrine was sure she could adapt her knowledge to a fine, sparkling rosé for Beauvais Cellars in Provence. And he would keep her safe!

Olivier gripped his thigh and fidgeted. Nobody had approached the dropbox. Staring darkly at the hotel's corner, he wondered how anyone could leave so much money undisturbed, waiting among the trash. The wind picked up. Debris was tossed around the street, flipping off signs and nearby trees in its trek through the alley near his car. His eyes strained to keep track of anyone nearing the dropbox. His head throbbed.

Trying to keep his mind busy, he remembered how sad he felt when Cendrine told him how Andres had lost interest in everything except the grapevines after losing his wife and son. Cendrine continued to learn about the vines from her father, but he was a ghost of the man she'd always known. She had turned to her uncle François for guidance and she had bloomed. When her uncle married Callie, she learned more about love, family and loyalty. She missed her mother dreadfully, but Callie, as her surrogate, made Cendrine whole again.

Olivier pulled at his sleeve and checked the time. One hour had elapsed. His belly hurt and his anger simmered. He wanted to race home, grab his family and leave everything behind. But, of course, he would never do such a thing. His mind meandered back to the time he'd fallen madly in love with Cendrine Frenot a few years after she returned from her studies in the Champagne region.

When they were together, there was magic. They'd married in France and honeymooned in Scotland, where three generations of his family tree lived. Cendrine loved his family and was delighted to learn that his great grandfather's good friend was William Grant, the original owner's son of a whiskey empire. They periodically traveled back and forth when their own grapevines didn't require all of their time.

When the twins were born, their trips slowed but didn't stop; she liked everyone except his cousin, Conall. She told Olivier his cousin stared at him with such malice, that she itched to knock him down. Olivier never took him seriously. One time, when the discussion involved the release of a 50-year old bottle of Glenfiddich, Conall acted proprietarily, working for a whiskey company. His jealousy was ridiculous and Olivier shrugged it off.

Just then, Olivier saw two men approach the dropbox and his breath caught. One lifted the lid and paused to look around him. The other man dropped a bag of trash inside. Olivier scrunched down in his seat and stared at the corner as the men walked on, holding their hats in the breeze. Where was the blackmailer? Was he going to wait until dark? Could he be that dumb? Olivier looked in all directions before he shook his head, angry still.

Squeezing his hands into fists, his mind turned to Cendrine, his fear of losing her intensified. Taking the vineyard's money made him shudder. Shaking his head, he forced his thoughts to her uncle François' death the following year. Cendrine had been devastated. Callie's hopelessness washed over her during the year her aunt grieved, but when she returned to America, Cendrine felt adrift. Although Callie transferred ownership of the old mill house to Cendrine and Olivier, she knew the unattached, renovated cottage was only a shadow of her home, but it would always be hers.

The wind died down and clouds darkened the street. Should he move the car closer? He didn't dare. Was the blackmailer watching him? If he was, would he look for Cendrine?

Someone knocked on his window and he jumped some inches off his seat. A policeman motioned him to move. "Move along. You've been parked too long and the lady who owns this house needs her parking spot."

Olivier nodded and took a deep breath. Smacking the steering wheel, he ground the gears noisily and inched away. When he arrived home, his hands shook as he removed his coat. Relieved to hear the sounds of the children's voices, he joined them in the living room as a plan began to form in his head.

Six

Cendrine watched Olivier chew his croissant the next morning and cut up fruit for the children. She prepared their morning coffees. Her brow rose when he plucked at his sleeve, anxious to get on with his day.

"Alright, Olivier, we'll go on holiday. I have the luggage ready to fill with clothes and I can make a lunch to take in the car. Let's go for three days instead of ten. Please? I must prepare for my *Chloe Rosé* paperwork and Papa wants me to go over everything with the crew. *Oui?*" She saw him look at her strangely. "Where are you taking us for our holiday?"

Olivier's eyes darted around the room, landing first on François and then on Bernadette before returning to his wife's face. "I have found us a place in Sainte Julien. Tomorrow. Can you be ready after breakfast?" His hand slid up her arm to find her hair and ruffle it.

"*Oui*, Olivier. I will tell Papa."

Later that morning, Cendrine drove the twins into town for last-minute shopping. After stopping for fresh vegetables and fruit, she stopped by the park near the central fountain to let the children run off energy. Her mind was agog with thoughts about her new label, but puzzled over Olivier's strange moodiness. When she had questioned him, he had smiled and patted her belly. When he left them that morning, he'd held her in a bone-crunching hug that took her breath away and she was worried.

When Olivier opened the vineyard's office door after lunch, he stepped on an envelope that had been slipped beneath the door. He froze an instant before exhaling loudly over his fears. Probably an invoice or a statement Andres brought by from one of the grape growers. Recently their Grenache grapes showed a bit of mold and they had contracted with a Co-Op until the mold issue was settled. But he was wrong on both counts.

As he read the paper, his hackles rose along with his blood pressure. Another letter. This time, it was focused on his children. More money or the children. He slumped forward and his mind went numb. He would call a police detective he knew in Pertuis. He should have talked to him before he tossed away the vineyard funds. Blackness erupted behind his eyeballs and his chest throbbed. "It will never end until I talk to….." No, he couldn't call him now because he didn't want to admit how stupid he was. Opening his laptop, he logged into the bank account at the same time his eyes fell on the blinking light of his phone machine. He angrily punched the button and then his knees turned weak as a stranger's words filled the room.

"Do not even think of calling *la Policia*, Benoit. I am looking at your little family playing in the park at this moment. Leave the money on the tire under the fender of the red Fiat at *la Poste*. Two o'clock. I will be watching. If you refuse, your family disappears." Click.

Olivier ran toward the house. He grabbed the luggage on the floor of both bedrooms where Cendrine left them. After frantically tossing clothes inside each bag, he grabbed passports and money from the safe. When he pulled the 35 millimeter gun from his bedside table, he heard a sound from below. Cendrine couldn't have returned from town yet and he knew that Andres was in the vineyard. Maybe she wasn't at the park at all. He couldn't be sure though.

He clutched the gun and inched his way down the stairs along the wooden balustrade. He listened intently. A creak by the front door didn't include the children's footsteps. He stopped another moment. When he touched the bottom step, a sharp pain in his side made him stumble and he swung his gun around. He fell forward when pain exploded on the back of his head, barely avoiding the boot aiming at his ribs. And then everything exploded as stars filled his head.

***

Cendrine drove into the garage with the children and pulled the bags of food into the house. Olivier's car was parked at the office but the lights were on inside the house. She opened the back door and entered the kitchen, anxious to get the bags packed. While feeding the children lunch and preparing for the trip, she told them about the holiday ahead of them.

"Sainte Julien is a very old, hilltop village and you can run up and down the streets. If you are very good, your Papa and I will allow you to climb the steps to the platform." The children knew of the platform because their parents had told them one could see mileage signs pointing to many places across the world. One pointed all the way to America where their *tante* Callie lived and one pointed toward GrandPapa in Scotland.

When Cendrine led them upstairs to pack their luggage, she noticed the curious scratches on the floor near the stairwell. When she walked into the children's bedroom, she saw the bags haphazardly stuffed with their clothes. Curious still, she flipped through the clothing and wondered why Olivier was in such a hurry? He knew she planned to get everything packed for the trip. When she walked into their bedroom, she saw the room in disarray, their clothes also stuffed into the bag, zipped closed and sitting by the door. She was bewildered.

The children ran into the bedroom playing tag and she shushed them as she tapped in Olivier's cell phone number. When his voice answered to leave a message, she bit her lip. After a moment, she called her father.

"Papa. Is Olivier with you? He is not answering his phone."

"No, *chérie*. I have not seen him yet this morning. Maybe he is in a meeting or on an errand so he doesn't hear the phone ring? You sound worried. Why?" Andres responded, quickly recognizing his daughter's voice and mirroring her concern.

"I don't know, Papa. Something is wrong. I can feel it."

"Do not worry, *chérie*. I will look for him and you will see he is fine. When I find him, I will call you and you can sit and rest that little baby again. You should stay calm. No stress, remember? I will call you soon." He hung up and headed toward the warehouse.

Cendrine stared at the phone in her hand. And then she herded the children into coats and out the door. Their short legs fought to keep up with their mother as she ran across the gardens toward the office. It was unlocked, which wasn't unusual. She forced herself to stop building what Callie called a mountain from a mole hill. Vaguely wondering what a mole was, she looked around his office, picked up a piece of mail and then glanced toward his laptop. It was black but purring, so she knew it was on. Touching the mouse, it quickly came to life and when it did, her face froze.

She turned around and spun her children out the door to look for her father. He would know what to do and maybe Olivier was with him. There must be a very good reason for what she saw on the bank statement showing the large withdrawal from the day before. There must be an answer and Olivier would tell her what it could be. She wanted to find him now.

Three hours later, Cendrine sat on the bottom step of the stairwell in the old mill house twisting the scarf in her hands. Her father had just left. He was very angry and she was shaking so badly, she couldn't think straight. And Olivier was nowhere to be found. The walls closed in on her and stifled her breath. Her mind darted in several directions, trying to think of the best person to contact. She would call the police. No, they would think the worst and arrest him. They would throw him into jail. Her Olivier would not steal from the family's vineyard account. She would find him first before upsetting everyone and…No police yet. If only she could call uncle François. He would have known what to do. She sniffed and wiped her nose with a shirt sleeve. Her mind settled with that thought and she sat up straight before reaching into her pocket. Shaking uncontrollably, she held the phone tightly to her ear and dialed her aunt Callie in America.

Seven
The Present

As the plane touched the ground in Marseille; goose bumps rose on Callie's arms. She was coming home. It was green and fertile and always seemed to welcome her like a mother's arms. From her earliest days in Pertuis where she spent her summers walking through the vineyard, she was happiest when she was in the French countryside. With a shuddering breath, she tapped open her iPad and typed another note. During her flight over the Atlantic toward the Mediterranean, she jotted down too many thoughts to keep in her head. She hoped she was now prepared to meet Cendrine.

After the Custom's official stamped her passport, she yanked her bag forward and started running. At the entrance doors, Callie was nearly knocked to the floor within Cendrine's solid embrace. As she hugged Cendrine, she could feel the bulging baby through her niece's heavy coat.

"Oh, *chérie*, it's so good to see you. Callie threw an arm around her as they walked toward the familiar blue Peugeot parked nearby. She fought tears from her choked throat, tossed her large bag into the trunk and settled into her seat belt. When their eyes met, the tears couldn't be contained.

"*J'ai peur.* I am afraid and I am very angry at Olivier." When Cendrine put the car into gear, she mumbled something in French.

"Let's practice your English, *ma chérie*. Tell me slowly as we drive home. We are less than one hour from the vineyard. Did you tell your grandparents yet?" Callie saw the negative nod, relieved that her niece had waited for her moral support.

Cendrine stopped crying, mid-snuffle, "I do not want to believe Olivier stole money from the vineyard. I cannot believe it. But when he left, so did the money. And he did not trust me enough to tell me about it."

Callie squeezed her niece's hand.

Long, golden-brown hair swished across Cendrine's shoulders. Gripping the steering wheel as she guided the little car toward Pertuis, she started talking. "When I came home with Bernadette and François from the farmer's market, Olivier was gone. We were going on a holiday. I saw he had filled three large bags with our clothes. An old man had visited him two days before. That morning, Olivier was upset but I did not know why." Cendrine reached for a tissue and blew her nose before continuing. "When I saw the bags filled already, I called Olivier, but he didn't answer, so I went to the vineyard office. Olivier's laptop was there and I saw a bank statement withdrawal on his screen. He took 50000 euros from the vineyard accounts. And now he is gone. He does not answer his phone. Where is he?!" She swiped away tears and maneuvered the car toward Aix en Provence.

"Who was this old man, Cendrine?" Callie was trying to digest the story, still confused.

"He said the man was a friend of his father's. Alexandre Benoit and this man were friends years ago at Vauvenargues, the chateau where Pablo Picasso lived for a few years. Alexandre and Fernando…I do not know his other names. He looked very tired when he walked to his car. I saw him crush his bag to his chest when he left. Olivier told me very little. He was quiet that night and….two days later, he wanted to rush us away for a holiday." Cendrine exhaled loudly and her lips trembled again.

Callie's chocolate-brown eyes stared ahead. As they continued on, it began raining. Heavy drops splatted on the windshield like exploding water balloons and she thought of Olivier, the man she remembered, and smiled. "Well, we will just have to find him now, won't we?"

"I want a day like any other and Olivier home again," Cendrine whispered. "There must be an answer. He would not leave us."

Callie patted her niece's hand as it gripped the gear shift beside her and smiled when she felt the fingers relax. Glancing out the windows a few minutes later, she was glad to see the rain had stopped. A beautiful rainbow arched above the trees. *A rainbow is a good omen. My god, how I have missed the vineyard and this family.* Her thoughts turned fleetingly to Nate back in Portland but she shrugged them away. *Not now.*

Nestled against the backdrop of the Mediterranean to the south and the French Alps to the north in southern France, was a region comprised of gentle rolling hills, rugged mountains, and a plethora of gnarly bush vines that dot the landscape as far as the eye can see. This wild, mind-expanding beauty is what led her father-in-law, Michel Beauvais, to fall in love with the land, take root there, and eventually produce some of the most expressive and elegant wines to emerge from Pertuis.

Miles of vineyards blurred her vision as Cendrine sped past the many acres toward the family home, the outbuildings, warehouse and the old mill house where Callie and François spent their summers renovating, laughing and loving. It always reminded her of a Renoir painting. Her heart swelled with the memories of the place and the man she had loved so much. She pushed away the memory of his death and her heart stumbled and swayed instead, toward the girl beside her and the reason for her flight to Pertuis.

When Callie saw their old mill house again, she turned a bittersweet smile toward the large stone terrace splayed out from the front door. The curving gravel driveway was still lined with oleander and ivy clustered against the fieldstone walls in thick tangles. She'd planted them as tiny plants and their growth surprised her. The four bedroom windows upstairs were tall and mullioned with light green shutters. Lavender still pushed out of small hillocks near the front door. A stone cluster of grapes stood tall beside the porch light that François had installed so long ago when they'd first purchased the old house. These small memories of her husband's existence embraced her and her throat closed again.

Cendrine looked toward Callie a moment before pulling her eyes back onto the curving driveway, stopping with the sounds of crunching gravel under the tires. She reached over and patted her aunt's knee. "You are home, Callie. Come inside and kiss the stones like always."

Callie grinned. "Yes, I always did that, didn't I? And I believe I will again."

"I am very happy you are here, Callie. The children have grown tall and by the time this baby comes....." Her lips trembled again as she smoothed her small hands across her distended belly.

"We shall have a glass of your famous sparkling rosé, *ma chérie*, and then we will get the children from the big house, *d'accord?*

" *Oui, mais seulement un peu. Je ne bois plus de vin depuis que je suis enceinte.*"

"Yes, I know you don't drink during your pregnancy, but a little glass? It might help us focus. There is a logical reason why he is gone. I share your fears and…I know your father loves Olivier too. What does he say about his disappearance?"

"He is quiet and will not speak of it. I told him everything I told to you. It is all I know. He saw the bank people yesterday. Papa said he will wait until you arrive, so we can tell *grand-mère* and *grand-père* together."

When they lifted flutes of chilled, sparkling wine, tapped rims and traded watery smiles, the air stilled. *"A votre santé!"* To your health. Callie had just touched her tongue to the cool bubbles when Andres' knock sounded on the front door.

Callie saw Cendrine's eyes widen.

When her father came into the room, he looked beaten; his eyes were swollen, as upset as his daughter. Callie put down her glass and rose to meet him where she was embraced with a big hug after kissing her on each cheek. He whispered, *"Bon jour, ma chérie."*

Since the children were at their great-grandparent's home, it was quiet in the old house as they sat and stared at one another, not knowing who should speak first.

"Where do we begin?" Andres Frenot gripped both knees and looked at Callie as if she had the answers, before lowering his head. After heaving a deep breath, he said, "Something is wrong. Olivier would not do this thing. I am very angry he did not trust us before he took the money from the vineyard account. And we must know why he did this."

Cendrine's eyes filled with tears and she sniffed loudly.

The women talked for two hours before the old man kissed them again, replaced his hat and tiredly left the house. It was agreed they would approach the owners of the vineyard together. The reason for Callie's visit was, of course, not shared with their in-laws; a big dinner was planned for the following evening. The welcome-home celebration would soon feel funereal, but tonight they would prepare to find Olivier.

As Callie sent Nate an email to say she'd arrived safely, Cendrine drove the short distance to pick up her children from their great grandparent's home. While she was gone, Callie walked slowly around the house that she and François had renovated with such care. She ran her hand along the top of the buffet she had stripped and stained. And remembered how François laughed when she had as much stain on her face and hands as she'd rubbed on the cabinet. He had reached to clean it off her chin and they had ended up in the shower together afterward to clean her up *properly*.

Glancing into the spacious living room, she noticed her Renoir prints still hung above the couch inside estate-sale frames. When she walked into the room, she was sure she could smell his muskiness and sank onto the nearest chair. Leaning her head back, she touched the flowered fabric with her fingers. Another memory. They learned to upholster the old chair together. This was home and not home and she would only allow herself these few moments to linger over the memories.

When she heard Cendrine's car return, she walked out quickly. The children had grown so much, they surprised her. They surged forward, pushing each other aside, vying for a glimpse of their aunt. Shyly, they approached *tante* Callie as their mother gently pushed them. Bernadette was the first to giggle and rush ahead to wrap her small arms around Callie's knees. She possessed her mother's coloring along with her father's red hair. Her thick hair fell in ringlets, tickling her face as she giggled. Callie reached down to smooth the girl's head with a hug before glancing at the little boy who'd been named after her husband. Little François watched his aunt from America with large brown eyes, cocking his small head as if to ask a question. She opened her arms, invited him forward and he approached a step at a time until Bernadette turned around and pushed him into Callie's arms.

Both giggling, the twins ran into the house; Cendrine and Callie followed, arm in arm. "Cendrine, they are such adorable sweethearts. We both know Olivier would never leave you or the children, especially with you pregnant and so beautiful."

Cendrine lips quivered and her body stiffened. "Where is he, then?!"

"Come, let's get the children settled. Then, we can do some serious talking, young lady." Callie followed the laughter into the kitchen where the children were both climbing onto the stools like little monkeys. Her eyes lingered on them. François, a handsome boy, sported dark blonde, curly hair with auburn streaks, dense lashes and freckles, utterly endearing. His shoelaces were untied and his shirttail had slipped out from his pants. His brown eyes were filled with curiosity. Callie smiled. Nobody was going to change her mind about Olivier. Where was he? He would never put Cendrine through this devastating fear or leave these children in such disarray if he had a choice. She was sure of it.

A few hours later, the children were bathed and tucked into bed. *Tante* Callie kissed them and painstakingly read each of them a story in French, determined to get back into the language so her head didn't hurt. When she heard them both say, "*bonne nuit, tante* Callie," she whispered back, "good night to you too." They both giggled, not understanding her words and she chuckled.

Slipping downstairs again, she found Cendrine in the large, open kitchen with a bottle of wine in her hand just beginning to pour the pink bubbling liquid into two crystal wine glasses. One hand caressed her bulging belly while the other poured.

"*Vous voilà*, Callie." Here you are.

They tapped rims and moved to the small chairs in the large living room where Callie sipped slowly. Although her eyes were on the Renoir paintings, her mind was on their conversation. She recognized Cendrine's weariness and anger. She also knew the young woman was so close to tears, she could hardly swallow.

Trying to sidetrack her, she said thoughtfully, "Cendrine, what made you decide to create sparkling rosé instead of the standard rosé that is so popular here in Provence? I don't think I ever asked you about that before."

A soft smile lit Cendrine's face. "François."

Callie almost choked on her wine as she looked at her niece quizzically. "François?"

"*Oui*. Yes, when I wanted to make my own wine label at the vineyard, he told me it should be different, stand alone. Since rosé had always been my favorite, I experimented. I knew what I wanted to do. You see, Callie, uncle

François explained that he believed there should be a sparkle in one's life always, both in wine and in women."

Callie paused, holding the base of the cool glass in her left hand while cradling the bulb with her right. "Oh?" Her brown eyes stared at Cendrine, perplexed.

Cendrine laughed at the expression on Callie's face. "Yes. He said rosé wine could be the sparkle in my life just as you were the sparkle in his."

"Oh," she said again. The room grew silent as vibrant memories swooped down upon Callie once again. Her throat clogged. She looked into the remaining pink bubbling rosé in her hand. When everything turned blurry, she smiled faintly and kissed Cendrine goodnight, turning toward the door that led to her private cottage beyond the gardens.

Cendrine followed behind, turning out the lights, and hoped she had not spoken too much. She loved the woman like a mother and the sadness she'd seen slip across her face made Cendrine's heart stumble. She also missed her uncle dreadfully, but knew it couldn't touch the pain that a wife must feel. She punched the pillow on the couch as she walked toward the stairs. She asked herself if their lives would ever be the same with Olivier gone too.

The next day, Callie pulled out her iPad and continued with her notes, listing everything she'd learned from Andres and Cendrine the night before. She knew it must be directly related to the old Spaniard who had been a friend of Olivier's father. Fernando. There were thousands of Spaniards named Fernando. She bit her lip and rubbed her fingers across her cheek. She tapped the small keyboard attached to her iPad and sat back to ponder the next step. Thinking about explaining everything to Janine and Michel Beauvais that night at dinner made her breath catch. It would kill the old people to think Olivier had used them, stolen from them, hurt their granddaughter. But of course, he couldn't have done any such thing, but...

Cendrine handed Callie a large cup of coffee, and then sat down with a determined look on her face as the questions began again.

"When did Olivier first start acting strangely?" Callie's fingers were poised above her keyboard as she waited for Cendrine. She worried about the anger etched on her niece's face. Hoping to prod her into thinking about the reason why, instead of her husband's absence, might smooth the stress lines. She watched Cendrine's hair fall toward her face before her shaking hands pulled it behind her ears. She tapped her lips in concentration and stretched her fingers outward across her pregnant belly.

"Two days after the Spaniard came to see him. The night after he saw the Spaniard, I noticed he'd finally opened the box of papers his father left him when he died six years ago. Before that, each time he tried to look through the box, he was sad and closed it up again. That night, I found a piece of paper beside the bed. I knew he'd opened the box."

"A piece of paper...? A letter? A document? What was it?"

"It was a small drawing of some sort...oh...an outline showing a Spanish woman sitting on the cork....on a bottle maybe?"

"You mentioned that on the phone but I couldn't imagine what you were talking about." Callie's brow creased.

Cendrine answered, "Yes, it was a pen and ink drawing...artwork that could be a wine label. I didn't recognize it and when I questioned Olivier, he took it away and placed it back in the box. He said it was about some old bottles his father had told him about and I remembered he'd mentioned it before. The story is that Olivier's father, Alexandre Benoit, was a friend of Pablo Picasso's. Alexandre saw old bottles in the cellar of the chateau. Olivier and I both thought it was just a story someone told to entertain...Picasso....really?" She sipped her coffee between words.

"Pablo Picasso had a castle in France? I thought he was Spanish." Callie was mystified, so Cendrine started at the beginning. After several more cups of coffee and a change of videos for the children, Callie contemplated the history that surrounded Olivier's father, the Spaniard and Picasso. *Was it real?*

Cendrine stared out the window and was surprised to see it already mid-day. "Lunch time already. I can't seem to think clearly."

"You feed the children their lunch. I have something to add to my lists. We WILL find him, Cendrine."

Cendrine laughed for the first time since she'd arrived. "You always were great for making lists, Callie. Isn't that how you and your friend, Livvy, finally figured out who was stealing your drugs to sell?"

Callie laughed along with her. "We were not selling drugs, *chérie*, we were trying to contract for a drug card from Canada...they were legal drugs for the people insured with our insurance company."

Although her list grew, nothing told them why Olivier would disappear without telling his wife. When Cendrine pointed out the severe scratches on the floor near the stairwell, they agreed it could be important, but still no answers. Why would Olivier be in such a hurry to leave town and stuff those bags full of clothes and then disappear? And where would he go? He left his car and his laptop behind. Why would he go, knowing Cendrine would be worried and the family devastated? Something clicked. He had no choice. There was someone else involved. When Cendrine came into the room carrying a tray of sandwiches and cookies, she was ready for her.

"Cendrine....do you have the password to Olivier's email address?"

"Yes, I did not think to look. Do you think we may find answers there?" She jumped up and grabbed her laptop and logged onto Olivier's yahoo account. Quickly scanning through the emails, one caught her attention because it was from Olivier to Olivier. When she opened it, she was perplexed to see an old photo with two men. On the table in the photo sat a bottle she had never seen before. Was that label showing a woman riding a cork? She leaned close and recognized it instantly, the finished product of the pen and ink drawing she'd found beside their bed. She moved to the couch and turned the laptop for Callie to see.

"I believe this man on the left is Olivier's father," Cendrine pointed. Her finger slid to the other man. "And I also think this may be the old Spaniard when he was young."

Callie studied the photo and the dark bottle on the table in the background. She knew it was significant because of the drawing Cendrine had found on the floor after Olivier riffled through the box his father left him. The label was unique and very Spanish. But it just added another layer to the mystery. "Can you print this out for us?"

Cendrine moved to do her bidding and gave Callie the printed photo of the small painting. "This photo looks like it was taken about 1960 or so."

"You're right…the ages of the men compared to the present makes sense. Do you know who Olivier might have discussed this with after he spoke with this Spaniard? Is he close to a friend nearby or a relative he could discuss his father's paperwork with?"

Cendrine's breath hitched.

"You know of someone?" Callie's heartbeat sped up.

"Yes, his GrandPapa in Scotland. This mysterious bottle story has been discussed often and he never believed Olivier's father was friends with Picasso. He laughed at the idea. Maybe Olivier's gone to Scotland??"

"Do you have his phone number?"

Cendrine found the number for Bruce Baird and dialed, but then her shoulders sagged when there was no answer.

Callie said, "We can call again later. What time are your grandparents expecting us for dinner?"

"Five for drinks. Dinner at six. Papa will arrive early, I think, as he has other things to discuss and he wants to…. how do you say, tile the way."

Callie chuckled. "You mean, pave the way?"

"*Oui*," Cendrine pulled at her smock top nervously.

Callie's iPad zinged, announcing an email. She tapped an answer to Nate but could not explain away her annoyance. He loved her. He was worried about her. He wanted her back in Portland, but he was pushing her. He was a gentle soul and she was crazy about him, his dad and his uncle. She smiled as she visualized what happened after she admitted her feelings for Nate, but then her brow furrowed. She had things to do, couldn't he understand that?

Eight

As she heard Cendrine herding the children into their beds for an afternoon nap, Callie tapped her fingers across the keyboard.

A few minutes later, Cendrine rushed into the room with a look of excitement, sat down and yanked the laptop open.

"What is it, Cendrine?"

"I found something, Callie!" She placed Olivier's laptop on the large round couch table and punched the keys. I logged onto his email from my laptop and found the painting, but I looked around **his** laptop and found a letter in his scanned document folder. It is from Olivier's father dated seven years ago, a year before he died. The letter talks about a map to Jouques, a village near here. But I cannot find a map on the computer……" Her eyes filled with hope, but she couldn't continue.

Callie reached over to tap a finger on her arm. "But, Cendrine, this is a big clue! Read the letter to me please." She knew Cendrine could print it out, but she also knew it was imperative to keep Cendrine focused. And every clue counted.

Cendrine enlarged the font. Sitting closely, Callie imagined an old man's voice speaking to his son. The letter was, of course, in French, so she asked Cendrine to read it aloud as she followed along with the cursive script. Although it was crooked and a little difficult to decipher, Cendrine's voice was clear, concise.

My dear Olivier,

If you are reading this letter, I am dead and buried. As I write this to you, I first want to tell you that you have always been a very good son and I love you very much. I have asked my old friend, Fernando Sanchez Ortega, to deliver this letter to you after I die and also asked him to wait until you were older. The reason for this is because my old friend, Pablo Ruiz Picasso, wanted his brandy hidden for as long as possible. This was our big plan. The brandy is very special and Pablo trusted us to follow his wishes. This I have done.

First, I will tell you the story he told to us. When the Spanish Civil War began in the summer of 1936 and lasted nearly three years, Pablo was a Republican, loyal to the democratically elected Spanish Republic. When the Nationalists, a fascist group led by Francisco Franco, won the war, he was frantic that his winery's new brandy not fall into the hands of the fascists. His friend, José Luis Alonzo, produced this brandy from a white grape called Airen. The small vineyard was one that Pablo held fifty percent ownership. It was located west of Málaga in the Province of Cadiz near Jerez de la Frontera in a small village barely seen on many maps. His friend and this brandy were both very important to Pablo and he wanted no fascist hands to touch them. So, he began to plan with his Republican friends. With many people helping, he was able to remove the brandy a few miles at a time toward the French border until he received five cases, sixty bottles at Vauvenargues.

I know this letter is long, my good son, but I must explain Pablo's passionate plea to save his brandy for a future promise. He asked us to taste it after he told us his story and it was delicious. At that time, it was about twenty years old. By the time you receive this letter, the brandy is probably seventy years old. Pablo promised that the brandy would be as good now as it was then and I believed him. He explained that in the cellar of the chateau, his brandy met all storage conditions, light, humidity, temperature and dark. Light will damage wine causing the degradation of stable organic compounds found in wine. Since these organic compounds contribute to the aroma, flavor and structure of the wine, the changes caused by UV light deteriorate the essence. You see, he explained this to me so often, I can remember each word from memory. These bottles of brandy were sealed with cork and wax. Since corks are far from perfect to seal a bottle of wine, the space between the bottom of the cork and the wine level in the bottle changes in almost all bottles stored for extended periods due to evaporation. If the cork is defective, low humidity will result in wine moving out of the bottle quicker over time and significant changes will develop faster. And then there is the temperature in the dark, humid storage area. Pablo's cellar was perfect to age the brandy. The chemical reactions taking place in the brandy must be consistent or chaos reigns in the bottle, he told us often. When the brandy was moved from Spain to France, it had to travel carefully, at night when the temperatures did not change radically to keep it safe from the chemical changes. He did not want the wine cooked along the way. And the cork? It cannot become dry! The bottles must stay at an angle to make it so. This is why I explain about preserving this brandy that so many hands have held to keep it safely for Pablo to continue his dream.

    Fernando and I were the keepers of the brandy and now it is up to you. I have enclosed a map to show you where we hid the brandy for Pablo after he left Vauvenargues to live in Mongins nearer the sea, where he died. He knew we would carry on that dream, so I ask you to do the same. Follow the map to Jouques and you will find the brandy. It should be very, very valuable now. Find a Spanish buyer. That was very important to Pablo. When you gather the bottles, sell them and use the funds to create a flamenco guitar school in Algodonales, the ancestral home of José Luis. He wanted the young people to keep the tradition to play the flamenco! The Prado in Madrid can help you to begin. If Fernando still lives in Málaga, he will be a good contact. I trust him explicitly.

    As I write this letter to you, I feel tears coming. This is a very big service you do and I trust it will not be too difficult.

I hope by now that you have a little family of your own and that you have a son that you love as much as I love you. I remain, as always,

        Your loving father, Alexandre Benoit

His words bumped the women speechless.

"So, it is true," Cendrine whispered. She leaned forward on the couch and pressed both hands against her face. She had no words to imagine her husband reading this letter. Leaning back, she laid her head against the cushion and smoothed both hands over her belly. As she sat shaking her head and swallowing tears, she saw Callie pull her laptop toward her quickly.

Callie's mind was moving fast. She typed frantically. "We must find the map. It has something to do with Olivier, of course. What must he have thought when he read this letter from his father? How far is Jouques from Pertuis? I do not know this village." She opened her browser and had her answer in seconds. "It's a thirty minute drive. We need that map. It would be impossible to go looking for these wine bottles without it."

***

Two days earlier, in another village about twenty minutes from Pertuis, Olivier Benoit sat on a cot with his head in his hands. He'd woken without the slightest notion where he was. Curled up on the bed, he wrinkled his nose and stared around him. The room was dirty. That much came dimly to him -- he could smell it. How long had he been there? A jolt of alarm brought him up on his elbows, but a bright stab of pain behind his eyes sat him down again, moaning and cursing. The bed was too short for his tall frame and his head had been wedged up against the wall. He couldn't remember what he had dreamt about, but vaguely recollected there were children. His body jerked when the door banged open.

"So, you are awake. Eat. Drink. Then we talk." When the door slammed against the filthy wall, dust and dirt swirled in the air. The man was gruff as he dropped a tray with a bottle of wine, a loaf of crusty bread and a white-wrapped package of cheese onto the wooden table beside him. Several Evian water bottles were on the table, empty bottles lay near the bed. Olivier looked out the small window. An inch of blue sky wedged across the top of a black oilcloth that covered the window. His head hurt and his shoulder did not feel right. Raising his fingers to the base of his neck, he felt a lump as big as a walnut, sore to the touch; he groaned and jerked his hand back onto his lap.

The man grunted and left as suddenly as he'd arrived. Olivier stared after him wondering who he was. And why had the man locked him in here? He looked around again. It appeared to be a storage room with shelves filled with small boxes. Disgustedly, he pulled his feet up on the cot, which was not too clean either. His head throbbed like a toothache and he was frightened; his mind was cloudy and he couldn't remember how he got there. Worse than that, he couldn't remember who he was.

He'd just fallen asleep when the door screeched open again. His jailer stood in the doorway, fists clenched at his side. He yanked a wooden chair off the floor and planted it knee to knee with Olivier and stared into his face. "Now, we talk. Tell me where the bottles are hidden and you go free."

Olivier stared at the man. He shook his head to focus. The man's face wavered, he was seeing double. He waited until his breath came easier, and then risked lifting his head again. "What bottles?"

"You know what bottles I'm talking about, man! The wine your Papa and the old Spaniard hid for Picasso. I saw the old Spaniard visit you the other day and I want them!" The man's face was twisted with irritation.

Olivier looked disgusted. "I have no idea what you are talking about. I can't remember anything at all, bottles, Spaniards or wine."

"I don't believe you!" Now belligerent, he angrily pushed his wild, copper-colored hair away from his face. "You know where that wine is and you'll tell me or I'll beat it out of you." He jerked away from the bed and kicked the empty water bottles across the room.

"Go ahead. There's nothing to tell." Olivier ground out.

"For a smart guy, you're still not getting it," the man hissed. "Things are going to change. I don't have to put up with your shit anymore. I'm giving the orders now. You will do as I say or I'll break you in half!" He gave Olivier's shoulder a powerful squeeze and shoved him backwards on the cot. "Have I made myself clear?" He stretched out the words, beady eyes daring Olivier to fight back.

Olivier rubbed his shoulder and glared at him with such intensity, the man stepped back. "You touch me again and we'll see who makes who clear. I. Do. Not. Know. What. You. Want!" Olivier enunciated with a fierce growl, not waiting for an answer. "Until I remember who the hell I am, you can go burp coins," he taunted.

The men stared at each other a few moments before the stranger slammed out the door. Olivier's head swam with the questions the man kept yelling at him. But he had no answers. He had no idea what the man was talking about and with each negative nod, the man had become angrier. How could he tell him where some wine bottles were hidden when he didn't even know his own name? He squeezed his temples with both hands and lay back on the cot, aching too badly to think further.

Half an hour later, a red Fiat idled at the curb not far from the old mill house. The driver turned off the ignition to wait as he formed another plan. There were no close neighbors and the vineyard stretched for miles in both directions. Worried his vehicle might be noticed, he hunkered down in the seat. His fingers tapped the steering wheel as he shook his head and pressed a palm against his leg. He'd hit him too hard. "Amnesia, for god's sake," he muttered a few unintelligible words. He really did not want to hurt the wife or the children. But he would get his answers. He'd waited too long to get his life right and wouldn't let the man's stupid Amnesia stop him now.

***

Later that afternoon, when Callie pulled the curtain back from her cottage window to gaze toward the old mill house, she felt a gnawing hollowness. When she first visited Pertuis twenty years earlier, the old girl was a decrepit mess but it had captivated her with its potential charm. In her previous life, she'd been an interior designer and the thought of bringing the beautiful stone house alive again was nearly as exciting as marrying François. She and her mother had worked together for years renovating, flipping houses and renovating again. After her mother was diagnosed with cancer, their lives changed radically. Callie moved her from Napa Valley in California to Portland, near the Oregon Health Sciences University. Callie joined the health insurance industry. Later, she'd moved to Larkspur Insurance where her best friend, Olivia, was the CEO. Then François died in the boating accident at their beach house, and then her mother had died.

She'd forgotten the thrill that came over her when she and François first walked into the old mill building so long ago. Now, looking toward the gardens draped in swathes of bougainvillea through the deeply-framed windows, gave her a bittersweet smile. She let go of the curtain slowly. Sitting down in the big easy chair, she lifted her feet to the cushion and sipped hot tea, staring into its depths. So much in her life had changed since then, she mused. She had been married and now she was single. She had been involved with decorating and now she worked as the sales manager for Larkspur Insurance in Oregon. She had been a country girl in the rural wine country of California and now she resided in a big Oregon city. Where did she really belong? Her musings placed a blanket on her worries about Olivier for the moment as she sipped tea and reminisced.

Showtime.

That evening, Cendrine and Callie helped the children into the car for the short drive to the big house. Janine and Michel expected the evening's dinner to be a celebratory feast welcoming Callinda home again. They certainly had a sad surprise in store for them.

As Cendrine drove through the brick columns at the vineyard's entrance, Callie recognized the sign embedded into the heavy, gray stones that read *Entre Privée*...private entrance. Her heart raced. She was part of this family. She belonged here. She thought of Nate so many miles away and knew he would never be able to share this part of her life. She swallowed hard. He would be fighting against her memories of François always.

After Callie was tightly embraced by both of the older people, she smiled. She was back where everything was beautiful and soft and smelled good. Her mind was calmer and the outside world fell away. Within minutes, the ladies were in the large colorful kitchen, leaving Andres and Michel to talk over glasses of wine. Callie did not miss the look Andres gave her when she entered the room and nodded as if to say, wait a bit please?

Janine handed Cendrine an apron to tie around her protruding belly and helped the twins into chairs at the table to taste freshly cut cheese and a few grapes. Happy with their snack, the children teased each other and grinned as they chewed, watching the adults work at the counters.

"Mmm, *Bon*," Good". Cendrine exclaimed, inhaling deeply. "Something smells delicious."

"We have salt cod with carrots, potatoes, green beans and fennel," Janine said with a smile as she stirred the vegetables and lifted a white cloth off a basket of bread chunks. "I also made the *aioli*, so we can move it around between the vegetables and fish. It is a magical emulsion with all the garlic and oil and I've already sampled it for you." She chuckled.

The younger women grinned and tried to dip a chunk of bread into the mixture but Janine tapped their fingers. "*Non.* No. You must wait for the *rillettes*. It tastes just fine. I tested it earlier." Her eyes danced.

Callie laughed. "I definitely remember *rillettes, Maman*. Pork belly and shoulder mixed with herbs and Swiss chard, yes?" Warmth began to creep through her body as she lifted her eyes to the older woman and they shared a smile. "And I see tapenade." Spreading it on a chunk of bread, she popped it in her mouth. "Mmmm."

The smells of Provence assailed her where the food was unassuming, simple and elegant. She glanced at Cendrine and saw her hands shake as she turned to help her grandmother unwrap the fromage.

***

After the never ceasing river of wine and piles of delicious food, Andres nodded to Cendrine. Callie reached for Janine's hand. She wished she could spare this dear old woman. She could see that Michel was not himself as he moved toward the living room before the group. He sat down as the children pushed toward him, but he studied his daughter in law, knowing something was amiss.

Janine looked at Callie with upraised eyebrows and then toward Cendrine. "What is it? You told me you would tell us why Olivier could not join us for dinner." She repeated, "What is it?"

When Cendrine began, her lips trembled and her father clasped her hand. He didn't have to shush the twins. Their heads jerked up and stared from one adult to the other with rounded eyes. The air stilled.

In between the women's explanations, Andres shared what they all knew. And it wasn't much.

Michel looked at Janine and filled the air with an angry expletive.

Janine quietly left the room and returned with a bottle of *Ricard Anise* and five small glasses. Her hands shook like her granddaughter's moments earlier, but she folded them in front of her and closed her eyes.

Callie reached for the bottle and poured each of them two fingers of liquor and then the questions popped and staggered around the room. After an hour of disjointed conversation, it was agreed they all loved Olivier and they must find him. They also admitted the mystery was daunting and they had no idea where to begin. And they were all very angry. Why couldn't he talk with them if there was a problem? Why take the vineyard money without trusting them? Where was he now? What should they do?

Michel's jaw tightened and his fingers turned slightly blue as he clutched his drink. Lifting the glass slowly to his lips, his eyes grew thoughtful, his mind spinning in a whirlwind.

Janine studied Cendrine. "You go home and rest. I will clean up without you. You must care for that little one you carry."

Callie tried to argue but Janine wouldn't have it. So she sipped her Anise, gripped the glass and thought of the old Scot again. She knew if she could learn anything from Olivier's great grandfather and find that map the letter alluded to, it could lead them to answers. And to Olivier.

An hour later, the group gathered at the front door to say their goodbyes. Andres hugged his daughter and helped her put coats on the children. They all agreed it was a serious matter and the only way to resolve the issue was to get started and work together. They also shared their anger at Olivier for not talking to them about something that amounted to 50000 euros. The vineyard would survive but family and trust was important too.

An hour later, Callie was speaking with old Bruce Alec Baird. He told her about his last conversation with Olivier shortly after Fernando, the Spaniard, had visited him, but he did not know anything more. He was frantic with worry and told her so. He also told her his friend had questioned him about the mysterious wine bottles.

Callie perked up. "How on earth did he learn about those bottles?"

The old Scot wasn't sure. "I tauld Olivier that my friend, William, was haur a few days ago askin' me if thaur was any truth tae those bottle rumors."

Callie rolled the information around in her head. "Does this man work at the same whiskey distillery where Cendrine's friend, Antoine, now works?" A connection was there somewhere but the thread wasn't finding its way through.

" Och aye, th' sam wee mukker works wi' a friend of William's."

Callie grinned as she struggled not to chuckle at the man's Scottish burr. She knew the wee mukker must be Antoine. "I cannot imagine there is a connection between Antoine unless he knows Olivier. I know he and Cendrine went to university together. I will ask her about him."

The old man said, "Olivier's coosin, Conaa, works thaur also but he an' Olivier hae ne'er bin close."

"Olivier has a cousin in Scotland? I had forgotten that. I will ask Cendrine about him also. Callie's unanswered questions brewed as the old Scot cleared his throat to say goodbye.

"Ye will please lit me ken abit Olivier as suin as ye fin' heem, yoong quine? If Ah hear frae heem, Ah will caa ye, but Ah hae a bad feelin' abit thes." The old man's voice broke suddenly.

Callie assured him she'd be in touch, hung up and headed for her iPad again. There were some answers in that discussion and she had to write everything down to find them. The house was quiet as she heard Cendrine tell little François and Bernadette good night.

Cendrine stepped down the stairs with a confused look on her face. "Callie, didn't I leave my book bag on the coffee table when we went to the big house for dinner?" She wandered into the room, pulling at her hair.

Callie glanced at the table and the surrounding area. "I can't remember." She turned back to Cendrine with a question on her face.

"I'm sure I did. When we arrived home, the living room light was on and I surely turned it off." Cendrine looked around the room, walked into the kitchen and saw the screen door ajar. Her eyes flew to Callie. "Something is wrong." Cendrine pulled a butcher knife from the side drawer and turned off the kitchen light immediately, inching toward the back door. It was unlatched and one small pane of glass was broken. Shards of glass lay on the floor and she used the knife to tap the knob. It fell off.

Callie stared at her very pregnant niece wielding the huge knife. The shocking hugeness of the situation thundered in her ears. She hurried to the kitchen window, relieved to see that nothing moved, not even the leaves on the trees.

They stared at one another a moment before they raced through the main floor of the house to check windows and to double lock the front door. Cendrine hurried upstairs to check on the children. When she stood at the door to their rooms, a flippy tingling erupted in her belly and she hoped it was the baby saying hello and not trying to come into the world too early. Her hands cupped her belly and she returned downstairs.

Callie picked up each piece of glass carefully, taped a piece of cardboard over the hole and wedged one of the dining room chairs under the bar of the broken door knob.. That is when she noticed smudges on the floor. She followed them through the kitchen, into the living room and through the house into Olivier's home office. It was a tiny alcove really, but it had playfully been called an office ever since she and François had purchased the old home. Now, twenty years later, Olivier did the same. She switched on the light. It looked like a small hurricane had bludgeoned the room. Goosebumps rose on her arms.

Cendrine found her staring at the mess. "*Oh, mon Dieu.* Someone was here while we were gone. Looking for something…what? I am glad we took both laptops to show *grand-mère* and *grand-père*. Now, I am really frightened, Callie. This tells me there is much more to Olivier's disappearance and this bizarre mystery."

Callie sat down in Olivier's chair. "We are missing something important here, Cendrine. And it might be in here or on Olivier's laptop." She started thrashing through the papers and looking into drawers. She tore through the books lined up on the shelf beside the desk. When her fingers lifted the carpet to peer under it, she said, "We can't do this alone, Cendrine. It is getting too big for us."

Cendrine studied her aunt. "The police?"

Callie glanced at her watch. "No. It's almost ten o'clock. We need a man to help us. We can't find Olivier or those blasted bottles on our own. And now we feel unsafe. With a burglar involved, it changes the dynamics. I'm frightened for you and the children. This creep has crossed the line into our home and…" She ran her fingers along the neck of her sweater, pulled it outward and let in some air. "Let's not call the police yet, though. Are we still agreed on that? I know we should, but dammit, I trust Olivier and…"

"Yes, no police. What is a creep?"

The women checked the upstairs windows. Callie's head bobbed up. "It's a disgusting person, like our burglar."

Cendrine sighed. "Ah…who are we going ask to help us, Callie? I can't stand this fear that stays with me every day and my anger at Olivier is growing." She clutched the door frame with clenched fists.

Callie sighed. "I know. Let's go to bed. I'll sleep in the guest room tonight." The thought of a stranger breaking into the house to hurt these innocents caused her to stumble on the stair. She wished she'd brought her 25 caliber gun from Portland. *I could scare the poop out of someone just holding it in my shaking fist. François said not to point it unless I was prepared to shoot. Maybe I could shoot it!*

Neither of the women slept. They heard every creak, the breeze at the windows, a faraway growl. It was a very long night.

Nine

The next morning, Callie sprawled on the bed and pulled up the notes she'd jotted down. Later, sitting at the dining room table amid the children's chatter, she ruffled Bernadette's hair while thoughtfully sipping her coffee. "Cendrine… tell me about this cousin in Scotland."

"Olivier has never been close to his cousin, Conall."

"What about the Grant distillery?"

GrandPapa's friend makes whiskey, but I had no idea he was related to William Grant. When Olivier said GrandPapa was a silent partner in the distillery, I was shocked. Then Olivier reminded me that the annual stipend that is automatically deposited into our bank account is from Grant & Sons."

Callie digested the information. "And Antoine. You trust him?"

"Absolutely. We are like brother and sister."

Callie's mind was awhirl with indecision. "We need help, Cendrine. Someone outside of the family, someone we can trust." They ticked off possibilities and then Callie's head snapped up.

"What?" Cendrine asked breathlessly.

Callie snapped her fingers. "I know just the man, *ma chérie*. Do you remember Jules, your uncle's childhood friend?"

"Yes, of course. They were always very close, but over the years I saw them grow apart. In fact, I remember they had a loud argument and Jules drove off so quickly that Papa raked the gravel smooth in the lane afterward…." Cendrine watched Callie's eyes sparkle.

"Well, we will see if he's still around." The next moment, Callie found the phone number. Within minutes, she smiled.

"Of course, I know who you are, Callie."

"I need your help, Jules. Could we….?"

"…..meet over a coffee?" he finished for her with a chuckle.

He heard the relief in her response, "*Oui, merci.*" Yes, thank you.

Two hours later, Jules Luc Armand's warm smile welcomed her at the *Bistrot Edin Café*. After kissing her on each cheek, they sat at a linen-covered table beside the window. As the morning sun laid a swath of gold across them, Jules asked, "So what do I owe the honor of meeting you for coffee, Callie?" His smile faded, however, when he noticed the look of concern on his friend's widow's face.

"I have a problem," Callie replied. "or I should say the Beauvais family has a problem. I instantly thought of you because you and François were friends since childhood. I also know you drifted apart over the years and I do not know why. Today, I do know he would have called you because he trusted you."

Jules sat up a bit straighter in his chair, his gray eyes wide open with curiosity. He had not seen the woman for several years and yet, he felt he was connected through his old friend, François.

As Callie told Jules about Olivier's disappearance over their espressos, she saw his face change. Jules was furious. He put down the small espresso cup and stared at his late friend's wife. "Do you mean to say Olivier has stolen the vineyard funds and disappeared, but you believe he is innocent of the theft, Callie?"

"Yes, he is!" She bit her lip before continuing and ran her hand through her silver bangs in exasperation. "He is a very good man, Jules. I called you because I knew you and François were friends for many years and I have nobody else to turn to. Please trust me when I say there is something not right here. Olivier loves Cendrine and his children. I just feel it here!" She placed her hand over her heart and tapped it repeatedly.

Jules noticed her ring, a large green stone surrounded by diamonds, sparkle in the sunshine streaming through the café windows. "Did you already call the police?"

"Absolutely not! The family would need to explain the missing money and they are not ready to do that yet because they fear for Olivier. They trusted him and still do, at least for now. Will you help us, Jules?"

"*Oui*, yes. I will help you find him but I will decide if I trust him when we do. Please continue. The challenge is intriguing." Jules sipped more espresso as Callie's assumptions took root and his eyes grew dark.

There was something about his genuine enthusiasm that made Callie trust Jules even more. She knew it was irrational but she was learning to trust her instincts. So, in that instant, she made the decision to share the mystery of the wine bottles with him, the Spanish woman riding the cork and the family story originally thought to be a myth. "There is something else you need to know," she whispered.

Jules looked into her dark, expressive eyes. Callie's mouth moved again and Jules leaned in to listen to the rest of the story. Her quick smile promised more and he was reluctant to look away. Why had he never noticed the woman's effortless charm and physical appeal before? Her features were gentle and her dark eyelashes brushed her cheeks. Slowly, chewing his croissant, he lifted a large piece of melon, organizing his thoughts. "First of all," he began, "I'm in charge. You and Cendrine must trust me to lead the way." He scanned Callie's face with keen interest, watching for her reaction.

Her jaw tightened, "Excuse me?" She pulled herself up and lifted her shoulders, instantly alert. Her brown eyes were riveted to his face, not quite sure she heard him right.

Jules lifted his coffee and did not answer.

She stared at him before breaking the silence. "What do you suggest? Olivier is **our** top priority. What is **yours**?" she ground out, as her eyes glared.

"Do you even have a clue about what you could be getting yourself into, Callie? If you have any hope of finding Olivier and keeping Cendrine and the children safe, you will agree to my terms or I walk away now."

Callie's eyes snapped sparks. *He is probably bluffing but can we afford to take that chance? Maybe we* **are** *in over her head.* Arguments rattled inside her head until her practical nature agreed with him, but she didn't like it. They sat for several minutes maintaining a tense silence as her pointer finger tapped the table top. As eager as she was to find Olivier, she needed a clear picture and a plan. She fought to suppress a bevy of emotions that welled up inside of her. This was the first time she'd met a man whose strength promised more than she bargained for. And she liked it. She sighed and held out her hand, inviting him to shake on the partnership.

He relaxed.

"The only facts we know for sure are about some mystery bottles of brandy that Picasso somehow secreted out of Spain. This was during Franco's reign because Picasso was a defiant exile from Spain and lived in France during the Spanish Civil War and afterward. The bottles may be close by in Jouques. His old chateau is not far from where we sit now, but the bottles are no longer there. They were moved, hidden, and that is part of this crazy story. The man who came to see Olivier, just before he disappeared with the vineyard's money, was a Spaniard named Fernando. Cendrine found information on Olivier's laptop. And why wouldn't Olivier have taken his laptop and his belongings if he'd run away? He left everything. Cendrine said his clothes were still stuffed inside his luggage."

"His luggage?" He eyeballed her with suspicion.

"Yes, he was upset about something a couple days after he met with Fernando. He planned to whisk his family away for a holiday in Sainte Julien, but he disappeared the day before they planned to leave." She exhaled loudly, lifted her cup and sipped thoughtfully. Before she could continue, a young woman with billowing blonde hair and a huge smile tapped on the window to get Jules' attention. Callie's breath caught and her eyebrows shot upward. She recognized François' eyes reflected through the glass as the girl looked back at her. If there was a clone for her late husband, she was staring at her. The hair on the back of Callie's neck stood on end.

Jules' intake of breath brought Callie's attention back to his face and she nearly dropped her cup. Her white knuckles squeezed its handle before she whipped a hand to her chest as if to hold her heartbeat in check.

The young woman grinned, spoke quickly to her friends and entered the café. She was pretty with wheat-colored hair and whiskey-colored eyes. She was dressed stylishly, a long silk scarf loosely looped around her neck.

She looked clean, fresh. And she had Callie's husband's eyes and her husband's smile.

Jules stood to open his arms. After kissing each cheek in the French fashion, she turned expectantly toward Callie. With a smile on her face, she was confused when her uncle did not introduce her to his friend. She offered her hand and said, "My name is Veronique Armand. I am this rude man's niece." She tsked toward him.

Callie lifted her hand and said, "I am pleased to meet you, Veronique. My name is Callie Beauvais. I was once married to your uncle's friend, François, before he died a few years ago. I am surprised we have not met before..." she answered gently before turning her face toward Jules once again with a look.

He took a deep breath and smiled wanly toward both women.

"I will see you tonight for dinner, uncle Jules….at *Gadoline's*?"

He nodded with a smile on his lips.

"Good, I will see you later," she confirmed, with a wide grin on her face as she adjusted her scarf. And then she was gone like the wind. They saw her join her friends on the sidewalk where she pulled the rich, yellow scarf around her pale head to tie it before the group disappeared from sight.

Unsettled, Callie let the strands of silence stretch between them. This couldn't be happening. How can this be true? And how in the world could she have misread a man she trusted with everything in her heart? She turned to Jules and whispered, "Tell me, please."

When Jules touched her with his eyes, she lost her breath.

Moved by Callie's sadness and the shock that crossed her face, he had no choice but to tell her. He delved deep as he told her a sad story about his sister, Aurore, and her daughter, Veronique. Quietly, he spoke for nearly thirty minutes, kindly trying to ignore the hurt in Callie's eyes.

"Aurore loved François from the time she was a teenager. He always saw her only as his best friend's little sister. Then he went away to college and returned to find a beautiful young woman who chased after him until he would see her, truly see her, as a woman. I did not like what was happening. I saw no magic between a man and a woman truly in love. She pushed herself at him over and over again. His parents did not realize what was happening, but I did. I talked to François many times but he told me men needed their flirtations. By the time he brought you home to Provence to meet his parents, Aurore was horrified, devastated and pregnant. And I was very angry. That is one of the reasons why François and I became estranged. He was ashamed and I stayed angry. Then, when I met you after your marriage, I was charmed and fell a little in love with you myself." His gray eyes softened.

Her lips quivered but her eyes smiled at his gentle admission. "I thought I knew my husband, Jules. He lied by omission. Protecting himself was more important than trusting me with the truth?"

Jules pursed his lips. "This is true. Although I remained angry still, François and I talked now and then. Our little Veronique was the bright spot in my life, but I pulled away from the Beauvais family. And I hated that. They'd always treated me like one of their own."

Callie's fist clenched. There was so much concern in his voice that Callie almost started crying, but managed to control herself. She reached up to swipe a wet cheek. "But why ignore his child? François and I could not have children. I always wanted a child and he knew that, and he already had one… My god, by now she must be…..?" She looked up at Jules uncertainly.

"Veronique is twenty years old." He tapped his finger against his cup. "I am sorry she chose that moment to look into the window. I cringed when I saw her, but we cannot ignore her existence now. She is beautiful like her mother, intelligent and thoughtful like her father."

Callie's look disagreed, too bruised to speak. With a watery smile, she rebutted him. "Thoughtful? How could he do such a thing?" She felt her coffee begin to rise upward in her throat.

Jules shook his head. "Yes, he was thoughtful; he just loved you too much to tell you the truth. Maybe he thought he might lose you? I do not know. He did, however, support her and pay for her living expenses while she attended the Sorbonne in *Paris*. He told Aurore he would do that on two conditions; his daughter must learn to speak English and she must never know he was her father."

His words swallowed Callie's thoughts. "Oh, my god." She rubbed her arms fiercely. "Aurore must hate me." She lowered her head before bringing it up again quickly. "Where does Veronique live now, Jules?"

"She lives within three miles of us," he answered, "and I am meeting her for dinner tonight. She is like a daughter to me and her laughter tinkles like a rainbow swelling across the sky after a rainstorm. You would like her very much, Callie. But, of course......"

"But, of course? Yes, probably, but why would François ignore this beautiful child? Why could he not trust me?" She groped for words and felt the walls close in on her, suffocating her, forcing introspection. "He was just a man after all, wasn't he?" Her eyes turned inward.

Jules sipped his coffee, smacked his lips and sighed. "Couldn't deal with losing you, I imagine." He watched the emotions flit across her face and thought he'd never seen anyone quite as beautiful.

Callie inhaled deeply, finished her espresso and raised her hand to order another. "Please bring me a warm chocolate croissant also?" Then, she turned toward Jules again. "We shall talk of this again but not now please. I cannot bear it." She pressed her hand to her belly and willed it to settle down. Would she ever remember François in the same way again?

Jules studied Callie, aching to help her. Instead, their discussion veered to Olivier, the missing man and the missing bottles. He noticed how her face glowed when she smiled and her chocolate-colored eyes lit up. He'd thought the same thing when François first introduced them twenty years earlier; the men had both just turned thirty. Now, he was in his fifties and François was gone. He missed his friend despite the family strife. And then he turned to Callie again, determined to find her answers if only to see that smile again.

"I asked Cendrine about her friend, Antoine. He and Cendrine went to university together near Paris; she left her internship to make her pink sparkling rosé here at Beauvais Cellars, but he stayed there. Until recently, that is. He is now working at a whiskey distillery in Scotland. It is probably just a coincidence, but his cousin, Conall Carson, also works there."

"Antoine's cousin?"

"No, Olivier's cousin. Cendrine told me his mother was not married to the father. She was Olivier's mother's sister, Aila, and she died in childbirth. Conall's father and his family raised the boy, but his great grandfather, Bruce Baird, kept close tabs on him. Cendrine tells me Conall is a bitter man and Olivier is not close to him. In fact, she said once during one of their visits to Scotland, she glanced across the dining room table and saw such a look of hatred on Conall's face, it made her shiver. He'd been staring at Olivier. I was surprised to learn he is now working with Cendrine's friend, Antoine. Coincidences do happen…it's a small world, really." She compressed her lips.

Jules pondered the information running through his head, wondering if it was really a coincidence or was there a connection? "Let's talk about the Spaniard again, Callie. You have his full name and where he lives in Spain?"

She tapped into her iPad notes. "Yes, we learned he is Fernando Sanchez Ortega and he lives in Malaga. We couldn't find the original letter or a map to the hidden bottles, but we know it's in Jouques. Cendrine is tearing through everything at the house and in the vineyard office. She is sure the Spaniard drove a rental car, but that could be from anywhere."

"Probably from Aix. Do you have the dates? I have a friend who works at a travel agency who might be able to do some investigating." He smiled and raised his eyebrows at her.

"Oh? I like the way you think, Jules." She grinned. "I will welcome your help with humility and gratitude." Something that Jules said had rung a faint bell with Callie. She frowned, trying to pinpoint what it was, but it slipped away from her. It would probably come back later.

Jules laughed. He hadn't had such an intriguing coffee date, ever.

***

That evening, Callie barely caught Cendrine as she slid to the floor in the kitchen. François and Bernadette's eyes bloomed round as pennies when their mother's body slowly eased toward the floor.

"François, run. Bring me a pillow from the couch."

The little boy flew to do her bidding and returned to push the pillow beneath his mother's head. His eyes were wide and frightened. His little fingers twisted into the pillow as Callie adjusted it under her head.

Bernadette started to whimper and her eyes pooled.

Callie rushed for a glass of water. Holding Cendrine closely, she patted her cheeks and whispered her name. The children did the same, tapping their mother's arms and whispering, "*Maman, Maman, Maman.*"

Cendrine's eyes fluttered open, surprised to have Callie and the children bent over her. "What?" Her hand lifted to push hair from her face and she stared at her children, before turning toward Callie.

"Stress, my darling. Let's get you to the couch." Callie pushed her into the cushions and lifted her niece's feet to the round table while little François pushed the couch pillow under her feet. He grinned as his mother patted his head. Bernadette watched her mother from the kitchen doorway, fearful. When Cendrine motioned for her to come closer, the little girl flew into her lap.

"You must rest. I know you are worried sick and haven't been sleeping. But, you have this little one to think about too," Callie whispered as she patted her large belly. Jules is trying to find an address for Fernando in Spain and when he finds that information, we will ask that old Spaniard a thing of two. You, my dear, must hold tight…"

Cendrine nodded and held her children close while she gently rubbed her belly with one hand and the children's shoulders with the other. She didn't want to tell Callie this wasn't the first time she'd fainted since the nightmare began. The room seemed to move around her and she made a note to call the doctor in the morning. The fear of losing Olivier and the baby too, was more than she could imagine. She closed her eyes and took a deep breath. She would worry about one thing at a time. She must!

***

Restaurant Gadoline in Pertuis was Jules Armand's favorite restaurant. It was where he and his niece always met for their monthly dinner dates. She looked forward to their dinners like chocolate candy because Veronique's uncle always treated her like a princess. The filmy ecru panels gently swayed between the tables and added to the ambiance. Music played through the restaurant like a whisper of a smile.

When he waved to her from the back table facing the large front windows, warmth spread across his face. As the beautiful young woman walked jauntily toward him, Jules shook his head to shake away the little-girl image he'd carried so long. She had the lithe build of a dancer, so like her mother. Her rich blonde hair was swept behind her ears and fell in waves that gathered naturally at the top of her shoulders. When she kissed him on both cheeks and sat down across from him, his eyes were drawn to the tiny flecks of gold encircling her irises that gave intensity to her gaze, so like her father's.

"Sorry I am late, uncle," Veronique whispered apologetically.

"Just glad you made it, *ma cheri*."

When a chilled pear cider was placed in front of her, she grinned.

"And I ordered for us, like usual, *oui?*"

"Perfect," she replied as she sipped her cider. Veronique looked across the table. Her uncle's grin seemed to soften his steel-gray eyes to a lighter shade of silver. And his dark hair fell over his forehead. He had a confident, easy smile that she knew must melt women standing in line since he divorced so many years ago. She smiled back at him. "Are you going to tell me about the beautiful Callie, uncle?" A pair of whiskey-colored eyes fixed on him and very slowly one eyelid dropped in a wink.

Ten

The Air France plane lifted off from Marseille the next morning, and landed at the Málaga–Costa del Sol Airport late in the afternoon via Paris. Callie's head was spinning with the mystery surrounding Olivier's disappearance and Jules' head spun with Callie's nearness. He shook his head to focus only on Olivier and getting answers from the Spaniard.

"You are amazing, Jules. To find the man and get us on the next plane has my head reeling." The whirlwind of activity made her wonder how she imagined she could find the man alone in the first place. He'd been right although it still annoyed her that he was 'in charge.' She smiled to herself and admitted it was working out well though she wouldn't tell him so.

He grinned and motioned her toward the transportation kiosk. As they waited in line for the rental car, Callie's phone beeped. Glancing at her phone, Nate's face lit up the screen. Nodding at Jules, she moved aside to take the call.

"Hey, gorgeous. How's the mystery going for you?" Nate kept his voice purposely calm, although Callie could hear his underlying frustration.

"We are sifting through several clues, Nate. Cendrine is overdoing it and I fear for her pregnancy. A pregnant woman can only take so much stress. And we've found a man who may give us some more information."

"We? I'm surprised Cendrine is with you if she's having problems..." His voice sounded confused.

She hesitated before answering. "No...an old friend of François' is helping us. We hope to find the Spaniard I told you about in my last email. Hopefully, we will soon have some answers. Jules lives near the vineyard in Pertuis."

"How old is he? And where is this man who might or might not give you answers?" Nate still couldn't believe Callie had lifted off into the wild blue yonder and he didn't like it. Some days he couldn't believe the euphoria of the week before had been replaced with such angst.

"Uh…we just arrived in Málaga. That's where the man lives," she rushed on. "He's an old Spaniard who was friends with Olivier's father."

Silence met her hurried explanation.

"Nate?"

"I'm here. I just wish *you* were here too. Good luck, Callie. We can talk again soon. Dad said to give you his best. Good luck. Bye for now." The phone went dead.

Callie felt like she'd been caught with her hand in the cookie jar. She didn't like the feeling. This shouldn't happen when you loved someone. She never felt that way with François. Her mind slowed. The François she *thought* she knew, that is. The François who didn't have a child.. She jerked her wheeled bag behind her and returned to Jules, who'd just been handed a key ring and a map.

Jules drove the small car onto the street and worked his way toward the city. Callie opened the brochure that came with his city map and read, "The city of Málaga is a fascinating city with a rich and unique history that gives visitors a great variety of interesting things to do and see. Apart from all the cultural attractions, Malaga is a perfect location to enjoy life. The relaxed Mediterranean atmosphere and the perfect climate, have during nearly half a decade, attracted many foreigners and tourists…."

"Uh-huh…." Jules moved into the outside lane.

She glanced across the seat at Jules, surprised she took a six hour plane trip with a man who was practically a stranger. She guessed his connection to François and the family made it all right. But then again, her ease with the man made her blink; she hadn't been so easy with a man since François died, other than Nate of course. "Spain, I've always wanted to visit. My friend's family is from a small village just outside Málaga. Her father built a round house they called *la casa redonda*. I must send her an email to tell her I am here. She'll be delighted."

Jules smiled and edged his way through the next light. His dark hair blew gently in the slight breeze flowing in from the lowered window. He adjusted his sunglasses and said, "I love visiting the city and sharing it with you will be my pleasure. Maybe a very nice dinner after we get settled. Tell me the directions to our hotel…I need to take one of the next exits soon, I think."

Callie watched him change gears on the little car and noticed how his hands had total control. Her fingers relaxed in her lap. "Okay, I will read the brochure to you. "You will find the Venecia Hotel in the center of the city, just 50 meters from the famous Calle Larios and at a short distance by foot to some of the main places to visit in Malaga. Discover the famous Alcazaba, the stunning Cathedral, the beautiful Roman theater or visit the museum dedicated to the famous painter from Málaga, Pablo Picasso…" She inhaled. "Oh! Picasso again." She continued, "at the Hotel Venecia you will stay in nice and luminous rooms, etcetera."

"But of course…and the directions to the hotel, Callie?" He down shifted and stopped at the light, gazing at her.

"Sorry! A-45 /Antequera-Málaga will lead you to the entrance of the city through Ciudad Jardín. You can also take the A-7, known as the Mediterranean motorway, which runs along the coast from Algeciras to Nerja. Once you arrive at Málaga, you can get to the Hotel Venecia from Avenida de Andalucía in the west and through Paseo del Parque in the east."

"Well, let's assume from the directions, we are looking for Avenida de Andalucía then." He chuckled.

"There it is," Callie pointed. He zipped off and they were quickly in front of the hotel. The building was comprised of gray marble blocks with beautiful glass doors that led into a foyer filled with flowers. Black and white checkerboard tiles led them to the front desk where Callie saw panoramic views of the bay surrounding the room along the top walls. She was enchanted.

Jules gave her a room key and led her to the third floor, where their rooms abutted one another. "Let's meet in an hour for a glass of wine or would that rush you? Spaniards do not eat dinner until nine, so we have a while for wine time and tapas."

"One hour will be fine, Jules. I can call Fernando and set a morning visit with him. I know just enough Spanish to get my point across.

Although, as I remember, Olivier doesn't speak Spanish, so maybe French will work. I may need you...." Her voice trailed off.

"I am just next door, Callie. If you need my help during your call, just knock on the door." His warm, dark eyes put her at ease. He lifted his hand with a slight wave and walked into his own room, leaving her to ponder the exchange.

What is the matter with me? First, Nate and now I'm enthralled with another Frenchman. Damn. She wondered where this trip would lead them. She heaved her bag onto a chair beside the lamp table and pulled out her iPad. Dropping onto the bed's pale green comforter, she struck a pose before she called Fernando. She was still amazed to see the contact information Jules received from his friend at the travel agency.

"*Hola*, Fernando Sanchez?"

"*Sí. Soy* Fernando Sánchez."

"This is Callie Beauvais. *Yo soy la tía de Olivier Benoit y necesito tu ayuda.* I am the aunt of Olivier Benoit and I need your help. *Habla usted Inglés?* Do you speak English?"

"Yes, I speak English. *Un poquito.*" A little.

"I am in Málaga. May I visit you in the morning?" She held her breath.

Fernando answered slowly, "What do you wish to speak with me about, *señora* Beauvais?" The old man thought he had closed that part of his life when he gave the young man his father's letter and the painting. Uneasiness clawed at his belly.

It is about Olivier Benoit and it is very important." She must talk with the man. She also worried he might refuse to see them after they flew all the way to Spain. She fumed. *That's what we get for assuming.*

Fernando rubbed his white mustache and gripped the chair back near him. His voice turned abrupt. "How do you know where I live?"

"Olivier." The lie escaped from her mouth faster than she could think. A little white lie, but it was so important to see the man.

She heard his deep sigh. "10 o'clock here. You have my address? I will have coffee."

"Yes. Thank you, *señor*." Callie let out her breath. Too relieved to wait, she rushed into the hallway and knocked on the adjoining door.

When Jules pulled it open, his bare chest peeked through the white towel slung over his shoulder. When a few drops of water slipped down his chest, Callie wished she hadn't knocked at all.

"Yes, Callie?" His gray eyes were fixed on her.

"I....I spoke with Fernando. Tomorrow, 10 o'clock...." She fisted both hands and damned the butterflies that danced inside her belly.

His eyes sparkled with interest as he lifted the towel to wipe his chest. "Excellent. Do I still have thirty minutes or is Spanish wine calling now?"

"I can wait," she mumbled and turned toward her own door.

"Sorry I threw you off balance," he chuckled. He liked her sincere, open face and the way it flushed when she was embarrassed. He also liked the idea of the shared adventure. He'd been so busy working more than sixty hours every week that he wondered if life was passing him by. He turned back into the room with a smile on his face. Yes, he decided this adventure with Callinda Beauvais would be a memorable one.

Callie let out a breath and pulled out her iPad to draw up her ideas and questions. The old man sounded reticent. She wondered why. Could he know something about Olivier's disappearance or was it something else? If he was friends with Alexandre, he should have answers. *If he and Alexandre both moved the wine, he knows where it is hidden in Jouques.* Her thoughts were just enough to frighten herself with hope. She wouldn't need the map. She needed wine. And she needed to whack herself for finding Jules so damned attractive. She'd found François attractive too. But learning this new secret he'd hidden from her lessened the heartstring hold on her. That loss engulfed her. *Will I ever really trust a man again?* She tossed the iPad on the bed and slipped into the black shoes that matched the checkered slacks and straightened her red shirt. Yes, wine sounded mighty good.

When Jules knocked on her door, she'd cleared her head. There was a young man out there with a pregnant wife and twins who needed her help.

His mysterious disappearance pushed her anger at François aside momentarily. She gritted her teeth. *Wine first, mystery later.*

Jules guided her around the corner from the hotel to a wine bar he'd heard someone mention in the lobby. The restaurant spilled light onto the dark street. The place felt like a cave, with a small bar, seating downstairs and racks of wine on the far wall. Jules ordered glasses of *Habla del Silencio* wine and asked to see the menu. But there was none, so the waiter, a moody sort with a thick mustache and thicker beard, listed the food choices orally. The only other person who spoke English in the whole place was the bartender. Luckily, Jules spoke Spanish and they ordered more than they could eat, mainly tapas of meats, olives and cheeses.

Two glasses of wine and the tapas sat on the wooden table as Jules told her about his childhood and his interest in the computer industry. "When my company grew over one hundred employees, my work week lessened from every day to having one day off and…"

Callie's head jerked up. "You're the owner? That's how you can slip away from your job so easily to help us?" She was impressed, but saddened to think of the broken friendship with François. She lifted her glass and picked up a handful of nuts.

Jules looked her in the eyes and nodded.

"Computers, hmmm? Nate is also proficient in computers."

"Nate?" He lifted a meatball with a toothpick and popped it into his mouth before reaching for a stuffed, green olive.

"Yes, he's…my friend in Portland who is the computer technician at Larkspur Insurance where I'm employed." She was unsure why she hesitated and it bothered her, so she took another sip of red wine. Sometimes she wondered if she was a slut in disguise. *Damn again.* She took another sip.

Jules pushed the plate of tapas across the table. "We do not eat dinner for another couple of hours; maybe you need to eat some of these little meatballs and rolls to go with your wine, *chérie?*"

She stabbed a meatball with a toothpick and studied the man across from her. She liked what she saw. He had dark hair that curled just below his collar and silvery eyes that seemed to dive into her head. There was a small Kirk Douglas dimple in the middle of his chin. She was mesmerized by that and the smile just above it. He stood about five foot, ten inches and carried himself with assurance. Jules Luc Armand was a man who took himself seriously and had an aura about him that reeked of strength. She smiled and wondered what really lay within. Did he have secrets too? Did all men?

    He studied her studying him as he lifted his glass and sipped, taking delight in every raised eyebrow and facial twinge. Her silvery bangs curled across her forehead in a fluffy bit of lovely brown that circled her head. Her hair and her bangs fought against each other in a way that made him want to run his hands through it. Her brown eyes were like pools he wanted to watch while he..... He sat up quickly. "Let's drive through the city at night and see all the lights before dinner, shall we?"

    Callie was relieved to move, do something, and she swiftly gathered her purse to follow the charming man outside. The air was sweet; the lights glowed on the stone buildings and streets like candle lights. Twisting around, she breathed in the sights, trying to soak up the city.

    A few hours later at El Pimpi Restaurant on Calle Granada, an idyllic atmosphere helped her relax. The white stone building was clean; an old fashioned gaslight glowed above glass doors and the black, filigreed gateway embraced them. As they stepped into a flowering courtyard, Callie stared at a beautiful bougainvillea climbing to the roof beside geranium-stuffed flower boxes. She was entranced. Once inside, they were led to a music-filled interior courtyard. Her eyes rose upward once they were seated and Jules saw her smile like an excited child. The inner walls were littered with too many bright-blue pots to count. Red flowers bloomed, fresh and fragrant, their inviting Moorish influence shone brightly around them.

    Callie laughed when she saw the colorful menu; a fisherman held two pots of seafood above the words, El Pimpi Mariscos. Jules ordered the Pimpi Platter, an enormous sampling of sausage, steak, potato croquets, roasted peppers and other vegetables. He suggested fried calamari but knew by Callie's face, they would not be appreciated. She requested Paella with Gambas, which she knew were shrimp by the photo on the menu, and, of course, a chilled sangría.

"My friend, whose father built the round house, told me about cozy bodega bars. She said they offer the best food and good wine. I will tell her about El Pimpi. Thanks so much for bringing me here, Jules. I would have been happy at the hotel restaurant although on a scale of one to ten in atmosphere, the hotel was about a four…"

He laughed. "And this is?"

"Eleven." She matched his smile, lifted the chilled sangría and danced her straw around the floating fruit. Listening to nearby Spanish conversations made her wish she'd paid better attention in Spanish classes all those years ago.

Flamenco guitar music flowed through the room as Jules raised his hand and a waiter appeared holding a small dish of green olives, bread and dipping oil. *"Gracias y más sangría para la señora por favor."*

"Well, I can remember enough to know you just thanked the man and asked him to bring me more sangría."

He nodded and the small dimple in his chin was back again.

Callie dropped her eyes to the tapas and reached for an olive. "When we see Fernando tomorrow, I may need you to ask the questions on my iPad. Since he met with Olivier, I hope there's something he can tell us. It's been five days since Olivier disappeared. He could be dead and it breaks my heart to think so."

Jules patted his lips with the cloth napkin before answering, his eyes never leaving her face. "Yes, of course. Don't lose hope, Callie. I also wonder if Olivier is hurt or dead since someone broke into the house looking for something. We don't know if the burglar found anything…" His deep sigh didn't bode well for the hope he was offering her though.

"Thankfully, Cendrine took both laptops with her that night. What are the odds of that? And what if she and I had been in the house with the children that night? The man must have been watching the house and saw us leave! I hadn't thought of that. Of course. Damn." She took a big gulp of her sangría and lifted bread from the basket to swirl angrily in the golden oil.

"I had thought of that but why mention it when you and Cendrine were already worried? Let's talk about other things tonight. Fernando and Olivier can wait until morning, please?"

Callie blinked moisture from her eyes and nodded. "Okay tell me about you and François when you were children and growing up?"

Jules' eyes shifted a moment before he began talking about two young boys running through the vineyard, each with a stick swatting at the birds that promised to eat the grapes. "Old Michel was in his early fifties then, and he could run as fast as the wind because he caught both of us boys in mid stride." He chuckled. "We never did that again."

Callie watched his features warm as he told the story. "And did you attend the same schools growing up?" She leaned forward, interested.

"Yes, we were inseparable when we were young. François loved the vines but he didn't want to work them when he grew up. His father wasn't happy about it but respected his wishes. So, he went to the Université of Reims Law School near Paris and I attended the Université Paris Diderot's Computer Science Training and Research Unit located on the Seine. I wanted to start my own computer business. François wanted to spread his wings. He did not want to remain in France forever, but I did. I love France and could never live anywhere else. I suppose I was the more serious one and he was more impulsive. But I loved him like a brother." He lifted his red wine and drank as she waited for him to continue.

"You see, Callie, there was a lot in our younger lives that you do not know and I do not wish to mention some of our disagreements. As I told you, once Aurore became pregnant and I met you, our lives moved even farther apart. But, before that, we were attached at the hip as I have heard Americans say when two friends are very close. I think that is how you and Olivia are, *oui*?"

She laughed. "Yes, I guess you could say that. Livvy and I have been friends since college. I promised to be her matron of honor in her wedding two weeks from now. I hope it doesn't hurt our friendship when I tell her I may not make it. It makes me sad, of course, but since I've stepped back on French soil, my heart sings. In America, it sputters. Nate is really more than a friend, Jules. Just before I left, he asked me to marry him. Now, being back in France, I wonder if I was in love with love. I had not allowed any man close to me since François died, but Nate made me laugh. I felt special again." She stopped and compressed her lips.

Jules reached for her hand and squeezed it gently. "Callie, everyone needs to laugh and feel special. Sometimes we can love a person without being in love with them and maybe the timing brought Nate into your life so you can live and love again. France makes my heart sing too and I know what you mean. I am sure Nate is a very nice guy if you became so close to him. I envy him, actually."

Callie's breath caught. "You envy him?"

"Yes, of course. To have a beautiful woman like you agree to marry him? I was married once. There was a woman named Solange who lives in Aix. She and I have been friends many years. She is a real estate agent and we thought we could make a life together. When I returned one day early from a business trip to surprise her, the surprise was mine. She and another man were in a, shall we say, very sensitive position. I left and never looked back."

Callie lifted her drink. "Well, that would do it for me too. I'd still be running in the opposite direction." She tried to imagine the pain of coming home to find your trusted spouse in the arms of another woman, but she couldn't quite get there. She'd trusted Francois their entire married life and the pain Jules must have lived through was beyond her. She wasn't so naïve to think marriages didn't end this way, but also thought how stupid Solange was to let this man go. How could the woman look beyond this man's goodness and charm? She gulped the wine and shook her head sadly.

They both laughed and then their eyes grew large as two huge plates of food were placed in front of them. The steam rising from her shrimp paella made her stomach yawn. When she saw him dip his fork into a platter so large she knew it would have fed the entire family, she tried not to snigger.

He rolled his eyes and they ate in silence, enjoying the camaraderie and food in tandem, both relaxing for the first time in days.

***

The next morning, Callie and Jules entered the small house on the outskirts of Málaga when a woman, about sixty, invited them inside. The room was large, airy and filled with religious art and flowering plants. An old man sat on a long gray couch smoking a cigarette and drinking a cup of black coffee from a very large cup.

"*Señor* Sanchez?" Jules asked as he reached out to shake the man's outstretched hand. The man's mustache was thick, white and curled at the ends. He had warm, brown eyes and a lined face that told of his hours under the hot sun. His handshake was firm.

"*Sí*, I am Fernando Sanchez Ortega." He looked at Callie. "And you are Olivier's aunt from America, *señora* Beauvais?"

"Yes, I am. It is good to find you." She smiled at the old man, liking him instantly. His eyes were kind and his French/Spanish accent an oddity.

"This is my daughter, Crescéncia. My grandson, Francisco, will be here soon. He buys fresh bread and some fruit. I am unsure how I can help you. I gave everything to Olivier from his father already." He seemed anxious as he flexed his fingers and pressed his lips together.

Crescéncia smiled toward them, listening, although she did not understand much of their conversation. Callie saw worry on her face.

"Yes, I know you visited Olivier. May I call you Fernando?"

"*Sí, señora.*" He crossed his leg over his knee and waited.

"Olivier disappeared two days after you spoke with him," Callie said quietly. She saw his face pale and he shakily replaced his large cup in a plate sitting on the small table beside him. "*Madre de Dios.* Please tell me what happened." His twitching fingers now changed to fists leveled on his knees.

"That is why we are here, Fernando. We hope you can give us some information that could help us find him. He has been gone five days. His wife is very upset. We are afraid something has happened to him." She watched the old man think a moment.

"Maybe he is following the instructions inside his father's letter?" He answered cautiously.

"We know about the mysterious wine bottles," she said.

Fernando sighed heavily. "He told his wife about the bottles, but he did not tell her where he was going?"

"He was upset about something but did not tell her why. They were preparing to leave town for a few days and had begun to pack. Then, he disappeared...and he took a large amount of money from the vineyard with him when he left."

Fernando's face was shocked. "This cannot be right. Do you also know about the man who has been following me and my family? The man who asked me about the wine bottles many years ago?"

Jules and Callie stared at each other.

Crescéncia brought their coffee and sat down near them. Fernando looked at her and she nodded. She did not speak English well, so Jules helped translate for Callie as she began to talk.

"She says her father is being followed. She took a picture of the man in a car one day and Fernando gave Olivier that picture. He did not recognize the man because it was blurry. Fernando thinks it may be the same man who questioned him twenty years ago. He looked about forty or older."

Just then, the front door swung open and a man walked into the house with two large bags. He nodded shyly and walked into the kitchen. He returned a minute later in a business suit that was creased perfectly, his crisp, white shirt, perfection.

"*Mi nieto*, my grandson, Francisco, Crescéncia's son."

Jules shook the younger man's hand and noticed the tender smile he gave to his grandfather at the introduction. "Have you also seen the man who has been following your grandfather?"

"No. My mother and *abuelo* saw him several times. When I find him, I will make him stop it. He has frightened them. *Abuelo* believes it is about the old wine bottles." He glanced at his grandfather worriedly and sat down beside him. Fernando patted his leg and shook his head.

"May we ask you some questions? You may know something that could help us." Callie looked at Crescéncia and she nodded toward her father when he shrugged.

"Yes, but what could I know that would help you?" He pushed his fingers through his dark hair and exhaled through his pursed lips.

"Jules speaks Spanish. I know English is difficult for you, so he will ask you questions." She lifted her iPad and handed it to Jules.

"Francisco, did you see the photo of the man in the car?"

"Yes, but it was blurry."

Jules recognized the frustration on the man's face, noticed his eyes dart toward his grandfather and back to his mother. His foot tapped on the floor as if he had a plane to catch. Jules switched his question to Fernando.

"What did the man look like who questioned you many years ago?" Jules stared at the list of questions and raised an eyebrow toward Callie.

"He had a pale face and hair the color of *zanahorias*. He said he knew about the bottles with the *señorita* riding the cork. He wanted me to tell him where the bottles were hidden. I told him I did not know what he was talking about." Fernando puffed his cheeks out and blew through his lips again.

Callie's brow furrowed.

Jules chuckled at her puzzlement. "Carrots. *Zanahorias* are carrots."

Callie nodded her thanks and noticed a look of confusion cross Francisco's face. He looked at his grandfather and his eyebrows rose into his hairline. And then he returned to the kitchen and jostled some dishes.

He knows something. Callie stared after the young man and tried to catch Jules' eye, wondering if it was just a hunch or more. He'd left the group so suddenly she knew part of the conversation obviously troubled him. She turned toward Jules, but at that moment he returned her iPad.

Fernando drummed his fingers on his thigh. "I am very sorry. Olivier is like his father, Alexandre….both good men. If the man followed me here in Málaga, do you think he followed me to see Olivier?" His hand shook as he reached for his coffee cup and his eyes filled. "This is terrible. I may have led the man to Olivier…"

"We had not thought of that, Fernando." Callie raised her eyes to Jules who stared back at her in agreement. She wanted to ask Fernando where the bottles were hidden, but he looked so distraught, she decided to shelve the question for now.

"We will contact you, Fernando, when we find Olivier." Jules could see they'd left the family more perplexed than when they'd arrived.

When Francisco heard Callie and Jules leave, he returned to the living room. His grandfather studied his grandson, wondering why he had not shown respect by saying goodbye properly. Seeing Francisco's agitation, he patted the couch beside him.

Francisco smiled hurriedly. "I must get to the bank, *abuelo*." He kissed his grandfather and mother, tossed his dark head toward them with a watery smile and left the house.

Eleven

"What do we do now? We have an approximate description of what the man looked like. Even if he followed Fernando to Pertuis, how could he have known it had anything to do with the brandy? Maybe he knows Fernando and Alexandre were involved with Pablo Picasso and the brandy? By the sounds of it, the mystery man could be Irish..." Jules tapped the steering wheel and stared at the traffic with the keys held loosely in his hand.

"Or Scottish... Red hair the color of carrots?" Callie turned to look at Jules before forming the next thought. "If he is Scottish, maybe there is a connection ... but following a Spaniard in Málaga. What's that connection? My head hurts..." At that moment, her cell phone rang and Cendrine's photo lit up her screen.

"Cendrine. How are you feeling, *chérie?*"

Jules pulled into traffic and headed toward the Venecia Hotel, half listening to Cendrine's voice. Curious, he tried to decipher the conversation but only got bits and pieces.

"Excellent! We will be on the next plane. We just spoke with Fernando and we have a small clue. I hope you told the doctor about your fainting the other day? Ok." Callie hung up and turned to Jules, her cheeks pink with news.

"She found Alexandre's original letter and the map." Her left hand touched his shoulder and her right hand tapped the window. "Sorry, I talk with my hands when I get excited."

Jules laughed. "That was a very long conversation just to tell you she found the letter and map." He laughed.

"She saw the doctor today and he ran some tests and everything was alright she said."

"I'll make our plane reservations, you pack and I'll check us out."

"Perfect, Jules," she said, as they rushed inside the hotel.

***

Francisco Garcia Sanchez squeezed the stapler on his desk as his call went to voicemail for the third time and his lips puckered with annoyance. A knot the size of a rock lodged inside his stomach, thinking he could be responsible for the mess. The collage of unpleasant memories swept through his mind, memories of his friend at university twenty years ago. Memories of their laughter, their pranks, their girls and their drunken conversations. He remembered telling his friend about the secret he'd promised his grandfather never to share with anyone when too much wine led to loose lips.

As soon as his grandfather mentioned the man had red hair, his antennae rose and fluttered there. He couldn't be sure, of course, but the coincidence was too strong. He knew he must get in touch with the man. He hoped he was wrong. Francisco had received emails from him about a month earlier and they'd connected again. He'd mentioned he lived with his mother and grandfather since his wife died. Did he give him their home address? He hadn't heard from him in awhile. He pulled his keyboard across his desk and after clacking a few computer keys, an email went out, hoping he'd get an answer since the man wasn't answering his phone. He closed his eyes and prayed he was wrong.

At two, Francisco left the bank, where his office kept him busy and often stressed. He hurried towards *Cañas y Tapas*, stepped inside and wiped his feet. The bodega bar was just across the street off Calle Molina Larios. It was a very popular bar; the barman knew him by name and knew his drink. He threaded his way to the back wall and before Francisco's butt hit the stool, a bowl of albondigas soup and a glass of red wine greeted him. He repositioned himself on the stool and ordered a second glass. Francisco knew shame was the only thing that could be silent and loud all at the same time.

***

After procuring tickets for the 12:30 flight, they ordered tapas and red wine in the airport lounge. As they sat back in their chairs, Jules twirled a splash of Cabernet in a slow circle around the bottom of his wine glass.

"Jules," said Callie. "I know we want to find these bottles and Olivier's father told him it was Picasso's wish to start that flamenco guitar school in Algodonales, but we must find Olivier and straighten out this mess first. Do you think we should just let the bottles sit wherever they are and puzzle out the mystery? I want to find Olivier, dammit."

Jules pondered in silence for a moment. "Good questions. There are two possible scenarios. The first is this mystery man has Olivier hidden somewhere and he may already know where the bottles are stored. The second is that Olivier is being pursued and he is trying to lead the man away from his family. Maybe he hasn't told the guy anything, but he's definitely a link to Olivier's disappearance since he burglarized the house after Olivier disappeared."

"I agree. But there's also a third scenario." She studied her fingernails and reached for her glass.

"Which is?" He leaned toward her and lifted an olive to his mouth.

"There is another connection we are missing. Today, when we were in Fernando's living room and he described this red-haired man, I saw Francisco's face change. He was nervous and went into the kitchen without a word. I think he may know something."

Jules sat up in his chair. "Why didn't you tell me this before?" He crunched down on a hunk of bread and chewed. After sipping the last drop of wine, he looked at her. "Ok, there's a lot going on. Let's think about it. Maybe we are lost in the forest instead of focusing on the trees."

Callie stared into her wine glass and smiled with a shake of her head. "Something like that. I think it's 'can't see the forest for the trees' but you have the idea and I think that is right.

Despite the heroic efforts of Jules to lessen Callie's stress during their plane ride back to France, she remained quiet. She tapped the cover of her iPad periodically and stared out the window across the wide expanse of black sky while gripping her armrest and sighed loudly.

Jules finally reached over and held her hand still. She turned to him after studying his hand over hers for about thirty seconds. And she crumpled, fear for Cendrine and Olivier at the forefront of her thoughts.

"*Chérie*, please have faith. With the map, we should find the bottles. It may not lead us to Olivier immediately, but it will bring us closer. I suggest you call the old Scot again. Maybe he knows something that can help us without realizing it?"

Callie nodded. "But who will take care of Cendrine? And the children? What shall we tell her if we can't find Olivier? Where could he be and… is he still alive? And I'm worried about Cendrine and the baby. Her color isn't good and she's already fainted once."

Jules wanted to hold her in his arms, to make all her fears go away. He caught himself reaching toward her but kept his hand, warm over hers. She let it stay and turned hers palm upward to clasp his warm fingers. He looked at her and she stared back at him. Before he could stop himself, he leaned over and pressed his lips to the top of her head.

***

Olivier stretched out on the lumpy cot and pulled the blanket over him. The food was gone and most of the wine. The crazed man had not given him a glass, so he drank it straight from the bottle, a cheap red wine. He was unsure how he knew this but somehow he was sure it wasn't the red wine he usually drank. He still had one bottle of water and sipped it sparingly. The man hadn't been back for two days and Olivier was very hungry. He'd tried to budge the door, but his headache had throbbed again. The window was too high and too small to reach, and he knew he couldn't fit through the opening anyway. His headache eased when he lay down, so there he stayed most of the day.

He squinted toward the small window, where only a few inches of daylight slipped through above the covering and tried to remember how many days he had been there. He still could not remember who he was or why he was there. He thumped his hands down on the cot in exasperation. When he heard the door hinges squeak, he knew he was no longer alone.

The door scraped open and the man stepped inside. "So, have you remembered anything yet? The bottles must be close. Your father and that old Spaniard wouldn't have carried them far. You know where they are hidden. I know it and you'll stay here until you remember!" The man's eyes probed, he appeared drunk. He pulled a gun from his coat pocket and tossed it back and forth between his hands.

Olivier just looked at him without saying a word.

"Talk to me, man…" the man slurred. "I can't believe you just forgot who you are. You know me. It just doesn't work that way." He shoved the gun into his pocket and ran his hands through an unruly bush of red hair before glaring at Olivier. His hands were shaking. He slid down onto the wooden chair six feet from the cot.

Olivier blinked. "What doesn't work that way?" He couldn't help but ask. Something wasn't adding up. He held himself rigid with the effort of appearing composed and cleared his throat, trying to dislodge the lump that had formed. The gun worried him but he wouldn't show it.

A flicker of anger turned the man's face red. "Amnesia, you fool! Do you think I've waited all these years taking shit, being second best? Do you think I will allow Amnesia to spoil my plans? " He slid his hand into his pocket again and fingered the gun.

Olivier glared at him through squinted eyes as the truth dawned. "You know who I am, don't you?" The man's words slipped into focus; Olivier's eyes started to burn and time stood still. This man had answers. He could help him, but would he?

The man's eyes slid away from Olivier's face momentarily and he smacked his lips. "So it's true you have no memory before you woke up here?" he asked, pointing to the cot. "I think you should remember by now. I didn't hit you that hard," the man spat out.

Olivier nodded with a knot of frustration. "*Oui.* Yes. I have no memory. I wish I did!" He looked down, squeezing the edge of the bed frame. He thought the man appeared to be about his same age but rougher and louder. His accent was familiar but his words did not make sense. His neck hurt and his head pounded. He lifted his fingers to squeeze his temples and closed his eyes, defeat washing over him.

The man pulled the gun out of his pocket again and ran his fingers across the barrel, smoothed the length of it and stared at Olivier. He kicked the leg of the cot and Olivier's eyes popped open. "Get up, man. Look at me when I talk to you." His breathing became ragged and he looked about the room agitatedly, swinging the gun around him.

"You make no sense. Who are you and why are you keeping me locked up in this room? Tell me who I am. I am sick of your yelling and I'm hungry. Go ask someone else your questions, someone who knows what the hell you are talking about. I told you! *I don't!*" Dazed and confused, Olivier closed his eyes again and didn't see the blow coming.

The man kicked him in the thigh and slammed his fist into his stomach. When he pointed the gun toward him and aimed another kick, Olivier grabbed his foot and yanked it hard. His chest heaved.

The man fell hard.

Leaning toward the man's inert body, Olivier worried only a little when he didn't move. It was then Olivier noticed the door was ajar. Forcing himself to sit up, he threw his legs over the edge of the cot and he ran. Several cars were traveling up a narrow street but nobody else was in sight. He limped as quickly as his raging head allowed, holding his gut where the man had hit him. His thigh throbbed too, but he didn't stop until he spied an alley where he could hide behind a dustbin and garbage bags. A street sign told him he was on Avenue Maurice Plantier. He wedged himself down beside the bin and pulled his shirt tight, trying to ignore the stench and the cold. He watched the mouth of the alley for a long time.

Twelve

When Jules and Callie arrived at the old mill house after landing in Marseille, Bernadette and François ran to greet them. Cendrine waved from the top stone step. The giggles and laughter of the children lifted Callie's mood as Jules' hand, on the small of her back, guided her forward.

Cendrine ushered them inside and shooed the children out of the doorway to allow Callie and Jules to enter the room. They saw nervous energy flit across her face when she brought in a tray with a fresh bread and fromage, (cheese) alongside glasses of wine.

"I know you are very tired, but I am too excited to wait." She reached into her pocket and retrieved the letter and map she'd found wedged between some old books on Olivier's bookshelf in his tiny office.

Jules reached for the envelope at the same time Callie stretched forward. They laughed as he slipped the map from the yellowed envelope and smoothed it open on the couch table in front them. His finger followed the road outlined on the map and he read the note scribbled at the bottom.

Callie lifted her iPad and typed in Jouques. "It says here that Jouques is stretched out in a very narrow line beside the river, with the ruins of a medieval chateau and imposing church-sized chapel overlooking the village. The town lacks good terrace cafés and a choice of restaurants, but it's an interesting place for an exploring visit. The town is separated from the small Réal River by a large, open space along the front of the town. There is a walkway along the far side of the meadow, following the banks of the river. For a number of centuries the river side was home to water mills for grain, olives and paper mills, along with tanning and wool workshops. The map shows the river and the palace," she said, placing her finger near Jules' hand.

"I have not been to Jouques for many years." Jules rubbed his hands together and listened to Callie continue.

"There's a nice little triple-arched stone bridge over the river into town, but barely visible, being paralleled closely by a modern footbridge. The layout of Jouques has long corresponding streets, including the main avenue with constant traffic; there are two back streets, and a higher road above it all. There are a limited number of traverses linking the long streets, so a wandering visit of the town requires the persistence to take a long walk along each of the streets which include old doorways, medieval arches and facades. The largest building in Jouques is the remnant of the medieval palace built by the d'Arbaud-Jouques."

Jules tapped his finger on the map. "This shows the triple arched bridge and the pathway along the river. What does it say about the chateau on the hill? I see a big star here," he tapped the spot, "marked beneath its stone steps." He licked his lips thoughtfully. "If that is where they hid the bottles, I'd be surprised if they are still there. Does the information say whether the chateau is open to the public?" He leaned toward Callie, who studied her iPad.

"The Chateau de Jouques was to be built in the middle of the western part of the village around a central court. Vaults to support the Chateau Terrace were built to support the Monumental Staircase, but construction was stopped for lack of funding and the chateau was never completed." She glanced up at them.

"So, there are probably not many people exploring the old place..."

Callie read the remaining piece, "Today the area around the Monumental Staircase is the outside area of the *Galerie des Baumes*. The gallery has free entry, so you can visit the chateau area and their offerings. Gallery items have a strong African theme and the inside rooms resemble a cross between an antique store and a museum."

Cendrine twisted her hands together. "Olivier would never have gone to this place alone. He would have taken me or Papa with him." She covered her face with both hands and the children stopped playing with their toys to run to their mother. She wrapped her arms around them, drying her tears.

A flicker of sympathy crossed Jules' face before turning to the map once again. His finger followed the map to where the brandy had been hidden, which might solve one mystery. Finding Olivier was the bigger mystery, but he'd already told Callie he feared for the man's life.

Callie's cell phone rang and she saw Nate's photo smiling up at her. She tapped the call open and walked into the kitchen. "Hello, Nate. We found the map. We are getting close. Please don't be angry. I couldn't bear it." She watched a hummingbird dart past the window as the sun set.

"I am sorry I was such a toad when I called you yesterday and I couldn't sleep all night. Please forgive me. I'm just worried about you and everything you are going through. It's hard for me to understand your strong attachments there, but I am trying. Please tell me you will come home as soon as you find Cendrine's husband and these bottles."

He sounded downcast and his voice was so warm, Callie wished she could answer him, but she had no idea when she could return. "Nate, I will be back as soon as I can, I promise. Please believe me when I say I just do not know, because I must be here for my family."

"That's just it, Callie. They are François' family. I know they are important to you and you love them, but…."

"No buts, Nate….I *am* staying. They need me and I will not let them down." Callie took a deep breath and closed her eyes, fighting tears.

"I wish you felt as deeply about letting *me* down, Callie."

She didn't answer.

"Sweetheart, I love you. Do what you have to do. I miss you."

"Yes Nate, and I will be in touch again very soon. Goodbye for now." She hung up and pressed the phone to her chin. Moments later, she joined the others in the dining room. She was sure everyone could hear her heart beating, so she reached up to quiet it, wondering if her life would ever be on an even keel again. She hadn't wanted to be pulled like a yoyo between France and Oregon, but she couldn't seem to stop the tug of war.

"We have a good chance if this map is correct and we can avoid the chateau police," Jules murmured.

"The chateau police? You're right. They aren't going to just let us waltz in there, pry open an old door and haul away bottles that have essentially belonged to them for so many years. All the yellow tape, the police, the questions, how will we manage it?"

Jules bit the inside of his lip for only a moment. "We don't get caught. They won't know what we are looking for. It's a tourist area and by the sounds of it, not many wander there anyway. At least, maybe they won't when we get there. We adapt. One can watch for the law while the other looks for the treasure." He grinned as he held the map between his fingers.

Cendrine looked up anxiously and said, "Okay. When do we leave?"

Jules and Callie said, "You don't," at exactly the same time.

"But I want to help you. It may lead us to Olivier," she cried. "I can take the children over to *grand-*…" Cendrine stopped talking at the look on Callie's face and the hand her aunt held up like a stop sign.

"Cendrine, you are seven months pregnant. Be practical. We are trying to take care of one thing at a time. We don't know if Olivier went to get the bottles. You told us he wouldn't go without you. You must stay home to hear from him….or if the police find him first, they will need to find you to tell you …" Callie whispered the last, knowing it would aggravate the ripples of stress already in her niece's head.

Cendrine sat in a chair and wiped her eyes. When she laid her head on the chair back, she heaved an exaggerated sigh. When she looked up again, she crossed her arms and stared at Callie and Jules. And then she got up, walked slowly upstairs to her room and closed the door behind her.

The twins watched her silently and then turned to look at Callie. Bernadette's curling hair hung in her face and she swiped at it with one hand and placed a finger in her mouth with her other. François did not take his eyes off the stairway.

"She will be all right, *mon petites*. Just let her rest. You can play for a while and I will make you some dinner, *oui*?"

They nodded as one.

"You'll stay, won't you, Jules?"

He laughed slightly. "I never turn down a home-cooked meal. Of course, I'll stay. I'll even help you." He followed her into the kitchen.

"You cook?" she asked in mock surprise, warmed by his offer.

He bent at the waist. "*Oui*, madam. If you ply me with red wine."

The dishes were washed and dried, the children were in bed and Cendrine had still not joined them. Callie prepared a plate for her, covered it, hoping she would eat later. Somehow the conversation turned to François and they sat with their *cafés au lait* after dinner.

"At the time, his death was devastating. Since then, I questioned whether I could ever have a meaningful relationship again. Nate helped me get past the barrier and I'd hoped he would be the next chapter in my life, but..."

"...But?"

She looked up at Jules. "But from this side of the ocean, that new chapter has paled a little. He cannot understand why I put the Beauvais family before his feelings." She lifted her cup and touched the tip of her tongue to the rim trying to catch a wayward drop. "And neither do I."

Jules could not take his eyes off the woman and for a moment let his mind play tricks. She looked vulnerable as her hair fell into her eyes.

"You see, Jules, after François died, I lived like a nun and always kept men at arm's length. It worked...until Nate wiggled his way into my life. He showed me life could be different." She ran her finger along the cup's base and sighed. "Now, knowing the secrets that François kept from me, new pages have unfolded and I do not know when I can digest this betrayal to either Veronique...or to me." She quickly diverted the spotlight back to Jules, asking, "What about your life? Other than Solange, I mean?"

"You are a strong woman, Callie. I believe you will find that strength will lead you to wholeness again." He sighed. "And one day, I will tell you about my boring life, *ma chérie*. But for now, I must leave. We have a big day tomorrow. I will pick you up early and we shall find some dusty brandy bottles, *oui*?"

She glanced toward the stairwell. "Olivier must be out there somewhere and against his will, I know it. I wonder every day how Cendrine goes through her day, knowing her husband might never come home," she whispered.

Jules looked at his clasped hands and then drew his eyes up to Callie's face. He didn't have an answer and didn't want to offer empty platitudes.

When Callie nodded, she thought she saw caution scamper across his face. Did he also have secrets in his past he refused to share? She tucked the thought away and turned her mind to tomorrow as she closed the door behind him.

Thirteen

Meanwhile, January's eastern sky was promising another fine day in Venelles, not far from Pertuis. The first blush of sunrise painted the scattered clouds with pastel pinks and orange. A cold breeze whispered through the alley, blowing softly to ruffle his tangle of blazing hair. Olivier's eyes flashed a light blue as he shifted his body. The smell of wet, fresh soil wafted toward him on the breeze and his head throbbed. He woke up, so stiff he could barely move. That's when he heard voices nearby and he scrunched down as low as he could in the cold alley. The sounds of scuffling in the steel bin beside his head unnerved him and he jerked away, slipping on the pile of boxes near his hip. The scuffling stopped abruptly and a shadow loomed above him.

"Are you hiding from the police?" An older man's startled question surprised Olivier into stillness. He tried to look beyond the stranger's words as he shook his head no. Olivier saw a flicker of sympathy cross the man's lined face. "You have no place to go? Are you hungry?"

Olivier had known that emerging from the alley to the crowded street carried considerable risk but looking into the man's eyes told him he no longer had a choice. He scooted as if to wedge himself into the bricks at his back. It was hard and his head slammed against the wall before he could stop the impetus of his lunge. His eyes lifted to the stranger and his body shook with an indescribable feeling of helplessness.

Again, Olivier shook his head no. "I do not know, *monsieur*."

"You do not know? You are homeless, hungry? Which is it?" The old man wiped his hands on the flour-splashed apron and reached a hand down to pull Olivier away from the garbage bin. "You reek with unmentionable odors, but I have smelled worse."

Olivier started shivering. "*Oui j'ai faim.*" Yes, I am hungry.

***

Bertrand Deniau nodded, satisfied. He pulled Olivier to his feet and saw the dirt and grime on his shirt. Sniffing in distaste from the young man's scent, he wrinkled his nose a moment before leading him toward a wooden door a short distance away. The brick wall beside the dustbin was a blend of gold and rust; the alley formed a French drain next to the door.

Olivier walked through it. Moving was difficult; he was sure his head looked the size of a melon, much too big to sit on his neck. He flexed his shoulders and groaned as he followed the older man inside. Olivier's stomach grumbled the minute he walked into the back room of the bakery. A large woman stood at a counter patting bread dough, fluffing it and squeezing it with her fingers. An apron covered her ample stomach and floated down to the hem on her dress. Mottled gray hair was stuffed under a small cap. Her dark eyes opened wide when her husband led the stranger through the kitchen.

"Bertrand?" Her face changed to concern as she watched the man nearly fall onto a stool beside her work counter. She stepped backward.

"I found him snuggled up to the dustbin outside the door. He is cold and hungry. I know nothing else," her husband answered as he moved to get a bowl of hot soup and a fresh baguette. "Bring wine, Christianne, and a warm blanket. I am unsure how long he has been out there." He ran his big hands down his apron, trying to determine what to do next. Wondering if the man was avoiding the police laid heavy on his mind. He did not want to get involved, but seeing the man hunkered down and shivering compelled him to help. There was something about the blank look in his eyes that pulled Bertrand and he nodded briskly at his wife again.

The woman bit her lip and muttered grumpily, "he is a reeking mess," before turning into a cupboard behind her. She lifted a bottle of wine and plopped it down beside Olivier. "I will get the blanket." She wiped the loose dough on a towel beside her work area and disappeared.

When Bertrand first saw the figure crouching in the ancient alley outside the back door of his bakery, *Christianne's Pain*, his first thought was a thief. The man's place of concealment between the dustbin and the alley wall appeared a perfect spot for a thief to hide, but now he wasn't so sure. Now, the man needed help. He didn't look like a thief. The old baker scoffed to himself, wondering what a thief looked like.

Christianne returned with a blanket and handed it to her husband.

Olivier lifted the soup spoon to his mouth as fast as he could scoop it in. And then he shivered. Sweat rolled down his face and inside his shirt. Sniffing loudly, he wrapped his arms around himself. He prayed the madman, who would undoubtedly look for him, didn't lurk nearby. The room wavered and spun in wide circles. He reached toward the glass of wine next to his hand, took a long drink and set it down. When he lifted the spoon again, it began to blur just before the floor rose to meet him.

Olivier Benoit woke in stages. He opened his eyes with difficulty and it took time to determine where he was. And then, a sharp pain jolted him awake. How long had he been in this room? It was nothing like the nasty room he'd run away from and for that he was glad. Diffused light crept through a grille and he heard the occasional muffled thump, footsteps. And the smell of fresh-baked bread. He felt safe for the first time in days.

Trying to keep his head on the pillow so as not to make any sudden movements that would aggravate the pain, he stretched out slowly. It was then he noticed he was naked and his uneasiness returned full blown. He fought against the thunder in his ears as he forced his brain to remember anything, something that would tell him who he was and why he was running from a maniac. He did remember the older man and woman though. And he knew they were good people. They'd given him food, something to drink and a blanket. He reached up to touch the knot at the base of his skull. Fingering the slightly-swollen bump, he twisted his neck an inch at a time and sighed in relief. The sharp stabbing pain was diminishing.

A knock on the door brought him back to his predicament and the man who had found him, walked in. "Ah, you are awake. That is good. We were worried about you and we have been checking on you every few hours."

Olivier responded with a weak smile.

"My friend is a doctor and he is coming to see you. You probably wonder what happened to your clothes." Bertrand chuckled at the look on the younger man's face. "I will bring you a clean shirt and if you can stand without falling down, you must take a shower. My wife refuses to serve your dinner unless that horrible smell is gone."

It was Olivier's turn to chuckle. *"Merci."*

"My name is Bertrand and my wife is Christianne. You are in a bedroom above our bakery. Over dinner, we must talk, but after your shower, and then the doctor will have a good look at you. This is good?"

"Oui. Thank you very much. There is much to talk about and also not much to talk about." Olivier rubbed his eyes and shook his head.

Bertrand's confusion was obvious. He gave Olivier an old robe and told him that a towel and necessities were in the bathroom just down the hall. "When you are clean, we will eat, my friend. I think this will be a good day. Now, go."

***

It was Friday, market day in Jouques, a medieval village built along the Réal River north of Aix-en-Provence, thirty minutes from Pertuis. An ancient road sign beside Blvd de la République, pointed out distances to Aix-en-Provence, Rians and to the border of the Bouches-du-Rhone department.

Jules and Callie entered Jouques beside the river. Ruins of the chateau and the imposing chapel overlooked the village. They drove past the boulangerie, a charcuterie and a café with tables and chairs set out on the pavement. The streets were crowded with cars intent on browsing the outside farmer's market. Jules squeezed his BMW beside a small square where a fountain bubbled. A bench stood beneath a canopy of trees, shaded by the luxuriant branches from an old oak. He began walking. "Let's compare this map with Alexandre's'."

Callie had a stupid grin plastered to her face. She couldn't help it. The adventure was intoxicating even though she was worried sick about Olivier. Attaching her fanny pack to her waist, she hurried to follow him across the grassy area. His long legs were no match for hers even though her ankle was finally working properly. She wondered if it would ever be right again after the clash with an angry co-worker wielding a gun the year before. She grimaced remembering the frightening encounter as she plopped down on the bench beside Jules.

"The layout of Jouques looks interesting with these long, parallel streets. I see two back streets and a higher road above it all. There are a limited number of traverses linking the long streets, so there doesn't appear to be any short cuts. I can see medieval arches and facades across the way and there's the remnant of the old medieval palace," he said as he pointed across the tops of the buildings along the main street.

"Amazing, isn't it?" Callie's grin hadn't left her face.

Jules laughed at her reactions. He glanced around him, ever watchful for a man with red hair who might be following them. They could hear musicians above the roar of the marketplace as the brisk breeze ruffled a few stall coverings. With the map's directions in her lap, Callie directed Jules as they drove toward the castle. It sat high on the hill overlooking the town near the imposing Notre Dame de la Roque Chapel. Passing one of several old stone fountains, they marveled at the fascinating stonework where four spigots spilled water over a trough. Green with age and not very appetizing, they moved on. When they saw an updated footbridge that paralleled the older bridge, they nearly missed the turn.

"Sorry, Jules, there's so much to see here and it's all so quaint. Turn right at the next corner. It's a long street but it starts uphill from there and we should be able to see the castle."

Blue and green shuttered windows winked out over the gaily striped awnings of the village shops and narrow cobblestone avenues shot out from the main road. "I think the marketplace is where all the action is, so we picked a good day to sneak inside. Let's watch for police as we get closer. The village only has about 3,400 inhabitants and I doubt they get up here much. Mostly, tourists I imagine." As he drove closer, the road began climbing upward and the castle came into view. The road narrowed along Rue des Baumes and hundreds of stones made up walls, houses and stair steps along the way. Jules slowed down at the next turn to avoid a large family of cats who stared at him indifferently. Callie laughed when the cats disbursed at the honk of the horn.

When his car purred around the last bend, a house caught their eye and they both laughed. A sturdy, climbing grapevine scampered up an ocher wall near a long window. Fancy black grillwork encased the delicate area where four black rubber boots languished upside down, destroying the effect.

Callie pointed a finger toward a stone wall. Jules jerked the car and slipped it through a break in the stones, pleased that it would be hidden from the road. "The map shows a door toward the back of the Monumental Steps." The breeze picked up and Callie wrapped her scarf tightly around her neck as she followed behind Jules. He turned and grabbed her hand and pulled her through a maze of tightly-packed cobblestones until they reached the courtyard. As they approached, they discovered a crumbling wall ran at the base of the hill that supported the castle like some ancient train trestle leading upward. Well-worn stone steps led up to the top on both sides, to the left and right of a three-arched bridge of a sort. Jules glanced around behind him, still wary of the mystery man, and studied the map. And then he headed off toward the right with Callie following close behind.

"This shows the doorway on this side, so let's…"

A voice carried up to them, "I forgot my camera, honey, will you get it from the car?" A mumble of response could be heard and then footsteps.

Jules and Callie stopped and pretended to study the stone wall beside them as a man joined them on the steps. A woman came around the corner after him, a camera hanging around her neck.

"Hi. Magnificent castle, isn't it?" The man asked, with a sharp UK accent. "We've been studying medieval castles and this is the tenth one we've found for our documentary."

"Yes, I understand this is part of the Gallerie Baumes. Ten castles must keep you busy." Callie said, not sure what to do next. She looked at Jules and he shook his head.

The couple focused their camera. She wrote in a notebook as her the man dictated. A slight breeze whistled between the stairwell and the landing, but the couple didn't seem to notice.

Jules nodded toward Callie and edged toward the corner of the steps Her eyes grew wide when he moved toward the door and she bit the inside of her lip as he moved into the shaded alcove. "Keep your eyes on them, Callie, and I'll see if I can nudge this open."

The couple continued up the steps above Callie to take more photos.

Callie called up to them. "Did you see the farmer's market in the big square? There's music and lots of food."

"Yes, but we were focused on the castle. If there's anything left when we're finished, we may stop by." They smiled down at her and proceeded to the top.

Callie followed them upward, relieved to see neither Jules nor the small door could be seen from her vantage point. Keeping her vigil, she lifted her phone and began snapping photos of the bridge and the buildings toward the river. She almost forgot why she was there until Jules called her from below.

He guided her down the steps, across the courtyard toward the car. "There's good news and there's bad news," he whispered. They slipped into his car and left their spot behind the broken wall to head back toward town.

"Well?" Callie's heart was beating hard; she was afraid Jules was going to postpone their outing and wondering what he'd do next. After all, they were this close. Would he really let two strangers stop the impetus now?

Jules didn't answer. He spied a quaint restaurant on the winding street and they were soon sitting at a window inside *Les Souvenirs de l'Avenir*.

Callie waited impatiently until the waitress delivered their tomato salad with fresh goat cheese and gratin de raviolis. Jules had ordered their main courses, a grilled steak on a bed of fresh vegetables and a Filet of Daurade along with glasses of Beauvais Cellars Rosé.

"Bad news first?" Callie drummed her nails against the tabletop.

Jules grinned and leaned toward her. The bad news is the door won't budge. The area looks like it hasn't seen the light of day or anyone around it for a very long time. It seems the perfect hiding place, *oui*?"

Callie sighed deeply, dejected. "And the good news?"

Jules winked. "I know how to pick locks."

Her face lit up. "You are definitely the man to hang around with, Jules. And let me guess. We are eating this beautiful meal and drinking wine while we wait for the professor to vacate the premises?"

He grinned at her again, reached for his wine and glanced toward the street periodically as he ate. Their food was delicious, their plates long empty before a green Citroën angled its way down the street. Jules peered through the window and lifted the napkin off his lap. "Let's look for the next piece of the puzzle."

The restaurant wasn't crowded earlier, but it was now teeming with hungry customers as they threaded their way toward the door. Jules felt excited and wondered if the movie, Ocean's Eleven, hadn't gone to his head. The adventure of the hunt, the excitement of not knowing if your plan would work and getting away with it all was uppermost in his mind as they jumped in his car. He wouldn't mention his crazy thoughts to Callie because she would think he was mad, not the George Clooney type at all.

After parking behind the crumbling stone wall again, they inched their way across the courtyard, where Callie sat at the bottom of the second stairway to watch for any surprises. The sun's rays were shifting across the stone steps where she inched her butt against the wall and she started counting as she held her breath against the dread that threatened to engulf her.

Jules whispered, "Watch for a man with red hair."

That said, an additional nervousness crawled up Callie's spine. As Jules made rattling noises above her, her eyes darted around the area, up and down the steps. Dusk was settling in as it became darker by the small door.

Jules maneuvered the small tool that he always carried in his pocket; it had three different blades. One usually worked. He smiled to remember how he and François used to break into the wine shed when they were young. He tested first one, then the next until a distinct click made him smile. Carefully replacing the tool back into his pocket, he pushed. Hard. When the door moved inward, his breath caught.

Fourteen

Cendrine glanced at her watch again and paced the length of the kitchen. When the phone rang, she sprang toward it like a tightly-wound spring.

"Cendrine, mah lassie. Ah am frantic haur wi' nae wuid frae ye. Still nae Olivier?"

"No, GrandPapa." Her words choked. She had hoped the call was Callie…or Olivier. "I am sorry for not calling you sooner, but events have moved from bad to worse since Olivier has been gone."

"Teel me whit Ah can dae fur ye, hen. Ah cannae jist sit haur twiddlin' mah thumbs. Ah want tae help. Ah want tae fly tae France tae be wi' ye but mah doctur willnae allaw it. Ah say tae heel wi' it, but Ah fear he is reit." The old Scotsman's words were frantic as they spilled toward her.

"GrandPapa, I know you want to help and I'd love to have you here. I would. But, right now, we have several people looking for Olivier and following a map, wondering if those damn bottles will lead us to him. I am sorry I didn't call you sooner and I promise to keep up with you. Your doctor is right. When I know something, I will call. I Promise." When Bernadette's small arms wrapped around her mother's knees, Cendrine smoothed a hand over her little head.

"Guid. Ah will bide an' pray tae th' heavens thaur is ah guid suin. Ah ken mah loon an' he is in trooble, Ah am sure ay it." His voice trembled with concern.

"Yes, he is a good boy and I also think he is in trouble. Try to think positive, GrandPapa. I will call soon." Tears squeezed from her eyes to drop onto her cheeks. The nightmare had to end soon. As she hung up, she smoothed her hand over her belly and sat down, pulling little Bernadette into her lap. The girl burrowed into Cendrine's arms and pushed her face into her mother's neck.

**

Francisco checked his email for the hundredth time. And then he checked his phone. No texts. No messages. His heart pounded. Two co-workers had already questioned him several times when they noticed his anxiety. He'd shooed them away, turned to his client file and tried to look busy. He couldn't remember being so angry since his wife died. Then, he knew there was no recourse. She was gone and he was alone. His family had opened their home and their arms. Like always. Now, his anger was at himself. He could no longer deny that his big mouth had led to this fear invading his home and family.

"Hey, Francisco, time to close the office. I'm off for a beer. Do you want to join me?" Diego Silván Hernández stood in his doorway, his jacket angled across his shoulder with a finger. "You look like you need one, *amigo*. Let's go."

Francisco said, "Let me make one more phone call and I'll join you, Diego. I need to speak to someone and I can't relax until I do." His friend shrugged his shoulder and left him alone. The click of the heavy wooden door signaled the outer room was empty. He reached for the phone, dialed the number and heard it ring.

"Yes?"

Francisco's heartbeat jumped. "This is Francisco."

The phone remained silent long enough for Francisco to wonder if the call had dropped. "Hey, Francisco." The man on the other end sounded tired and apprehensive.

"Where are you, man?" Francisco's voice was icy.

"I'm on holiday. Why?"

"Where *are* you?"

"Okay, I'm in France. Why do you want to know?"

Francisco's rage was palpable. "Because, I think you and I need to talk and soon. Today is Friday and I do not work on the weekend. Meet me in Málaga at our old place tomorrow by seven o'clock or I will call your grandfather."

The man's voice hitched. "I can't be there that soon. How do I know if there are any planes leaving…?"

"You make it happen. Or I make the call." Francisco slammed down the phone so hard the files flipped off his desk. Now he could use that beer.

***

Christianne beamed at Olivier when he entered her kitchen smelling like a rose instead of a spoiled cabbage. The pants were too short but the shirt fit. She nodded toward a large cup of coffee on the table beside Bertrand. They'd waited for him, whispering to each other as they wondered about this young man and his troubles.

"*Asseyez vous s'il vous plaît.* Sit please. You frightened us this morning when you fainted. My wife," he nodded to Christianne, "and I helped you to your bed. I took off your clothes and she threw them in the dustbin. Now, eat and then you can please tell us how we can help you."

Olivier placed his hand over his heart and tapped it. "Thank you both for helping me. I will tell you all I know." He drank the dark coffee and picked up his fork to dig into the rich soup. Croissants and fresh fruit sat beside his plate and the smell of fresh bread filled the kitchen. He inhaled deeply, feeling safe again. He knew the old couple watched him and waited for him to speak, but he wasn't sure how to begin.

"*Encore du café?*" More coffee? Christianne nudged more fruit toward him. It was obvious the young man had not eaten properly in some time. Reaching behind her, she brought a hot baguette toward him and pushed butter across the table. He smiled, ripped into it and began his story.

"When you found me this morning, I was hiding from a man who had locked me in a dirty room not far from here. When he kicked me because I could not answer his questions, I grabbed his foot and he fell to the floor and he didn't get up. The door was open and I ran. When I saw the alley, I hid because I was afraid he would find me."

"Why did this man lock you up? And who is he?"

"I do not know who the man is and I could not answer his questions. I woke up with a violent headache and I could not lift my head for the pain. It still hurts. He said he hit me but I do not know where I was when this happened." He shoved another piece of buttered bread into his mouth and lifted the soup spoon to his mouth.

The couple stared at him, stunned. They wondered if they could be vulnerable. He could see it in their eyes. Olivier reached toward the woman and placed his hand over hers. "If I thought you would be hurt by helping me, I would leave right now. My biggest problem is that I have no memory before I woke up in that box-like room several days ago."

Bertrand's eyes widened. "Maybe my doctor friend can help you. Please tell us what this man looks like so we can watch for him. You must stay here in the kitchen until my friend arrives. You are welcome to stay in our spare bedroom until we puzzle this out. This is good with you?" Bertrand's face was a mirror of concern.

Olivier's throat clogged with tears as he bit into the delicious bread again. "He is about the same height as I am. He has reddish hair and a gravelly voice. He wore jeans and a red sweatshirt the last time I saw him. He has a short red beard and mustache. His eyes are blue. And he is very mean." Olivier's jaw tightened.

The next morning, the bell above the bakery door, jangled and Christianne raised her eyebrows. Although very early, she had not been watching the clock. She hurried into the front of the bakery where a glass case offered baguettes, croissants, sweet rolls and breadsticks.

Bertrand turned toward the oven to remove fresh baked bread and fill sacks with orders. He nodded toward Olivier. The timer beeped just as Christianne entered the kitchen again. Her hand covered her throat. She whispered, "The man you described is here...He asked me if I saw a man with reddish hair in this area recently."

Olivier's fork stopped midway to his mouth and his eyes rounded. Before he could move, Bertrand held up his hand and followed Christianne out with a loaf of bread in his hand. He entered the room and glanced at the man in front of the counter. Olivier hid in the doorway and watched the man step from one foot to the other as if keeping time to music nobody else could hear. His hair was in disarray and his eyes darted around the room.

Christianne handed him a loaf of bread and the sweet roll he pointed toward. As she held out her hand for his coins, the man lifted his head to stare at Bertrand with narrowed eyes. One of his hands remained in his pocket as he paid her. "*Bonjour,*" he mumbled and turned to leave the bakery.

Bertrand placed fresh bread in the glass case and did not look up again. When the bell's jangle told them the customer had left, he looked at Christianne and gave her a look. Then he returned to the kitchen to see Olivier still watched the man from the doorway.

"What shall we call you? If you do not know your name, we must give you one until you remember your own." Bertrand thought a moment with a finger to his lips. "Alexandre. We shall call you Alexandre, which was my brother's name."

"Alexandre sounds very familiar to me, Bertrand. I am unsure why, but that sounds fine. I have to remember. There must be someone who misses me, who wonders where I am, who is afraid because I am not home. I feel it." Olivier sat down again, reached for the remaining piece of baguette and crunched it between his teeth. He'd eaten the entire loaf.

An hour later, Olivier washed pots and dishes. He had already peeled a pot of potatoes and he was drying some large pans when there was a knock on the back door. He froze.

Bertrand hurried to the door and glanced through the tiny window. "Ah, it is my doctor friend, 'Alexandre.'" He opened the door and pulled the man inside.

Doctor Denis Colbert entered the kitchen and sniffed deeply. "Fresh bread, yes I will have some, thank you," he laughed. He was a small man, barely five feet five with kind eyes and a ready smile. "This must be your new friend," he said as he headed toward Olivier.

"*Oui,* we call him 'Alexandre,'" Bertrand beamed.

The doctor raised his eyebrows. "You are calling him 'Alexandre'?" Bertrand placed a plate of hot bread with butter and strawberry preserves before his friend and pushed Olivier into a chair across from him.

"We are calling him 'Alexandre' because he does not remember his name. He was hit on the head some days ago and…well, 'Alexandre' you please tell him the story."

Olivier shook hands with the doctor and told him everything he could remember. The doctor listened intently, swallowed the last piece of his bread and then reached over to explore Olivier's head. Probing the knot at the base of his skull with deft fingers, he sat down again. Reaching into his shirt pocket, he removed a tiny flashlight and shined it into Olivier's eyes as he held open each eye lid. "It appears you are suffering from Amnesia, young man. This is a condition that sometimes happens after hard bumps to the head. Usually, a mild concussion leaves a serious headache but sometimes there is also memory loss, vomiting, that kind of thing. Have you suffered from anything besides memory loss?" He looked at Olivier hard.

"I had a headache for many days and I had chills when Bertrand found me but I'd been in the alley for a long time and it was getting cold."

"He fainted yesterday when we fed him but we checked on him every few hours to make sure he was still breathing." Bertrand squeezed Olivier's shoulder.

Olivier chuckled. "Thanks for that, Bertrand. And what would you have done if I hadn't been breathing?" Olivier smiled at the older man. "I have dreams but I don't know if they mean anything. I remember thinking the cheap red wine the man gave me wasn't something I normally drank. And I have dreamed about children and this morning when I woke up, I was in a vineyard reaching down to pick grapes. Sometimes I see a woman but it is blurry and as hard as I try, I can't see her face." His hands gripped each other in agitation.

"Well, that is good news, then. These dreams are probably your memories trying to surface. I believe, since you are already having these thoughts while you sleep, you will soon begin to remember. Unfortunately, it is difficult to hurry this along. The vineyard dream may be important, though. There are only a handful of vineyards around this area. We can do some research, eh, Bertrand? Make a list, make some calls, and ask questions?"

Olivier looked hopeful for the first time in days. He wondered if it could be that easy. He tried to squeeze the answers out of his brain as the two men talked about his missing memory, but knew it was something he had to work out. The more he thought about the faceless woman, the more he knew she was very important. The grapevines? Not so much. Was he a vintner? A farm worker? He looked at his hands and counted that out. He had no blisters to show he worked on a farm or a vineyard. In fact, his fingers were smooth. He must work inside, not outside. He reached his hands up to his temples and pressed his fingers, probing, rubbing and wishing he could find the answers.

"….yes, I agree. 'Alexandre' should remain inside. If the red-bearded man looks for him here, he must be looking for him in other shops. I will go visit my friend, Gaston, to buy his cheese. His shop is four buildings down the street. He has contacts all over the village and if this man is asking questions, we will make sure he gets no answers. We will also call the police." With that, Bertrand pulled his coat on and left them.

Dr. Colbert turned to Olivier. "We shall figure this out, young man. For now, drink lots of water and eat some of Christianne's good food. If you have more dreams, or if any hazy memories begin to surface, ask Bertrand to call me. I know of a doctor who specializes in this condition. I'll call him for you if things start opening up for you. I will also call Bertrand if I think of anything new. For now, *au revoir*."

When Olivier closed the door behind the doctor, he surveyed his surroundings and slumped into the nearest chair. Compressing his lips, he wondered where his jailer had got to. Pressure built up inside his chest; he rubbed his fingers across his eyes and then through his hair. "It's a beginning," he whispered before his deep breath whisked flour from the work table. He watched a handful whoosh toward the floor before he shrugged and picked up a broom. He would earn the food he ate to show these people he appreciated everything they were doing for him. A free room, free food and free kindness. His shoulders tightened at the memory of hiding in the cold alley before Bertrand found him hunched there, still afraid. The broom moved across the floor briskly, his fingers nearly white as he squeezed the wooden handle. He thought about asking Bertrand to take him to the police station. Telling them about the man who held him locked up in that room would be a start, but first he wanted his memory back.

Fifteen

The musty odor emanating from the small room nearly knocked Jules flat. Holding his breath, he pushed the door open until it touched the wall. Rats scurried near him and he pulled his hand off the door and reached around looking for a light switch. He was relieved to find one close to the doorway. The meager light bulb blazed from a single cable in the center of the room. Sliding out the door again, he walked to the top of the steps and looked over the stone edge way where Callie stood sentinel.

"Callie?"

She looked up quickly, hardly daring to breathe. "You're in?"

"Yes, everything is quiet." He looked like a little boy who had just received his first little red wagon.

The door beckoned them inside. The light barely illuminated the room but it was enough to see shelving and buckets along the inside wall. The room was cool, dark and perfect for aging wine. Callie took a deep breath and coughed jaggedly before she slipped through after Jules.

Edging along the shelves, they made their way toward the center of the room. It was a storage room with a door on the opposite wall. Jules knelt down beside the far door and opened it just a crack, peeking through the gap. He was surprised it was not locked, but guessed nobody thought to do it since the outer door was locked. He chuckled. The outer room was a large, deserted warehouse. It was filled with old furniture covered thick with dust; nobody had been inside for many years. He turned around to see Callie squatting down before the deep shelves. She held a dark, dusty bottle in her hands.

"Holy shit." She covered her mouth contritely.

Jules' face wrinkled in a grin.

"The label does have a Spanish woman riding on a cork." Callie pulled her shirt out of her waistband and gently rubbed the bottle before holding it up to him. "I feel like I just had a baby," she laughed.

Jules joined her and together, they counted fifty nine bottles. "Well, we need a plan to remove them. We can't carry them out of here today...."

"Why not?" Callie stared at him. "Your car is big enough. If we can get them down without anyone seeing us, we can do it." Her hands tightened around the bottle protectively and her eyebrows furrowed.

"Callie. We need a plan. It's almost dark outside. First, I must make sure I didn't break the lock since I unlatched it without a key. If it still locks, I can get us in again. If it won't, we have a problem. Nobody has been in here except rats, so either way the bottles will wait for us..."

She jumped toward him. "I hate rats." Callie looked around the floor and peered into the dark shelves. "Maybe you're right..." She stared at him in the dimness.

He snickered and handed her two bottles. When he pulled the door closed, he was relieved to hear the latch click. He jiggled the handle and was glad to feel it fight against his hand. "Good, it's locked."

They turned toward the steps. She was disturbingly close and Jules found it impossible to tear his gaze away. He had long ago acknowledged her undeniable attraction and wasn't surprised to feel a familiar longing inside. She held the bottles close to her chest as he guided her downward. It was now nearly dark, making it difficult to see the stone steps. As they got to the bottom, Callie slipped. The momentum of her fall propelled her into the stone wall. Although she banged her elbow, she held the bottles tightly and fell into Jules' chest. "Ooh..." She whimpered as she was pulled into his arms with the two bottles of seventy-year old brandy between them.

"You are a fireball of fierce energy, Callie Beauvais. And you saved the brandy." He kissed the top of her head. When she laughed up at him, he cupped her cheek carefully with his hand and his thumb ran under her chin.

The corners of her mouth lifted in a small smile. She was astonished and had to remind herself to breathe as he leaned down and their lips met in the twilight with Picasso's brandy wedged tightly between her breasts.

"That's the sweetest feeling in the world," she said softly, her voice filled with pleasure, her mouth so near his he had to kiss her again.

He leaned forward. Her lips were warm and soft, and her brown eyes were filled with so many gold flecks it made him dizzy. Something wild and hot flooded through his stomach, and the feeling grew. She lowered her eyes and transferred her gaze to the brandy bottles, smiling at his tenderness.

When he lifted them from her arms and they slipped between the antique stone arches, Callie's mind was in turmoil. She tried to make sense of what just happened. Without a doubt, his kiss had taken her by surprise. Smiling, she recalled Jules' scent, his strong embrace and his firm lips against hers.

Some minutes later, Jules drew in a long breath, stared out the window to think for a moment as the last glints of warming sunset slanted across the window.. The sky above had turned mauve and then dark blue-gray.

Forty five minutes later, the bottles were bookended on her lap with her fanny pack nudged between them as they arrived at the old mill house. The last thing she wanted was to break them after being coddled and hidden so long. She could hardly wait to show Cendrine and Andres.

Beside her, Jules was quiet, hoping he had not made a mistake. He valued Callie's friendship and never imagined he could feel quite like this. No wonder François made that rash and unpredictable decision so many years ago. It wasn't right, not by a long shot. But, would Jules do the same thing in his position? No. He would not. He would have trusted Callie's love and laid it out in the open. He would never have given up his daughter. He would have shared her. Callie would have understood. Seeing Veronique had scorched her heart, but he hoped she would understand that François was only a man with human frailties. He also admitted he wanted to be part of her life. He turned off the ignition and turned toward her.

"Callie, maybe I shouldn't have done that, but..." he began, but she cut him off.

"...Jules, don't you dare tell me you regret that kiss. Because I don't. Even though I'm angry at François and feel guilty because of Nate...I feel drained, but that was...Cendrine's waiting. Let's analyze our emotions later."

Before she could open the car door, he reached his arm around her and pulled her toward him. Looking into her eyes, he whispered, "Make that a promise and I will let you out of my car."

She laughed, lifted three fingers in a Girl Scout salute and reached for the door handle. His laughter followed her into the old mill house.

***

In Málaga, Francisco Garcia Sanchez glanced at his watch again, nursing the *Mahou* beer in front of him. It had long ago lost its chill and he had just ordered another. It was 6:45, the lights on the street were bright and the traffic was thick with cars, not surprising for a Saturday night.

The men had met at the University of Málaga when they were nineteen years old and they'd become fast friends. They had spent so much time together; another friend teased them about being gay. They were the odd couple, he with dark hair and brown eyes and his friend with red hair and blue eyes. He'd grown up in Málaga and was proud of his Malagueñan heritage. His friend spoke Spanish, but soon learned to chop off his words to fit into Andalucía. After graduation, Francisco started his banking career and his best friend left Spain to return to his homeland and eventually work in the whiskey trade. They'd lost track over the years. Until recently.

Francisco squeezed his glass of *Mahou* beer until it nearly disappeared in his palm. Another cold one was delivered at 6:55. Gulping down the beer incited more anger as he admitted alcohol had probably been his downfall when he was a university student. That was when he'd spilled his grandfather's secrets about Picasso, the old brandy, the *señorita* label; all the words he'd promised never to repeat.

He stared at the glass in his hand. He did not want to call the old Scotsman but he would if he had to. He stared at nothing and imagined the conversation and the old man's fury. Would his great grandfather remove his friend from his will? Even a bastard grandson usually got something.

When Francisco's third beer was set in front of him, he watched the girl move away with a sexy sway to her walk. His gut knotted, wishing he was there just to drink a beer and flirt with a woman. When did life change from the simple things? He wished he was a little boy again, sitting at his *abuelo's* knee, feeling the old man's hand tousle his head. But now, he had to watch over his *abuelo*, the tables were turned. He'd just swallowed the last drop when the door opened and Conall Baird Carson walked in, pulling a flat cap from his head.

***

Meanwhile back in Pertuis, Cendrine stared at the woman on the wine label the havoc created such turmoil in her body, she could not stand. She sat down fast, the air left her lungs and she whipped a hand to her mouth to keep from screaming. Her fingers danced across the artwork as she stared at Jules and Callie.

They took turns telling her everything after Callie washed the bottles and sat them on the coffee table. Well, almost everything. Callie gave Jules a look, both remembering when she'd almost dropped the bottles and the kisses that followed.

"Now, we need to prepare to get the rest of the bottles. Nobody followed us. If someone had, he would have shown up when we were inside. I watched all day for anyone with red hair," Jules said with pride.

Callie's head popped up. What would she have done if the man had followed them, demanded the bottles? She would have given them to him in exchange for Olivier. Her shoulders slumped at the thought.

After Bernadette and François were both in bed, Cendrine called her father. She knew he was fighting his anger at Olivier for not talking to either of them before taking the money. Regardless of why he disappeared or where he was, he should have told them! Where was he now? Was he afraid or hurt or worse? Her mind thrummed with questions, fought against the justifications she was sure must be in the mystery somewhere. She took a solid breath, glanced at the brandy bottle again. She hoped it might ease her father's frustrations. But did the old bottles lead to her husband's destruction? His death? She put her hand to her head and sat down again, admitting the most intense thoughts she had was about her husband; her worry for him escalated as she waited for Andres to arrive.

Within minutes, he knocked on the door and entered with a question on his face. Seeing the old wine bottles centered on the couch table wiped it clear. He walked slowly toward them and sat down next to his daughter. And then he lifted a bottle in his hands and stared at the label. "I couldn't believe it without seeing them with my own eyes," Andres said slowly. "Whoever frightened Olivier and broke into your house was looking for these. That man knows they are real and now we have them to prove it. Now he will come back." His lined face sagged. He squeezed his hat in his hands and allowed his daughter to massage his shoulders.

"What now, Jules? Now that you and Callie found the brandy bottles, how will you get them out? How can you be sure the mystery man is not nearby....maybe watching Cendrine? Special care must be taken to keep everyone safe." He glared at the bottles and compressed his lips. "If old Picasso wanted this brandy hidden and saved so badly, why choose a Frenchman as its keeper?" he demanded. "Alexandre must have known how dangerous it could be for his son. And for his family!" The vintner looked haunted, fisting his hands into both pockets. He stood up and stared out the window before he paced back and forth, mumbling to himself.

"Papa, we will gather the brandy another time. And we can follow Alexandre's instructions another time. The selling and disbursing of the funds can wait for Picasso's flamenco guitar school too. Now we know the bottles exist, we are closer to understanding what upset Olivier. I do not know why he wanted to take us away on holiday though... Jules and Callie got this far, we must trust them to find him...." Her words dwindled into a whisper and he stopped pacing. And then her father's callused hand caressed her small one as it lay across her pregnant belly protectively.

Sixteen

Olivier had eventually drifted off to sleep the night before as unanswered questions continued to trouble his mind. Amazed at how eager Bertrand and Christianne were to help him, he wanted to be of some use to them. His brain might not be working, but he was strong and able. Beams of light brightened the room and Olivier felt hope brighten with them. The doctor he'd seen the day before had given him a little more information but he still could not remember much.

His jaw tightened as recent memories slid through his mind. The crazy man who'd held him in that dingy room had not come back to the bakery and for that he was grateful. Would he again? Would Olivier be stuck inside, fearful of walking out into the brisk air of the village he now knew was Venelles?

When Bertrand told him he'd spoken with the police to learn that nobody had reported him missing, Olivier didn't want to believe it and depression descended like a heavy quilt. He slid his hands beneath his head and stared up at the ceiling. Counting the small blue flowers painted on the ceramic light cover above his head, his eyes swung to the chest of drawers and the tidy crocheted doily that rested beneath a small lamp. There were books stacked near the lamp, on the floor and beside a chair by the window. His lips curved in a smile. Someone liked to read. His forehead creased, wondering whose room he was sleeping in. The sun was creeping into the room and he told himself to get up. Perhaps today he would get his life back and the answers eluding his befuddled brain. He was sure there was someone looking for him, family, and the woman. Maybe the children belonged to the woman? To him?

"I just hope they find me soon, before that crazy bastard comes around again." With that thought, his feet hit the floor. The aroma of frying bacon wafted from the kitchen. And then he smiled.

***

When Conall Carson slid into the booth across from Francisco, his features were calm despite the anger that simmered below the surface. He forced a grin. Reaching a hand to Francisco, he said, "Hey, old friend. What is so important that couldn't be discussed over the phone? Ye knew I was in France." His eyes challenged Francisco, wondering how much the guy knew. Raising his hand and wiggling his fingers, he caught the attention of a young woman delivering drinks to the table next to them. He pointed at the beer glass in front of Francisco.

Francisco's heart rate spiked. "You know exactly what is so important, Conall. We had visitors at my grandfather's house yesterday and I could see you right in the middle of the mystery!" Francisco's hand hit the table, shaking his beer.

The woman delivering Conall's beer jerked her hand and spilled it on the table. She glared at Francisco and he quickly apologized, "*Lo siento mucho.*" I am very sorry. She marched off but left with a forgiving grin.

"What mystery, Francisco?" Conall drawled as he sipped his beer and stared at his old friend. How much could the guy know? He'd been very careful to stay clear of Francisco but now that the avalanche of motion had begun, he worried he'd been less careful than he'd hoped. He could see Francisco's chest heave. Ignoring Francisco's anger, he took another sip of beer and raked his fingers through his red hair.

Francisco looked around quickly and then moved forward and hissed, "Those old wine bottles. The story I told you when we were at university. It was just a family legend, nothing more. Now, I have learned that you questioned my grandfather about it twenty years ago. Yesterday, he described you perfectly. Then, my mother took a photo of a man inside a car who has been following *abuelo*. I know it was you!" When he squeezed his glass between his fingers, Conall's eyes were drawn to the beer spilled across the table between them. "I want you to leave my *abuelo* alone. He knows nothing. What are you trying to do? Why do you care about some old wine bottles anyway?" He looked like he wanted to jump over the table and grab Conall's neck and squeeze it into silence.

Conall drained his beer and put the glass down on the table none too gently. His eyes drilled into Francisco's when he replied, "Ye'r auld *abuelo* knows where those bottles are. I followed 'im to France and saw 'im meet with Olivier Benoit. Your *abuelo* carried something in a wee satchel. He probably told Olivier where the auld bottles are hidden. Why am Ah interested? Man, we could be rich. Do ye have any idea how much those old bottles of brandy are worth by now? They must be ab'ut seventy years old, aged, prime and extremely valuable."

Francisco scoffed. "*We* could be rich? You think I want any part of this stupid scheme? I don't give a damn about those bottles. And I'm telling you to stay away from my family or I will call that old Scotsman you call a grandfather. You leave my *abuelo* alone and I will leave *your abuelo* alone." He picked up his beer and drained the last few drops, his eyes never leaving Conall's face.

The muscles worked in Conall's jaw and his lips tightened as if he'd eaten a sour lemon. He knew his Scottish brogue broadened when his emotions were high. Conall drained his glass and sat it down very lightly to the table, planning how he would handle this stupid Spaniard. Despite being friends in school years ago, now they had nothing in common except graduation documents and some childish memories. After feeling second best all his life next to Olivier Benoit, he'd given up trying to get his great grandfather's attention. His disappointment changed to anger and then to revenge. He knew if he could get the old brandy, sell them out from under Olivier, he would kill two birds with one stone. His great grandfather would acknowledge his success and his cousin would lose whatever his father had promised him. Either way, Conall would be the winner. But of course, that meant Francisco had to be silenced. The last thing he needed was a wrinkle in his plan.

"I ha' always wanted to find the bottles because Ah thought the story was true all those years ago when you first told me. Olivier's father told my great grandfather about them, including the label showing a black-haired *señorita* riding a cork on her butt called *Sueño España*. I knew it must be

Spanish. That old wine was made in the province of Cadiz, at a small vineyard a few miles from Jerez de la Frontera."

Francisco's eyes rounded. "How do you know all this, Conall?"

Conall laughed. "After we left university, I wasn't backpacking around Spain for two weeks before I wen' back to Scotland, like I told you. Hell, no. I was lookin' for information about the brandy." He leaned forward with his elbows on the table and grinned. "Ye know what else I found out? The vineyard with the label of the babe on the cork… was owned by a friend of Pablo Picasso's. Tha's when I knew it was troo…" He called for another beer.

Francisco looked dumbfounded.

Conall exhaled deeply and unconsciously rubbed his thumb against the table. Running his fingers beneath his curling red hair at the base of his neck, he tried to ease the stress building, but no matter how hard he pressed, it stayed put. "So, we have a vineyard in Spain farmed by a friend of Picasso's and bottles of brandy produced and sealed near Jerez. And a label with a woman ridin' a cork." He snapped his fingers and stared shrewdly at Francisco. "I also learned nobody in the area knows anything aboot the bottles. Oh, really? Of course they do, but remember this was during General Franco's dictatorship in Spain. Nobody admitted to anything about anything that could get them arrested. Picasso was their countryman, a Republican-thinking Spaniard and a well-known artist. I blended your story with my findings an' pieced the facts together. Somehow, he was able to get that brandy from Spain to France. There must have been many people helping along the way. They had to take th' lower route, probably through La Línea and then by water from Gibraltar, Valencia or Barcelona. I would be shocked if they managed it by land."

"I don't care! Don't you get it? The bottles mean nothing to me. I have a good job at the bank and I do not need money from stolen bottles. I need peace. And you are not going to drag me into a stupid adventure that makes no sense, like you did when we were twenty years old. We are forty now, not children!" Francisco held his head in his hands. He rubbed his temples and glared. Brown eyes held blue until Conall broke eye contact.

"Okay, okay, Francisco, I give up." Conall fisted his hand in his lap and moved it to his side pocket to assure himself the knife was still there. He lifted his head after fingering it a moment and smiled across the table. When he saw Francisco's shoulders relax, he ran his tongue across his lips. He'd always liked the guy and he didn't want to hurt him but a plan was a plan after all. And it didn't include Francisco or the mess he could make if he made that phone call to Scotland.

"Hey, still friends? I'll go home. You go back to your bank job. An' those wine bottles will remain a mystery. Sorry I got you so angry. I didn't mean to make you so crazy. Just like auld times, now, right?" He reached over and ruffled the top of Francisco's head and saw him smile feebly.

Francisco studied Conall. "Yes, and I will go home now too. You will leave Spain and my *abuelo* alone. I want to trust you, Conall. Stop this or you will have more people than just me yelling at you!" Francisco slid off the bench seat and stood looking at his old friend a moment before walking away and out the door.

Conall slowly counted to ten, dropped some euros on the table and fingered the steel in his pocket again. Yes, a plan was a plan after all and he had work to do before his plane returned to *Marseille* at ten.

***

Francisco heard quick footsteps behind him on the empty street. He hurried his pace. A group of people rounded the corner from the *plaza mayor*, laughing loudly and giving way on the sidewalk. He nodded to them briefly, too focused on getting to his car and home to notice the footsteps had picked up the pace behind him. He was once again alone on the street.

Digging out his car keys, he neared his Peugeot and flicked the remote. The lights blinked and the shrill sound of his door unlocking made him walk faster. As he reached for the door handle, he was stunned to see Conall Carson's face reflected behind him in the glass, his eyes mean. As he started to turn around, he was grabbed around the neck in a vice-like grip and thrown against his car. A screaming pain slammed into his side and all coherent thoughts left him. Francisco slid down the side of his car onto the sidewalk as he heard his attacker run into the alley while blood drained from his body.

***

The next morning, instead of her khaki pants and pullover sweater, her usual attire, Callie pulled on soft gray slacks and added a fuzzy, hot pink sweater. At the last minute, she added a long chain that held a heart shaped locket. She tried convincing herself that it was because she was eating breakfast in town. But the truth was she wanted to look good for Jules. And it bothered her. Could she possibly handle any more emotion?

The moment she twisted the door handle of her cottage, her laptop chimed. Skype call. She tapped the screen and Nate's face appeared.

"Nate." She looked at her watch. "It's 1:30 in the morning in Portland. What on earth?"

"Hi. I was hoping I'd catch you before you were off and running this morning. It's what, 9:30 in the morning there?" His smile looked tired.

"Yes. I'm meeting Cendrine for breakfast in town. We found the bottles and brought two of them home yesterday. Now we need a plan to retrieve the rest of them."

Nate's face looked pained. "Home? Is that your home now?" He saw Callie's expression and brushed the hair off his forehead in frustration. She could see he was tired, but she didn't deserve his grumpiness. He began again, "Callie, I think about you all the time and I am trying to be patient. I love you."

Callie sighed and tried to smile at him. "I know that."

"But how close are you to finding Olivier? That's why you flew all the way to Provence; you didn't leave me to find old bottles of wine." Tiredness lined his face and he lifted a bottle of water to his lips. "I miss you, dear heart. I want you here in my arms again. Please come home." He hadn't meant to say the words out loud but they escaped anyway.

"Nate," she said as she looked into his dear face, "there is no greater thrill in life than to find that you are not only useful, but that you can help, and that your help matters. It's as if I hold a magic fairy wand and I want to use it." She was disappointed her humor had not cracked a smile on his face.

He compressed his lips and she marveled that he could appear so close to her in the cottage in Provence when he sat so far away in Oregon. He was quiet a moment before starting, "Callie….."

She knew by the tone of his voice that what he was going to say wouldn't be good. She was right.

"How did we get from making love in your hot tub …to you being in France thinking François' family needs you more than I do?" His sleepy face stared at her across the miles.

Callie placed her hand to her throat considering Nate's words. He was sapping her natural optimism and sense of humor. She had always seen humor in most things. This key facet to her personality had been eroding since François died and she had to find it again. Nate's voice jerked her back from introspection.

"Callie?"

Her eyes met his again. "I'm here and to answer your question, I guess I don't know how to answer it. I love you, Nate, but there is…"

Nate snorted and his voice hardened. "Haven't you heard that when you follow a statement with the word, 'but', that it negates the statement?"

A mist of guilt settled around her for a moment but it dissipated when Nate repeated, "Please come home, Callie. This is where you belong. François is gone. You don't need to be Superwoman for his family." A nervous chuckle followed his words. "You can be Superwoman back here though…"

Callie's eyes watered and she wiped them with her hand. "Nate, I have a breakfast date and it's important. You are right, I don't have to be Superwoman, but I've promised to see this through. I'm committed and I have work to do. Please tell everyone at the office hello for me." She glanced at her watch again and her hand hovered over the end-call button. Nate got the message, tossed a kiss toward her and the screen went blank.

Pressing a hand onto her chest, she tried to knead the heaviness away, to ease the crumpling feelings that hovered there. Sometimes she wished she was sitting on a chaise lounge chair, beneath a palm tree with her toes drawing pictures in the sand. Life was just too damned uncomfortable sometimes. Struggling with her wayward thoughts, she ran out the door just as Cendrine honked outside her door. She'd tuck her Oregon worries aside to concentrate on the worries in France for now. No, she wasn't Superwoman although sometimes she wished she was.

Seventeen

Le Tourne Midi Café, in Pertuis, was tucked off the central square and embraced its patrons with the aroma of coffee, fresh bread and more. The room was abuzz with chatter as the ladies arrived. Grimacing, Cendrine shifted her belly trying to slip into the booth. "I can barely squeeze through!"

Jules grinned at her. "Shall we move to a table instead?"

"No, I just need a *café au lait*, a buttery croissant and lots of fruit." Wriggling to adjust her body, she shook her head in despair.

Jules said, "We should involve the police, Cendrine. They have access to official connections to look for Olivier. We do not know what else to do. It has been nearly two weeks and the clues are cold. In fact, the police will probably be angry we waited this long."

Cendrine pushed her plate aside and reached for her coffee. "I think you are right. I've been lying to myself, hoping we could keep the police out of it. By now, if he was d....dead...the police would have told me. They would have found him..." She sniffed and pulled a handkerchief from her purse. Blowing her nose hard, she continued, "Papa told me the same thing last night after he saw the bottles. He is very worried and talked to *grand-mére* and *grand-pére* about it. They agree." Her lips trembled as she lifted the cup again, sipped it and sat it down slowly. "I know if Olivier could contact me, he would have. Whoever broke into the house must know where he is. I would like to think the burglar is gone but I have a terrible feeling he is just around the corner."

Jules reached for her hand and squeezed her fingers. "You are probably right and that is why you must keep the house locked tight when you are alone. I am surprised the man hasn't contacted you. If he's kidnapped Olivier, he'd be asking for money. If he wanted to blackmail you or Olivier, why hasn't he done that? It seems since you've arrived, Callie, there are mysteries dancing around Pertuis everyplace." His brow furrowed and his eyes lifted to the ceiling in thought.

"The mystery brought me here, Jules; I didn't bring it with me. How can we narrow down the clues? Is there anyone, other than the police, who could help us?"

He stared at the women and tapped the table top with his hands. "The money." He snapped his fingers. "Maybe this man was blackmailing him… and that is why he took the vineyard money?"

The women stared at him as he reached for fruit.

Before they could respond, his cell phone rang, catching his fork mid air and the melon dropped back into his small plate. "*Halo?*"

Callie saw his face crimp in concentration, his eyelashes shadowing his cheek bones. She tried to look away but couldn't stop looking at his fingers as they held the phone, long and sensitive. Glancing upward, she saw the dimple in his chin and the way his hair was perfectly cut, dark and waving across is forehead. What was she doing? She'd just talked with Nate and now her thoughts were on silver eyes, a winning smile and charming banter. When Jules caught her staring at him, her face flushed as pink as the sangría he'd bought her a few days earlier.

"No, Claude. Just send the forty laptops to the school and get one of our people there to accept the delivery. I want those children to put their hands on them in three days just as I promised. I told Ailsa it would be Tuesday. No, I am still unavailable for a couple days. You can handle it. That's why you're the manager. Don't take no for an answer, dammit. I committed to Tuesday and I meant it. Okay, okay. I will trust you. Call me back if there's a problem and I'll make a call." He looked at Callie and shook his head. "Business interferes with our lives sometimes…."

"Jules, if your business is suffering, we can do this. Cendrine and I can go to the police station. We must find Olivier. Repeating those words over and over again is beginning to sound like a litany!" Callie's voice shook and she reached for Cendrine's hand as it twitched beside her breakfast plate.

Cendrine's face mirrored quiet desperation. Closing her eyes, tears seeped from her eye lids and her throat closed up tighter than a drum.

Jules turned to place his arm around her shoulders. "Cendrine, don't lose hope. You are right. If Olivier was found by the police, they would have told you. The silence from the police tells us he's still out there somewhere and," he gave Callie a look, "we will find him together. I know I have not been around in your life much in the past twenty years but I am here now. You are like a niece to me and you are not alone." He patted her arm with his fingers and she dropped her head on his shoulder.

"*Merci beaucoup*, Jules." Thank you so much.

Callie twisted the cup in her hands. "If Olivier was being blackmailed, it may be the reason he tried to get his family out of town. But, why disappear...?"

"It was just a thought." Jules tapped his fingers on the table.

Callie looked at his phone. "It sounds like you have a project involving school children, Jules?"

He smiled. "Hmmm? Yes, my company has donated laptops to the first year high school class in Venelles. The shipping company wanted to change the delivery date but the event is set for Tuesday. I hope we will find Olivier by then. If not, my manager, Claude, will meet the students in my place. He can explain the laptop's functions very well."

Callie was impressed. Another chink in her armor slipped away. Eating her croissant in earnest, she licked crisp flakes from her fingers. A brief euphoria engulfed her from the combination of the scent of the roll, Jules' aftershave and the fresh *café au lait*.

***

The Gendarmerie de Pertuis Police station was located at Avenue Jean Moulin, not far away. Jules accompanied Callie and Cendrine toward the tan building below a bright blue sign that displayed *Police Municipale*. Two windows hung above the door, one tall with a grilled balcony and one small square; each framed with white, wooden shutters. The French flag flapped in the wind alongside the flag of Vaucluse. The early winter sunshine tossed shadows from the tall bushes along the wall as they walked in the doors, which added a vague feeling of doom.

Callie marched up to the front desk in front of an amused Jules and placed her hands on the desk, tapping her fingers nervously. Cendrine huffed up beside her out of breath. Jules laid a calming hand on her shoulder.

"May I help you madame?" The officer was young, his dimples alight on his face as he surveyed the group. His navy uniform was starched to perfection, the collar standing at attention.

Callie said, "We want to report a missing person." She pointed to Cendrine, "my niece's husband has been missing nearly two weeks."

His confused glance was focused on Cendrine, who was pregnant. "This is the first time you bring this to our attention? Your husband has been missing and… by now the clues will be cold," he said. His eyes turned dark and he compressed his lips, losing his smile. He motioned to another officer at a nearby desk.

"*Oui*. Yes. We thought we could find him by ourselves," she finished lamely. Callie looked back and forth between both officers who returned her look with narrowed eyes.

The second officer approached Cendrine and introduced himself as Officer Boulieau. He tipped his head toward her and asked her to join him in the chair beside his desk. When Callie and Jules followed, he put up his hand to stop them. "Wait please. I only have the one chair and since it is her husband who is missing, only one at a time for now."

Jules pulled Callie toward a chair alongside the wall. He watched her eyes follow Cendrine. "You must let them handle it now, *chérie*. Cendrine is a strong woman. I know you want to be a mother hen, but let the man do his job."

She snorted and crossed her hands in her lap. Jules shook his head and smiled. What distinguished Callie from all the other women who had walked through his life was her sheer presence. Though she stood only five foot, three inches tall, she oozed charisma. He thought the first officer fell in love with her the minute she tapped her fingers on his desk. He'd seen heads turn when she walked by. Her pretty heart-shaped face was framed by a mass of dark curls with that silver streak interspersed through her bangs. She was glittering with eagerness, jittery and anxious. He was charmed.

Half an hour later, Cendrine looked faint after she signed the missing person's report. "The officer was upset because I waited so long to come in and he wondered why. I didn't have a good answer. I did not tell him about the missing money. I stuck to our plan. I am glad it is Sunday because it is not crowded in the station. Beavais Cellars is well known and the less notoriety the better for *grand-mére* and *grand-pére*. They are already keeping the children a few hours each day while I work in Olivier's office, answering the phone, invoicing orders, accepting truck shipments."

Callie squeezed her arm.

"I feel lost when I sit in my husband's chair. Olivier's aroma settles around me each time I walk into his office and it follows me home again each day. These have been the longest days of my life." She leaned into Callie.

The trio was so intent on their conversation, they missed the lone man leaning against the light post in the parking lot, his cigarette smoke rising slowly as he inhaled. His blue eyes followed the grouping until they got inside the BMW and then he quietly opened his Fiat's door and slid behind the wheel.

***

Later that afternoon, the sun shone brightly through the cottage windows. Jules left after promising to return in the morning. The bottles would be gathered and brought back to the cellar in the old mill house. He would look for a buyer without telling the entire story, putting feelers out into the brandy-buying community. He'd been told vintage brandy could sell for nearly 1400 euros per bottle. It didn't take a math genius to calculate how much money fifty seven bottles would total; 80000 euros should certainly fund a school to teach students to play the flamenco guitar that Picasso envisioned. Two bottles would remain with the family; Cendrine gave one to Callie and saved one for Olivier, of course.

Callie looked at her watch again. Livvy was due to Skype just after lunch, Pertuis time. She had just enough time to shoot off an email to Nate. She was still uneasy about their call earlier and her emotions were such a mess, she wanted to talk to Olivia. She knew she would miss her friend's wedding and she hated disappointing her.

The women had been friends a very long time; they shared their thoughts and feelings, kicking off ideas with each other during both good times and bad. Olivia had been the one she'd turned to when François died. Then, again when her mother died a year ago, it was Livvy who held her up and pressed her on. Callie stood at the window and stared into the gardens, lost in her memories. Assuming she'd finally crossed the edge of grief after losing François when Nate came into her life, she'd been relieved. Now back in France, not so much and it scared the hell out of her.

The chiming of the Skype call broke into her thoughts and she popped it on to see Olivia's welcome smile. Her short blond hair was cropped close and her eyes sparkled. Callie's stomach knotted and she gripped the edge of her laptop as she leaned in.

Both women grinned at each other. "Techies now, aren't we?" Livvy quipped. "From my fight against using the internet to someone hacking my computer from anywhere in the world to Skyping my best friend all the way to France..." She looked at Callie's worried face.

"Yes, we are techies alright. My iPad and laptop have been burning the midnight oil trying to figure out what happened to Olivier. Keeping Cendrine's psyche up, and mine along with it, is like tossing balls in the air. The only problem is my balls keep falling on the floor."

Olivia laughed. "Now that does sound like a personal problem, dropping one's balls on the floor."

Callie laughed. "Thanks, Livvy, I needed that. How are things going in Portland?"

"Well, I'm getting ready for my wedding. Our friend, Janine Vinnier, has been flitting around ever since I asked her to help me plan it. She needed something to keep her mind busy since her husband went to prison and Bram has been a jewel staying out of our way."

They stared at one another. "I am disappointing you, Livvy. I know that. I dreamed of being your matron of honor on your special day, but…..Olivier is still missing and my in-laws are so disturbed…and

Cendrine's pregnancy worries me. She's so stressed, she fainted the other day. The children are...."

"Whoa. Stop. I called to tell you something very important."

Callie's fingers covered her trembling mouth and she leaned toward the computer screen. "Oh?"

Her friend raked slim fingers through her short blonde hair until it stood up like spikes. "Don't think for a minute you're getting away with missing my wedding, Callinda Larkin Augustine Beauvais!" Olivia's face belied the censure behind the statement. And then a look of concern surfaced at the anguished look on Callie's face.

"I feel horrible. I know I promised, but that was before Olivier went missing. If I could hurry this along to find him, I'd wave my stupid, magic wand." Tears welled up in Callie's eyes and she angrily swiped at them.

Olivia compressed her lips and looked away from the monitor. Bram's face popped on the screen and they both beamed at her.

"Shhhhh," he said.

Callie's face was a riot of confusion. Where was the anger and disappointment? She stared at the monitor and tapped her fingers on the table, bereft of words. Her heartbeat sped up and she reached for a handkerchief to wipe at her eyes.

Olivia leaned in toward the screen. "Remember, Callie, that my daughter is house-sitting in Nice?"

Nodding yes, Callie said, "I remember, but I haven't had a moment away from this mystery to contact Nicole...."

Olivia glanced over her shoulder and Bram's face came into view again. He pulled up a chair and put his arm around Olivia. "Callie, we've decided to go to Spain for our honeymoon. We've both marked our calendars for ten full days to play in the sun and drink sangria and eat tapas and listen to guitars and...."

"Bram!" Olivia bumped his shoulder before he added sex to the list.

"Wonderful!" Callie moved her hand to her throat, happy their plan was moving forward. She leaned in shrewdly. "And......?"

Olivia and Bram gave each other a look. "Well," she said slowly, "we don't want to be too jetlagged to enjoy our honeymoon...."

"She means she doesn't want to tire me out with flying time, so she can use me up during the honeymoon time, Callie." He snickered when Olivia tapped his arm in mock agitation again.

She stared at Callie again. "If the matron of honor won't come to the wedding, then the wedding will come to the matron of honor!" She finished with a lopsided grin on her face. Bram placed his hand on her shoulder and Olivia reached up to caress his fingers.

Callie was stunned speechless. She grinned, smooched her fingers and tossed the kiss across the miles. A slow grin remained on her face as Olivia continued.

"It gets even better, Callie! Janine has planned the wedding from cake to flowers. Can you imagine her excitement when I told her we'd moved the wedding from Oregon to Provence since she's tried to get us to visit France with her for several years?"

"I thought since that horror of a husband of hers was thrown in prison, she would be working with Senator Donofrio in Washington, D.C." Callie knew the poor woman had been gob smacked after she learned her husband had killed a man in Portland. He'd fought Olivia over a Canadian prescription drug card option for Larkspur Insurance. The women wondered if Janine would ever get past the shock of his betrayal after learning what he'd done to Olivia and Callie, but she'd proved them wrong.

Bram kissed Olivia on the top of her head and wiggled a finger at Callie before leaving the women to chat. "I enjoyed sharing our surprise, but once you women start chatting, I know you'll be an hour or more."

Olivia glanced over her shoulder to make sure Bram had left the room before leaning in again, "And my friend, what's happening between you and Nate?" She was worried.

Callie covered her face with both hands. The sun shot beams of light across her hair to give her an ethereal look. "I am a mess, Livvy, I love Nate, but since I've been here, I'm not sure I'm *in* love with him. Am I so fickle as that, I wonder?"

Olivia looked pained.

"You see, my dear friend, my heart has definitely been misbehaving."

Olivia's head jerked forward. "What do you mean, misbehaving? Are you having heart problems? Pain? Shortness of breath?"

"No, not that." Callie laughed. "Jules Luc Armand is what I mean."

The light dawned on Livvy's face as frustration fought with delight. "Another Frenchman? How delicious."

"Yes, delicious… and I am at a loss to understand it. Nate was moving me forward, but compared to Jules?" Callie shook her head. "I've analyzed my relationship with Nate until I'm blue in the face. He was there and everything was good. He makes me laugh, he's sweet and he's gentle, thoughtful…but…" Callie groped for words.

Olivia studied her friend. "But? Maybe," she said slowly, "Nate helped you budge the door open, but Jules is the one who will invite you to walk through it?" A look of exquisite pleasure showed on Callie's face.

"Okay, hold that thought. I need another cup of coffee. I want to hear about Jules. His name sounds familiar. Do I know this guy? Oh, forget the coffee, tell me about him…."

"He makes my heart sing. It's like magic. I feel like I've known him forever. He grew up with François, but they had a falling out about the time we were married…" A faraway look came into her eyes and she wasn't sure how to continue.

"Do you know what they argued about? You'd think with a friendship that long, it had to be something darned important." Olivia pursed her lip. "I remember when our friendship wavered for those few minutes and I hate that memory."

"Oh, it was important alright. Damned important. I'm so furious with François, I could spit nails. But, for now, I must focus on finding Olivier. We went to the police today and Jules is looking for a buyer for ….I'll tell you another time. There's too much in my head. Cendrine is doing Olivier's job at the vineyard office and running after her four year old twins. Her new baby is due in a couple of months and she's stressed to the gills planning a new pink rosé. It is exciting and frightening around here…and you know what? I haven't felt so alive in ages."

Olivia laughed. "Sounds like it. Email me a photo of Jules. I like visualization." She laughed again. "Keep in touch. I want to hear what François did that has upset you so much…"

After Callie hung up, she leaned her chin on her hand, content to let her mind wander. The conversation had dredged up the image of Veronique. Just imagining Aurore's crushed spirit, raising the child without a father's moral support or love, gave Callie heartburn. *How could François do that?* She screamed inside her brain. The man she loved for twenty years wouldn't have done this. It was then she remembered a conversation with Jules on that first day. She curled her lips trying to put together his words. Now that she thought of it, he'd said François' refusal to claim Veronique was one of the reasons their friendship died. *I wonder what else tore up their friendship?* She made a note to ask him.

Eighteen

Janine and Michel gave Callie a warm hug and the twins ran for their box of toys while the adults started talking simultaneously.

"Then we went to the police station….."

"……And they were disturbed we hadn't reported him missing the first day, especially after the house was broken into…."

"But what did they say they can do? Is the trail too….?"

"…..cold? It might be," Cendrine said sadly.

Everyone looked at her, afraid to share their worst fears.

"Jules and Callie reminded me that if Olivier had been found already, the police would have alerted me and these policemen did not know anything about him. So, I continue to hope and maybe….."

"Of course, *ma chérie*. There is always hope. We have lingered over this disturbing conversation without a glass of wine. What am I thinking?" Janine stood and Cendrine followed her grandmother into the kitchen.

Callie sighed deeply. Michel drew her hand into his and sat there staring into her face. "Callinda, I see sadness cross your face at times when I least expect it. Thank you for coming so far to help our Cendrine. Andres is relieved and worried about her pregnancy, the stress and the little ones are a handful. We are happy to keep them some hours during the day while she works in the office. But, the days are dragging by and I do not want to say it, but I lose hope every day." His eyes were so sad, Callie squeezed his fingers. He forced a smile when the women returned with a tray filled with glasses of bubbly wine beside chunks of bread and various cheeses.

"What can we do, Callinda?" Janine lifted a glass and sat down near Michel. Her eyes kept shifting to Cendrine, upset for the girl, helpless. She gulped her drink and refilled her glass. Callie knew running the vineyard all these years had not prepared her mother-in-law for the events of the past week. She saw her glance at her husband; he was not handling it well either. Although they both knew in their hearts that Olivier was trustworthy, sometimes their heads disagreed. She knew the old people wondered where he could be. The vineyard could deal with the money loss. Although they were furious, they trusted their instincts and both agreed Olivier would not do this without a damned good reason.

As Callie drank her second glass, the bubbles tingled inside her mouth and lifted her spirits a notch. A wayward thought made the air quiver. "Cendrine… remember when I told you that Fernando said the man who followed him had red hair the color of carrots?"

Cendrine nodded as she pulled little François up on her lap. He laid his head on her shoulder and nuzzled into her neck. Rubbing his little butt with one hand, she lifted her flute in the other.

Callie's mind clicked as the idea hit her like a brick. "You told me that Olivier's cousin was ornery and you said the men dislike each other. Didn't you also tell me that your friend, Antoine, works at the same company where Conall works in Scotland?"

"*Oui*, yes. He left the Champagne area and moved to Scotland to learn whiskey making. He told me that Conall mentioned Olivier's name when he learned Antoine was French. Conall told him that his cousin married a French woman. That was all." Bernadette decided she wanted on *Maman's* lap too. Cendrine shook her head. "You two play a little longer there. We will eat soon." She pushed François gently off her lap, trying hard to remember anything else. "Why, Callie?"

"Does Antoine like Conall?" Callie knew she'd missed something and struggled to puzzle it out.

"Not really. When Antoine mentioned the new pink rosé, Conall told him his cousin's wife also made sparkling wine. Antoine had been stunned to discover his cousin was married to me! He told me that Conall made a snide comment at the time."

Everyone listened intently. Bernadette had moved over to her great grandfather and burrowed into his chair beside him. The old man's hand swept her hair from her face and his eyes turned warm.

Cendrine continued, "One day, when Antoine left the building later than usual, he overheard Conall talking to someone on the phone. He was yelling to someone about some bottles. When he saw Antoine in the hallway, he hung up and glared at him with a nasty look in his eyes."

Callie pursed her lips. "Well, now…since Conall is also Scottish, can we assume that he has red hair the color of carrots?"

Cendrine took a sharp intake of breath. "Yes, he certainly does. Conall? Of course. He was raised as the bastard grandson. He probably heard about the family legend. Could Antoine have heard him talking to someone about *that* wine?" She started shaking. "Could Conall really hurt Olivier? If he broke into our home, that means he could have Olivier somewhere right now and….." Her frightened face turned to her grandmother and she crumpled into her open arms.

Michel spoke from the corner of the room. "The police should be called immediately. Also, we must call Bruce. Now that we may have narrowed down the scoundrel who caused the terror in our family, we should get some answers." His determined face and strong voice surprised Janine, who had worried about her husband's health for awhile. She studied him astutely. The events of the past week had perked him up instead of weakening him.

Callie thought of Jules, wondering if maybe a quick call… No, she would call the police and Cendrine could call Bruce Baird. She would tell Jules and Andres everything in the morning when they had their rendezvous with a Spanish lady and her brandy. An image of Fernando and Francisco came to mind and she wondered if she should warn them about Conall. But they probably had no idea who he was. She decided scaring them any further was useless. However, remembering Francisco's agitation that day gave her second thoughts. What to do? Making the decision, Callie walked into the kitchen and dialed Jules' number. "It may be nothing, Jules, but…."

"I will call Fernando right now. *La vache*! (Holy cow) This gets more complicated by the minute. I will see you in the morning about nine. Andres will follow us in his truck. He has crates in the back and between the three of us we should be able to unload those magnificent bottles of brandy by noon. Does that work for you, Callie?"

"I'll be ready, Jules, but this revelation about Olivier's cousin scares us. Cendrine is going to call Olivier's great grandfather. Maybe we can learn Conall's whereabouts to relieve some of the tension around here. He sounds mentally-challenged and I certainly hope he's no longer hanging around here. But, he must know where Olivier is…" She broke off and stared at the shadows outside the windows. And then she jumped back. *Is the man watching us right now?*

"Callie. Stop. We will get the answers. Be sure to lock everything, house, car and your cottage door. Until we find the man, who knows what could happen. I am going to call the police right now. I know the man's name is Conall, but what is his last name? And do you know anything else about him that would help the police?"

She thought a moment. "Carson is his last name. He's about forty years old and he works at a whiskey company in Scotland. I think he attended the University of…Málaga…. That's what we're missing, Jules!"

"He has a Spanish connection? Isn't Francisco also about forty? Francisco has heard the legend about that old Spanish wine for years, I'm sure, because of Fernando's involvement with Picasso and Olivier's father. Callie, I will call him right now. See you in the morning."

Callie was quiet when she entered the living room again and all eyes turned her way. She wasn't sure how to begin but the logical pattern was falling into place. And everything clicked. "I just spoke with Jules. He is calling the police to tell them about Conall. He will also call the old Spaniard, Fernando. We think there might be a connection between his grandson and Conall. Same age. Same university. And the man was nervous when we saw him in Málaga."

Cendrine began to shake and her hands gripped her belly.

Callie and Janine both reached her at the same time and their eyes met. When Cendrine started moaning and pushing at her belly, everyone moved quickly.

"I will take her to hospital once we get her into the car. The children can remain here, *Maman*? Callie and Janine lifted her and she walked carefully out the door, as Michel held both children in his arms.

Within an hour, Cendrine was surrounded by a doctor and nurses, the baby's heart beat was on a monitor and Callie and Janine were pushed out of the room. Cendrine was frantic with worry for her baby and her eyes pleaded with the nurses when they poked her arm for an IV.

"We will keep you overnight. You need rest now and we will watch the baby. It is too early for your baby's birth."

Callie and Janine were frantic as they waited down the hallway and both jumped up as the doctor approached them some time later. "Please go home and come back in the morning." He was firm, but allowed them to peek into the room and toss a kiss to her Cendrine.

When they left the room, Cendrine squeezed her eyes shut as the many worries bombarded her and her belly tightened again. She watched the dripping fluid flow into her arm and prayed Lulu would survive.

***

Thunderstruck, Jules gripped his phone and plopped down on his bed while he listened to Fernando.

"My grandson was attacked last night, *señor*. He is in the hospital and my daughter has not left his side. Someone stabbed him and left him for dead. Luckily, it was near the *plaza mayor* and the *paseo* brought many people walking by Francisco's car soon afterward. He was in surgery several hours and we do not know if he will live..." Fernando's voice broke off.

Jules could hear the man blow his nose, knew he was crying. The man was hurting badly; and Jules wanted to reach out and embrace him. "Fernando, I am so sorry to hear this. I have a bad feeling this attack could be related to those old Spanish bottles."

"What? How could this be? Nobody knows about them. I wish I'd never heard of those bottles of *Sueño España*...ever!"

"I know, but Fernando…I am calling because we think we know the rogue who is behind everything. And I believe he could be the same man who attacked Francisco." Jules paced back and forth, agitated.

Fernando did not answer.

"Do you know if Francisco and Conall Carson went to university together in Málaga about twenty some years ago?"

"Yes, of course, he was the boy from Scotland. I never met him because I was still in France in those days. They were best friends and got into a little trouble together, drinking, girls, that kind of thing. You are saying this boy, his friend….attacked Francisco and maybe hurt Olivier too?" He was quiet a moment before adding, "*Madre de Dios*, he followed me to France when I met Olivier. I led him there. But Francisco…he is a good boy. He would not be involved in this danger. I know this, *señor*."

"Fernando, did Francisco know the story about the old bottles?"

The old man hesitated before answering. "Yes, he heard me talking about them. I tried to keep it secret, but it was difficult to be silent. If he is the same man who questioned me so many years ago…it was about the time the boys graduated from university…Francisco must have told Conall."

"Did you know that Conall Carson and Olivier Benoit were cousins?" Jules shook his head as the pieces fell together.

Fernando's surprise was evident in the quick intake of breath that raced across the phone. "No," he whispered.

"It is more complex than any of us realized. Jealousy, money, betrayal, cheating and now attempted murder. I am calling the police here in Pertuis now. What hospital is Francisco in, Fernando?"

"*Hospital Ciudad Jardin*. I go there now. I will call you if there is a change or…if….."

"Thank you, Fernando. Please tell Crescéncia how sorry I am."

Jules wondered what could have happened in the young Scotsman's life that could make him try to kill his friend or his cousin. Even though he and François had arguments, and some of them were big ones, neither would have hurt the other. Conall was definitely unstable and that made him even more dangerous.

Nineteen

That night, the police would not accept Jules' statement over the phone, so within minutes, he was standing inside their building. The officer behind the desk pointed him toward a cubicle. As he rang for someone to assist him, Jules bunched his hands into his jacket pockets to wait.

"Come this way, sir." The officer's starched blue uniform was unwrinkled, even though it was the end of the day. He walked briskly, aware of everything around him. He led Jules into a wide-open space in the middle of the floor that housed four desks that were separated by panels and shielded from the public view by fica trees planted in wooden containers.

Armed with all the information Callie shared with him, he met the officer head on. It was over an hour before he drove home again. His head was in such turmoil, he wondered how he'd gotten himself into such a situation. His life was typically slow and easy, just the way he liked it. Ever since the fiasco with François a few years ago, he promised himself a more relaxed life. He learned the hard way when you get in too deeply and let emotion rule your decisions, friendships could wither and die. His thoughts were filled with François and his betrayal. He shook his head, refusing to dig into the past. Of course, thinking of François also brought his beautiful widow to mind. He needed to be alone. Things were becoming suffocating and he needed to breathe. And that was damn hard to do around Callie.

He'd never met a woman who listened to what he had to say without wishing he'd hurry up so she could talk. She actually listened. She was sensitive, caring. Look what she'd done as soon as Cendrine called her. She'd flown across the ocean to be with her family to take their burden away and try to solve this hellish mystery. Two mysteries, actually and he was glad one was already solved. When they solved the second one, he would no longer have an excuse to see her every day. He slammed the door of his BMW and wondered if he would get any sleep that night at all.

***

Christianne's Boulangerie-Pâtisserie stood on a street corner in Venelles; its big front windows were filled with baskets of fresh bread, long, skinny, fat and round loaves. There were smaller baskets with bread sticks and two large trays filled with croissants. Olivier had watched Christianne stuff croissants with chocolate at dawn that morning and he laughed at the memory of her face watching his. She'd wiped her flour-covered fingers on her large white apron and tossed him a chocolate croissant that he caught in mid air. She'd laughed when he demolished the pastry in just a few bites.

He filled the display-window baskets as instructed. He doubted he'd known so much about bread before he'd lost his memory. The tray of cookies looked overfull, so he snagged one and popped it into his mouth on the way back to the kitchen. Olivier was earning his keep; having a big man in the bakery seemed to demand all sorts of little jobs.

"Please bring down that large box on the top shelf? We have a large order, much too large for the sacks." Bertrand pointed above his head and Olivier obliged by reaching up, lifting it with ease and plopping it on the sideboard. Bertrand smiled at him and tapped his back. "*Merci.* Our doctor friend will be here for lunch, 'Alexandre,' and I think your dreams make him hopeful. Maybe you will know who you are very soon….and where you belong." Olivier smiled and hoped he was right. He would miss the old man. He knew Bertrand and Christianne had grown to like him a lot and having his help in the bakery was an added plus, with their son gone.

The front bell jingled. Christianne was taking the morning, Bertrand would take the afternoon. They shared the time in front as well as the back. Both were bakers and their lives had been filled with the aroma of fresh baked bread for many years. Their son had not been interested in baking. He'd left the flour, sugar, chocolate and customers behind when he fled to the university. Bertrand told Olivier they didn't blame the boy; he'd hated his own father's trade. How could anyone be happy making shoes all day?

Doctor Colbert got to his feet and rubbed his chin. "Perhaps we are going too fast, 'Alexandre.' Sometimes memory takes time to return, other times a person or an instance triggers the memory gates. Don't worry about it now," he said as he finished his espresso and pushed away the fourth cookie Christianne gave to him with his lunch. "I know it's easy for me to say, but going slowly is better than rushing it."

Olivier nodded, disappointed. He had hoped for a magic potion. Time was moving forward and his gut told him something important was happening and he had no idea what it could be. He wished something would lubricate his frozen mind to unravel his memory.

Later, after dinner with the kitchen cleaned up, Olivier said good night and walked slowly up the stairs to the room he now called his own. He'd learned it had been their son's room. Olivier smiled when he remembered his first morning, seeing all the books. He'd been right. Their son, Claude, loved to read and after attending the University of Aix-en-Provence, he now had a thriving business creating *santons*.

Olivier's thoughts turned inward. What had he done to earn a living before his mind went blank? Did he live in Venelles? If so, wouldn't someone have recognized him by now? He shifted his shoulders and entered the bedroom. How could anyone find him when he hovered inside a bakery? The police didn't seem interested and he was still wary about leaving, worried he'd run into the man who brought this nightmare on. He pressed his fist into his thigh and sat on the bed a moment before grabbing the old robe and heading toward the shower.

He put his hands to his face and literally shook his head, trying to shake out memories. As the steam filled the bathroom, he closed his eyes, lifted his face to the water and stayed there until the tension left his body. When he switched off the spigot, another blurred memory returned as if through a fog, the children again. He was lying on a large bed in a big room. A boy and girl rushed into the room. He heard them laughing. Olivier's body became rigid. They'd called him Papa. He sat on the toilet seat and cried.

***

After Callie hung up her cell phone after talking with Olivier's GrandPapa, she sat down heavily. The world sat on her shoulders as she looked at Cendrine and whispered, "He is so angry, I fear for his health. He told me his friend said that Conall asked for a week's holiday and they had not heard from him. He should have returned to work on Friday. The day Olivier disappeared was the third day after Conall left Scotland."

Cendrine shook her head, anxious to leave the hospital. The doctor entered the room. When he placed his hand on her belly and listened to the baby's heartbeat with his stethoscope, he maneuvered his lips as if to speak. When Cendrine stared up at him, he smiled only a little. "Your baby sounds good but I worry about your blood pressure. It is too high for my liking. I want you to go home and sit, rest and be less active." He stared into her face. "I mean it. You do not want this child born for at least another four weeks or I can't promise a good prognosis. Do you understand?"

Cendrine nodded mutely.

He spoke with the nurse outside her door. Callie tried to eavesdrop but couldn't make out the words.

When the nurse came in a few minutes later, Callie held tightly to Cendrine's hand. When the nurse grinned at the women and tapped the IV bag, she knew her hospital stay was at an end. When the nurse removed the IV, she checked her watch and promised to bring a wheelchair to the bed, refusing to allow Cendrine to walk out of the hospital on her own. "We don't want you back here for another two months. You must rest and relax or it will be difficult for your baby..."

"*Oui.*"

As Cendrine pulled the car door closed, Callie revisited her conversation with the old Scotsman. "Evidently, Conall has been doing sloppy work and he's within an inch of losing his job. Olivier's GrandPapa told me if it is true that Conall is behind this, he will wash his hands of him. I told him everything we knew."

"With his Scottish brogue and the old slang he uses, it was difficult to get every word, wasn't it, Callie? It's always been that way." She smiled wanly. "Thank you for being here, Callie. I do not want to lose this baby."

The women stared at one another. "And where is that horrible man now?" Cendrine spoke the words that filled Callie's every waking moment.

***

The following morning, Callie dreaded the date on the calendar. Her mother had died one year ago today. She smiled into her pillow. Her mother always promised that every time Callie thought of her, she was just whispering hello. "Hello, Mom," she said to the empty room.

Padding over to the window with her hands wrapped around a steaming cup of coffee, she sat down to stare at her old gardens. Sipping the brew, she thought of her mother and wonderful memories cascaded through her mind. "You taught me love, compassion, a sense of humor and you refused to admit Santa wasn't real, the importance of equity for all, to value myself, a joy for life and perhaps the most priceless gift, a love of reading. I will always be grateful for the keys you gave me to explore the worlds that exist between the pages of books. Oh, and your ability to make a recipe twenty different times, twenty different ways. May you continue to dance, name inanimate objects, sing, grow plants from nothing and pick weeds out of other people's gardens because they don't belong there. You were one of the classiest women I've ever known." Callie whispered toward the winter flowers that blew in the breeze to dazzle her view. The day had to get better.

Determined that Cendrine would not gaze out a window to reminisce about a dead husband, she rushed to get dressed. They had a big day ahead of them. They would get the brandy bottles and store them in the cellar of the old mill house. It was the right temperature, there were shelves to lay them at an angle and nobody went down there. It was the perfect storage place, just as Alexandre's letter described.

Shimmying into her jeans before pulling on a bright, blue shirt, she dug her feet into her tennis shoes and grabbed a jacket. Jules was due any minute for coffee. Then, they could begin. Andres would follow her and Jules to Jouques after he picked up the vineyard mail. Although he hated leaving his vines, they couldn't load all the bottles without him. She secretly believed he needed to see them to believe the cache existed despite seeing the bottles on the table two days earlier. She chuckled.

Conall Carson watched the house from a discreet distance. Shivering, but stoic, he knew he'd made the right decision. He didn't give a damn where Olivier had run to since the man had lost his memory anyway. Francisco wouldn't bother him anymore. His great grandfather was unaware of his activities and Conall would soon be rich. A bellow of a laugh erupted from his gut, knowing the waiting would soon be over. Yes, following the others was better than chasing around town looking for a man with a blank mind. Olivier's gun was in the glove box of the Fiat and his knife was still in his pocket. He pushed away the unsettling thoughts of hurting Francisco as his conscience raised its ugly head.

It started to rain and the cold morning turned his mind gloomy. The house appeared quiet, but he knew someone knew something. Yes, he'd chosen right this time. He watched an old man climb into a truck and drive past him, a cigarette hanging from between his lips. The man had looked at Conall as he drove by, but Conall shrugged. It was the women he had to worry about, not some old man.

***

Andres slowed at the next corner. He'd seen that red Fiat twice in the past week and he was sure the man wasn't a local resident. He'd asked around and nobody knew who he was. Andres had the sinking feeling that he did though. He couldn't see red hair because the man had a wool beret pulled over his forehead, but he had a bad feeling. After picking up the mail for the vineyard, he had an errand to run and the timing would work out perfectly to follow Jules and Callie to Jouques. However, seeing the red car in his rearview mirror, he made some changes to their plan. He lifted his cell phone to his ear before leaving the postal parking lot.

***

Jules replaced his empty coffee cup and watched Callie drift away from the table to linger at the counter and embrace Cendrine. He smiled when he saw Callie lean around the baby bump that seemed bigger today than it had been just a few days earlier. The only experience he had with pregnant women had been his sister, Aurore, when she carried his sweet Veronique. He pondered the vision, remembering Aurore at this stage, the anger that filled her, the depression and the bitterness that never seemed to leave her even today. He was sorry for that. Veronique loved her mother but he didn't feel Aurore had given her daughter the mother-love he'd hoped for. He had the terrible thought that Aurore blamed Veronique because François chose Callie over her love and her daughter. What a stupid idea, he thought, but then he revisited it slowly in his mind. Could that be?

"Okay, big boss. I'm ready," Callie waved a hand in front of his face to get his attention. Her bright, blue shirt was opened at the neck and a heart-shaped locket dangled just below the first button. She cinched the belt to her jacket and peered into his face.

He looked up, eye level with her breasts and took a deep breath. He threw his head back and laughed. "Big boss? Ha! Just because I wanted to be in charge of this investigation doesn't mean I'm really the boss and you know it." He snorted at the look on her face and reached for her hand.

She went willingly. The touch of his warm fingers around hers energized him with a wild and willing warmth, he felt steam.

Cendrine watched the warm camaraderie and stared as they clasped hands all the way to the front door. Smiling, she smoothed a hand across her belly absently, happy to be back home again. She watched the BMW leave the house, without noticing the red car that sped after them. She put in another video for the children and started making crepes for their breakfast.

***

Jules did not share the early-morning phone call from Andres with Callie, but his eyes darted to the rear-view mirror several times. When he caught sight of the small red Fiat, his shoulders tightened. As the road ahead shimmered in the distance, he told Callie about his phone conversation with Fernando the night before. He'd called the hospital early that morning but the nurse would not tell him anything. He'd called Fernando's home but there was no answer.

Callie was shocked. "This man is a monster, Jules. Attacking his old friend is more than I can understand. Even when Livvy and I had a run-in last year while fighting a creepy doctor in Portland and an alcoholic senator in Washington, D.C., I never felt this threatened. This man is fighting against his own family. Francisco *must* live through this. I wonder if he knows it was Conall? Wait a minute. If Conall was in Málaga, he couldn't be in France. And he's obviously AWOL from his job in Scotland." She thrust her hands tightly between her knees as the road took them closer to Jouques.

Jules glanced over at her, confused. "AWOL?"

"Yes, that means absent without leave. It's an old military term that Americans use to describe people not being where they should be."

"Ah," he answered as his eyes tracked the little car behind them. He wondered where Andres was by now. Their plan had to work and the timing had to be absolutely perfect. The wine bottles would be the catalyst and the lure they needed to trap the fellow. Jules wished he was twenty years younger, more fit, and reminded himself to start running daily.

Callie glanced into the back where Jules had laid down the seats and stuffed the wine crates neatly, side by side. She knew Andres had the remaining crates in the truck. While she idly wondered if he was behind or ahead of them, they passed the antique road sign announcing Jouques. Her stomach got queasy. "I'm not sure why I'm so nervous. We didn't see much traffic around the castle Saturday and that's usually when tourists are around. You brought your trusty little lock picks again, right?"

Jules chuckled, nodded his head at her, and looked in the mirror once again. The red car was two cars behind them. There was no doubt he was following them to their bottle rendezvous. How the hell did the man think he could fit all those bottles into that small Fiat? He snorted. Jules trusted Andres to do his part and soon they'd have the bastard. If luck was on their side, they'd have Olivier soon also. And then Callie could go back to America. Acid backed up in his stomach and he gritted his teeth.

When his cell phone rang, he fumbled in his pocket and flipped it on. "Claude?"

"Jules, bad news. I fell over my son's bicycle this morning and broke my leg. I'm in the hospital." His manager's gruff voice was full of apology. "You know what that means for tomorrow, right?"

Jules groaned. "Yes, Claude. I am sorry about your leg though. I get to sign your cast, right?" He heard his manager's slight laughter and knew he was embarrassed to put Jules into this predicament. "Well, be nice to the nurses, Claude. Tomorrow at nine, you say?" When he heard the muffled agreement, he agreed to drive to Venelles to gift the laptops to the teenagers.

Callie looked at him. He circled the ornamental fountain where water bubbled, turned off the main road and then maneuvered the BMW up the winding cobblestone streets toward the castle. "So, you are not off the hook after all? It's a wonderful gift you are offering those students, Jules. You must be very proud to be able to donate so many laptops to those kids."

"You better stop patting me on the back or I'll have to take you with me to fight off those teenage imps." He laughed before turning toward the broken stone wall and the courtyard area.

"Of course, I'll go with you, Jules. A break from the frantic activities of the past week will be good for us...between worrying about Olivier, and then Cendrine's scare over the baby and these bottles." She took a deep breath. "I've never been to Venelles even though it's so close to the old mill house and I look forward to seeing the excitement on the children's faces."

Jules pulled behind the broken stone wall and set the brake. "Callie. I don't want to frighten you, but I want you to get out of the car and run across the courtyard fast. Run up the steps to our little hidey hole and watch out for Andres. Please don't ask questions because I don't have time to explain. Move now!"

Stunned, Callie jerked the door open. She rushed across the cobblestones and swung around the corner without being told twice. Jules' face told her he wasn't kidding. She skidded toward the old stone steps, taking them two at a time until she reached the upper level. After running into the shadows by the small door that housed the brandy, she held her hand up to shade her eyes. Looking downward, she held a hand to her chest to catch her breath. She could see Andres' truck across the courtyard, but he wasn't inside. She shook her head trying to clear her head.

Within a few moments, a small red Fiat pulled in behind the BMW and she groaned. Another tourist, she thought. That would throw their plans awry. She shrugged and pulled back toward the turn in the wall. That's when she heard the shouting. Craning her neck as far as she could, she watched in horror as a bearded, ginger-haired man got out of the car holding a black gun in his fist. She heard whimpering nearby, stunned to realize it was her own.

"Thanks for leading me to those wine bottles. Now, take me to them right now." When Conall saw the man nonchalantly braced against the dark car, he yelled, "Do you understand what I'm saying?!"

Jules leaned against his BMW clipping his nails. He raised his head to look at Conall. The man's veins bulged in his neck and his eyebrows rose beneath his thick hair. Blue eyes blazed as he swung the gun erratically in Jules' direction.

Callie watched in fascination as Conall brandished the gun and shook it in the air. Partial words floated upward and she simmered. *He must have known Conall was following us from Pertuis and he didn't warn me.* With her body shaking, she stuffed her hands into her pants pocket to still them and felt a kind of terror. It was like a sickly sweet insanity, lapping at the edges of her mind.

Jules slouched against his car, watching Conall getting angrier. The man's gun was twitching back and forth between Jules and where she hid above the stairway. Conall couldn't have seen her. Her fingers gripped the stone wall as Jules stood eerily composed, ignoring the man and his gun.

Callie seethed. What was he doing? Had the man lost his mind? He was acting like he didn't have a care in the entire world, like he didn't give a toot about a gun being waved in his face. A tingle of fear raced along her spine, heavily spiced with confusion, wondering what she could do. Callie danced from one foot to the other, trying to think of options. Movement from below caught her eye to instantly jerk her focus away from Conall.

She saw Andres creeping along the tumbling, shallow stone wall near his truck. Stealthily, he made his way toward the Fiat and now crouched, hidden from view. The next moment, the air was filled with crackling noises and bright lights as fireworks flipped in Conall's direction.

When Conall's head swung around at the clamorous noise, his gun went off and Jules lunged toward him. Callie slammed a hand to her breast. Willing her heartbeat to slow down, she watched the panorama below her. Wishing she could help, but knowing she could not, made her stumble, mind and body.

Andres ran toward the men, a baseball bat held high above his head. When he came closer, she saw him hesitate; probably afraid he would hit the wrong man or the gun might fire again in the melee. Andres watched Jules wrestle Conall for control of the gun. Callie stood above with a fist to her mouth, sure a bullet would find its mark.

"Let it go, you bastard," Jules yelled. His knuckles turned white as he tried to pull the gun from Conall's hand. You're finished hurting people and now you're done." Jules bent his knees to get a tighter stance and gripped the man's wrists but the man was strong and held his own.

"No, you are not going to steal those wine bottles. I've hunted for them too long. I know they are here somewhere…" Conall twisted his face into a snarl and a growling sound came in spurts as he struggled. Kicking his thick leg outward, he rammed his heel into Jules' instep, knocking him backward against the BMW. When he aimed the gun toward Jules, he was too slow.

With his hands still fisted around the gun, Jules head butted the man and heard a loud crunching sound. Conall's scream rent the air. Before he could catch his breath, Andres brought the bat down on Conall's knee, who squealed as he turned toward the new adversary. He was stunned to recognize the old man from the truck that he'd ignored earlier that morning.

"Dammit. I want those bottles!" Thick veins bulged in his neck, his face flushed a deep red and his hair flopped over his snapping eyes. When he hissed angrily, spittle spewed into the air.

Jules laughed in his face. "What bottles?" He asked very quietly.

When Andres swung the bat again, Conall went down. The old man was breathing hard, shocked at the depth of his anger.

"What took you so long, Andres? *Mon Dieu*, I thought my heart was going to hammer out of my chest counting the seconds away. Jules reached down for Conall's gun still clutched loosely in the man's hand. When he glanced upward again, he saw the look on Andres face and they both started laughing. They laughed until tears ran down their face.

They didn't see Callie race down the steps toward them. "You've killed him? Now, how in the hell are we ever going to find Olivier?" Callie screamed and slapped Jules across his face. Hard.

Andres shut up and watched the stunned look on Jules' face.

"You two scared the crap out of me, fighting with a man slugging a gun in your direction while one clipped his fingernails and the other played with firecrackers and a baseball bat?" Her face was pale and then she started shaking again. "Well, hell, you were...." She blew air out between her trembling lips. "..... both fabulous, but...."

The men started laughing again. Jules rubbed his jaw and then turned to tie up Conall. When he hauled him toward the truck and lodged him against the stone wall, he said, "He's not dead, Callie. If Andres and I wanted him dead, the bat would have hit him over the head. A knee replacement surgery maybe and probably a concussion, but he's alive."

Once he was trussed up, Jules gave Andres a look and the old man nodded. Timing was still a loaded question as the men hurried toward their vehicles. They didn't have time to explain anything further to Callie.

"Okay, now for the brandy." They grabbed the boxes and made several trips up the steps. When all the crates stood alongside the chateau's stone wall, Jules picked the lock and the old door creaked open.

Callie read somewhere that the past whispers to those who listen and she wondered how many feet had passed through the small door etched into the wall of the castle. The words made sense in that moment as she waited with Andres before walking into the dark room.

Jules ran his hand over the smooth stone, searching for the light switch he knew was there. Inch by inch, his fingers crept along the dirty surface until the dim light popped on in the center of the small room The area had a slightly damp and very mysterious atmosphere, probably holding any number of critters on the floor and all around them. Pale, eerie shapes on the shelves beckoned from the dark shadows. If there were rats, mice or other critters, nothing stirred while they stood in the doorway, no sounds apart from their footsteps echoed on the flagstone floor. They stood silently in the doorway, trying to accustom their eyes to the dark. Edging along the shelves, Jules invited Andres behind him with a motion of his fingers. He and Callie watched the old vintner stare at the bottles.

Callie pulled the crates into the dimly-lit room and the men began filling them, twelve in each box. She was holding her breath as Jules lugged the first crate into the archway, checking to make sure nobody was going to surprise them before reentering the room. The second, third, fourth and fifth crates were filled before Andres started muttering to himself. Jules raised his eyebrows and Callie held her breath. She was still frightened and she wanted to get back on the road. Fast.

"Okay, this is the fifth crate, fifty seven bottles. The letter described sixty, they drank one and we have two in Pertuis. Callie, please keep watch from up here and let us know if any cars come winding up that cobblestone street. Can you whistle?"

She rolled her eyes. "No, never could."

"Well, just give a yell then." Each man reached for a crate and balanced them carefully down the steep stone steps. "Watch out, Andres, Callie tripped at the bottom. I think a stone is uneven just there…"

Within fifteen minutes, the bottles were stored in the front of the truck. They were ready to roll. The old door was locked again and birdsong surrounded them as they emerged, blinking, into the bright sunlight. Not quite believing their good fortune, they didn't want to push it. When they came around the stone wall, everyone was glad Conall was still unconscious.

Andres nodded significantly to Jules and reversed the truck, inched out from the hiding place and drove slowly back the way he came. When he reached the bottom of the incline, he saw the police car angling its way toward him with sirens screaming. He started whistling.

"What do we do now? Conall is still out like a stone." Callie worried a chipped nail and stretched her fingers as she waited for Jules to answer. When he looked up and grinned at her like a mischievous child, she was confused, wondering what he was up to now.

"We untie him and very quickly." He heaved and pulled the man out from behind the wall.

"What? We untie him?" She ran her befuddled hands through her hair. Watching Jules loosen the rags Andres had tied around Conall's wrists, she stared at him totally perplexed.

Her eyes rounded in surprise at the sounds of a siren just before the oncoming car clattered up the stone roadway toward them. Police. She glanced back at Jules and blew out air. Her hands twitched nervously at her jacket when the police car pulled across the courtyard, parked, and both doors popped open.

When the blue and whites arrived, their lights blazing, their doors flew open. "Thank you for coming so quickly officers. This man attacked my fiancé while we were exploring the old castle here," he said as he pointed toward the stone steps and the courtyard winding toward the huge stone tower. "I was able to stop him but it was scary for us because he had a gun." Jules lifted it from the top of Conall's car and handed it to the closest policeman. "He fired it once before we disabled him."

His partner was crouched down beside Conall, feeling for a pulse in his neck. "Have you ever seen this man before, *monsieur*?" Jules and Callie both nodded their heads, no. "Well, we must make a report and we will take this rogue to the station and lock him up. Please follow us."

"How long will you keep him, officer? We do not want him coming around Pertuis in case he knows we live there. Someone broke into her house. Maybe it was this man? He will wake up very angry because my fiancé had to hit him with my baseball bat." Jules handed the bat to Callie and she automatically took it from him, assuring her fingerprints littered the handle.

The officers looked at Callie with new respect before lifting Conall into the back of the police car. After they taped a notice on the Fiat's windshield, they motioned for them to follow. Jules and Callie got into the BMW and he put the car in gear.

"And, Mr. Armand, when were you going to tell me that Conall was following us and that you'd managed to get the police here to clean up the mess?" She asked sweetly, trying to compose herself.

Jules licked his lips. "I can't think of a good lie, Callie. I never intended to tell you because you had enough on your shoulders." He shrugged as he took the next bend. The graceful tree at the corner bent toward them as he followed the police car's brake lights.

She rubbed her hands over her face and exhaled dramatically in capitulation. She knew he was right but wouldn't give him the satisfaction of telling him so. It was one of those days that you only dreamed about; and hoped it never happened. Her thoughts were on the police car and the man who had a lot to answer for, especially about Olivier. She looked at Jules and watched his fingers grip the small steering wheel as the car rolled to a stop in front of the police station.

She marveled at his composure earlier when he calmly waited for Conall to attack brandishing that gun and again when she slapped his face. She allowed herself a small smile. "Okay, Jules. You win. You were right. I would have been too afraid to leave you alone with him, but if I'd known Andres was your backup…well, hell. I'm impulsive sometimes, but I can fight. Use me next time."

He laughed at her. "Use you? What, for backup? Or did you have something else in mind?" He watched her stare back at him. Her brown eyes had a doe-in-the-headlights-kind-of look.

"Callie, despite the heroic efforts of Andres and his baseball bat, knowing you were above gave me the strength to fight back and win." He touched her cheek, wiped the look off her face. "Don't worry. We'll find Olivier. If I can lighten the mood with a little humor, why not?"

Scattered emotions burned her face. She mumbled something he couldn't hear and he chuckled. The sun emerged from behind the clouds again like a huge gift, its burst of warmth like a kiss; she raised her head to feel it caress her face as the policemen dragged Conall from the car. She was pleased to see he shuffled along with them, not dead after all. Now if he will only tell them what they needed to know. He needed medical attention, so it wouldn't be easy to question him. They gave their witness statements, assuring the police that Callie had been the intended victim. Their impatience was palpable when they learned they couldn't talk with Conall until the next day, although they were unsure why they were surprised.

A calmer atmosphere prevailed on their way back to Pertuis, but Callie's hand still hovered over her racing heart. She saw Jules' eyes dart toward her from time to time, dark and intense, but he didn't speak again. By the time Jules pulled into the circular drive in front of the mill house, Andres had already unloaded the bottles from his truck. Both men carried the cases into the cellar where they'd already prepared shelves for their storage. Cendrine kept the children out of the way.

A while later, when Jules and Andres rehashed their exploits with Conall, Cendrine's head whipped around toward Callie. She couldn't imagine the fright going through her aunt's head as she watched the men entangled below her. They sat around the table discussing what ifs for a long time.

Cendrine said, "I'll call Olivier's great grandfather. Now that the police have Conall, we'll finally find Olivier…"

Jules smiled tiredly. His hands throbbed. He twisted and stretched his neck to loosen the bruised muscles. His instep was swollen and he limped slightly. He let out a loud sigh. "I asked the officer to let me know when we can see him. The police know how important it is to us. He thinks we want to question him about burglarizing the house and following Callie."

"Yes, Cendrine, we told the police the story." Callie finished.

"All of it?" Her belly skimmed the dining table and they all worried at the look on her face. "I'm fine. I'm resting. The children are running their little legs off for me since I'm being lazy, like the doctor ordered."

"Glad to hear that, Cendrine. Well, we didn't tell the police the entire story. We told them that Conall may have followed Callie and he may have broken into your house. We also told them there is a possibility he attacked Francisco in Málaga and may have hurt Olivier. They know he's been missing for two weeks. But, your father battered Conall's knee and his shoulder. I think I may have given him a concussion. I imagine the man is in a lot of pain about now."

"Good!" Callie and Cendrine both said vehemently.

Twenty

Conall watched the nurse place an IV in his arm, who assumed the narcotic would slide him into sleep. Despite the excruciating pain in his shoulder and knee, he welcomed the drugs and wished he could sleep and forget everything. He lifted a hand to his head.

When he groaned, she glanced up, "I hope that didn't hurt too much," she said and patted his arm. "The officer said you might be dangerous, but with that damaged knee, I knew you weren't going anywhere. The surgery room is being prepared now." When she left the room, she nodded to the officer sitting in the chair beside the door.

Conall watched her go. The drugs flowing through his IV made him sleepy, but he fought it. He knew he had to get out of the hospital because going to prison wasn't an option. His great grandfather would be furious if he heard about his lack of common sense. But the man was in Scotland, after all. Now, he agreed with Francisco: He wished he'd never heard about the stupid wine. He wished he didn't need money to prove his success to an old Scotsman who didn't seem to care anyway. His eyes drooped and he slept against his will, thinking of an old man with red hair and blue eyes.

Promptly at eight the following morning, Callie fluffed her hair, smoothed her pantyhose and slipped into low pumps. After all, it wasn't every day a classroom of teenagers received free laptop computers. She walked over to check on Cendrine while she waited for her ride.

"*Bonjour*, Cendrine."

Her niece stretched a cheek upward to receive Callie's kiss.

"Glad to see you are relaxing this morning."

"*Oui*. I don't want my auntie to take me back to hospital."

Callie grinned. Anxious to see the BMW drive up to the door, she walked nearer the window. Seeing Jules' pride in his computer business told her he respected education and also, young people. He was more than just a friend to François. He was now her friend too and she liked the thought.

Cendrine saw the smile on Callie's face. "I think you are thinking of Jules again." She tapped her pregnant belly and pulled down a long curl of hair when Callie didn't answer. When the BMW pulled up in the yard, Callie's grin widened. The children ran to the door to welcome Jules inside and he laughed as they wrapped their arms around his legs. They missed their father and confusion met them each morning when he was not yet at home. Though very young, they were sure this man and their auntie Callie would find him. Their mother said so and they believed.

Callie's eyes lifted to his and they smiled at one another. He bowed and swung his arm outside. "Your carriage awaits, madam."

The children giggled as they ran to their mother. "*Comme Cendrillon, tante.*" Like Cinderella, auntie.

Everyone laughed.

Callie hugged the children and glanced toward Cendrine. "Maybe we will know something today, *ma chérie*. Conall should give us answers. Keep the hope-light burning?"

Cendrine's chest burned, thinking about Conall and his answers that would surely lead them to her husband. As she watched Jules drive away with Callie, she dropped the curtain back in place and whispered, "Yes, maybe, Jules is the one. I can only hope."

Jules' fingers tightened around his steering wheel, wondering what his life would have been like with little children running around his legs, hugging and laughing and being children. He thought he would have liked it very much. Watching Callie's face, his next thought was how amazing it would have been if he'd had a woman like Callie to be their mother.

Wondering at the contemplation in Jules' features and the stillness in the car, she ventured a few questions. "Tell me about the school and how it happened for you to donate forty computers, Jules. I don't believe it was just for a tax expense. In the past few days, I have learned that you are more than you appear. How do you spend your time when you are not chasing around the country looking for a missing stranger with a woman you hardly know? Why, Jules?" The air became thick in the car. Her hands twisted the handle on her purse. His answers seemed important as she waited.

Jules glanced toward her and turned the corner, narrowly missing another car. Its loud horn made them laugh and lightened the mood. Pertuis was growing and the road to Venelles, though only twenty minutes away, was more difficult to traverse as more people moved to the Provence area. The buildings blurred when he shifted into higher gear and sped ahead. Trees that would soon be bursting with buds stood dormant along the way. Winter wasn't bleak, but Provence was waiting for the beauty spring promised just around the corner.

"Actually Callie, when I began my computer business, I had no idea I would be as successful as I am." He paused cautiously before continuing, "I had two financial backers and in exchange I gave each of them stock in my new company, hoping one day their money would expand...multiply and make everyone happy. I worked hard, sometimes fifteen or more hours in a day and never relaxed on the weekends. Times were hard and the principal of this school is one of my dearest friends. She had faith in my dream and faith in me. As I found more clients to believe in my idea, she told others about my wish to educate through the internet. She was my English teacher when I grew up, originally from the UK, and has taught in France for thirty five years. Now, as principal, she contacted me about her dream. I trusted it and I have made it my own. Children will have a chance to learn via the internet regardless of their financial ability and family lives."

"And you offered to help her with her dream because she believed in yours?" Callie's chest expanded as she gazed at the man beside her. How could it be? It seemed she had known him her entire life. She'd really only known him two weeks despite meeting him years earlier. With Nate, it took her months to agree to date him and longer to open her heart again. But, not like this. Nate was sweet, kind. But was it enough? Jules was more. Much more. She was dismayed to admit where her mind was going.

Jules honked his horn and passed the Volkswagen in front of him on the narrow road as it pointed into Venelles before he continued, "When Ailsa asked me to donate a few laptops, I was happy to find a way to thank her after all these many years. I wanted Claude to accept the accolades from the class because I was embarrassed by the attention, but I can no longer get away from it. You will stand beside me, *oui?*"

Callie reached over and squeezed his upper arm. "*Oui*, I will clap as loudly as everyone else. You amaze me, *mon ami*." She wondered if he also had secrets that could wound like François did. She pulled her mind back and sighed deeply as she stared at the old buildings. She enjoyed the cobblestones and trees with long fingers of leaves that drifted toward them. She saw shop owners sweep their front entrances, lift window coverings and prepare for the new day.

"We are very early, Callie. Shall we stop for a *café au lait* and a bakery before we arrive?" He slowed down when he saw a sign and pulled into the alley by the front door. "This looks inviting, *oui?*"

Callie nodded toward *Christianne's Pain* and grinned. "I never turn down croissants, especially if there's chocolate inside." She started to get out and Jules pressed his long fingers to her arm.

"I will grab us some wonderful *pâtisserie* (pastries) and we can eat them at the café there," he pointed.

The bell above the door announced his arrival, and an affable woman with considerable girth appeared behind the counter to take his order. The bakery smelled like heaven and he marveled at so many baskets of various breads. He turned to see a man with a ready smile welcome him. Jules bent his head a moment to stare at the man before the bakery's aromas pointed him toward chocolate-filled croissants. Mesmerized by the numerous choices and seduced by the smells, he surveyed the display case. His eyes wavered with indecision until the man he'd first thought he recognized offered his assistance.

Callie glanced in the front glass window and spied a tray filled with delicate, swan-shaped pastries. She knew the children would love them; they were the most charming little people she'd been around in so long, she heaved a sigh of contentment. She loved them dearly.

Jules held the small sack and guided her to a table in the café across the street. She bit into her chocolate croissant with relish. "Mmmmmmmm. Jules, you make a woman happy enough to kiss."

He laughed, put his own croissant down and leaned toward her.

She was nonplussed only a moment, before she planted her chocolate-covered lips to his cheek. "Thank you, Jules. Perfect." When she pulled away, his face remained close and she didn't move away.

"I could get used to this, Callie. I cannot get enough of you. Forgive me. I know you have Nate at home, but you charm me beyond reason. And then he kissed her lips and let his tongue gently remove the chocolate left behind.

Callie didn't move. "Jules. Something is happening and I fear I may not be able to stop it. I am confused by my feelings, yet unashamed that I want more." She kissed him gently on the lips and tasted her own chocolate. When she lifted her face, he smiled gently and touched her lips with his fingers. With his hand on the back of her head and his face inches away, life slowed and her temperature soared.

"You, *ma chérie*, take my breath away. We must talk about....."

His cell phone rang and he hesitated to answer it, but she pointed to his pocket. He lifted it slowly to his ear, never taking his eyes from her face.

"*Hola*, Jules?"

"Fernando! How is Francisco?" His voice cracked and he feared the worst. With everything that had happened, he hadn't had a moment to call Málaga since the events of the previous day. Berating himself, he was happy to hear the old man's news.

"Francisco will live, *amigo*. The doctors tell me and Crescéncia that the knife missed vital organs. I call to tell you this, but also to say he told me and the police that Conall Carson attacked him. He saw the man's face reflected in his car window that night. He is in shock. It was about the wine bottles. Francisco threatened to call his great grandfather in Scotland if he did not stop following me. Francisco says he should have known Conall would not go away easily." Fernando's voice was jubilant.

"Well, Fernando, more good news. Conall attacked me yesterday in Jouques. No, he did not hurt us, but we hurt him. He is in the hospital with some damaged body parts, but will soon be jailed in Jouques. If the Málaga police call the Jouques police, they can add attempted murder to his crimes."

Fernando's response was loud, "*Madre de Dios, gracias*, Jules. I will call the police now. I am very happy to have this terrible time over for all of us. Did he tell you where Olivier is?" The old man was obviously unnerved by the situation but hadn't forgotten his old friend's son in the crux of it all.

Jules held the phone close to Callie's ear to hear their conversation. At the mention of Olivier's name, her lip trembled a little, wishing she could answer his question with something positive.

"No, Fernando. We hope to question Conall later today. He was injured when he attacked us and the police took him to the hospital. They promised to call us when he is behind bars again so we can question him later today." Jules touched Callie's hand, caressing her little finger ever so slightly as he spoke.

Callie turned toward him and lifted her *café au lait* to her lips, wondering for the hundredth time how this could be happening. She'd promised Nate she'd Skype him that evening. She shook her head and closed her eyes, dreading the conversation. On the phone was one thing but seeing another's face and trying to hide emotions on Skype was impossible.

Jules hung up the phone, glanced at his watch and nodded toward the car. Within minutes, they were walking into the *École Langue*, (language school) where Madame Ailsa Murphy waited.

Jules followed Callie down the school hallway. He watched her dark hair bounce from side to side as she walked. Her smell filled the hall like the lavender blooms that used to fill his mother's garden.

The minute Jules and Callie turned the corner, they were bombarded with a group of teenagers holding signs painted with *MERCI BEAUCOUP*. Thank you, thank you, thank you was everywhere. And then Jules was being hugged by an older woman with silver hair and a smile as big as the moon.

"Jules, we are ready for the celebration. Come with me." The woman pulled him down the hallway after linking arms. Callie laughed because he looked like a small boy being taken to the principal's office. He gave her a look when she laughed and he motioned her to follow.

The laptop boxes were stacked near the podium and there were four chairs beside them. When Ailsa Murphy motioned for him to sit in one of them, he pulled Callie along with him. "Ailsa, this is my good friend, Callie Beauvais."

Ailsa looked at Callie trying to place the name. "Are you any relation to Beauvais Cellars?" She tilted her head, trying to recognize the woman who was obviously very important to Jules.

Callie nodded. "Yes, François Beauvais was my husband before he died a few years ago. His parents own the vineyard." Her voice was soft, vibrant.

The woman took her hand and held it in both of hers. "I was very sorry to learn of François' death. He and Jules were in my classroom and sometimes very naughty…but they were also my favorites." She smiled and glanced up at Jules. The woman turned toward the large group of fifteen year olds as they marched in and took their seats. She beamed at Jules before reaching for the microphone.

***

Afterward, they walked lazily back to his car. He reached for her hand as they crossed the street and she didn't let go. There was a warm tingling in Jules' fingers as he walked beside Callie. He was sure he'd been transported somehow, into a new place. The past couple of weeks seemed to have awakened something deep inside him; a new chapter opened up and it amazed him how her steps were synchronized already with his.

Jules could still hear the laughter, excitement and handclapping in his ears as they pulled away from the curb. He loved seeing their insatiable interest in his instructions when he explained some issues on the laptops. His business was doing well, regardless of the nasty chaos that reigned just before François died. He shook his head, trying to keep that awful time from invading his memory. Instead, he reached for Callie's hand clasped in her lap. "Well, now you know more of what I do. Creating the computers was exciting for me, but sharing them and seeing the interest in others who want to use them, makes my heart speed up."

Callie squeezed his fingers in response. As they drove down the street toward Pertuis, she turned toward him. "Jules, would you mind terribly if we go back to that little bakery? I saw some pastries shaped like swans I'm sure the children would love to eat... and so would I."

"Absolutely." He turned the car around momentarily and sped back the way they'd come. People were looking into the bakery's enticing windows filled with pastries waiting to be packed up and carried home. Jules turned toward her. Gently, he took her shoulders and raised her chin with his hand to look at her. "Hurry…"

She laughed. "I'll run in and be back in a heartbeat," she said, leaping from the car and entering the bakery at a near run.

***

The tantalizing aroma that filled the air and tingled her senses made Callie's mouth water. There was only one customer ahead of her; an octogenarian gripped his long loaf of bread between both hands and pointed to croissants. As Callie gazed at the pastries, she watched a man replace some loaves in the front window and return to the glassed-in counter. She stared unbelievingly.

"Here, 'Alexandre.' Would you please wrap these croissants for *monsieur* LeBlanc?" The big woman smiled and he lifted the croissants to wrap them in thin paper for the old gentleman.

Callie walked slowly toward the glass case as if she was in a trance. She demanded, "Alexandre is your name?"

The red haired man looked up quickly. His hands slowed and the paper stilled. "I am called Alexandre….but….." He froze as she stared at him as if she'd seen a ghost.

Her eyes snapped fire. Both hands were splayed across her cheeks, her eyes opened wide. "But, how can that be? You look exactly like our Olivier!" She stepped back a few steps, speechless. Her heart thumped and she placed her hand over her chest to quiet it down. Her eyes never left his face. The walls seemed to crush in on her and she needed a chair. Turning to glance through the windows, she saw Jules sitting patiently in the car. The world was right-side-up out there, but in here? She wasn't so sure.

The customer left the shop with a hastily-wrapped package of croissants and his bread and the older woman moved from the register. She stood beside the younger man with a look of confusion plastered on her face. They both stared at Callie.

"Bertrand," the woman called urgently. An older man joined them and he placed a protective hand over Olivier's arm, where he felt the muscles tighten.

Olivier watched the emotions scamper across the woman's face while he held onto the counter, a stranglehold on his brain. And then everything started moving like the colored squares on a Rubik's cube. His blue eyes filled with tears. Ripping his apron strings loose, he took hesitant steps toward Callie from behind the counter.

Christianne and Bertrand saw in his eyes the wealth of remembering. They looked at one another, each admitting with their eyes they'd hoped to keep him longer. They had grown so used to his smile, his help and his honesty. It was like having a son around again.

Olivier's mind came out from the fog as he stared at the woman with dark hair, the odd silvery bangs and large brown eyes. Vivid splashes of remembrance returned of a time before his life had become unglued. The memories bowled him over; he gripped the glass case so hard that his knuckles turned white.

"Callie.....Oh, *mon Dieu*. At last, I remember...." His hands whipped through his hair and he came around the glass case to grab her with both arms to swing her off her feet. "Callie....Callie....Callie." He laughed and danced around the room and then pulled Callie toward the back of the bakery. Christianne and Bertrand followed close behind. Olivier sat her in a chair and pulled another over, their knees almost touching.

Callie's chest hurt, not quite believing she'd found Olivier. Walking into a bakery to find this man who had eluded them for so many days... Her eyes brimmed over. She stared at the man as his ginger-colored hair fell across his brow and his clear eyes bored into hers.

"I am Olivier." He looked up at his two saviors and said, "My father's name was Alexandre. You named me after my own father! It was magical." He reached for both of Callie's hands. "We have a lot to tell you, Callie. But, how did you find me?"

"And I have a lot to tell you, Olivier. Jules is waiting. We must call him." She stared at the two people above her and saw the love on their faces for Olivier. She heaved a sigh, thankful she'd been right to trust her instincts.

In the meantime, Jules had been tapping his fingers on the steering wheel until they were nearly numb. He stared into the glass window but it was too dark to see inside. After he saw the old man leave, he shrugged but was too curious to sit still. Within moments, the doorbell jingled and he was inside. But there was nobody to greet him. Uneasy, fear slid into his head. Then, an older man came from the back area and asked if he could help him?

"Yes, you can! My lady friend walked in ten minutes ago and now she is not here. She did not come out the front door. Where is she?" He demanded, close to panic.

The man grinned and motioned for Jules to come around the glass counter and enter the back room where Jules saw touches of flour spilled on the work floor.

Jules stalled. Of course it could be a trick but why all the subterfuge in a little bakery? He followed the man cautiously through the door and stopped in his tracks at the sight of Callie with a red-headed man's arms wrapped around her. They were both crying. What the hell?

Twenty One

Olivier's breath was so short, he was sure he was going to faint as Jules drove them to his own front door. He stared in disbelief, stunned that he was alive and so was his family. Callie turned around and nodded her head urgently toward the front door with an excited grin on her face.

He didn't waste another minute. He rushed out and ran up the flagstone steps as the front door was thrown open. They stared at each other. Cendrine's mouth shaped an O and then she was in his arms. Olivier promised to never let her go. When the children flew around the corner to hug his legs, he leaned down to encase both of them in his arms. Everyone was crying. He was sure his heart would explode.

Jules and Callie watched the reunion with hearts so full, they were unsure whether to let them be alone or stand aside. When Callie grabbed his arm and led him around to the side of the big house, she pulled him into her cottage and closed the door. And then she burst into tears.

It took two seconds for Jules to wrap his arms around her, pull her close and marvel at the feel of her in his arms. Callie wrapped her arms around his waist and cried herself out.

When she stepped back, she wiped her face and then laughed as she headed toward the small kitchen. She pulled out the coffeemaker, but then put it back again. "Oh hell, it's almost noon, this deserves a flute of sparkling rosé... or would you rather have Cabernet?" She pulled glasses down from the cupboard. Jules did not answer. Twisting around, she saw him walk slowly toward her. She put the glasses down on the counter and her knees turned to rubber.

He swept her up in his arms and kissed her breathless. "You are one amazing woman, Callinda Beauvais." His hands caressed her back and surrounded her waist. His eyes were so silver, Callie wondered if they changed color on demand or only when he was most vulnerable.

She swallowed hard and leaned back against the counter. She rubbed her lips with her fingers and knew she wanted more. Much more. "Jules, without your help, we would never have found the bottles or Olivier. I never would have gone to Venelles and who knows how long it would have taken to jog his memory awake? If that kiss was thanking me for showing you an adventure, I'll take it…but I think if you are acting in haste, I might read more into that kiss than you expect." She finished in a rush.

He laughed, reached for the glasses and the bottle of red wine near his hand and turned to her. "I act in haste at times, but wanting to kiss you was not, Callie. I've wanted to kiss you again since Saturday at the chateau." He poured their wine and handed her a glass, before leading her to the couch.

He tapped the rim of her glass and they each sipped. And then he took her glass and placed them both on the table in front of them. Taking her hands in his, he leaned in so she didn't miss a single word. "Callie, you are very important to me and I've liked spending time with you from the day you called me for help. At first, I wanted to help you because you were my friend's widow. That lasted about fifteen minutes. Since then, I knew I wanted to help you, period." He placed his hands on hers and looked into her face. "Please tell me you share my feelings? I've been a bachelor for a very long time. I've lived for my business. I now want to see life through your eyes as I have done the past two weeks."

"Jules, I am…"

He pulled her fingers to his lips and kissed them gently before turning her hand slightly to place another kiss in the palm of her hand. His gray eyes probed her face and then warmed as she leaned toward him and placed her lips oh so gently on his.

"I thought you were happy being a bachelor," she breathed, placing small kisses along his lips, his chin and cheekbones.

"No," he answered. "Not anymore. Too late." And then he laughed that husky laugh. Her eyelashes tickled his face and he pulled her close. "*La vache*, Callie," Jules whispered. Holy cow.

A knock on the cottage door broke them apart. Cendrine's voice was calling, "*Halo?* Please join us, you two. Olivier and I want you inside with us for a celebration and a long talk. *Oui?*" Yes?

Jules lifted his wine, drained the glass and touched Callie's lips with his thumb. She finished hers quickly and he pulled her up to stand beside him. She couldn't hide the small smile that lingered where she'd tasted the last bit of his red wine and he got the message. Her feet barely touched the flagstone walkway between the house and her cottage when he guided her inside with a hand on her waist. She had questioned her relationship with Nate long before Jules kissed her. Now those questions thundered across her mind like galloping stallions.

As they opened the old mill house door, Andres pulled his truck in beside the BMW, beaming with excitement. "Yes, Cendrine just called me," he said as he came up the steps and joined them. "It is a miracle and now we will hear the story." He almost knocked the couple down going into the door.

The children were tightly entrenched on Olivier's lap and Cendrine was perching a tray on the table that held glasses and two wine bottles. Several types of cheese, grapes and two long baguettes joined them with napkins flying off the edge when the children grabbed for the grapes. He laughed at his children through misty eyes. They'd been trying to call him back home through his dreams. And now the faceless woman had a dear face. He couldn't take his eyes off of her.

Cendrine's face was rosy pink. Sitting beside him, Olivier pulled her hand into his while he looked at his father-in-law, Callie and then toward Jules. Olivier slipped his left arm around Cendrine and placed his right palm over her belly as if to reassure himself she and their baby were safe. The gesture was tender and intimate and Callie wondered if anyone else noticed.

"I have not met you before, *monsieur*," he said as he looked at Jules. "Cendrine tells me you and François were good friends and you have helped Callie find me. I thank you with all my heart, both of you, for having trust in me and bringing me home. I know you want to hear the story and I will tell you everything. But first, let's eat." He lifted his glass in the air and everyone joined him. "Salut!"

"I know I should have gone to the police when I received the blackmail letter instead of panicking and taking the vineyard money, but it was too late. I didn't know it was my cousin, Conall, until today because by the time I woke up from his attack, I had no memory. My head was as big as a monster and felt like one too. No matter how hard I tried to remember who I was or how I got there, nothing."

He explained how he'd been locked inside the small, dark room in Venelles, how Bertrand found him in the alley, their kindness, the doctor, everything. "I was still in shock about the letter Fernando Sanchez gave to me from my father and I should have shared it with you, Cendrine," he said, looking contrite before continuing.

As he told them about his days at the bakery and the owners who cared for him so well, he knew they would return to the bakery soon. Callie told them why she'd gone back to the bakery. Cendrine laughed because the children perked up, wondering where the little swan pastries were. Of course, she'd forgotten them.

Cendrine said, "We found the letter on your laptop but it wasn't until after Jules and Callie met with Fernando in Málaga that I found the original letter and the map. That is how they knew where the bottles of wine were hidden."

Olivier looked up quickly. "Well, we must get them from Jouques before Conall learns they are there. I do not know what happened to him after I knocked him down and ran away." He bit harshly into the chunk of baguette while his mind raced ahead.

Everyone looked at each other and smiled indulgently.

Olivier's face showed his confusion and he turned to look at Cendrine. She nodded toward her father.

Andres took up the story with nods here and there between Jules and Callie. When he talked about the baseball bat, Olivier couldn't help himself when a grin sneaked across his face. "My baseball bat, Andres?"

"*Oui*, so you helped us in spirit also, Olivier." Andres looked smug. "But I must tell you, Olivier, I am very angry you did not trust us when you received the first letter asking for the money. You should have had faith in me and in your wife. I am very happy you are back but you must know this."

Olivier nearly choked on his bread and washed it down with the wine. Clearing his throat and shaking his head, he let Andres continue. The old man was talking fast, trying to tell Olivier everything at once.

"I know that, Andres." He sighed deeply. "So, you found the castle, picked the lock…" He stared at Jules who grinned back at him. "You went back a second time but saw Conall following you, and you got yourselves nearly killed over these bottles of brandy. Am I right so far?"

Jules and Callie raised their eyebrows and reluctantly agreed.

"Andres called his old friend in the village and asked him to call the Jouques police exactly ninety minutes later. We knew it would take thirty minutes to get there and another thirty minutes to load up the wine. We gave ourselves thirty minutes to out think Conall and well, that's exactly what we did." Jules finished and Callie jumped in.

"I was watching from above the castle steps and nearly died watching them fight. Conall had a gun. He shot it once and these two stupid, wonderful men knocked him out. I thought they'd killed him and I was so furious because I thought we'd lost the only chance of finding you….that….well, I…uh…."

Jules turned toward her. "Yes, Callie…please tell Olivier how you thanked me for getting Conall out of our hair so we could gather all those wine bottles?"

Andres snickered.

Callie brushed her dark hair away from her face, pausing to answer just a moment. "Well… I slapped his face off," she said quietly.

Cendrine's eyes rounded and Olivier struggled not to laugh. But when everyone laughed, even the children joined in because they assumed someone said something very funny. And then Callie laughed too.

Jules turned serious when he told Olivier about Conall attacking Francisco with a knife. He told him he was Fernando's grandson and he'd told Conall about the bottles during their university days. When he saw Olivier sit forward with horror on his face, Jules held up his hand. "He is going to be okay. I spoke with Fernando this morning and if my guess is right, the Málaga police have already spoken with the Jouques police and Conall is not going anywhere.

Olivier ran his hands over his face, trying to take in everything. He thought his time away was tough, but listening to the adventures that went on without him, he wondered if he hadn't been the lucky one. Holding Cendrine's hand tightly, he reached over and rubbed her belly. "In all this craziness, I hope the baby is safe in there?"

She dropped her eyes a moment before Callie answered for her. "We were worried, Olivier. She fainted one day. She spent overnight in the hospital, but the doctor assured us the baby is fine but to avoid stress..."

At Olivier's frightened look, Cendrine whispered, "No, I have worked in the office and *grand-mère* and *grand-père* have watched the children each day. Papa has been struggling without you and so have we. Olivier, there are no words to tell you how happy we are to have you home again. We must call *grand-mère* and *grand-père* and also your GrandPapa. He is very worried for you and he is very angry at Conall."

Andres spoke quietly, "I knew this man must have hurt you, Olivier. Taking my aggression and frustrations out on him seemed easier than I ever imagined it could be." He sighed. "And I didn't break your bat."

Olivier shared a moment with Andres in silent understanding and shook his head, imagining the frantic fight between the men.

When Jules' phone rang, he excused himself to walk into the kitchen. He returned moments later, his face like thunder. "Conall is missing. He had a security guard outside his hospital room..." He glanced at Olivier. "We hurt him badly. His knee and shoulder needed attention." He slammed his fist into his hand. "The guy slipped out the window and the police are combing the town for him. He can't possibly go far with that battered knee, but until he's found, we watch very closely for anything out of the ordinary."

"He must know you probably hauled those bottles of wine away by now, Jules. He'll be coming back here, I'm sure of it. Where are the bottles hidden?" Olivier asked worriedly.

"In your cellar," Andres answered grimly.

Twenty Two

Olivier jumped up and hurried into the cellar. Andres and Jules followed, showing him the area they'd cleared out with the bottles lying on their sides on several shelves. Olivier pulled one of the bottles off the shelf carefully, tried to see the label and walked to the small window for light. Lifting his shirt tail, he gently rubbed across the paper and stared at the infamous label. "It is real, then?" He turned to the two men silently. After gently replacing the bottle, the three men hugged one another silently. Olivier's shoulders shook and the men did not let go.

It was several minutes before Olivier could gather his wits and the men returned to the living room. Callie and Cendrine sat together whispering, their faces eager to know Olivier's thoughts and hear him talk about the bottles he had so long denied as myth.

"I can't expect you to continue helping me with this massive project, but I would appreciate it if you would. The bottles can't stay here. Conall's on the loose. We need to find a buyer. It is brandy, not wine and its age tells me it is very valuable. Conall told me we could get as much as $1,000 American dollars for each bottle. We have sixty bottles?"

"Well, let's say fifty seven. We kept two for celebrating and your father and Fernando drank one with Pablo Picasso," Cendrine said. "I'm sure he would have financed this endeavor and my idea of financing is letting that aged brandy touch my tongue."

Olivier grinned and touched her cheek with his hand before continuing. "A buyer must be discreet and solvent. We can't sell them on eBay or at the farmer's market," he said with sarcasm.

Jules said, "Olivier, I may be able to help you. But it won't be easy to tell anyone we have Spanish brandy over seventy years old without proving you have a right to sell them."

Olivier held up a hand and rushed upstairs to his small office. Underneath his bookcase was a small slot just large enough for a folded sheet of paper. Pulling the envelope from the hiding place, he returned to the living room. "I do not speak Spanish. When I found this document with my father's letter, I knew it was a legal paper, so I hid it."

Cendrine was surprised. "It wasn't with your father's letter."

"No, I have another stash in the little office," he said sheepishly.

Jules raised his hand and Olivier slipped the document toward him. Not knowing the man, he had to trust him since he'd helped from the beginning. He was sort of family since he was François' friend. He'd known the paper was important, but hadn't had time to decipher the words before Conall knocked him out.

Jules tried to translate the words from the beautiful cursive script. The paper was very old, the document dated 1962. Everyone hushed as he began reading,

"I, Pablo Ruiz Picasso, entrust these bottles of Sueño España brandy from Colinas Ocultos Vineyards to my friend, Alexandre Sylvain Benoit, or his descendant, in the event of his death. It is my wish that these bottles of brandy, produced by José Luis Alonzo near Jerez, be sold to finance a flamenco guitar school in the ancestral home of José Luis, my friend from Algodonales. These funds are to be used to establish a school in Algodonales where poor students from all over España can learn to play flamenco guitar and carry on Spanish traditions.

This is my explicit wish and legal approval to create a foundation in my friend's name for this school. I give you authority to hire a trustee to maintain the foundation and estate to watch over the school.

Signed, Pablo Ruiz Picasso

Witnessed by, Phillippe Mouret, Solicitor, Avignon, France

Goose bumps rose on Callie's arms and she rubbed them, feeling the mighty Pablo Ruiz Picasso in the room. She glanced around and noticed everyone's faces mimicked her own. "Well, that answers your question about validity, Jules. What an amazing journey this has been."

"And it is not finished yet," Jules whispered beside her with a soft chuckle. He loved watching her face blush and he inched his fingers to clasp hers, smiling when she didn't pull them away.

Olivier shook his head in agreement and called his GrandPapa Bruce Baird. He paced through the kitchen, trying to calm his grandfather down, explaining what happened and assuring the old man it was Conall who pulled the rug out from under him, frightened his family and stabbed his old university friend in Málaga. When he told him that Conall had escaped from his hospital room and the police were searching for him, he caught his breath. He knew it stunned the old man to learn this but he told him everything. Conall must be stopped.

When Olivier hung up the phone, his face was grim. He was worried about his great grandfather; neither could understand Conall's motives. They could only surmise it was money, as Conall had suggested to Olivier during his ranting. Olivier handed the telephone to Cendrine. She called Antoine in Scotland to relate what happened. Her call didn't take long; he was horrified and agreed to talk with his employer about Conall. They surely would not expect him back again. Antoine told Cendrine they wanted to fire him from his job anyway.

Antoine continued, "Be careful, Cendrine. If Conall has already tried to kill someone, it could be easier for him the next time. Once you get back to a normal life, you must get started on your *Chloe Rosé*. It will be a new beginning for you and I want to buy some of these bottles from Beauvais Cellars very soon. *A bientôt*." See you soon.

When Cendrine hung up, she returned to Olivier's side. As one, everyone stood to leave. Both Conall and brandy bottles could wait. After Cendrine and Olivier closed their front door, they put the children down for their naps. They had a lot to catch up on without the little people around.

***

"I should get back to my office. Everyone will want to hear about the school children's responses to those laptops and Claude won't be coming in today. Tonight, I am meeting Veronique for dinner again to discuss a new venture she hopes to begin. She wants to start her own interior design shop. I told her that you once had a shop. Would you like to join us?" Jules watched the discomfort that showed in Callie's stance. He could tell she was struggling with the idea of sharing an evening with Veronique. To learn that her husband fathered a child was one thing, getting to know the girl might be more than Jules could expect.

Something clicked in her face and her shoulders sagged a little. "Yes, of course, I would be honored to be part of your evening, Jules. Where…?"

"I will pick you up about seven o'clock? She lives near the restaurant, so she will walk and meet us there. When I mentioned you and your mother's interior design business, she was excited and I didn't know how to respond."

Callie soothed his arm with her hand. "It's all right, Jules. I have been avoiding the topic since I learned of this….liaison with Aurore. But as Mom used to say, meet it head on or run away, one is hard and the other easy, but facing the issue is the only way to resolve it."

He covered her fingers with his own and inched toward her just as Andres joined them. She interlocked her arm with the old man on one side and Jules on the other.

As the BMW and the truck left the yard, she paused. Today she would listen to her mother's wise words and trust them. Today, she would try to understand why François would give up a child of his own blood instead of trusting her love. Maybe seeing Callie's disappointment over the years because they did not have a child of their own kept him silent? Was he ashamed of his actions? Or was he unfeeling? The boating accident on the lake during that horrible storm crept through her mind. And then she thought of the dream at the lake house telling her to move on with her life when she thought Nate was the answer. *Too much wine? Maybe a short nap will prepare me to spend an evening with my husband's child.*

As she lay on the bed, twisting to get comfortable, the Skype call rang from the main room. Rolling her eyes, she hurried to answer, relieved to see Livvy's face on the screen.

"Good morning, Callie. Well, morning here, afternoon there…I have news. Janine is thrilled we've moved the wedding. Our date is set and I am packing. Bram's schedule was moved up because of a court deposition at the end of the month. We arrive in four days." Olivia's green eyes shone and her short cap of blonde hair danced as she talked, her hands expressively moving in the air.

"The time is great, Livvy. We found Olivier this morning."

"Was he alive?" She frowned, afraid for the answer.

"Yes, alive and well. He had Amnesia from being attacked by his cousin. I will tell you all about it when you arrive. Email me your itinerary and I will pick you up from the airport in Marseille. That's where you are flying in, right?"

Olivia nodded. "Do you want me to run by your house to pick up anything special? I still have the key."

"Yes, that would be wonderful, Livvy. I will send you a list with instructions where you can find things. We can shop for a special dress for me to wear once you arrive. Aix has some beautiful dress shops and..."

"And have you spoken with Nate yet?"

"No, I am calling him at tonight."

"And?"

"I am going to tell him I can't marry him, Livvy. He is a wonderful guy and so sweet and caring. He was there when I was so lost in my life....."

"But?"

"But, he is not my future, Livvy. We can talk when you arrive. Why don't you and Bram stay here at my cottage and I will move into the guest room in the big house? I'm sure Cendrine will not mind and you two can have privacy, your own little love nest. Oh wait, of course, you won't be allowed to sleep together until the wedding, what am I thinking?"

Olivia burst out laughing. "Holy shit, Cal, do you think Bram would fly all the way to Provence and not have me warm his bed?"

The friends had a big laugh and then Olivia shrewdly asked, "What else is it, my friend? You've found Olivier, you're breaking it off with Nate and you think Jules is the man. What else?"

Callie sighed heavily. "I will tell you *that* when you arrive too. In fact, instead of telling you, I will show you. Just get your butt here. I miss our girl time." She smiled goodbye and clicked off.

When she crawled onto her bed again, questions lingered and swirled through her head. Five minutes later, she was snoozing as birds chirped outside and a chilly breeze slipped through the partially-opened window.

***

Conall Carson was stumped. He'd slipped away from the police, just barely. When the officer checked on him the last time, he'd faked sleep and it had worked. He'd been prepared to overpower him if necessary, but knew with his injuries, he'd probably have hurt himself further if the man had tried to stop him. His throbbing knee was swollen, but he'd managed to slip out the window. He was lucky his hospital room had been on the ground floor. But when he landed on his good leg, he'd jammed his damaged shoulder when he let go of the window ledge. With precious minutes to spare, he'd limped behind the hospital away from prying eyes and hotwired an old Volkswagen. Wedging himself behind the wheel, he thanked his luck again. With his good knee, he could still work a clutch; otherwise he'd be dead in the water.

When he'd maneuvered the little car into the street, two police cars had just arrived at the front doors. Jerking away, he knew he had to think. He had to retrieve the money he'd stashed, so that was the first place he needed to go. Damn Olivier! It was his fault. If Olivier had given him what he'd wanted, he wouldn't be in this position. And if he'd been more aware, an old man with a baseball bat wouldn't have… "Oh shit in a basket, I'm screwed. Think, man! Think. First get the money, then back to the big house and wait to see if someone will lead me to the bottles or back to Venelles and look for Olivier again?" One thing for sure, he had to leave Jouques before one of the coppers got smart. He left the town behind him and headed toward Pertuis, thinking up one plan and discarding it for another.

Twenty Three

Callie braced herself for Veronique's arrival. She'd worn the pearls François had given her for a wedding gift. She'd hesitated to clasp them around her neck because that was a time when his child was growing in someone else's womb. She forced the dark thoughts away and tapped her fingers on the lightly shaded table.

She knew that Jules worried he'd asked too much of her. He loved his niece dearly and he wanted them to become friends. He told her it would fill him up, already overwhelmed with the feelings Callie invoked within him. She knew he'd been single for years and he'd decided long ago to remain that way. She saw more than a mild interest in his eyes, knew she could not ignore the feelings. She needed to face this young woman, regardless of her own vulnerability. Callie wished he'd waited longer to bring them together, let her warm up to Veronique before sharing a meal with her. Now it was too late.

The young woman in question rushed over to them as she had before, a bit out of breath and still beautiful. Her dark blonde hair was curled around her face, touching her shoulders; her eyes were alight with pleasure. She pulled her brightly-colored scarf from around her neck and held it tightly in her hands. Giving her uncle a quick kiss on each cheek, she turned to Callie, fascinated.

Callie stood and pulled the young woman toward her, kissed her cheeks and grinned, "Did you run all the way, *chérie?*" She could feel the girl's giggle in her hug and was delighted to see the impish smile she sent to her uncle when he pulled out a chair.

Facing Callie across the table, Veronique reached over and squeezed her hands. "I am so happy you could join us, Callie." She pronounced her name Cal-EEE, a song in her voice. "When uncle Jules told me you and your mother were interior designers, I knew we would be great friends, *oui?*"

Callie watched the young woman's eyes sparkle as she spoke and a wave of anger nearly knocked her flat. *How could he give up this delightful, beautiful child? She wasn't allowing her circumstances to define her. She appears tough and vulnerable, clever and reckless and compassionate, utterly real.* Callie's eyes lifted to Jules, who nodded his understanding. He lifted his hand to the waiter and ordered drinks quickly, gathering menus for the three of them.

"What is it you have in mind, Veronique? Are you planning to have commercial clients or individuals? Will you specialize in the entire house or a specific room? Inside or outside?"

Veronique's face registered surprise. She turned to look at her uncle and whispered loudly, "You were right, uncle Jules, she is rather awesome, isn't she?"

Jules tried to keep from smiling when Callie winked at him. He coughed behind his hand and welcomed the bottle of wine placed in front of him. He poured their glasses and held his own up as if to indicate he would make a toast. He did not. And then Callie and Veronique began talking fast, in low-rumbling English.

"Individuals, entire houses, inside," she spoke with much animation, her sentences punctuated with her hands moving in front of her face to make a point. Veronique looked at Callie with a soft, forgive-me-for-running-on face and she smiled apologetically.

The waiter brought plate after plate of food to the table. A large crock of pâté and a steaming loaf of bread were deposited in front of Callie, followed by spit-roasted pheasants, golden brown and fragrant, with rosemary. A chafing dish of white fish, redolent in the garlicky *aioli* sauce of Provence now sat beside a large salad of greens glistening with olive oil and liberally sprinkled with *Herbes of Provence.*

The heady, red wine bottle was nearly empty as the women chatted the evening away over their delicious dinner, leaving Jules to watch them in wonder. It had taken them all of five minutes to become fast friends and his head was awhirl with its magic. Callie had already agreed to meet Veronique the next day for coffee and share a quick look at a prospective shop for lease.

"I suppose it's time for me to go back to *Compagnie des Machines Armand.* I have work waiting and since my company is a full service computer company that includes IT services, software, hardware and consulting services, it is time."

The women nodded in agreement, forking their food in between bites, trying to chew quickly so they could talk more. As the women chatted, Jules ate his dinner thoughtfully. He took a deep sip of the red wine and nudged his niece under the table.

Veronique glanced at her uncle. He pointed to his watch and she was stunned to see it was already ten p.m. "Oh, Callie, forgive me for talking so much. And uncle Jules, we have left you out…next time you can do all the talking, *oui?*" She winked at Callie and turned to give him a squeeze.

The dimple in Jules' chin deepened and his eyes smiled.

Callie was utterly charmed by Veronique and stole a quick glance at Jules. Her look was a bittersweet acknowledgement that a fierce battle had been fought and won.

Once outside the restaurant, the women strolled to the curb with their arms interlocked. "Until tomorrow, Callie. I shall pick you up at nine? We shall have our coffee and then meet with the solicitor? The shop is not far away from my favorite café." Swiftly re-wrapping her bright scarf a few times around her neck, she hurried down the street.

"Whew….that girl can talk, *oui?*" Jules said with a chuckle.

Callie's thoughts were far away and she did not answer. They did not speak all the way back to the cottage. When he parked the car, she said, "Thank you, Jules. What François did not start, I will finish." She turned toward him, her eyes shiny with unshed tears. "She is so sweet and spending these few hours with her cements my decision to remain in France."

He was dumbfounded. "Remain in France?"

She shook her head slowly. "Yes, being back makes me realize that America is no longer my home. My mother is gone and that was the biggest reason I refused to live in France. François liked America, so we had two homes, one in Portland and a cottage at Devil's Lake near Lincoln City on the ocean. That is the lake where his boat took him away. I love both places but not nearly as much as I love being here. I have decided to sell them and move back to France."

"And what about Nate?" he asked quietly.

"I will tell Nate I cannot marry him. He is a good man, Jules, but I know in my heart, I do not love him. If I did, I would not enjoy your kisses. You told me that you saw no magic between Aurore and François. But he and I shared magic and even though I am angry with him for his decision about Veronique, those memories will always be with me. Now, I am moving forward and it feels very good. I've hidden behind my grief far too long. I read somewhere that when your true love smiles, the wind bends. If it is possible to love like that again, I shall wait." She reached out two fingers and pressed them to Jules' lips before opening the door, just barely beating his gentlemanly race around the car.

She felt Jules behind her, his chin resting on her head and one hand caressing her shoulder. His arm tightened around her, pressing her closer. "I am very happy you are staying in France. I am not as good with words as the romantics in the movies, but I will say you move me beyond those words. Let me help you return to the living."

Without replying, she closed her eyes and sighed deeply. Turning around slowly, she reached up to pull his face down to hers. "Thank you, Jules, for everything." They kissed deeply. *Slow down. Make it last.* But everything goes faster when time swallows moments like this in the night, among the vineyards, flowers, cold breezes and too much wine. She knew in Jules' arms she could forget about grief, losing her mother, angst over François' unnecessary boat accident and tomorrow.

Jules pulled her closer, and kissed her again before he drove away.

Callie Skyped Nate that night, as she'd promised. It was 1:30 in the afternoon at the Portland office. Her heart hammered, her breath was short and she knew her face would tell the story. She'd never been one to hide her feelings. Her mother told her even as a child, Callie couldn't lie about anything without everyone seeing the truth of it.

When Nate responded, his face was wreathed in smiles. "Hello, Callie. I've counted the minutes waiting for your call this afternoon. The office was busy, so I kept my mind burning through it all. How are things going? How are *you*?"

Callie smiled at him. "I am good. We found Olivier this morning."

Nate's face changed to uneasiness. "Was he alive?"

"Oh, yes. He'd been attacked and locked away by his cousin from Scotland. But he didn't know him. The knock on his head gave him Amnesia. He couldn't answer any of the man's questions and it was several days before he was able to overpower the man. Olivier escaped and hid in an alley close by. An old man found him the next morning; he and his wife cared for him inside their bakery. That's where we found him this morning." She heaved a sigh. "I went in for some pastries and found him. Seeing me brought his memory back. I couldn't believe it."

"We found him? You and François' old friend? Or you and Cendrine?" He tilted his head, plainly jealous.

"Does it matter, Nate?" she answered wearily. "The good news is we found him. The bad news is that his cousin was captured, but escaped from his hospital room afterward. The police are looking for him now. Everyone is worried sick because he is most likely still watching…"

Nate heaved a relieved sigh. "So, now that Olivier is back, you are coming home?" His eyes shifted a moment, waiting for Callie's answer.

"No, Nate. I…I'm going to see this through. There is more to this story than just finding Olivier. The brandy bottles will fund a foundation for a flamenco guitar school Pablo Picasso wanted created in Spain and…"

"…..And a wedding? When were you going to tell me Bram and Olivia moved their wedding to France? Is the world moving around at your whims, Callie? I guess I'm not as important as you led me to believe a couple of weeks ago." His sad face filled the screen.

"Nate, I am sorry. Being here has filled me with so many memories that I think…I…" She exhaled loudly. "Your friendship and love helped me see life was worth living, Nate. But, being in France again has helped me go beyond that. I am staying in France. Please forgive me, Nate." She burst into tears and swiped her eyes, pleading with him to understand.

Nate's stunned face gave her a hard, stony stare. She saw the sting of disappointment. "So, guess I'm not invited to the wedding?" His sarcasm could not hide his turmoil. "If that is what you think is important, I will have to live with it, Callie, but I don't have to like it. You know I love you. You also know I could never live in France." He hesitated a minute. "Or maybe you hadn't included me in your plans when you decided to stay there? Maybe this man you've been jetting around the country with....?" He left his words hanging.

Callie's face fell and her cheeks flamed.

His face stilled. "Life is full of strange and wonderful things, Callie. And sometimes some hellish things too…hold on to the good ones. I know you aren't trying to hurt me but I'm just…" The screen went blank.

He'd hung up and she couldn't bear the pain she saw etched across his face. Breaking her relationship off with Nate crushed her, but she was determined that he deserved more. Remembering Jules' kiss drenched her heart in wine, just like the Norah Jones' song…And she would not change her mind. She wanted Nate to find that magic too.

***

The following morning as Olivier kissed Cendrine goodbye and walked to his vineyard office, Veronique's small silver Fiat drove into the lane. Callie waved at them and jumped into the car, anxious to spend time with the young woman. *What will happen when these girls learn they are cousins?*

"*Maman* told me she wanted to see the shop also, but she was unsure if she could meet me there. We shall see. For now, let's get coffee and I will ---as the American's say--- pick your mind."

Callie laughed, "that's pick your brain."

"*Oui.* That is it." Veronique's face dimpled.

Callie wasn't sure she wanted to meet Aurore yet. One surprise at a time was sufficient. Gripping her purse, she bit her lip and sighed deeply inside her mind. *I don't want to like the woman François slept with, teased and laughed with, impregnated with a child and then left.* Her head hurt. *But she is Jules' sister.* Callie tried to see the good in people, but in the past few weeks, she'd fought against the glass-half-empty mentality. She grimaced, hoping the woman wouldn't show up at all.

Veronique drilled Callie with questions as they sipped their *café au laits* and lingered over their *petite dejuner*, breakfast. She scribbled Callie's answers in a tablet plus her thoughts, ideas and experiences with her new business; budgets, advertising, supplies, connections, marketing and business cards.

"This is much more than I imagined." She pulled her wheat-colored hair back from her face and stared at the list on the table. Touching several bullet points with her pencil, she tapped the eraser against her chin.

Callie sipped her coffee and looked at the girl's fingers. They were long, just like her father's. Her hair was lighter. The lips and smile, along with the eyes, were such that Callie couldn't quite believe the similarity. How could he have looked at this girl and not instantly fallen in love with her? She jerked her head. Had he seen her? In all those years, of course, he must have. Photos? *I cannot accept your decision, François. I wish I could ask you, slap you and knock you down. What other secrets did you keep from me?*

Veronique said, "What do you think, Callie?"

Callie looked up blankly. "What?"

"Time to meet the solicitor. If you think the shop will work for my new shop, I will sign on the dotted line. I am so happy you are willing to help me. I have read many books and searched for information online. And I have listened to my professors at university, but just one morning with you and I already feel more confident.

When they walked across the street, a tall woman with long straight hair waved a set of keys in the air. Holding a folder beneath her arm, the stranger opened the glass door of a small shop sandwiched between a hair salon and a wine shop. Callie glanced up and down the street and thought it was a perfect location.

After Veronique hurried across the street, Callie followed her through the door. Open rafters greeted them. One wall was completely bricked and light fixtures hung down in an eclectic mixture of old and new. Callie could envision shelving and racks on one side, but on the brick wall, she anticipated Veronique's framed samples, décor to feed the imagination of prospective clients. She clasped her hands in front of her and leaned her chin on them, turning slowly to stare in every corner.

Veronique looked at Callie.

Callie grinned. Clapping her hands in delight, she said, "Yes, this could work very well for you, *ma chérie*. It is exciting to imagine and I will help you with some ideas that already fill up my head."

"I'll take it, Madame LaRusse. Where do I sign?" She laughed and hugged Callie, before stopping near the woman.

Laureline LaRusse removed papers from her folder and pulled a chair to the table. "All I need is your signature on the annual lease agreement and a check for first and last month's rent.

"Wait one moment. Veronique, are you being too hasty, child?"

Callie turned. She didn't know what she had expected, but the woman in her late forties who stood in the doorway was attractive, perfectly coiffed and manicured. Wearing an expensive, elegant trouser suit, she stood about five feet six and shrewdly appraised Madame LaRusse and Veronique. She marched up to them and stared at the paper waiting for a signature.

"*Maman*, it is what I want. I have looked at three properties and Callie...oh, I am sorry, *Maman*. Let me introduce you to uncle Jules' friend, Callie Beauvais."

Aurore turned very slowly toward Callie. Her lips pressed into a thin line. Neither woman spoke for a heartbeat. "You are the widow of François Beauvais?" Her arms hung straight at her sides and her face closed up. Her unfriendly eyes skewered Callie with a long look and she didn't flinch at her daughter's sharp intake of breath.

"Yes, I was married to François Beauvais." The tension in Callie's shoulders beat a tattoo against her backbone as she felt the woman survey her from head to toe. She swallowed hard to stop from crying and simmered quietly instead. *How could François put me in this position?!*

Annoyed, Veronique jumped up, horrified and confused at her mother's rudeness. "*Maman*, Callie is an interior designer. She and her mother once owned a business and she is helping me decide......."

"*I* will help you decide. You should not sign anything until I look at the legalities." Aurore straightened her posture and walked toward the table, ignoring Callie altogether. "Let me read this." Pulling it off the table, her knuckles turned white as her finger followed each line.

Madame LaRusse watched the tableau with concern, tapping her foot and drumming her fingers on the table.

Veronique calmly removed the agreement from her mother's hands. Staring at her mother without blinking, she told her, "I am signing this. I am a grown woman and I have made my decision, *Maman*. I read the fine print as you instructed so many times and the shop will be my new business."

Aurore huffed loudly. Biting her lip for only a moment and jerking the white sleeves at her wrists taut, she yanked her long jacket closed, as if hiding her heart behind it. Tight lipped, she stalked out.

For the next couple of hours, Callie and Veronique measured windows and walls, considering where to place her antique furniture. "I have several pieces; a tall bookcase and a three-legged pie table." She rubbed her hands together anticipating the placement laid out in her head.

"And don't forget the library table you told me about. That could be your work table, the focal point right here," she pointed, "and the place where your clients hand over all their money." Callie grinned.

The women laughed. "What do you think? Put my catalogs on the bookcase or on the large display table in this corner?"

Callie pointed as she watched the girl walk around the room and remembered when she was in her shoes with Millie Augustine sharing it all with her. *I wish this young woman had the camaraderie with her own mother that I had with my mom. Life is so unfair sometimes.*

Jules called Callie later that afternoon. "*Halo*. How was the shop? Did she like it?" Peace rolled over her when she heard his warm voice like soft music in a dimly-lit room.

"She loved it and so did I. We are going to make a plan and she is filled with ideas that I planted in her sweet head."

"But? I hear a *but* in your voice."

She chuckled. "Yes, well....I met Aurore."

"Ah. My sister is pretty strong-willed."

"Is that what you call it?"

"What happened?" Jules heard tension cut across the line.

"After she deduced who I was, she erased me from the room but Veronique stood her ground." Callie answered fiercely.

"What did Veronique do? She's had to fight her mother every step of the way for years." His voice shared her frustration.

"You would have been proud of her. I sure was. She signed the papers against her mother's wishes. Aurore stormed out."

Jules rolled his eyes. His sister was a lawyer who crossed hot coals to win a case. Jules never saw the joy in it. He remembered the sweet girl his sister used to be, before François riveted her world. She'd fought phantom enemies ever since and Veronique was caught in her web. He was disgusted, but remembered how he'd started his company. When two people believed in him, trusted him with their money, the company was born. That was François and Aurore, his best friend and his sister. In exchange for their financial backing, they each held twenty percent stock in his company. It seemed the perfect solution. One day, he had assured them, their stocks would increase in value and they would be rich. Until one of his trusted backers betrayed him. Without Aurore's backing, his company would not exist. Life was a paradox at times.

"Are you still there, Jules?"

"*Oui*. I found a Spaniard who might be in interested in buying the brandy. Shall I call Olivier with his name or should I drop by?"

Callie's lips twitched. "Hmmmmm, let me think. Drop by and I will walk you over to his office. I've seen Cendrine walk over three times since I got home." She chuckled. "I guess she wants to make sure he's still there."

"I can arrive by 6:30. If I am lucky, I'll be invited to dinner."

"Tonight, I'm cooking, so consider yourself invited. I'll pour your Cabernet when I see you drive in the lane…"

"Ah, a woman after my heart." He'd finagled that dinner invitation so smoothly. Maybe he was learning how to be romantic after all.

Twenty Four

Olivier still couldn't believe he was home or that his memory was intact. When the children ran to him when he opened his door, he almost cried. Cendrine unwrapped a bag of something at the kitchen door and Callie sat at the table stirring something. He didn't give a damn what either woman was preparing, he was so happy, he could drown in it.

The children wrapped their little arms around his knees and he leaned down to hug them. Joining them on the floor, laughter spilled from Bernadette and François, adding to his contentment. Once the hugs were over and they changed direction, he walked into the kitchen, smoothed his hand over Cendrine's belly and kissed her before turning to Callie. "No calls from the police yet?"

"No, nothing. The Málaga police are talking with the Jouques police and now the Pertuis police are involved, what more can we do? Conall was in very bad shape when Jules and Andres got done with him, how far could the man go?" Callie mixed the salsa and cleaned up all the debris.

Olivier looked at the bowl in front of her, leaned down to sniff it and wrinkled his nose. "What is that?" Their eyes met and she smiled.

"Fresh tomato salsa for our white fish. I am cooking tonight so you take you pregnant wife into the living room and start kissing on her. She's in my way," she said with a laugh.

Cendrine lifted her arms and Olivier held her close. "We're gone."

Twenty minutes later, Jules knocked on the door. He had a bouquet of flowers in his hand and a bottle of Tempranillo his assistant found for him. "If we are going to find a brandy buyer in Spain, we should drink Spanish wine, *oui?*"

Olivier took the wine, Cendrine grabbed the flowers and Callie handed him a glass of Cabernet. Everyone sat at the table while Callie worked her magic in the kitchen. When Cendrine started to rise, Callie shooed her back and Olivier pulled her to him. "Rest, *ma chérie*. I am afraid

Callie might hit us with my baseball bat if you get in her way… although your father has not returned it yet." He chuckled and kissed the top of her head.

Just then, Andres knocked on the door. Callie shushed them and pulled him inside. He grinned when he saw the tomato mess on the apron tied around her waist. "I am here for dinner. Cendrine tells me come to dinner anytime. Today is anytime." His face lit up when he saw his daughter's face. Callie hugged him and pointed to a chair around the table.

"So, Jules, it seems this is now your second home," Andres said with a smile in his voice. I wonder what brings you here so often, my friend, could it be the food? The wine?" He glanced at Callie and grinned. Kissing her on both cheeks, he whispered, "*très bien*." Very good.

After the fish, salad, rice and cheese plate was cleared away, Jules pushed a piece of paper across to Olivier. "I found two buyers in Spain who may be interested in the brandy. One is near Jerez by the old vineyard that produced it and one is near Campanillas, a small town near Málaga. Since Picasso stressed using a Spanish buyer, I knew you would want to follow his instructions. Once you decide, I suggest you ask a lawyer to study it. Since the brandy could be well worth over 80000 euros, you should be very cautious. Once word gets out about the brandy, all hell will break loose."

Olivier looked at the list. "I did not have time to call Fernando today but I will soon. Also, the letter said the Prado Museum might help us, but a good attorney should be able to set up the foundation in Picasso's friend's name. Do you have anyone who might help us research the people involved in Algodonales about the guitar playing school?"

Inspiration popped Callie's head up. "My friends arrive from America to be married here in Provence. They will stay in my cottage. Bram is an Oregon lawyer with connections here in France. He could be very helpful. They are honeymooning in Marbella, not far from Málaga. Livvy loves an adventure as much as I do. Why not ask them to drive to Algodonales and speak to the people who make flamenco guitars?"

"Yes. This sounds good. You have helped us so much. I do not want you to leave again, Callie," Olivier said fervently.

Everyone looked at her.

Callie grinned. "Okay."

Cendrine screwed up her face. "What?"

"I'm staying in France. I have not told your grandparents yet, Cendrine, but my heart is here. So, I am not leaving. You won't mind having a full-time resident in the cottage?"

Cendrine jumped up and hugged Callie. "*Parfait!* Perfect. My dream is to have you close once again and you will be here for the baby." Her eyes brimmed over and she could not speak except in a whisper. "My husband is home, my baby is safe and my auntie will stay in France. What more can I ask for?"

Olivier's phone rang, interrupting the excitement. After listening for several minutes, he hung up and stared at the table. "That was GrandPapa. He had a stroke and he wants me to fly to Scotland. He's in the hospital." He looked at Cendrine. Fraying nerves and pain were plainly etched across his face. "It is this thing with Conall who has put him in danger! When I see my cousin again, I fear I will kill him!"

"You must go, of course, Oliver." Cendrine blew out excess air and sat down. You must go make the reservations now."

At 7:30 a.m. the next morning, Cendrine and Callie waited for Olivia and Bram's plane to land in Marseille. They'd arrived early since Olivier's plane left at 6:00 a.m. for Scotland. When Callie saw Livvy's blonde head bobbing above a group of children, she ran to her friend and embraced her with enthusiasm. Seeing Bram, she also wrapped her arms around him, welcoming them to Provence. "The car is nearby. You have all the bags? Does Nicole know where I live? Did you find everything on the list I sent to you? When is Janine arriving?"

Olivia rolled her eyes and grinned at Cendrine. "Callie, take me home and give me coffee. Yes to everything. Janine arrives tomorrow. My children haven't seen each other for awhile and they are both excited. Roger arrives one hour after Janine. Nicole is driving from Nice. He's going to Nice with her the morning after our wedding. And they are all staying at the Hotel Ibis Styles Pertuis and I'm starving. Where's the car?"

Cendrine was caught up in a big hug. She loved Callie's friends already. Her grandparents were thrilled to host a wedding in the old home place instead of a funeral, as they'd feared Olivier was dead. As they sped back to Pertuis, her mind switched back to her husband. She hadn't wanted him to leave, but of course, he had to. He adored his great grandfather and Conall's actions had nearly killed the old man. The baby kicked her so hard, she let out a little cry and all conversation stopped.

"Cendrine?"

"I am okay, Callie. Lulu has decided to be part of the welcome."

"Lulu? That is the first I heard this name. Is it a girl, then?"

"No," Cendrine laughed. We just call her Lulu because I have a feeling it is a girl. I have no idea what name to give her in order to nickname her Lulu, but we shall see. My doctor appointment is later today. I have only seven weeks to go and after the last problem, my doctor is watching me very closely. But I am good at being very lazy, just like he demanded." She pulled a hand off the steering wheel to caress her belly and grinned at Callie.

That evening, Jules met Bram and Olivia. He'd arrived on the pretext of discussing the document with Bram, and to ask about possible connections to solicitors in Provence.

Olivia pulled Callie aside after dinner and whispered, "I see what you mean. He has charisma and is a man in charge. I agree with you that as sweet as Nate is, this man is more." When she watched Callie's face as she glanced across the room at Jules, Olivia continued. "And that is a look I've yearned to see on your face since François' death, Callie."

Later, Olivia and Bram were ensconced in the cottage while Callie walked Jules to his car. "They are very nice and the friendship I see between you and Livvy is easy to watch," he said as he neared his BMW. "Bram is very smart and I think he is probably the answer to Olivier's wish to find a good attorney for the foundation legalities. By the way, I believe I should be invited to this wedding so I can protect you from Conall."

Callie smiled in the darkness. "Oh? Well, I just happen to have an extra invitation lying around so I'll put your name on it."

He wheeled her around and backed her up to the car. His face was inches from her face. "Callie. I want you."

She drank the excitement like wine and took a deep breath. *Oh, God, I might be a slut after all.* She wanted him too. Wrapping her arms around his neck, she said, "Well, why the hell are you telling me this now when I just gave away my cottage?"

He laughed. Kissing her, he held her tightly, enjoying the way she folded into him. Their kiss deepened and her breasts were crushed against his chest. "Oh Callie, Callie."

She bit softly at his lip, "There is always tomorrow," she whispered, "but I have a wedding to plan and," she pulled him toward her by his lapels, "then we can talk about this."

When he started to answer her, Callie rose up on her toes and pressed a finger to his lips to silence him. When he groaned, she pushed him into his car.

The next two days were a whirlwind of activity. Their friend, Janine Vinnier, arrived from Oregon with napkins, small vials of bubbles, ribbons and laughter. She was one of the most joyful women Callie had ever met and her husband was the scoundrel of the century. The Frenchwoman hid her recent sadness, focusing instead on Olivia's wedding plans.

The next day, Olivia and Callie found the morning to themselves. When Callie introduced her to her favorite café, they agreed the ambiance reminded them of their old favorite, Three Lions Bakery in Portland, Oregon. Reminiscing, they also agreed Three Lion's chocolate croissants were good, but not the heavenly pastry they now ate in Provence. Her *café au lait* was still steaming when Olivia said, "Okay, tell me what is hovering through your mind. I know something is wrong. I see it all over your face."

Callie sipped her coffee to put off the conversation. Her lip trembled just a bit when she sat the cup back in its saucer. When she looked at her best friend, her face was grim. "The day I met Jules to ask for his help, his niece tapped on the window of the café and he invited her to join us. She is a lovely young woman, just over twenty and smart, sharp and sweet. She's interested in interior design and I helped her make a decision to lease a shop two doors from where we sit right now." She pointed toward the flowering pot hanging above the sidewalk and lifted her cup again.

Olivia was unsure where this conversation was going. She could see her friend's mind searching for words.

"When she came into the café, I'd already seen more than I could fathom; her eyes and smile were so familiar; my body turned numb and my mind stumbled." She looked at Olivia and took a deep breath. "I knew immediately. Her eyes and smile both screamed pure François."

Olivia's eyes rounded. She asked slowly, "Are you saying this young woman is his daughter?" Disbelief was etched across her friend's face. When she reached over to cover Callie's hand to still the twitching fingers, she felt the anger emanating from her like a small breeze.

Callie nodded mutely. "She is Jules' sister's child. Aurore was younger than Jules and François. She was crazy about him and he evidently succumbed to her charms. Jules was angry with François for toying with her, but François would not listen. About the same time Aurore realized she was pregnant, François had met me and brought me here to meet his family. Jules said Aurore was devastated."

"How could he keep this secret from you for so many years?" Olivia demanded. She was spitting sparks with her eyes, unmistakably ready for battle.

"It gets worse, Livvy. François told Aurore he would pay for her schooling and he would support the child on two conditions. His daughter must learn English as a second language and she could never know he was her father. Aurore took the deal because she had no other option." Callie finished her coffee and heaved a sigh. "I do not know who the young woman thinks her father is. I've met Aurore and she, of course, hates me to pieces; Veronique can't understand her mother's animosity. And I can't blame her, for pity sake."

"But why would he...?" Olivia spread her fingers on the table.

"Every time I think of it, I shake all over. You must meet her. Then we can talk some more." Callie looked at her watch. "Come, I told her I was bringing my best friend to see the shop." They slid out of the booth and Olivia followed her, still astonished.

Lights shown through the glass window and Callie tapped on the glass door. Within a few seconds, the shade lifted and Veronique's smiling face shone at them. Greeting them with kisses on each cheek, she welcomed them inside with a dramatic dip of her head.

Olivia felt a kick in her stomach as they walked inside.

Veronique pointed to the shelving being installed and the fake wall she'd designed to hold her samples near the front door. "This is good?"

Callie studied the wall and pointed. "Why not place your lavender logo above the banner with your samples over there? That way, your banner will be the first thing customers see when they come in the door."

Veronique's bubbling enthusiasm filled the room as she leaned over and hugged Callie. "What would I do without you? When uncle Jules said you were awesome, he was right…I say it again!" Her hair swung across her shoulders as she snagged some fabric off the corner table and rushed to hold it up on the wall. "Like this?" They were immersed in design talk.

Callie could see that Olivia's mind was awhirl when they left Veronique's shop nearly an hour later, experiencing a gamut of mixed emotions, just as Callie knew she would.

Callie did not speak as they returned to the car.

"Callie, she is beautiful and sweet. Her resemblance to him is uncanny. François could never have denied fatherhood for this child. I always thought a lot of François, but this certainly muddies the waters. I marveled at the camaraderie between the two of you back there. Now, you can enjoy the closeness of both Cendrine and Veronique. I will be sad with you living so far away, but a new chapter is opening for both of us, so how can I complain? But how could he…?"

Callie pounded on the steering wheel before starting the car. She ripped out her words impatiently, "I know! Why couldn't he trust me with this? He must have known I would find out! And I am sick with the burden. That child will probably hate me when she learns her father chose me over her. And I have no idea who the man I married really was. I've been grieving for a man who didn't exist..." Her voice died away and she thrust the key in the ignition without waiting for Olivia to reply.

Bram walked through the Beauvais vineyards with Andres while he explained about the grapevines, explored the warehouse and visited the cool cave where their wine was stored. He tasted different varietals. Andres was the perfect teacher since he loved the vines and thrived on sharing his knowledge. Both sitting on overturned barrels late one afternoon, Andres handed him a stemmed glass and winked at him. "Here, Bram, you must taste our newest blend. I have not shared it with Cendrine yet. Tell me what you think of this." He dribbled a small amount of wine in the glass.

Bram swirled the glass, smelled the aroma, and then tossed it back. Within seconds, he said, "Andres, I can't believe it. This is magnificent."

Andres face crinkled in a smile that lit up the cave. "Yes, I believe it is also. Cendrine will like it very much." He walked behind the barrels and returned with two bottles. Handing them to Bram, he bowed. "For you, my new friend. You and your bride can toast each other and share a virgin wine no other lips have tasted except ours."

Bram hugged the man and held the bottles to his chest as they walked back through the vineyards toward the cottage. The women were still making plans. Joining the ladies wasn't really what he wanted to do. "The women are still there..." he mumbled.

Andres laughed. "Come to my place. Eat simple. Drink wine."

Bram didn't hesitate to follow Andres across the vineyard.

Cendrine was on the phone when Callie came down the stairs the next morning. Her face was a bit pale as she nodded for Callie to join her. She motioned toward the table filled with fruit and croissants. The children had cereal with sliced bananas and were riveted to the cartoon video on the television. As Callie slid into her chair and reached for the coffee, Cendrine joined her.

"Olivier is flying home tonight. GrandPapa is doing well and will be released from the hospital this morning. He is very angry at Conall and told

Olivier he will remove him from his will. Olivier sees the pain it gives his great grandfather to do this. Greed has destroyed a family." She shook her head. "Will you stay with the children while I go get Olivier from the airport tonight?"

"Of course."

"You are not leaving us to spend the evening with Jules, then?"

Callie laughed. "Okay, matchmaker. Out with it."

Cendrine drew Callie's hand to her own. "I have wanted you to stay in France for a very long time. When uncle François died, I thought I might never see you again when you flew back to America after I had you to myself for a year. I have wondered if Olivier's disappearance created a silver lining for me. I missed you so much, I ached sometimes. When I watch you with Jules, I see magic again, Callie. Am I wrong?"

Callie looked at her. "No, you are not wrong. I feel the magic, but I am cautious. I do not want to jump into a relationship. When I arrived, I was engaged to a man I thought I loved. But within a few days, I ached for France more than I missed Nate. And then I met Jules and his energy lit a fire inside me. I will return to America to clean out my houses and put them up for sale. I am here to stay, *ma chérie*. I will love living close to you and François and Bernadette and little Lulu."

Cendrine eyes sparkled. "But there is something you are not telling me, Callie. I feel it here," she said while thumping her chest.

Callie glanced at the children, each mesmerized with Mickey Mouse on the television. She swallowed hard and reached for her coffee. And then she told Cendrine about the secret that her uncle François kept from her and his family for twenty years.

***

Olivia's daughter, Nicole, arrived from Nice the night before and her son, Roger, drove his rental car into the vineyard three hours later. Both of Olivia's children loved Bram and had for years. He had been a friend of their mother's nearly as long as they'd been alive, so it was a blessed event.

They both loved their father but they admitted he was unfit to be a husband and barely passed the rules of fatherhood.

The morning of the wedding, the Beauvais house was beribboned and soft music flowed from the speakers in the living room. Janine and Michel Beauvais had been so delighted to have the wedding in their large home; they thanked them for the adventure. The special event went ahead despite everyone's nervousness, because nobody knew Conall's whereabouts. And although the police were still empty handed, the day was all excitement and ever-flowing wine. It was a vineyard, after all.

The twins were dressed in their finest. Michel kept them busy with toys and stories. His wife, Janine, fussed in the kitchen and the baker had just delivered a glorious wedding cake iced in light yellow, covered in miniature, fresh flower petals.

Janine Vinnier, who arrived in a flurry of activity, hugged Janine Beauvais. "We are kindred souls because we share the same name. I hope we will become friends." The ladies smiled at each other and anxiously waited for the musicians to arrive.

Olivia, Nicole and Callie dressed in one of Janine's guest rooms while the men nervously sipped glasses of sparkling wine. Olivier stood near Jules. Bram spoke quietly to Andres and introduced his new stepson, Roger, as the musicians arrived.

Two men in their seventies lugged in a bass and a guitar, an amplifier and their own chairs. Janine's eyebrows rose as they sat their musical instruments near her large fireplace just before the cleric arrived. The room was filled with a sense of delicious anticipation. The men began playing big band music amid French favorites as Callie peeked into the big room. Her mother in law nodded and Callie ducked back inside the guest room.

Nicole added the final ribbons to a small, intimate bouquet and kissed her mother's cheek. "I love you, Mom. You look truly beautiful today and I can't believe you are getting married in Provence!"

Olivia hugged her daughter tightly and choked back her tears. "Knowing you were close made the decision so much easier, darling." Her daughter was twenty four years old but still a child in her heart. She felt all of her fifty years when she saw her little girl walk toward the door in her pale, lace dress and spiked heels. Nicole turned around to give her mother a last-minute grin and thumbs-up sign.

"Livvy, you are about to become a bride again. Are you sure you want to go through with it?" Callie laughed at her friend's response. "Oh, so that's a yes?" The friends laughed and Olivia's chest heaved.

"I am nervous and surprised that I'm nervous. Marrying Bram is a melody and here in this beautiful home is a dream come true." She took a deep breath and placed the small, yellow-laced hat on her head.

The music beckoned.

Callie adjusted the flowers on Livvy's hat and thought her friend looked like a yellow vision from head to foot. When she'd given Livvy her mother's small pansy pin to wear, they'd cried off their mascara and had to begin again. After the tears were dried, Olivia thought of Callie living so far from her and it robbed her of speech.

Their long-time friend, Janine, popped in. *"C'est l'heure,"* she whispered. It's time. "Who is the most excited? Is it the bride, the matron of honor or the wedding planner?" She grinned and left the room.

Olivia's son, Roger, stood in the doorway with his arms open and she walked into them. Squeezing his arm, she put her cheek firmly against his shoulder and smiled when she saw his pant's leg shaking nervously.

Suddenly, the musicians began to play *May I have this Dance for the Rest of my Life*. Roger, a foot taller than his mother, pulled Olivia toward him. Putting his fingers over his mother's hand etched into the curve of his arm, he led her toward the fireplace beside the musicians where Bram waited. Roger grinned at Bram, delighted to see the look of devotion on the man's face and overjoyed his mother was finally marrying the right man.

Callie stood beside Olivia as the cleric asked who would be giving the bride away. Holding hands, her children both said "we do." And then Nicole joined Callie and Roger joined Bram. It was an unusual ceremony. Olivia and Bram decided they wanted to hold hands, light a candle and exchange rings with ribbons.

The cleric took the lighted candle, blessed them and tied a ribbon around their wrists. His bald head shone. It had taken him some time to agree. No typical wedding vows. Now, he was touched by its simplicity. Tying the yellow ribbon into a loose bow, he said "I now pronounce you man and wife. You may kiss your bride."

Olivia and Bram couldn't stop grinning at one another. Bram looked at his wife and leaned in to give her a chaste kiss. But Olivia grabbed him and didn't let go until the crowd's clapping erupted in hoots of laughter. Reaching around her waist, he pulled her tightly to his side; sure his face would crack from smiling.

Jules stood beside Callie as the group inched their way into the kitchen for wine, cake and refreshments. He reached for her hand and her fingers curled around his. "That was very nice, I liked it. I have never seen such a simple and spiritual wedding with everyone standing."

Callie turned toward him, pulled by the scent of his aftershave. She thought he was quite a beautiful man, not handsome in the typical way but strong and easy to be around. She let him lead her to the bride and groom and stood aside as Cendrine poured her special pink rosé into crystal flutes. Everyone picked up a glass as the bride and groom linked arms and lifted their glasses in the air.

Callie cleared her throat and everyone turned toward her. "I want to thank Bram for finally turning this woman around." Everyone laughed. "And I toast the beautiful life you will share because you are finally together." She turned to Roger, who took the gauntlet.

"I also want to thank you, Bram. You have been part of our lives so long, it seems only right that Nicole and I christen you. From this day forward, we will proudly call you Pop and we welcome you to our family."

Bram's face turned soft as he raised his glass. He and Livvy twisted their arms together and started to sip, but gulped it down instead. And then he turned to his new stepchildren and opened his arms. Olivia held a shaking hand up for a refill as her eyes met Callie's charmed smile.

Janine Vinnier was in her element. The beautiful cake was pulled aside. Photos were taken from every angle as wine flowed and more toasts were made. Bram did not let go of Olivia's hand except to eat his cake and sample tastings from each small plate on the table.

The party wound down by eight, the children were put to bed, Cendrine and Olivier had settled in for the night.

Their friend, Janine, didn't want it to end. "Callie, let's find a place to have more wine and talk, shall we?"

"Tomorrow, Janine, I am quite tired. Forgive me, but I must go put my feet up and find quiet."

Janine eyed Jules across the room. "He is your new friend, Callie?"

"Yes, he is an old friend of the family. Did you meet him?" They began walking toward Jules who was in deep conversation with Andres.

"*Oui*, he is intriguing. Hold on to him, Callie. But get to know every corner of his personality. Do not make the mistake I did and have blind eyes." She hugged Callie and slipped out the door after kissing Janine and Michel and promising to return tomorrow to clean up the debris.

Jules wandered over to Callie. "May I drive you home Callie or will you be staying awhile?" His eyes said more than his words. After kissing her in-laws goodbye, she allowed him to lead her away. They sat in his car a few moments when they returned to the mill house. When the cottage lights blinked out, they grinned at each other.

"I am very happy for my friends. It is a good day. Bram and Livvy fly to Málaga tomorrow morning, Jules. I am driving them to the airport, but Veronique has invited me to lunch afterward. Can you join us?"

He held her hand clasped between both of his and groaned. "No, *chérie*. I have an all-day meeting in Aix. I have fallen behind in my work and must catch up. Ask me again soon? I am tempted, but work demands my attention." Lifting the dark hair from her cheek, he leaned down and kissed her neck, his firm lips moving toward her lips. "Callie, soon, *oui*?"

Callie snuggled against him and smiled in the dark. When she entered the house after he drove away, her insides tingled and she leaned her head against the door. Over fifty and feeling like a teenager. She knew she was being swept away. The man was so much more than she remembered, but then again, she'd been married when she saw him last. Married to a man with secrets… *Enough.* She pushed away from the door and entered the guestroom, clicking the door behind her.

Thinking about the past two weeks kept her awake for hours as she tossed and turned, threw off covers, pulled them back over her and wished for dawn. She hated when this happened and tried to talk her way into sleep but it just wouldn't work. Finally, she switched on a lamp and began another list, this time on a pad and paper so she could give it to Olivia to take with them the next day for their trip to Algodonales. Every time she thought about Jules, she lost her train of thought all over again. "This is ridiculous," she whispered. She fluffed her pillow and turned off the light.

By the time she finally fell asleep, the sun was slipping into her window and little footsteps tapped outside her door. Whispers and giggling sounds made her grin. She shook her head at the sounds. *I can sleep tomorrow night.* She reached for her robe.

Callie drove the new bride and groom to the airport in Marseille just before noon while Olivia jammed the scrawled to-do list into her bag.

"Yes, we will have plenty of time in between honeymoon stuff," Bram promised. Olivia's smile was so radiant, Callie was unsure if it lit up the car or if the sun's weak rays reached inside to shine on them.

"Neither of us has been to Marbella or anywhere else on the Costa del Sol. And even though we have a fabulous honeymoon beach waiting for us, we promise to call you when we find answers to the questions on your list." Both smiling like children, Livvy pulled Bram away from the car and yanked her rolling bag behind her. Bram winked at Callie and then followed.

***

Inside the vineyard office, Olivier and Andres discussed the bottles locked in the cellar. They planned to carefully clean all the labels in preparation for the projected sale. After the escapades they went through to find them, they hated to give them up at all. But, of course they would. So much work had backed up in the office and the vineyard, they were unsure when Picasso's project could begin.

"Bram found a contact in Málaga who might help you create the foundation, Olivier. They will be staying in a hotel only an hour from Málaga. Also, they will drive to Algodonales to prospect for you. With Cendrine pregnant, I doubt you will want to leave again. Shall we ask Callie for help after Livvy and Bram fly back to America? The lovebirds can't spend much time on this research, but at least they will get you started." Andres pushed his beret on his head as Olivier nodded agreement and they each returned to their work.

Not far away, an old, black Volkswagen idled at the curb. Conall tapped the steering wheel rhythmically with his fingers. He looked up and down the long, broad road toward the vineyard. By the time he saw the old man leave Olivier's office, Conall was sweating profusely, and his knee was swollen twice its normal size. It was so tight and hot, he was sure if he stuck a needle into it, his leg would pop. He had driven with his left hand because his right shoulder was too painful to lift his arm. When the chills started again, he turned off the ignition and laid his head back on the seat. Was it all worth it? By now, the damn wine bottles must be here, hidden in that big house or somewhere on the grounds. He knew he was close. So far, he'd eluded the Jouques police. He snorted, wondering how they resolved any crimes at all.

With his left foot, he stashed the thick packet of money beneath the seat and used his fingers to push it another few inches to make sure it was hidden. He'd wanted to deposit it into his bank account at the Royal Bank of Scotland, but there were no bank branches in France. When his friend in Edinburgh lent him the key to the old storage room in Venelles, he hadn't believed his luck when he learned its proximity to Olivier's home. How ironic that it was exactly what he needed. It had been unused a long time and smelled bad, but he'd slept there until Olivier needed the cot. He pulled at his lip, remembering how difficult it had been to drag his cousin out the door of his home and stuff him into the small car. Olivier had been unconscious for so long, Conall had worried he might have killed him. And he hoped he was wrong! Although he had Olivier's money, he wanted those old brandy bottles too. How could he prove his worth to the old Scot if he couldn't even make this plan come together?

He exhaled loudly and shook his head. What a fiasco his great plan turned out to be. His thoughts turned to his old friend, Francisco. He bit his lip again. He shouldn't have stabbed him. His fists curled into his lap. "Dammit, he should have stayed out of it…hope I didn't kill him." His heart hammered tightly against his chest, wishing he was back in Scotland just doing his job. But seeing Olivier walking beside his beautiful, pregnant wife and their small children running around them had inflamed him weeks ago. Why did his cousin always get everything that was good? When would it be his turn? He groaned as he answered his own question: never.

The fiasco of the past two weeks exploded in his mind. His head was throbbing, his knee was on fire. Maybe if he just slept a little, he could think up a new and better plan. Just a few minutes were all he needed.

Twenty Five

Callie's mind was spiraling with design ideas for Veronique's new shop as she drove back to Pertuis from the airport. She maneuvered the car through the town's slender streets and cruised by, hoping the girl was there, but noticed the lights were unlit. Shrugging, she stopped by a bakery and picked up some pastries before returning to the old mill house. Just before turning into the vineyard's lane, she noticed a man slouched over a steering wheel in an old Volkswagen at the mouth of the drive. When she recognized Conall, she nearly ran into his car.

Horrified, she sped up. And then she walked into the house as sedately as possible, knowing Conall was watching her. With shaking hands, she got out her phone and punched in the number.

When Cendrine heard her conversation with the police, her eyes widened. She pulled Bernadette to her chest and moved quickly to the window to look across the lane. Sure enough, the car was still there and she could see a man sitting behind the wheel.

"Yes, *monsieur*. Conall Carson is the same man who broke into the house, attacked us in Jouques and is wanted for attempted murder in Malaga. Yes, we have already filed a report. I do not know if he is sleeping or unconscious, but I am afraid he might hurt us. He is sitting at the end of our lane right now in a black Volkswagen! Thank you."

Callie joined Cendrine at the window, willing the man to stay there until the police arrived. "Call Olivier, Cendrine. If we don't tell him what is happening, he will be angry that we kept silent."

Cendrine ran for her phone.

A moment later, Callie saw Olivier open his office door and motion toward them. Then he marched straight toward the Volkswagen.

"No, don't approach him, Olivier! What are you doing?" Callie stomped her foot and gripped the window curtain.

Cendrine was livid when she saw Olivier storm toward Conall. She was headed for the door when Callie grabbed her elbow. "Oh no, you don't...You are not taking Lulu out into that mess. Olivier is a big guy. One crazy person is enough out there. Please wait for the police. Olivier probably knows what he is doing. Conall can't still have a gun. The police have it. Please stay here with me." They looked at each other for a heartbeat before Cendrine nodded and joined her at the window again.

Olivier was nearly to the car, when Conall's head lifted from the steering wheel. The cousins stared at one another. Olivier continued toward him, fists clenched, his face blazing with anger. Conall opened the car door, but his knee had frozen in place and the slightest movement ripped a pain through his leg all the way to his hip.

Reaching the door, Olivier tried to haul his cousin out of the car, but then he noticed Conall was feverish, his eyes so glassy they couldn't focus. The man was unable to hold his head upright. "When are you going to leave us alone?" Olivier shouted. "You are one stupid bastard. If you think...." Conall curled forward on the seat. Sweat glistened on his forehead.

Loud sirens jerked Olivier into silence. Two police cars pulled up behind Conall's car and four policemen jumped out. Waving Olivier away, they approached with guns drawn.

"He isn't going anywhere, officers. He needs to be in a hospital." Olivier kicked the side of the car and loped toward the house. Cendrine threw herself into his arms. Soothing her, he whispered, "It is finally over. He is like a wilted flower. He's no threat to anyone. Shhhh...."

Callie heaved a huge sigh of relief and watched the police pull Conall out of the car and half carry him into the police car. After a few minutes of deliberation, both cars drove away, leaving the Volkswagen where it sat. She rubbed her forehead and lifted her silver bangs with a shaking hand. "Well, we can breathe easier now. The worst is finally over. And maybe the family will eventually retrieve the vineyard's money too.

***

By the time Jules left Aix after his meeting, he was exhausted, but as always, he checked his phone messages. His lips lifted in a grin when he saw Callie's voicemail. The grin changed to a full-fledged smile when he heard the news. Conall off the streets would put a smile on anyone's face. Driving straight home, he called Fernando Sanchez.

"*Mil gracious*, Jules." A million thanks. "*Francisco es bueno.*" Francisco is good. They chatted a few minutes, both relieved to know the problem was resolved and then Jules returned Callie's call.

***

Marbella, Spain is touted as a destination for the rich and famous. Bram chose it for the beach and the beauty promised in the tourist brochures. The Meliá Marbella Banús Hotel was perfect, beside swaying palms and citrus trees that turned the city into paradise. The landscape was so different from Oregon, he and Olivia could only stare like country bumpkins. They'd both traveled before, but Marbella sang a different beauty. When they arrived, they turned their faces to the sun.

"Sangría and tapas," Bram murmured. They walked along the wide boardwalk as the red and yellow Spanish flag flapped in the breeze. Marbella was full of history. Its origins dated back to 1600 BC, so Bram knew there was a little part of history in every corner of the old town, with its Moorish castle and famous Orange Square. The historical, old quarter with the Andalusian/Moorish mix could still be seen with its flower-filled balconies and narrow streets.

They saw hammocks for rent, with umbrellas made of dried grass, on the beach where sand stretched for miles. They walked along the boardwalk as the Atlantic Ocean lazily slurped up sand nearby, and they enjoyed the quiet in each other. The aroma of grilled fish wafted toward them and Bram studied the man behind the small stall. "Shall we eat fish here on the sand or find a restaurant? Not sure I want sand in my food, but it's up to you." He glanced at his bride.

Olivia grinned.

"Oh good. The hotel concierge told me there's a flamenco dinner show in the main room at 9:00 tonight. Let's make a reservation. We have four hours..." He raised an eyebrow and she gave him a sultry smile. He grabbed her hand and they walked toward the hotel again, no longer noticing the fisherman, the hammocks or the beach. It could all wait.

***

Meanwhile in Pertuis, inside the apartment she shared with Aurore, Veronique stared at her mother in exasperation. "*Maman*, what is it? You act like Callie is a devil. She has experience running a shop like mine and I can use her expertise. Why are you being so ugly about her?" She ran her fingers through her hair and yanked it in a knot at the back of her head.

Aurore ignored her. "Why do you need this woman? You learned enough in your classes and the mentor who befriended you. There are YouTube videos everywhere and there is the internet. I will find you some connections. You hardly know her, Veronique. I think it is inappropriate to hang on to her for new ideas. You should have your own ideas." Aurore's voice rose in anger. She would never allow her daughter to befriend her father's wife. Never!

"I do not understand you. Uncle Jules likes Callie very much and she has offered to help me. I see no sense to your words. And I want her help. She has experience and has already given me excellent ideas. Getting help from books and the university is only part of it, *Maman*. Please! It is something I want to do. I like Callie. I do not know why you are being so unreasonable and rude." Veronique took a deep breath. "I am going to the shop now. I will see you later if you have time to come around for dinner. If not, you can find me at *Gadoline's*.

Aurore simmered, standing in the middle of the room. She hugged herself harshly, squeezing her forearms until they hurt. When she released her fingers, her hands tightened into fists.

Veronique savagely twisted a long scarf around her neck several times, grabbed a notebook and tossed the car keys into her purse. Shaking her dark blonde head, she puzzled again at her mother's strange attitude. They had never been close, but she loved her and wished things were different. Veronique refused to allow her mother to run her life or her new business. Glancing at her watch, she had just enough time to meet Callie for lunch. She certainly hadn't wanted to tell her mother she was on her way to see her today after her mother's nasty remarks.

When Veronique entered the café, Callie beckoned toward her. They kissed each other's cheeks and then both began speaking at once. The canvas awning shaded them beneath the wintery sun as Veronique shared the morning's news. "The shelving is finished. I added the fabric as you suggested to the *faux* wall near the front door and my banner is promised to me within two days." She took a deep breath.

Callie's teeth gleamed behind a wide smile, enjoyment palpable on her face. After ordering two Beauvais rosés, the women tapped the rims of their glasses. "I am happy to hear it. You have not told me the name of your new shop…"

Veronique grinned. You will be surprised when you see the banner," she said mysteriously. "And I ordered my business cards. When I have a date for the grand opening, my good friend at the *La Provence* will place a photo and advertise in the newspaper…for free!" She was ecstatic.

Callie laughed and sipped her wine. "Veronique, when I opened my shop, it was one of the most exciting days of my life because I was sharing it with my mother. We both loved interior design. I love all those memories and listening to you, I get goose bumps remembering all over again."

A cloud rolled across Veronique's face. "Well, my mother never liked my choice. She wanted me to become a lawyer, like her, but it never appealed to me. I was more creative and leaned toward art and design. She never forgave me, I think." Lifting her flute, she sipped her wine with a faraway look on her face. She reached for her notebook after pointing to the salad on the menu and the girl sped away. "Tell me again, your ideas about the color design compared to the less-is-more suggestion you gave me at the shop. It intrigues me. The American viewpoints are not the same as the French and I want to blend the two together."

Callie nodded her approval. Leaning over, she explained her ideas, pleased she was making a difference in this girl's life. Their conversation flowed onto other topics and minutes slipped by unnoticed. The women were so focused on their discussion, neither saw Aurore stop and stare stonily at them through the window.

***

Aurore's angry face would have stunned them. She flipped her bag over her shoulder and walked away, muttering. Hardly believing that her brother would introduce his niece to that woman was bad enough. But seeing their instant connection rubbed her heart raw. A nasty gleam in her eye followed an idea brewing in her head but she wasn't sure if she could go through with it. The bitterness she'd carried inside for so many years still simmered although she tried to keep it from bubbling over. Surely this woman must know her husband fathered this child? Or, maybe not. Maybe she didn't know and maybe she should learn more about the not-so-saintly man she married. Her mind was abuzz with thoughts, trying to erase the entranced look she'd just witnessed spread across her daughter's face.

That evening, Callie's laptop rang. She shivered, hoping it wasn't Nate. She couldn't go through the turmoil again. Instead, she grinned and tapped the screen. "Don't tell me you two have run out of things to do on your honeymoon already?" she teased.

Olivia held a glass of sangría aloft. "We are fitting everything in that needs to be fit in," she answered with a wink.

"Ha ha...so cute, aren't we?" Callie pushed her hair behind her ear and leaned closer to the screen. "Feeling good every moment?"

Olivia's face didn't need words. "I am calling because we found you a law firm. Malaga Law Solicitors is independently regarded as the premier firm of English-speaking solicitors in Spain. The English side of the business is managed by *Paloma España*, being one of only a handful of dual-qualified solicitors in Spain entitled to practice as both a Spanish lawyer and also as an English solicitor. Bram and I are driving over to Fuengirola tomorrow afternoon to see if he will handle the arrangements on the buying end of those infamous bottles. Bram says you can scan the legal document from Picasso later." Olivia took an exaggerated gulp of her sangría. "Wish you were here...."

"Ha Ha. You are so full of it. I'm sure Bram would love having me share the honeymoon." She snickered. "Thank you, Livvy. This means so much to Olivier. Seeing his father's letter was emotional even without the Picasso story or brandy. Once he sells the brandy, he can fund the foundation and students can begin learning to play that flamenco. Thank the stars that Conall is out of the way…"

"What? Good news. The police caught him?"

"No, I did." She laughed at Livvy's face. Callie didn't realize eyes could get so big. "Well, not literally…go back to that gorgeous old man and stop thinking about lawyers and brandy…" Callie grinned widely and hung up.

When her cell phone rang a few minutes later, she was languishing in the positive energy from Olivia's phone call. She was so happy for her best friend, she could spit.

"Hey, you. Can you sneak away for dinner with an old friend?" Jules' voice sounded husky with intrigue.

"An old friend? Who's joining us?" He was so easy to tease that she took advantage of it every chance she got. She was pleased when she heard him chuckle. "Yes, I'd love it, Jules. I have some news I must give to Olivier and Cendrine. Can you get away by six and have a drink with us at the mill house before we leave?"

"I'd love to. As much as I like Cendrine's sparkling wine, though…I like Cabernet better. I'll bring my own bottle, hmmmm?" His voice was warm and soothing to her ears.

It was getting easier to admit that she hungered for this man.

When Jules arrived later that evening, Cendrine padded to the door to let him in. The children raced to welcome him. He laughed when he saw the apron stretching over her very pregnant belly covered in tomato sauce and a number of other stains.

"Come in, Jules. I'm making dinner, but the children can play by themselves," she said while she motioned for the short people to head back to their video. Find a seat and I'll bring you some wine. Callie is talking with Olivier in the living room."

He handed her a bottle of Cabernet and she looked askance at it. "So, are you telling me you'd rather have Cab instead of my pink…..?" She laughed at his contrite look. "Just teasing, this red is more a man's drink, right? I'll bring you a glass."

When he entered the living room, he found Callie and Olivier talking in earnest. The light from the lamp shone on her dark hair, making the silver streak in her bangs sparkle. When she turned toward him, her eyes smiled and he caught his breath. They shared a look and then Olivier was standing with an outstretched hand.

Cendrine brought two cabernets and two rosés and turned to Jules. You aren't the only one who chooses red over pink…"

Olivier grinned.

Jules lifted the glass to his lips and then remarked, "I wonder when the police are going to tow away that old Volkswagen they pulled Conall out of?"

Everyone shrugged.

After Callie repeated Olivia's conversation about the attorney, she saw Olivier smile. It seemed one more peg was placed in the board to connect the dots. The burden his father had placed on his shoulders was leaving its mark. Pablo Ruiz Picasso definitely knew a man he could trust when he asked Alexandre to carry out his dream. He was lucky that his son was as trustworthy. The mystery had impacted the lives of several people; changed some, hurt others and definitely would enhance the lives of many young, indigent Spanish people in the art of playing flamenco guitar.

"Livvy will call again tomorrow to tell me what the lawyer says. Another piece to the puzzle is their meeting with the owner of a guitar shop in Algodonales. The two should work together, don't you think, Olivier?"

Reaching his hand to touch Callie's arm, he responded, "Callie, any ideas to help finish this story helps us. Cendrine told me you never lost faith in me, even when the money was missing and nobody knew where I was. You are a special lady and I am very happy to hear you will stay home this time. France is where you belong. I see it in your face every time you look around. We appreciate you more than you can ever know." His eyes were moist as he lifted his wine glass in a silent toast.

When Callie's eyes filled, Cendrine leaned in and whispered, "Olivier just wants to smooth the way for you to babysit the children when Lulu arrives…"

The room erupted in laughter.

"Lulu?" Olivier teased. "I think you mean Bertrand. I am sure it is a boy. But, for a girl, I like the name of Chloe or Christianne, but I think it might be a tough sell."

"Chloe maybe…"Cendrine smoothed a hand over her belly, glad she'd removed the offending apron, and turned to Callie and Jules. "We have invited Bertrand and Christianne to dinner on Sunday. We want to invite you to join us when we invite *grand-mére* and *grand-pére* next time. I am anxious to meet them with Papa first. Olivier tells wonderful stories about his time with them except for trying to remember us…" Her face paled a bit.

"Only if I can help you cook, Cendrine. I do not want you waiting on me. There are only a few weeks before Lulu arrives," she added, rolling her eyes at Olivier's face. "I also believe it is a boy, Olivier, but…"

He solemnly agreed but followed with a wink, "Well at least we know it is one or the other…or twins again?" He laughed at Cendrine's face after she smacked his arm and nodded a vehement NO.

A couple hours later, Jules and Callie entered the candle-lit *Restaurant Gadoline*. Sheer panels swayed from the ceiling to add a romantic ambiance to the evening. She thanked Jules with a pensive smile when he led her to a table near a violinist who played French soft music.

"*Salut*, Callie, *enchantée*."

She tapped his glass and smiled at him over the crystal rim.

Halfway through their dinner, as Callie chewed on her lamb tempered with marmalade, she heard Jules groan softly. Lifting her head, she saw Aurore slipping through the tables toward them, like a storm cloud brewing.

"How nice to see you, Jules. You seem to have more time for Veronique and your friend's wife than you do for your own sister." She ignored Callie.

Jules' face paled at her rudeness. Turning toward his sister with a look of innocence, he responded, "Aurore, will you join us? I know you have already met Callie," he responded, forcing his sister to acknowledge his guest by reaching a hand across the table.

With disdain, she turned just a hair and nodded, but her face was filled with angst. "Yes, we have met. Veronique appears quite taken with you, madam. I understand you are visiting from America." Not waiting for an answer, she turned to leave when Callie responded.

"Actually…no, I am not visiting, Aurore. I am moving back to Pertuis. So, we will see each other again." Callie dabbed a napkin to her lips and dared to continue, "Maybe one day, we might become friends?"

Aurore's look of horror did not escape either of them. Wordlessly, she shot Jules a grim look and disappeared as quickly as she had arrived.

He rolled his eyes and pressed his lips together. Lifting his red wine to his lips, he shook his head. "I am sorry, Callie. There is so much history she is dealing with…."

Callie sighed sadly. She knew it would be a tough road to cross into friendship with the woman. She wanted to enjoy the new camaraderie with Veronique, though, and Jules. Hoping the woman's bitterness would not hurt her relationship with either of them. She drank the last of her wine and licked the remnants off her lips.

Aurore Armand thought her heart would burst from her chest as she left the restaurant without even telling her dinner date goodbye. Her heels clicked along the sidewalk, a staccato sound echoing behind her, sharp and mean. When she slung open her car door and slipped inside, she leaned her head on the steering wheel. "She stole François from me, but she can't have my daughter and my brother too!" She spat the words out harshly and pursed her lips. And then she smiled spitefully and drove home. She knew exactly what it would take to send the woman back across the ocean.

Veronique was stretched out on the couch when her mother returned from dinner. "You are home early, *Maman*. I thought you and Gaston would be much later. He is not coming in for his usual after-dinner drink?" Surprised at her mother's flushed face, she sat up and studied her.

Aurore appeared fragile for the first time that Veronique could ever remember. Her mother smoothed shaking hands down her dress, carefully replaced her coat in the closet and sat on a chair. Her eyes darted about the room and she reached over to straighten the framed photograph on the table beside her. When she leaned her head back on the chair, she closed her eyes and continued to tap her fingers in her lap. "No, Gaston is not coming tonight." Her eyes focused a moment and she grimaced. "I left him at the restaurant and he probably thinks I am still wandering around inside *Gadoline's* somewhere…*Merde.*" Shit. Aurore fidgeted a few more minutes, kicked off her shoes and carried them in her hand. I am going to bed," she said and slammed her bedroom door.

Veronique stared after her.

Meanwhile, still inside *Gadoline's*, Jules listened to Callie tell him about her ideas for Veronique's store. "She asked me to mentor her as a consultant for the shop. I was thrilled because it will be lovely to be part of that industry again, but with Aurore's feelings toward me, now I am not so sure." Her chocolate, brown eyes glistened. "Just when things were looking brighter, there is a fly in the ointment."

Jules chuckled only a little, as her words reflected her sadness. "Callie, now that you have met Veronique and you have become friends, how will that change your relationship with the Beauvais family? Will you keep her a secret from them? I fear if you recognized François in the girl, someone else is bound to also. I am actually very surprised nobody has noticed the resemblance before now."

She took a moment to answer. "She is their family, Jules. I shudder to think how she will respond when she learns about her father. For me, it was a shock because he betrayed her and lied to me by not telling me about her. For her, it could open the flood gates and children have been known to go either way. They are either so angry, they run from those who held it from them or they reach out and embrace their new family members. I have only known Veronique a short time, but I have a feeling she will take the latter road. She's been raised as an only child. So was I. And I hated it. But," she looked at Jules with determination, "it is not my story to tell. I will be there for her and for the family, but of course, I have no idea what the future holds for any of us."

Jules nodded. "And Aurore would never allow it. She should hear herself, see herself and get over the old hurts. It has been over twenty years. When will her bitterness end? I try to put myself in her place, but I think the answer is probably never. With Veronique at the center of the mad pull for control, she would indeed be the one hurt."

Callie slowly twirled her nearly empty wine glass, contemplating the thoughts rambling around in her head. And then she lifted it to her mouth and sipped the last dregs.

He glanced at Callie and said softly, "I think a quiet place would be nice... Now that Livvy and Bram are gone, you have your cottage alone again?"

She carefully replaced her glass and slipped the small, chocolate after-dinner mint into her mouth. When she lifted her face to his, silvery eyes were asking a question and she was unsure how to answer. When she saw the lines around his eyes crinkle in a smile, she decided a quiet place was exactly what she needed. Reaching her hand across the table to touch his fingers, she said, "are you ready, *monsieur*?"

He lifted her fingers to his lips.

The night was clear as they drove into the lane beside her cottage; Callie's thoughts were already inside. Following her, Jules saw her tap a finger to the side of a small black box. And then she plugged a cable that was attached to her iPad. "Pandora," she answered his look. When the soft music drifted from the speakers on the portable Bose receiver, Jules held out his arms.

She flowed into them and they began to dance. Sweet music, the music Callie loved best, filtered into the room. The living room was large and easily accommodated the gentle two-step as he guided her around slowly. Her head dropped to his shoulder and his hand moved to the back of her neck. When she snuggled closer, his lips dropped to her cheek and traveled around until their lips were a hair breadth apart. He cupped her chin and angled her mouth, nudging her lips open to deepen the kiss. The smell of fresh air clung to his hair, the taste of red wine lingered on his tongue and mingled with the taste of chocolate remaining in her mouth.

"Callie, you feel like magic. I want to make love to you. Tell me you feel this way too. Tell me I am not rushing you…tell me what you want, *ma chérie*." At fifty two years old, he'd seduced women, but it had been a game, none seriously, and it worked for years. Tonight, he admitted the game was off and he didn't want to play games with this woman.

Callie closed the distance with her lips and they continued dancing in a slow rhythm. Kissing deeper and deeper, Jules folded her tightly against his body. His arms tightened around her and she met his kiss when his tongue slid along her bottom lip.

"Jules," she whispered. "You know what I want." Her arms held him tight against her chest and she felt his breath on her face. The tiny flutter of emotion yanked her heart so hard, that she feared it would stop beating. Still, she found it difficult to push past the fears and vulnerability that had plagued her for so long. Still, she hesitated.

"Say it, Callie." His lips brushed along her cheek bone and she lifted her head, willing him to continue along her neck and farther. "Tell me."

She whispered his name again. "Jules, I want you to make love to me." When the words slipped out, his arms tightened and he pulled her to the couch and down onto his lap. Callie kissed his forehead, his eyelids, and the tip of his nose before finding his mouth again. When she pulled her head back, their eyes finished telling the story.

When she led him into the large bedroom, he tossed the decorative pillows off the bed and turned toward her. She was reaching for the hem of her sweater when he touched her hands and replaced them with his own.

Gently pulling the top off, he cupped her breasts, kissing them while her hands held his head firmly to her chest. When she arched toward him, he pulled her onto the bed and whipped her around beneath him.

"*Oh, mon Dieu*, Callie, I have wanted you for too long….." His dark hair fell over his forehead and his eyes turned silver as his body clung to hers. Warmth suffused his everything and his tongue touched the tip of hers in a mating ritual as old as the ages.

"You taste delicious and feel even better. I want…….." He stopped her with kisses and their clothes were soon piled on the floor beside the bed. Her sweet music continued to tinkle and waft through the bedroom as if she were taking part in someone else's love story. When his arm pulled her closer toward him and Jules made her his own, she knew the love story was truly hers.

Twenty Six

The hospital corridor was quiet when Olivier entered the wing. He saw a policeman sitting on a chair three doors down on his left. Conall. He tried to keep his mind from racing ahead, tried to pull back his anger for all the reasons he could smack down the man and walk away whistling. But his mind didn't behave as ordered when each step took him toward the room that held his cousin. He'd been told the knee replacement surgery went well and his cousin was awake.

When the officer looked up, he stood and braced himself against the door leading into the room. "This man is not allowed visitors, sir."

Olivier held out his hand. "I am his cousin. I must speak with him."

The officer stared at Olivier. "You will need official permission, *monsieur*. He has already escaped once. I am responsible to make sure this does not happen again. His shaggy eyebrows rose into his hairline, his hands braced on his hips.

Olivier saw a chair across the hall and pulled it over to sit beside the officer and asked him to sit down. After fifteen minutes of deliberation, the officer rolled his eyes. "Ten minutes and if you are not out, I will come in to get you."

When Oliver grinned, the officer tapped his arm and opened the door, leading him into the privacy of the room. Everything was quiet, the drapes were pulled and it was not quite dark in the room. Olivier saw Conall lying on the bed, his leg in a machine raising his knee slowly, an inch at a time. His knee joint had been demolished. His bat had done its job and Olivier felt just a bit guilty for not being sorry he was hurt so badly. Conall's shoulder had been damaged, but the surgery had not been life threatening.

He pulled a chair near the bed and touched Conall's arm.

When Conall turned his head toward Olivier, his eyes widened.

"Yes, your favorite cousin has come to visit, Conall." Olivier smirked, wanting to beat the man until he couldn't move. Instead, he looked into his cousin's blue eyes and said, "Why? Why would you jeopardize your life for some money when you have your whole life ahead of you? Why would you attack me and my family when we have never hurt you in any way? I know we have never been friends, but we are family, Conall." Olivier's eyes were sad, angry, confused and snapping mad.

Conall continued to look at Olivier. "How can I answer you, whom I've hated all my life? Ever since I was a child, you've taken the love I'd wanted so badly…for granted." He stared into blue eyes that matched his own and red hair only a shade lighter than his. Suddenly nervous, his eyes darted toward the door.

"No, the officer has left us alone for a bit, so don't expect him to walk in to save you. Your actions have given GrandPapa a stroke, Conall."

Conall tried to sit up, visibly stunned. "Is he…."

"He lives, but he is very angry. He does not understand why you would do this thing, Conall. And neither do I. We are family, for god's sake. This is not what families do to each other. I ask you again, why?" Olivier pulled the bed covering into his fist and stared into his cousin's face.

Conall exhaled loudly when the machine pulled his leg up too high and he grimaced. "My knee is hurting so badly, my brain can't function."

"Do you think I give a damn? You are such a slug for what you've done, Conall." Olivier's fingers itched to strangle the man, imagined pushing the writhing machine off the bed and his cousin's knee with it.

Conall exhaled again. "I have been jealous of you forever. You were always the one GrandPapa smiled at, the one he told others about, the one who could run fast, and the one who did well in school without trying. I struggled with every class, sometimes wondering if I would pass to the next grade. I worked hard but he didn't notice. Why should he? He had his precious Olivier." Conall's eyes filled and he squeezed them shut, refusing to allow unwanted tears to flow.

Olivier hardened his heart. "And I say again, do you think I give a damn? For that, you blackmailed me and frightened my family? Beat me, locked me up and treated me like an animal? Where is the money I gave to you? That money was the vineyard's funds and I want it back. Sure, I could run fast and all the rest, but I was willing to be your friend and you never wanted that. You always pushed me away. Again, I ask why? For money? For GrandPapa's notice? That doesn't make sense. My god, you even attacked your friend. You acted like a monster and frightened my wife and hit me senseless. If I hadn't found some good people to help me, who knows where I would be now? This just does not make sense. I was so angry, I wanted to kill you!" Olivier struck the bed beside the machine that continued to raise and lower Conall's leg, where his new titanium knee joint worked its way into his system. "And I want the vineyard's money back! Where is it?"

Conall turned toward him again. He reached his hand toward the fist that pounded the bed and gripped it hard. "Olivier! Saying I am sorry will not help right now. And I don't know if I'm sorry at all. I know I will go to jail and now GrandPapa will probably disown me…"

"….He has already disowned you!" Olivier rasped toward him.

Conall closed his eyes a moment. "In the car."

"What? What's in the car, the money?"

"Yes, under the driver's seat. I couldn't lock the car because I don't have a key. The Volkswagen is stolen. I hotwired the car at the hospital in Jouques. The money is in the same envelope you gave to me…under the driver's seat. It doesn't do me any good in here and it won't when I go to jail either." He laid his head back on the pillow, exhausted.

Olivier glanced at his watch, expecting the policeman to come in any moment. "In the car…" He shook his head and started to get up. Conall grabbed his hand.

"Do you know if my friend, Francisco, lives?" Conall's agitation was evident in his face. Staring at Olivier, he was afraid of the answer. "Tell me he is not dead, Olivier. Tell me it is so."

Olivier stared at the man. His red hair flicked down over his forehead. Conall's eyes begged for an answer. He got up, replaced the chair against the wall and turned to go, without answering. He didn't want to give his cousin the satisfaction or relieve his mind to know his friend lived.

"Olivier?"

Olivier stopped at the door, his hand on the wall, and turned to his cousin. "You could have killed me, Conall. You could have killed your friend. I wanted to kill you myself, but you know what? You have a life to figure out and maybe, just maybe, you will figure out what is important. No, your friend did not die." And then Olivier left the room, ignoring the sound of Conall's intake of breath and the sob that escaped his cousin's throat.

He shook the policeman's hand and hurried down the corridor. He had a date with a Volkswagen. He couldn't remember if he'd seen it still parked at the curb when he'd left the vineyard on his way to the hospital. He hastened his steps. Questions raced through his mind as he drove toward home. Would the police find the money and keep it for themselves? Cendrine had not disclosed the blackmail part of the story when she met with them. Would they believe him when he told them it was his money?

Twenty minutes later, he turned onto his lane and relief washed over him. In the headlights, he saw the old Volkswagen. He was stunned the police had not towed it away already. Olivier glanced around him, to make sure nobody was out on the street. Few houses were in the area where Conall had parked. Could he really be so lucky?

He turned off his headlights and rolled up behind the Volkswagen. He checked around the car again, looked in his rear view mirror, down the street toward the little shop on the corner. Nobody. When he slid out of his car and opened the Volkswagen's door, he wondered if Conall had lied to him. It would be so like him to do that. He clenched his jaw, got on his knees and reached his hands beneath the bucket seat. When he felt the fat envelope filled with euros and heard the crinkling sound beneath his hands, his chest expanded and heat filled his face. Wedged between the seats, he also found his cell phone. How could the police have left everything here? The money could have been stolen by anyone. The car could have been stolen. Pulling the envelope open, he counted the money. Despite seeing 700 euros missing, a relieved grin replaced Olivier's anger. Anxious to make up the difference and deposit the money back into the vineyard's account, he headed to Michel and Janine's.

***

Sunday afternoon, Olivier opened the door to pull Christianne and Bertrand Deniau inside. He put his arms around them in a huge hug as little footsteps raced around the corner from the kitchen and skidded to a stop. Two pair of wide eyes stared at the strangers.

Christianne reached a hand down to their level and they crept forward, their eyes on their father. When they saw his nod, they moved toward her tentatively and their surprise was replaced with shy grins.

The men laughed and Olivier closed the door. "Cendrine will be here any moment, please sit. It is very good to see you. You are both welcome in our home. Now, it is my turn to share my food with you." He drew them into the living room and they sat, smiles fixed to their faces.

"*Merci*, Alexandre…I mean, Olivier." Bertrand tightened his hands against his knees and the air seeped out of his lungs as he relaxed against the easy chair.

Christianne lifted a large box toward Olivier at the moment Cendrine rushed down the steps, holding her belly to guide the way. All eyes watched her as she walked toward them and her eyes smiled. "Ah, you are Christianne and Bertrand, our new best friends." When she reached the old couple, she motioned Bertrand to remain seated. She turned to each of them, bent her bulky body down and hugged them soundly, kissing each of their cheeks.

Olivier beamed and reached for his wife's hand. She clasped it, held it tightly against Lulu and turned to the old couple. "Wine! We must have wine. I will serve you my specialty…" She started to move toward the kitchen, but stopped and turned. "You do like pink sparkling wine, *non*?"

They nodded yes and then Christianne followed her into the kitchen. "I can help you, Cendrine." She placed the bakery box on the long counter, grinning when Cendrine eyed it curiously. "Yes, please open it. When Olivier was with us, we learned to love him and he helped us in the bakery. He also learned to bake bread and small cookies. I was sure the children would enjoy these and there are baguettes in there also." She proudly opened the box to display the pastries and bread inside.

Cendrine rubbed her hands together with excitement after peeking inside. "Oh, I might share some...*Merci,* Christianne." She closed the box and patted the older woman's shoulder. "Let's gather our wine and then I want to learn all about the two of you. You saved my husband from that beast of a cousin and I thank you always." She touched her lips with her fingers and smacked them, tossing a kiss toward the woman.

Christianne placed a hand to her trembling mouth and smiled. "We helped each other, *chérie,* and we are very happy to be here, meet you and these beautiful children. And now, there will be a new child soon."

With a happy nod, Cendrine lifted the tray of chilled rosé and invited Christianne to bring the small plate of grapes and fresh brie.

The men's voices were deep in conversation, but when they saw the wine and food, they abruptly stopped and the women laughed. Food usually won over words any day. While the children eyed the newcomers, the adults enjoyed learning about each other.

"Our son lives in Aix," Bertrand answered Cendrine's question.

"He makes *santons* and loves creating the hand-painted figurines to look like characters in all the villages for the Christmas nativity scenes. He tells us the small figures sell faster than he can make them, and it is not just to observe the midnight mass celebrations," she added. "His figurines are so popular, many shops now sell them and he also sells them on the internet." She beamed, fiercely proud of her son's success.

Cendrine sipped her wine. "We have several *santons* for our Christmas celebrations. The children love placing them around the animals in the nativity. I wonder if he made any of our figurines? Does he sign them?"

Bertrand glanced at his wife for an answer. "*Oui,* you will find *Deniau* in black paint on each one he creates.

Olivier and Cendrine invited everyone into the dining room at the same time Andres knocked on the door. The aroma was enticing and the table was set beautifully, a testament to Cendrine's love of cooking.

He pushed the door open. "Sorry, I am late...did you eat without me?" The old man's eyes danced. "I had to get something...." He stuffed his hat into his pocket before hanging his coat on the hall tree by the front door.

After introductions, Andres thanked the couple for watching over Olivier and stashed a small box behind a picture frame. The conversation among the group did not slow down the children's eating or the teasing between them.

"*Non*, François! I asked first." The little girl's eyes filled with tears. "Mine." Her long red curls slipped over her face and she pulled the bread from her brother's hands.

"We have more bread, children...." Christianne scooted back the chair and lifted the top from the box she'd delivered. When she scooped the miniature bread loaves from the box and placed one on each small dinner plate, she was awarded with small smiles through the tears. She lifted a hand to her heart and smiled at Olivier.

Andres explained the vineyard's processing to Bertrand, but his eyes soon glazed over. When the conversation turned to *Petanque*, the game of boules, perhaps the sport that is closest to French hearts, the men found an instant camaraderie.

"We meet in the park near our bakery in Venelles every Saturday morning." Bertrand clapped Andres on the back. "You come and I beat you, agreed?"

Andres laughed, lifted his glass of wine and caught his daughter's eye. As he swallowed the sparkling wine, he grew impatient to show her the box on the shelf near them.

Soon, the old couple kissed and hugged everyone goodbye amid promises to see everyone again very soon. "Saturday, Andres!" Bertrand called as the door closed behind them.

Olivier and Cendrine stood with clasped hands while the children waved small hands from the window.

Andres reached for his daughter's hand. "Now, you sit. You have been standing too long in the kitchen, *ma chérie*." His lined face was animated and one would think he was much younger than his years. Cendrine raised her eyebrows and let him lead her to the couch.

"What, Papa? Now I am a wilting flower?" She laughed.

Olivier sat down beside her, equally as curious, when Andres dropped a small flat box into her lap. Lulu kicked against her belly and it slid toward the floor, but she caught it deftly causing everyone to chuckle.

Looking at her father's face, Cendrine knew it was something momentous because his eyes were nervous. He promptly dropped into the chair next to them. When she looked inside the box, her hands shook. She let the lid slip back over the contents and went to her father to kiss him on the top of his head.

"What is it?" Olivier was at a loss.

She grinned, handed him the box and he looked inside. When he saw the wine label, he knew why his wife had turned to jelly. The Beauvais label template had been placed over the words, *Chloe's Rosé*. When Olivier's head snapped around toward his wife, both her hands covered her flushed cheeks.

"Now, that Olivier is home again, you can begin the new wine just about the time your baby is born…and I will help you all the way," Andres told her. He cleared his throat and stood up to gather his coat. When he pulled his hat from the pocket, he said, "Now, it is time to put these old bones to bed."

Cendrine pressed the label template to her chest. Throwing her arms around her father, she felt another dream soon to be realized; she would add another label to Beauvais Cellars. She kissed him on the cheek loudly and danced him in a circle.

Just a little embarrassed, Andres grinned at his daughter, nodded to Olivier and then whistled as he left them.

Twenty Seven

When the sound of a Skype call floated into the bedroom from her laptop the next morning, Callie rolled over on her side and held her hands beneath her pillow. She was staring into Jules' face as his dark eyelashes flickered and lay on his cheek like butterfly wings. When the music chimed again, his eyes flicked open and he smiled at her languidly.

"Good morning." He wrapped his arms around her and pulled her on top of him, laughing when she giggled. Tingling sounds drifted in from the living room. "We left music on?"

She laughed and rolled off of him. "No, it's a Skype call. It's probably Livvy. She told me she'd call this morning to tell me about the meeting with the lawyer yesterday. How great is that... for her and Bram to do Olivier's leg work, even on their honeymoon?" She slipped out of bed and opened the laptop. When she saw Nate's photo on the screen, she dropped the laptop lid, holding her breath a moment to compose herself.

Jules stood in the doorway. "Olivia?"

"Missed it. We can connect later. I can, however, pour us some steaming coffee." She walked toward him and wrapped her arms around his waist. When he dropped his chin to the top of her head, she mumbled, "...so good."

Sighing deeply, he whispered into her curls, "I have an early meeting but coffee first would be excellent. In fact, I might have a bit more time than it takes to drink a cup of coffee..." He grinned.

"Really?" She glanced at her naked wrist. "Hmm...as it happens, I have some extra time too." Her heart thumped. She was surely home at last.

***

The children had been wild all morning. When Cendrine glanced out the window, her face changed from frustration to surprise and then to delight: Jules' BMW was parked discreetly along the side of the cottage. As she served the children their fruit and croissants, she couldn't erase the smile from her face. "Yes!"

After Jules drove away, Callie wandered through her old garden. Her mind drifted. *I will see the buds burst into bloom in the spring and the bright poppies flap their wispy petals in the breeze. The landscape will soon green up and the house will be ablaze with color along the borders and the lane. And I will be here to see it.* She wrapped her arms around herself and did a little dance, happy her ankle was completely healed from the craziness last year. There was a cool wind flicking gently at Callie's cheeks when she glanced up and saw Cendrine's grinning face watching her and motioning her inside.

When Callie got to the door, Cendrine wrapped her arms around her and pulled her into the kitchen. Protecting her baby belly from the edge of the counter automatically, she handed Callie a cup of coffee, a container of cream and pushed her into a chair.

"Okay, tell me." Cendrine's enthusiasm was alive with curiosity.

Callie's face was worth a thousand words. "So, you have been spying on my cottage activity?" She stirred the cream in her coffee and laughed at the slight pink that rippled across Cendrine's cheeks. Reaching over to tap her niece's hand, grins split both of their faces.

"So, the cautious wait you worried about, is gone?" Cendrine was eager for details, hoping to hear the big love story. When Olivier left that morning, she was thinking of her own, but seeing Callie like this was more than she had hoped for.

Wanting to hold onto the feelings just a while longer, Callie didn't answer. Instead, she sipped her coffee and her brown eyes shone with happiness. For now, that was all she would offer Cendrine. *For now, the beauty of the man is all mine.*

When Olivia texted Callie to alert her to their Skype call, she left the house and returned to her cottage. She hoped she could keep her face from sharing it. *It will be hard to keep this from my best friend but damn, I am not ready to share this intoxicating feeling.*

"*Halo* from *España*," Olivia said immediately. "I am going to email you all the pertinent information, Callie. Bram is positive this man will be perfect for the job. You can just forward it all to Olivier; Bram forgot to get his email address. We are driving to Algodonales for lunch. We've contacted a man to translate for us and the guitar shop's owner is curious to meet with us. Do you want me to take photos with my phone?"

"Perfect to everything, Livvy. We can't thank you enough. How's the honeymoon going?" Callie asked wickedly.

Bram's face filled the screen. "Perfect and now we're off to the beach, although I'd hoped it would be warmer. Honeymoon here we come."

"Oh, a honeymoon on the beach?" Callie teased.

"You are wicked, Callie." He shook his finger at her.

After they hung up, she laughed and decided to look for Andres in the vineyard. It was time for a walk through the vines. He always let her taste new brews and Bram whispered something about a virgin wine.

Several hours later, Callie returned to the cottage with the taste of Andres' new blend on her lips. In her rush to visit her in-laws with Cendrine and the children, she hadn't noticed the brown envelope wedged into the grille work of her kitchen window.

Michel and Janine were sipping coffee with their new friend, Janine Vinnier when Callie, Olivier, Cendrine and the children arrived in the late afternoon. After rehashing the beautiful wedding, Callie brought them up to date on Bram and Livvy's research in Spain. Afterward, they were blessed with another sumptuous meal in the old home place's brightly-tiled kitchen.

"Janine, I knew you would make Livvy's wedding fabulous and I wasn't wrong. I'll be anxious to hear about the next part of your life. Maybe go into wedding event planning?" Callie was awed by her French/American friend's talents, but she also worried about her every-day life since her husband sat in an American prison.

Pausing to answer, the French woman lifted a tremulous smile toward Callie. "I have sold the condo in Portland. Vincent will be in prison forever and I am divorcing him. Nan Donofrio offered me a job in her

Senate office and I may do that. I will find a house near my sister in Alexandria, Virginia. For now, I will remain in France for a few weeks. Living among my native people will help my wounded heart. And I can watch over you, *ma petite*." She laughed and squeezed Callie's hand. "I am happy you are staying here, but we shall miss you in America."

Callie noticed how much more relaxed her friend was now that her husband was out of her life. The man had not only cheated and hurt people, but he let another man die and then attempted to kill the man's wife afterward. But that was last year in America…Here in France, Callie would also start a new life. She watched her friend and mother-in-law chat about cooking, wine, the vineyard and the old home place.

The younger Janine said, "Callie, your family is woven together like a fine tapestry. I wish my life had been different, but it is never too late to push us toward new horizons. You seem more relaxed here than you were in America." Janine sighed. "Life is a crazy puzzle sometimes and I hope you will fit the puzzle pieces into the correct holes like I plan to do."

Callie reached over to squeeze her friend's fingers.

As the children tired, Olivier pulled his son on his lap and raised an eyebrow to Cendrine. She nodded and lifted Bernadette to her feet. After hugging everyone, they all turned to leave and asked Callie if she was ready?

Callie's eagerness to leave did not go unnoticed. Her in-laws wondered if Callinda was possibly finding a life beyond their beloved son, François. Bittersweet though it was, they wanted to see her happy. When Janine Beauvais walked Callie to the door, she pulled her aside and placed a hand on each of Callie's shoulders. "Callinda. Thank you for making an old man and woman happy by staying in France. You will always be our daughter. We want you to find happiness. We love you." She kissed Callie's forehead.

Callie's eyes filled with tears and she held the old woman tightly. Rocking back and forth a few seconds, she leaned back, kissed her on both cheeks and smiled at Michel who nodded from his chair. And then she squeezed into the back seat between two little people who were determined to have all her attention. She laughed all the way back to the cottage.

Entering her cottage a few minutes later after goodbye kisses and hugs for the children, she stood with her back pressed against the door. Closing her eyes, she exhaled slowly before peeking at the clock. Turning on her Bose receiver, music softly filtered through the rooms. After fluffing her bangs, she decided to use the extra minutes to gather her old fabric samples and the photo book. Veronique was arriving at ten in the morning to go over last minute details. *I wonder who is more excited to open this shop, me or Veronique? The days were so full of exciting new ideas when Mom and I started our shop and once we set a date to open, time raced by.*

Why she brought both books to France was a mystery. *Was it really twenty five years ago that the ideas propelled me to balance colors, sizes, shapes and contrast?* She smiled. *Mom was so full of excitement; I wonder who drove who to make it happen?* Sitting on the couch, she pulled her fabric sample book onto her lap. Touching the self-made cover, she rubbed her fingers across the label, caressing the raised letters. *Augustine's Taste of Life.*

When Jules knocked lightly on the door, she jerked out of her reverie and felt a bubble expand in her chest. When she pulled him inside, he reached down to nuzzle her lips.

Jules was grinning at her. "*Halo, ma chérie.* I did not bring flowers or wine. I just brought me."

"Well, I wonder if I should let you in then?" She teased.

"But of course you should..." He sat in the nearest chair and pulled her onto his lap. "Now, tell me about your day."

Air crackled around them as Callie and Jules talked softly for over an hour before she put her head down on his shoulder. "Jules, I am so comfortable with you."

His husky voice mumbled something into her curly hair. She lifted her face to look into his gray eyes. The wanting was obvious as he kissed her, softly at first and then more demanding. The romantic voice of Charles Trenet serenaded them as he lifted his questing hand to the ties that held her satin caftan together. When she groaned softly, he unfolded himself from the chair and pulled her chin up, his lips were nearly touching hers. She reached for his hand.

In the bedroom, Jules lifted the hair from her neck and kissed her so gently she thought of butterfly wings. The thrill racing through her body rooted her to the floor. Everything inside her dipped and swirled before exploding outward in a million points of sensation. She felt alive and vibrant, connected to another man for the first time since François, a place where Nate had never touched.

Grinning, he lay down and pulled her on top of him. "Callie, you make me want to do things I haven't thought about in a long time. I have a business to run, clients to woo and your face slips into my thoughts all day. What am I to do with you?" His eyes saw her face warm at his words.

"*Monsieur* Armand, must I tell you how to do everything?" she demanded. She dipped her face close and brushed her eyelashes across his cheek, inhaling his musky smell. Her lips touched his cheeks, his neck and then came back to his mouth. When her tongue gently touched his lips, he drank in the sweetness.

Early the next morning, with their clothes and bed linens in disarray, Jules whispered against her hair. "Callie. People say you can't be mesmerized by another this fast, but they are wrong." He inched his torso up and smiled down at her mussed hair and black, mascara-drenched eyes.

Pulling herself up on one elbow, she looked at him. "I agree. My heart has been flapping in the wind like the petals on a spring flower." She pulled his head down and he wrapped his arms around her. When he saw the clock, he yelped.

She jumped.

"I have an important meeting this morning and I am the speaker. It's seven already. I must leave by eight thirty." His eyes swung between her and the clock. When he saw her face, he pulled her down into the sheets and Callie felt his hand on her hip. Not long afterward, Jules closed his eyes as she exhaled a rasping, long breath and kissed the side of her head as she shuffled down in bed to rest on him.

Twenty Eight

Thirty minutes later, the sun beat through the curtains while Callie changed into a loose wrap, smiled at the man who filled her bed, and left him to prepare coffee. *I cannot imagine a day without him.*

Before the pot finished perking, Jules walked up behind her and kissed the back of her neck. When he lifted a bright red cup from the cupboard, he noticed a brown envelope fluttering on the outside of the window. Perplexed, he turned to Callie. "Your mail is delivered to the cottage?"

"No, why?" She looked at him while she inhaled the delicious aroma of fresh coffee permeating through the cottage. Her brow furrowed.

"There's an envelope in your kitchen window..." He opened the front door, pulled the envelope loose from the grille and gave it to her before he returned with their cups.

She shrugged when she saw the envelope had no return address. When Jules handed her the coffee, she sipped a little of the hot brew before unsealing it. "That is so strange." When she slid the piece of paper from the envelope, she started reading the letter and put her cup down in slow motion. When she finished it, her brow creased, sending her pulses spinning. A date stamp showed the letter was hand delivered to the recipient. She lifted her eyes to Jules in alarm. And a new anguish filled her heart as a soft gasp escaped her.

"Callie? What is it?"

Her hands shook so badly that she dropped the letter.

His face clouded with uneasiness. "Callie. Tell me, *ma chérie*."

Staring at Jules, a swift shadow of anger swept across her face. She was unsure what to do. She'd made a terrible mistake once by assuming the worst of someone she cared for and she didn't want to make the same mistake again. She would not cry. She would not scream. She would not faint. She would talk. Handing the letter to Jules without a word, she lifted her cup of coffee again, carefully balancing it on her lap as he read the words that could damage everything they'd held dear.

Violation de L' Avis de Marché

M. François Jacques Beauvais
4362 S.W. 35th Place
Portland, Oregon 97221

RE: Rupture de Contrat

Monsieur Beauvais,

    Se IL VOUS PLAÎT PRENEZ AVIS que vous êtes en violation de notre contrat intitulé « Accord de soutien financier du 30 Septembre, 1992 (la contrat). Plus précisément, vous avez violé l'obligation suivante (s) en vertu du contrat:

    Se IL VOUS PLAÎT AVIS EST ÉGALEMENT DONNÉ que sauf la violation est corrigée dans les dix jours suivant la date de cette lettre, je vais prendre des mesures pour protéger mes droits en vertu du contrat et en vertu de toute loi française applicable. Tous mes droits sont réservés par le présent avis.

    En vendant votre vingt pour cent la propriété dans mon entreprise à mon concurrent au lieu de m'offrir la première offre d'encaisser, je n'avais pas d'autre choix que de poursuivre ton cul. Vous pouvez me contacter si vous avez des questions.

Cordialement,

Jules Luc Armand.

Jules Luc Armand
Compagnie des Machines Armand
23 Rue Benjamin Franklin
Pertuis, France

Callie was numb. The end of the letter was blatantly seared into her mind. 'By selling your twenty percent ownership in my business to a competitor instead of offering me the first offer to cash you out, I had no choice but to sue your ass.' Jules had sued François for breach of contract. The day François received the letter, he'd raced their boat across Devil's Lake in a terrible storm and didn't live to tell about it. The day he received that letter was the day he died on the lake.

"Please tell me there is a mistake, Jules," she whispered.

His luminous eyes widened in astonishment and his expression darkened with an unreadable emotion. He reached for her hand but she pulled it aside. "It is true, Callie, but it is also not true. François threw me under the bus. When I started my business, I told you I had financial backers. That was François and Aurore. Each gave me money and in exchange, I gave them stock in my new company. Both Aurore and François accepted twenty percent stock. They both agreed that if either wanted to cash out of the company, I would buy their stock and they would have cash immediately." He looked at her wearily as he ran his fingers through his dark hair, just turning grey at the temples. His eyes were silver with emotion as he continued, "One day, one of my competitors contacted me. He said he'd just purchased twenty percent of my company from François and asked when the next Board meeting was being held. I was stunned and hurt."

Callie's eyes explored his face as she searched anxiously for the meaning behind his words. Her silence loomed between them like a heavy mist.

When she didn't speak, he went on, "I called François that day and he apologized. He said he needed money fast. I asked why he didn't ask me first, as he'd promised. He said I was already furious about Veronique and Aurore. He didn't want to add to my misery by admitting he was in a fix. It didn't make any sense. And I was devastated." He leaned over and placed his elbows on his thighs, making the jeans stretch tightly over his knees. He hung his head.

A cold knot formed in her stomach and she clenched her jaw to kill the sob in her throat. Her hair was awhirl around her head and her face shone with anger. She closed her eyes and shook her head to remove the image of François' boat racing across the lake that day. *Why would François do that to his best friend? And why didn't I know he held stock in Jules' company?* The questions mounted, but she was too overwhelmed to look for answers.

"But Callie, I did not do this."

Her eyes widened and anger lit her eyes. "This letter is a fake? You are telling me it's a lie?" Her voice was hoarse with frustration.

Denial flew from him. "I told my lawyer I was angry at François' betrayal, but I have never seen this letter. My lawyer wanted me to sue him and for a heartbeat, I entertained the idea, but I changed my mind. I never signed this. That is why I am shocked to see it. I would not sue François. He was like my brother. I walked away from it. The company that purchased his twenty percent eventually blended into our company and now he is a friend. Please believe me, Callie," he asked with deceptive calm.

She heaved a deep sigh. "Well, your lawyer evidently chose to ignore your wishes, Jules, and I believe this letter contributed to François' death. I could never understand why he went out in the boat that day. The storm was terrible, black clouds, strong winds…"

"Callie, I was angry. As a businessman, I had every right to send this letter to a man I'd trusted all my life. He betrayed me as a friend and as a business partner. My business was successful and he knew it. I could have given François the money easily. After this happened, I had difficulty trusting anyone for a very long time. When he died in that boat accident, my heart was broken. I loved him and not being able to say goodbye to the man was devastating…" He sniffed and shook his head while searching her face.

She looked up at him, her brown eyes still flashing. "You better talk to your lawyer to find out what happened. Why was this letter left for me?" Her head jerked and she sat back as light dawned. "Who *is* your lawyer, Jules?" A tinge of exasperation had entered her voice. She was afraid she already knew the answer.

His eyes shifted momentarily. "Aurore."

"Aurore... Why am I not surprised?" Her lips thinned. "Jules, you are going to be late for your morning meeting." She stood up, tossed the letter into his lap and walked into the kitchen.

Jules' face had a wounded expression, like she'd kicked him. He shut the door loudly behind him. As he rounded the front of his car, a thought escaped his lips, "François, you are reaching out to wound me again." He wrenched open his car door and drove away.

When gravel flew from beneath his wheels, the flowers were not so bright, the day was not as beautiful. She had a raging headache. And Veronique was due to knock on her door within two hours.

By the time Veronique arrived, Callie had showered and dressed, although she moved like a robot. It happened a long time ago, she told herself, and nothing would bring François back to answer all the questions she had building up inside her head. She pasted on a smile and opened the door.

Veronique nearly danced into the room wearing a brown tunic over black leggings. The varied-colored scarf entwined around her neck was bright yellow with black polka dots. She looked like a bumble bee. "Good morning, Callie. I have good news. I have set a date for the grand opening and my inventory has started to arrive. I do not want to create my samples book though, until I see yours, *oui?*" Her light hair swung back and forth in excitement as she rearranged the long scarf looped double around her neck.

Callie laughed a little, glad she'd pulled out the books the night before. "Here, you start glancing through these and I'll get our coffee. Cendrine made some banana bread. I want you to meet her before you go back to the shop, once you devour my books." Uplifted by the young woman's enthusiasm, Callie's gloom began to slide away.

As Veronique turned each page, her excitement mounted. Pointing to the top of one page and the middle of another, questions mounted in her brain. "Callie. I want to sell two specific items in my shop, different from many. To make it stand out, *oui?* When I was a child, *Maman* always let me choose a *santon* at Christmas. They are little saints, painted in vibrant colors and always placed in Provencal nativity scenes. You know this tradition?"

Callie smiled, "Yes, François and I have some in a box somewhere."

"Well, they emerged in the 18th century after the French Revolution suppressed observance of Christmas Eve Midnight Mass and families created their own nativity scenes in their homes. These nativities were enriched with figurines representing characters of the village. I had a baker, a cheese maker, the meat man and candy man. It is something I have dreamed about including in my shop since I was at University. I must find a *santon* artist." She clapped her hands like a child.

"And the other item you want to include?" Though there was a pensive shimmer in the shadow of her eyes, Callie was riveted to the young woman's energy.

"Lavender. I want to plant an acre of lavender. Uncle Jules knows someone with space in the back of a vineyard, where old vines were just removed. I want lavender scents in my shop and customers will leave with bouquets tied with raffia. I may even move on to selling it to perfumeries."

Callie was stunned to hear the big ideas coming from the girl. Sitting down with her hand on her chest, she breathed a sigh. "And I shall help you. We have a vineyard on three sides of us. And there must surely be a free acre. I like this idea very much, Veronique!" Sitting beside the young woman, she snapped her finger across the cover of her sample book. "Do you see anything in here that might help you?"

"Oh, the sample pages are just what I love. Remember, I told you I wanted to offer a design shop different from all the others? It will be French and American, a hybrid shop. *Maman* thinks it is silly, that only French will sell. She says in America, everyone wants French and here in France, they scoff at American designs. I think she is wrong." She ran her fingers across Callie's swatches and imagined the book she would create for her own.

"I cannot keep it a secret from you, Callie. My shop is called *Hybrid Designs*, because I am weaving French with America. Do you like it?"

"I love it! Yes, it is unique too. When is your grand opening, Veronique?" Callie stirred creamer into her coffee and lifted a slice of banana bread. Her throat was still a little clogged but she staved it off. "I have a surprise for you in my mind that will take some planning."

Veronique lifted her head and grinned at Callie. "*Oui?* I love surprises. What is it?" Her wheat-blonde hair fell over her shoulders, her eyes anxious for her response.

Callie grinned. "Well, it wouldn't be a surprise if I told you, now would it? The other book has photographs of our old shop." She was pleased to see Veronique begin thumbing through the photo book pages. *Augustine's Taste of Life* shop held so many memories that she decided to look through the book again when she had time. There were photos of the shop inside and out with her mother and with….." Her eyes rounded at the next thought.

Veronique turned the next page and drew in her breath. "Who is this man, Callie?" Her finger traced the side of the brick building in the photo. Near the front door swung a grand opening banner across the window. The man pointed to the banner, but his smiling face stared into the camera. His dark blonde hair was rumpled by a soft breeze and his knee was bent as if holding up a heavy sign.

Forcing herself to appear calm, Callie glanced at the page. "That was my husband, François Beauvais." Heat rushed through her as she watched Veronique.

The girl's face moved from the photo and stared at Callie, disoriented. "He has my face," she whispered. Her heartbeat sped up and she pressed a hand to her lips. She whispered again, "How can this be? Callie?" Her whiskey-colored eyes tore away from the photograph and the question on her face burned into Callie's heart.

It wasn't Callie's story to tell, but she couldn't bear to lie to Veronique. She took a deep breath and moved to sit beside the girl, knowing she had no choice. Licking her lips to hold them steady, she lifted the coffee to her mouth and looked at her over the rim. Then, she replaced it on the table very slowly as she had earlier that morning. *Another pile of poop to wade through.*

"Veronique. Tell me about your father."

The girl was surprised by the question. "He died before I was born. That is why I have the Armand name; *Maman* was not married to him yet. It was an accident somewhere in Paris. She had no photos of him. And she never married. It has just been me and *Maman*. Always. Why? Did you know my father?"

"Yes. I learned about your father the day I met you."

"Oh, uncle Jules told you about him?"

"No, you did." Callie's eyes stared into her face.

Veronique stared at her and stammered in bewilderment. "I d-did? What do you mean?"

Callie whispered. "You have his smile. You have his eyes. And now you have just seen his face. Your mother should have told you a long time ago but he made her promise not to do that. And this revelation should not be coming from me, Veronique." She placed her hands over the girl's fingers where she clutched the edge of the photo album.

Animation left Veronique's face as she stared at Callie for a beat before returning to the photo. When she looked at Callie again, her eyes were filled with tears and her mouth worked. "François Beauvais was my father?"

"*Oui.*" Yes.

Veronique slammed the book shut. Her eyes were blazing. Hurt and shock had just been upgraded to anger and she wanted answers. "I had a father all my life until a few years ago and he did not want to see me? He did not want to know me? How could you love such a man? How could *Maman* love him? She would never tell me about my father except to say he was beautiful and made her heart sing. When I asked why there were no photos, she said it was because he was very poor and they had no money for photos. Of course, I believed her. All this time…I believed her…"

Callie gave Veronique a handkerchief and the girl blew her nose hard. Still snuffling, she squeezed her hands around the photo book now clasped against her chest. All these years….." Veronique's sniffle hid the remaining words.

During the next hour, Callie told Veronique about her father. She repeated everything Jules had told her about a young Aurore and François, about François supporting his child without raising her. She explained her own thoughts about François possibly feeling ashamed and guilty that his love for Callie took his love from his child. Wanting children of her own and not being able to carry a child was heavy on her heart and Veronique reached her hand to soothe Callie. At that point, they both burst into tears and ended up looking at one another in a new way.

Veronique tried to force her confused emotions into order. "Callie, thank you for telling me; this means you are my stepmother, *oui?*" Her blonde hair swished across her face and she flicked it off one shoulder before leaning toward Callie. Her pale eyes glanced again at the photo of her father.

The smile that lit Callie's face at the thought, changed the day from shit to flowers with those few words. To think this beautiful child could have had two parents and a stepmother in the bargain was an amazing thought. Veronique didn't hate her after all, and her troubled spirit quieted.

"My mother and I will have a long conversation. And I will have the whole truth from her." She pinched the bridge of her nose and sniffed again.

"Try to remember she loved your father and when he brought me home to marry, imagine her pain. That pain has evidently stayed with her and grown into a great bitterness." Callie thought of the breach of contract letter again and cringed. "And one more thing, Veronique...You have much more than a stepmother to add to your new family." She grinned, all of a sudden excited, as anticipation raced through her.

"What do you mean?" She squeezed the handkerchief between her fingers, perplexed.

"Only a few steps away from us at this moment, is a woman named Cendrine Benoit who is your cousin. She has adorable twins named François and Bernadette and she will soon have another baby."

Veronique's breath caught. Joy bubbled in her laugh. And a golden smile filled her face. "Oh!" She hugged herself in delight.

"And grandparents, Veronique. They will all want to meet you and I promise they will love you." Callie laughed and finished with, "And I am so happy to be part of it."

The women hugged one another soundly.

***

Just after lunch that same afternoon, Jules stormed into the offices of *Armand and Dubois*. "Is she in, Colette?" He was past her desk and opening the door to his sister's office before her secretary could respond. The older woman started to stand in confusion, but he waved her back.

Aurore had her face buried in papers strewn across her desk. When he burst in, a look of annoyance crossed her face. When she saw who it was, she placed her hands on top of the papers. Her stomach had been in knots since she'd left the envelope, so she wasn't surprised to see him.

Jules put both hands on her desk, leaned toward her and stared in her face. "Do you think you are the only person betrayed by a false lover, Aurore? I thought ethics played a part in this office? You know I told you not to pursue that breach of contract issue and dammit, you sent the letter anyway! And you forged my signature too. I'm sure you realize the day he received it was the same day he ran his boat into a storm and died?" His face looked like thunder and his breath was ragged.

Aurore stared at him, the knots in her stomach growing from the size of a walnut to an orange. Her lips compressed and high color stained her cheeks. Seething, she ignored his questions and responded through clenched teeth, "I can't believe that woman has you under her spell too, Jules."

Her brother stood up straight and shook his finger at her. "Do not change the subject. We are talking about your conniving, underhanded use of the law. I know I had a right to send that letter but I did not want to do that," he snarled. "And I told you that!" His hair fell over his forehead and the veins in his neck stood out.

"I do not want Veronique to be friends with that woman. Sending the letter to François was necessary. He was wrong and you were right, so I made the decision to override your concerns as your lawyer and silent partner," she answered stolidly. When her dark hair slipped over her cheek; she pushed it behind her ear, smacked her lips and they stared at one another.

Jules sat in the chair hard and grunted when the springs embraced his butt. His eyes turned dark. "Speaking of Veronique, Aurore, I know you have blamed her for François not loving you all her sweet life. Personally, I don't know how she can love you at all. If you keep treating her like shit, you will lose her. I love you because you are my sister but right now, I do not like you at all. Stop meddling in our lives or I will tell your daughter everything!!" Jules whipped around, slammed his palms on her desk, and flipped the papers onto the floor before he slammed out.

***

When Callie knocked on the old mill house door, they heard little footsteps racing toward them. Callie grinned and raised her eyebrows toward Veronique. When the door swung open, Cendrine tried holding the twins back so the women could walk inside.

After kissing cheeks, Callie introduced Veronique to Cendrine who invited them to the table before making fresh coffee. Shooing the children into the side room, she flipped open their coloring books before rushing back to learn why Callie's face was animated with secrets.

Veronique nervously sat at the dining room table. Tears were gone, evaporated as if by an onrushing wind. The children pulled up chairs to their small wooden table by the window. They began coloring now that their guest had been properly welcomed and Veronique couldn't take her eyes off of them.

Cendrine served coffee and a plate filled with small sandwiches, fruit and chocolate candies on the side. She could tell there was something Callie was bursting to share. The young woman she'd brought with her looked familiar, but she couldn't remember meeting her previously. Surreptitiously watching Callie in a striped gray and black tunic and black long pants, Cendrine wondered what had put such a glow on Callie's face. After placing small sandwiches on the children's coloring table, she pulled up a chair.

Veronique watched Cendrine as a child would look at a new toy. Cendrine admired the way the young woman dressed, especially the bright scarf circling her neck. But she was curious, wondering why her black-clad feet nervously tapped the floor. She reached for a croissant sandwich.

Callie leaned forward and pulled Cendrine's hand across the table toward her. And then she reached for Veronique's and lifted her outstretched hand to cover Cendrine's. She laughed at Cendrine's face a moment, drawing out the suspense.

"Cendrine, I want to introduce you to your cousin, Veronique Armand." Her impish smile settled on her niece, willing her to respond with a smile. And she was not disappointed.

The surprise rocked her. "My cousin?" Her face showed her excitement. She glanced at Callie and then swiftly brought her face back to Veronique. Smoothing her hand over her belly, she leaned in to stare into Veronique's face. When the girl smiled at Cendrine, she knew the answer. Shock engulfed her. Despite knowing uncle François' daughter existed…seeing her in the flesh added so much more to the story.

"Uncle François….why did he never tell us?" She looked at Callie for help, lifting a hand to her trembling lips. "I hope so many shocks in the past few weeks do not stunt Lulu's growth."

Laughter erupted between the women and the children's heads popped up. "Bernadette and François, come meet your new cousin." Cendrine guided her children toward Veronique and lifted their hands to the girl's lap. When Veronique lowered herself onto the floor beside the children and kissed the cheeks of each child, Cendrine was touched beyond words. The tide of excitement carried her toward her next thought and Callie nodded, knowing she was thinking about her grandparents. The children returned to their lunch, trying to manage eating and coloring in their books without dropping either the sandwich or the crayon.

As they ate lunch, Callie watched the young women enjoy the newness of their relationship. Trying to fight the ominous despair in her stomach when she thought of the letter Aurore had left for her, the gloom remained and her stomach gurgled. *I only wanted to mentor a sweet young woman, a woman who could have been my own child. How could François have generated so much hate in one person? And how could he have ignored such a beautiful woman as his daughter? What was François really made of?* She bit savagely into the remaining corner of her croissant, not tasting the chicken salad stuffed inside.

She was staring into nowhere land when Veronique touched her arm. "Callie, I must now meet with my friend from the newspaper. And then I am going to see my mother," she said meaningfully.

Cendrine pulled her cousin into a fierce hug and laughed when Lulu chose that moment to kick Veronique, as if welcoming her newest cousin into the family. Veronique smiled and reached her hand to touch her cousin's belly, delighted and unbelieving how the day had progressed.

After Veronique left, Cendrine and Callie talked for a long time. "I will call *grand-pére* and *grand-mére*, but I want to tell them in person. Please come with me, Callie. I do not want to shock them. I know they will be very surprised, but happy to have a bit of uncle François.... She saw the look on Callie's face too late to stop the words. "Oh, Callie, forgive me…I…."

Callie shushed her. "It is all right, *ma chérie*. I have had more than three weeks to prepare for Veronique's appearance in your lives. It was bittersweet to learn François had a child. I admit that. And I was angry. Maybe I still am just a little. But, you know what? Instead of gloominess and doom, I made my mind right…because now I have a stepdaughter and we have another woman to share sparkling rosé with at family functions!"

Cendrine's arm swung around her aunt's neck and she kissed her loudly. So many events would surely bring her baby sooner than later, but she scrambled through the thoughts in her head like a squirrel on a limb.

"Call your grandparents and we will tell them before we introduce them to their new grandchild. You are right. A shock like this might knock them silly. I must Skype Livvy and Bram. I received an email to set up the time and Olivier wants to talk with me later today. I suppose I will just have to return later for that wine," she teased and turned toward the door.

Cendrine reached a hand out and pulled her aunt back a few steps. "Callie, are you sure you are all right with all this? You seem a little sad…" Cendrine wiped her hands down both legs of her jeans. After realizing she had jam on her fingers, she screwed up her face and said, "Argh…."

Callie laughed. "I am fine. Call them. I will see you later."

Back in the cottage, when Callie's face filled the Skype screen, Livvy knew instantly something was wrong but also recognized it wasn't open for discussion. When Callie's eyes wavered, Livvy turned toward Bram and pulled papers in front of her. "We had a wonderful drive to Algodonales, Callie. We met the owner of *Valeriano Bernal*. When we walked in, we loved the wonderful cozy smell of milled wood. There was a man playing a flamenco guitar in the store front and we saw flamenco guitars displayed on the walls. The owner is excited to hear young people will be able to enroll into an art colony to learn to play flamenco guitars. We didn't tell him anything except to ask if he'd be willing to be part of the endeavor. He was happy, happy, happy. Bram emailed the information to Olivier this morning."

"That must be why Olivier wants to talk with me tonight. Another free dinner and more wine, how could I not accept?" She smiled wanly.

"What's going on? When we left, you were sitting on a magic carpet. What's happened?" Livvy's emerald green and blue blouse was as bright as a peacock. Her forehead creased and her eyelashes swept upward. Callie could see her mind moving fast through all the possibilities. "Callie?"

"Just a little boulder in the pathway of my life," she said philosophically with a weary shrug. "Until I know more, let's leave it there, Livvy. Thanks for helping Olivier. I suspect he feels he's walking beside his father with this venture. He's so happy to be home, his feet haven't touched the ground since we found him." Callie offered the shadow of a smile.

At that moment, someone tapped on the cottage door and she flinched, tossed a kiss across the miles. "Must go, Livvy." Callie walked towards the door and saw, through the stained glass, the silhouette of a woman framed against the mid-day sun. As soon as Callie opened the door, Aurore Armand stepped past her, nudging her shoulder impatiently.

Twenty Nine

"Stay away from my daughter or you will be sorry you returned to France." Aurore spit the words out like hammered nails.

"Are you threatening me?" Callie snapped back, as her eyes bored into the woman who'd shared her husband's bed so many years ago. The woman who carried the child she'd always hoped for. Her face showed an exaggerated incredulity. The mad thought flashed through her mind that she should pound some sense into this woman. She visualized slapping her and not stopping for breath.

Aurore didn't answer. She let the silence build up and they stared out a tug of war that neither wanted to lose.

Callie blinked. "I can't quite believe you have come to my door." She licked her lips, feeling her nerves exposed. Then she remembered what she had told Veronique earlier. This woman had been spurned and used in the worst way and raised a child alone afterward.

Aurore turned her dark eyes on Callie. Looking at the smaller woman, she saw a silver swathe of hair drop across her forehead as dark hair swished at her chin line. Her hands were braced on her hips and anger seeped from every pore of her body. Aurore swallowed hard and felt a knife twist inside. "I will give you money to return to America. You would have a good life. Veronique is my life here and I will not share her with you."

Callie looked off toward the horizon, at the trees and the fields of grapevines. She turned to Aurore, who looked ready to bolt.

"Aurore. Have a seat. You and I have much to talk about."

Dumbfounded, the elegantly-dressed woman pulled herself up straight. Her short hair slid from behind her ear and she pushed it back with a shaking finger, nonplussed. Taking a deep breath, she stared at the woman she'd hated for more than twenty years. And as she sat down, dull resignation bloomed somewhere deep inside her.

***

Late that night, Callie had still not heard from Jules. She frowned and groaned. Lying on her bed, she curled into the pillows and hot tears left the edges of her eyes and ran down the side of her head. She remained still, feeling the stinging heat of her face. Several hours later, she still had not slept. Angrily, she closed her eyes tightly, not allowing any more tears to flow. One minute she was crying silently, the next she was sound asleep.

When she woke up the next morning, she thought about the breach of contract letter. She'd believed the worst. Why? That was totally against her nature. Maybe she thought sleep might have rearranged the words on the letter. She snorted. The dark knowledge that François had kept another secret from her stood her hair on end. She didn't want to know anything about it. And sleep had not made François' deceit any more clear. The facts were there. The day François was served the letter was the day he climbed into that boat and struck across the lake in a dark, roiling storm. The day he died. Jules did not force François into the boat that day. It was his choice.

Staring at the ceiling above her bed, she remembered the day clearly but at the time, hadn't understood the complexities. Betrayal was a dark word. She'd felt it in her gut when she first looked into Veronique's face, but something lovely had come from it for her. The betrayal Jules must have endured when his best friend sold him up the river must have been devastating too. *Now I know what Jules meant that day when he said François' rejection of Veronique was* one *of the reasons their friendship splintered.*

She sat up and everything turned blurry as the thoughts rushed into her head. Then she stood up as another thought bit into her brain. *What did François need that money for? We were quite comfortable. Oh, spit, there is still another secret flitting around out there in the great beyond. And do I really want to know what it is?* She ground her teeth in irritation and slammed her hand against the back of his favorite chair.

Exhaling deeply, she let her eyes move around the room, visualizing François sharing it with her. She tortured herself creatively, staring for minutes at the space above the deep chair cushion, the foot stool jammed against it, François sitting there sipping morning coffee near the window. Next, he was sitting on the edge of the bed, looking at her, with hooded eyes.

Then she pushed away her imaginings. Instead, she let a series of memories slide through her. François standing in the doorway adjusting his tie, slipping out of his shoes. When he studied papers at his desk at their home in Portland, pulled her on the water skis from their boat across the lake. Laughing at something she said, always laughing, never appearing to have troubles they couldn't handle together.

Callie screwed up her face, finishing the tableau with a final thought. *François was a great pretender.* Yes, he loved her but he had not shared his deepest concerns, his secrets or his soul. The François she had known was dead and so was the man she never knew at all. She must walk away from the pain in her mind and now her heart. He was gone and she couldn't ask him questions. She would make her life count for something, more than a sales manager at an insurance company, something special in Provence. She had returned home and her heart yearned to stay.

***

The night before, when Aurore had placed her key in the lock to slip inside the house, she found Veronique simmering drunkenly. Callinda had tried to prepare her for the onslaught, but nothing could have surprised her more when her daughter whipped herself up and stood nose to nose with her mother.

"I've been waiting for you for several hours, *Maman*. You weren't at the office when I showed up, so here I have waited." Veronique's pale eyes flicked in agitation from her mother's stunned face to the glass of wine in her hand. "Come, *Maman*, join me. I've just opened another bottle."

Aurore's eyes strayed to the empty bottle of wine on the side table and the half-empty one beside it. Her daughter's wine-soaked breath hit her in the face like a freight train. She removed her jacket in slow motion and lifted a stemmed glass from the side cupboard. Without a word, she slipped into the chair beside her daughter and lifted the glass. Veronique's hand shakily filled it nearly to the brim and she giggled, wiping the edge with her finger and sucking it loudly.

"Veronique, I want to….." She wasn't sure where to begin and wasn't sure she really wanted to, but she had no choice. She knew her daughter already knew about François. Her chest grew heavy and her misery was like a steel weight. She lifted her hand and let the glass's contents drift onto her tongue as she prayed for strength.

"Yes, *Maman*? You want to tell me something now? Maybe about my father who died before I was born? Or wait… maybe about the father who didn't die then, but died a few years ago? The one I could have known so I could have asked why he didn't want me? That one. Yes, tell me about the second one, since I found a photograph of him and you don't have any of the first one," she added with a snort of defiance. "How could you do this thing?!" Veronique glared at her mother and drank some of her wine.

"Veronique," Aurore repositioned herself on the chair, kicked off her shoes and curled her legs beneath her. She might as well get comfortable because she knew the girl would want to hear it all. Loosening her top button, she pulled her blouse loose and began the story she should have shared long ago. She could see that Veronique was like a volcano ready to erupt. She swallowed hard to stop herself from crying and pinched the cushion beneath her. She'd cried herself out so long ago, she didn't think she had any tears left, but now she wasn't so sure.

Veronique waited, infuriatingly tight lipped as her mother described a young girl chasing after her older brother's best friend. She did everything in her power to catch his attention but he went away to the university and forgot all about her. She pined for him and grew up in his absence. When he returned from the university, she knew by his face, that he liked the woman she'd grown into, blooming straight into womanhood. But again, he wasn't interested as much as she'd hoped, so she stretched herself. She made a picnic lunch and she'd dressed in the shortest skirt and highest heels she could walk in. And he'd noticed at last, once she'd slipped off her shoes and then he'd slipped off her skirt.

Veronique braced her chin on an upraised knee. "You seduced him." Her eyes were glazed and she finished off her glass. Shredded tissues littered the glass table, but she pushed them aside to reach for the wine bottle.

Aurore did not stop her, but continued with her story. "He didn't call me very often, so I called him. Still living at the old home place until he found his own apartment, his mother sometimes answered the phone. I could tell she was not happy but I was desperate. Sometimes he didn't return my calls and I blamed his mother. I was sure she hadn't told him. I kept after him and tried to snare him with the only thing I knew would work."

"Sex. You just…threw yourself at 'im…" Veronique was slurring and Aurore grimaced. "What man turns a willing woman away? You've told me that for years to warn me agains' men. You said a man will say anything to get you in bed to do the wild thing. You spoke from experience, *Maman*?"

"That is correct. We spent more time in bed naked than anywhere else. I was very angry when he went to America to work with one of his professors in California. I waited and waited. Jules told me over and over to forget him. When I missed my second period, I was happy because I…thought he would finally love me. But then, François returned from America with Callinda Augustine hanging on his arm. When I saw the way he looked at her, I wanted to kill myself and you with me."

Veronique sucked in her breath, her eyes glaring. Reaching up, she pulled her dark blonde hair away from her face and twisted it up on her head. "You wanted an abortion?" She was whispered, horrified.

"*Non*." No. "I wanted to die. You just happened to be inside me. He didn't want either of us. You see, I managed to catch him without his lover on his arm one day and told him I was carrying his child. He laughed nervously. I could tell he was sorry because he held me by the shoulders and looked at me seriously. He told me to give you all the love he could not because he was going to marry Callinda. That is when he also told me he would pay me money to raise you, but only on two conditions: You must learn to speak English as a second language and you must never know he was your father." Aurore swiped her nose with her wrist and looked around for a tissue. Sniffing, she said, "I always hated her. I'd watch them sometimes when they renovated that old mill house. When I'd hear them laugh or see him reach his arms around her, I kept dying little inches until I suppose I forgot how to love at all."

Veronique sat motionless. "*Maman*, you should have told me long ago. I met my cousin, Cendrine and her little children today. And I have grandparents….." Her eyes filled. "You should have…."

Aurore's eyes blazed. "No! He would not let me. I wanted to be everything to you. Even your uncle Jules was angry with your father…but now he hates me too. I tried to frighten Callie away this morning by giving her a letter to read. I knew it would make her very angry." Aurore lifted her glass and finished the red wine, shaking her head wearily. "I knew it was wrong, but I wanted her gone ---- back to America."

Veronique sat up and stared. "She didn't mention a letter to me. I like her very much, *Maman*. You must try harder because she is remaining in France and I have asked her to be a consultant for *Hybrid Designs*.

Aurore breathed deeply. "*Hybrid Designs*? That is the name of your new shop? Why do you call it hybrid?" She raised one of her shapely eyebrows and leaned forward for another glass of wine. Her voice had drifted into a hushed whisper.

Veronique poured wine into her mother's glass without spilling it this time and then sipped her own wine reflectively. "Because, *Maman*, it will be French interiors with a touch of America. I shall use my initials for my logo…." Veronique smacked her leg and wiped tears from her cheeks. "You did not give me a father and since I do not have his name, it will be *VA*, Veronique Armand…It would have been so wonderful if….."

Her daughter's simple words moved her. Aurore set down her glass and moved to the couch. When she opened her arms, Veronique tunneled in until her sobs turned to whimpers. Her mother rocked her and stroked her tawny hair. Aurore finally admitted she could be heart-broken, but hearts mend and without love she had nothing. Better to risk it than stay a dry and bitter person with no center.

Thirty

Olivier offered Callie the scalloped potatoes before twisting around to cut Bernadette's roast pork. François pulled at his father's shirt to remind him he was next and Olivier laughed. When he looked up and met Callie's bemused smile, he grinned.

"Tell me about this new cousin. Cendrine wants to rush over to *grand-père* and *grand-mère's* house to share the news. It is unbelievable that François had a child all these years. She sounds like a very nice person. Her mother is also, *non?*"

Callie and Cendrine laughed.

"We aren't sure yet…" Callie sheathed her inner feelings.

Olivier raised his eyebrows. "Callie, I received the email today from Bram and Livvy. She gave me information about the guitar shop in Algodonales and I have spoken with the attorney near Marbella. The ball is rolling, as you say." His eyes twinkled at her. He loved using Americanisms every chance he could.

She laughed.

"I have a great favor to ask of you. Since you will be staying in France…I am very happy you will be close to us again…" He hesitated before continuing. "Callie, do you speak Spanish?"

Surprised, she choked on her wine. Grabbing a napkin, she caught the drips on her chin. Her heart-shaped face turned to his with utter blankness. "No, not much, why?"

"Would you be open to learning the language?" He grinned.

Cendrine kicked him under the table. "Olivier, get on with it."

"The *José Luis Alonzo Foundation* needs a trustee to manage the financials. Also, the man in Algodonales speaks only a little English. Bram and Livvy took a translator when they met with him. He is very happy to work with us. But of course, we need to decide which person to sell those *Sueño España* brandy bottles to. There are two people interested."

Cendrine gently kicked at him again.

"Ouch!" He raised a red eyebrow and raised an arm in mock pain.

"What are you asking me, Olivier?" Still surprised at his question, she searched for a plausible explanation.

Olivier laughed at her expression and pulled his leg in to avoid getting kicked again.

"We would like you to be the trustee, Callie, and help us choose the buyer. It would mean spending some time in Spain. So, of course, speaking the language would be important."

She blew out a breath. "I may be too old to learn a new language. Would the timeline fit, since I'm returning to Oregon to sell both houses and training my replacement at Larkspur? The thought of brokering those beautiful bottles is exciting. Sometimes, I run my hands over my brandy bottle and talk to the Señorita riding her cork across its label."

Olivier studied her as he chewed his dinner.

Cendrine quieted the children.

Olivier eyed Callie and turned to give a Cendrine a look.

Pulling a chunk off the end of the warm baguette, Callie said, "I will think about it seriously, Olivier. When do you need my answer? I can't make promises until a few things in my life are cleared up. And I don't want to let you down."

"Take all the time you need. It's been seventy years already."

They laughed.

Later, the women swapped kisses on both cheeks. "Thank you for bringing Veronique into our lives, Callie. I will see you in the morning to tell...?" She watched her son jump off the chair. Rolling her eyes, she held her belly and turned to Callie.

"Absolutely. I'll be over about nine." Callie waved to the children, tossed a kiss to Olivier and left the house. As she followed the flagstones back to her empty cottage, she was blown forward by the sudden wind. It whipped around the grapevines and tossed the bougainvillea aside, nearly pulling it from its stake beside her door. Pushing inside and slamming the door, she steadied her breathing. She hadn't seen weather like this in some time and didn't like it. But, back in Oregon, she'd seen it all. Why was she surprised? She thought of her roses in Portland and the camellias and azaleas that would soon bud. The gardenia had died from too much rain, but the flowers were beautiful there. Would she miss them? Not really. She wanted to stay and regardless of her problems with Jules, she would do just that.

Leaning against the door, she glanced at the chair where she'd sat on Jules' lap the night before last. And then she walked across the room. She swallowed the despair in her throat and sat down, caressing the cushion with a heaviness centered in her chest.

Walking slowly into her bedroom, she stripped and stepped toward the shower. The past two days were unbelievable. First Jules finding that damned letter and then Veronique finding the photo of François and learning he was her father, meeting her cousins… Callie smiled as she relived the events, but then her face turned chalky. And then Aurore. Dammit, she could like the woman; she felt her pain. *I wish things could change.* When Aurore left after their heart-to-heart talk, Callie had held a germ of hope.

Flinging herself into the shower, she turned the water on hot, covered herself in soapsuds and rubbed herself raw. Turning her face to the water, she let it drench her hair, run in rivulets down between her breasts and flow down the drain. She stood there like a statue for some minutes before turning off the tap and grabbing her towel.

***

Just before six, Claude had limped into Jules' office on crutches. "Need your signature, Jules." His manager's freckled face was harried. Jules scribbled his name on the line and Claude was on his way again. Business was so busy, Jules' skull beat against his brain. He wondered what his life would have been like if he'd just followed in his father's footsteps. Vineyards. In retrospect, they appeared a hell of a lot more enticing than computers, software, hardware and breach of contract letters. *"Mon Dieu,"* He put his chin down on his chest and groaned.

The wind had picked up and tall trees swayed on the street, debris was flying and dogs were barking, playing havoc with the umbrellas on the nearby café tables. The waiters were hurrying to roll them down in order to save damage. He thought the wind and chaos matched his mood. Swiveling in his chair to face the dark window, Jules sat in his office with lead in his belly. He'd told his sister off and slunk away from Callie. He wondered if either of the women would ever give him peace again.

The dregs of emotions had followed since he'd left Callie yesterday morning. Then, after yelling at his sister who was still trying to hold her life together the only way she knew how, he'd slammed out of her office like an angry child. All day long, people had come in and out of his office until he wanted to scream. He needed a vacation. He thought about how long it had been since he'd taken off and left Claude in charge. Screwing up his face, he thought hard. He couldn't even remember when he'd skipped town last.

The wind buffeted the window, bringing his mind back to his present frustration. Damn, he loved the woman. He grabbed his jacket, locked his desk drawer and walked out of the building. The wind still kicked up debris around him as he neared his BMW and he had to hold his coat closed before it took off into the city plaza.

Callie shook out her wet hair and padded into the kitchen to turn off the lights, wearing a long Hawaiian dress that hugged her body. When she turned around, she saw headlights pull into the lane and a car screeched to a halt behind the cottage. Her heartbeat accelerated and her hand fisted against her chest.

When the pounding started against her door, she pulled it open so fast that Jules nearly fell inside. They stared at one another just a moment before she reached for him. "You, *monsieur*, are exactly the man I wanted to see walk through that door."

He looked at her with amused wonder. "Callie, I love you and I'll be damned if that stupid letter or François' ghost is going to stop me. So there it is." He leaned against the door and ran a hand through his windblown hair that fell over his forehead.

Without another word, she sagged against him, hungry for his nearness. With one hand, he smoothed her damp hair from her forehead and pulled her head back to look into her face. "You can't live without me, *oui?*"

"You *know* I can live without you," she sniffed, leaning her head against his shoulder for a moment. His chest rumbled and his arms tightened around her as he chuckled, and she could not resist a poorly aimed punch to his shoulder. She whispered, "But I don't want to, Jules."

His husky laughter charmed her.

He wrapped his arms around her until he could feel her heart thumping against his chest. Jules held her face between his hands and studied her closely before kissing her and pulling her down on the couch. "This was probably the longest day of my life, Callie. Work piled up and I didn't care. The employees came and went and I didn't care. It was ridiculous. I decided you weren't going to get away from me. We have a lot to talk about, but not now…" He kissed her again, slowly and thoroughly.

Callie adjusted herself securely in his arms and kissed his neck. "Well, now I guess I need your help again." She inhaled his scent and her belly flip flopped against her backbone.

"Did you lose another nephew?" He chuckled.

"Very funny. No. But I need to learn how to speak Spanish. Are you up to it?" She turned out the lights and let him guide her past the couch, down the hallway past her artwork and into her bedroom.

"I'm up for whatever you want, *mon amie*, why? He was slipping off his tie and toeing off his shoes, not really caring about Spanish at all.

"I'll tell you why later." Her voice changed and softened.

As they lay down on the bed and watched each other's faces, she wrapped her legs around his and reached up to kiss the tip of his nose. He pressed his body to her and inhaled the intense lavender soap she'd lathered over her skin. And no words were spoken except to whisper delight in one another.

"*Yo te quiero mucho,*" he whispered into her hair.

"Mmmmm…A Spanish lesson already?" She tugged his head toward her, flinching at the emotion in his voice.

He chuckled and then he embraced her until her breath whooshed out. "Yes, that means I want you very much." His breath was short and he could feel her warmth beneath him. Whether saying it in Spanish or French, he loved this woman. He wondered again, fleetingly, why she wanted to learn Spanish but when she curled herself around him and touched him, all thoughts fled.

***

The following morning, as always, Janine and Michel were delighted to see the twins race up the steps with Cendrine and Callinda following close behind them. Family was so important to them and having their daughter-in-law back in Pertuis filled them up. Michel pulled the children toward their toy box, lifted the small girl onto his lap and gazed up at the women with a look of pure joy on his face. When François used his great grandfather's leg as a road for his small car, the old man laughed, sure that life couldn't be any better than this. He was wrong, of course.

Cendrine's face could not contain her excitement. "Please tell them, Callie." She reached for her grandmother's hand and led her to a chair across from her grandfather.

The old people thought they'd had enough surprises for their lifetime until Callie started talking. With each word, their faces paled; their ears heard the words but their minds couldn't quite grasp them. It was as if her words sucked all the oxygen from the room. Janine gripped the upholstered arms of her chair, fighting a dizzying rush of disbelief while she stared at Callie.

"François had a daughter with Aurore Armand and never told us this?" Michel's face flushed the color of a boiled ham.

"*Oui*. I have met this beautiful child, explained to her what her uncle Jules told me and I have spoken with her mother. Your granddaughter's name is Veronique. She is twenty years old and just graduated from the Sorbonne with a diploma in interior design. She has leased a shop near *Gadoline's* and has asked me to help her. And I am delighted…"

Janine reached for Callie's hand. "Are you all right with this, *ma chérie?*" The creases around her eyes deepened as empathy fought with excitement. Pressing her daughter-in-law's hand to her own heart, she whispered, "Callinda, as we have always known, you are a brave and strong daughter. We do not want this wonderful news for us to be painful for you." The older woman fought tears as she stared into Callie's face.

Callie smiled, loving Janine more than she could possibly know. She squeezed her fingers. "Yes, she has decided I am her stepmother and I am happy about it….once the shock went away. Thank you, *Maman*."

Michel's face was still and he said not a word.

"She is having a grand opening in her shop. It is called *Hybrid Designs*….because she is offering French and American samples. She is very smart and I already love her. You will too, when you meet her." She reached for both of their hands and looked at them seriously. "*Maman* and *Papa*, I want to order a personalized banner for her new shop with the name of Beauvais and I ask your approval." Callie waited breathlessly.

Michel's voice filled the room. "But of course, she is a Beauvais and it should say so. Why her mother would deny us….Why François wouldn't tell us that…." His voice hitched, sounding broken.

Callie went to his side and hugged him closely. "*Papa*, François did not trust my love and evidently he didn't trust yours either. He did not realize the love of a parent for a child. I cannot understand it either. But this girl is a Beauvais and you will love her as I do. Please do not be angry at François. He made a bad decision. If I can forgive him, you can also, *oui?*"

The old man held Callie against him. "*Oui.*" He whispered into her hair. "But I am still angry."

Cendrine's face was wreathed in smiles. Rubbing softly against Lulu's kicking feet, she hugged her grandmother. No words were required and the planning began. A family reunion would fill the house with ribbons and good news once again. With the wedding just ending and two new grandchildren joining the family, Janine rubbed her hands together with enthusiasm.

"I want to meet her soon. Please bring her to us."

The next afternoon, Michel and Janine stood at the window with their veined hands clasped tightly. Michel pulled his wife away from the pale, wispy curtains and looked at her closely. "I am very angry at François and it is hard to forgive him for keeping this child from us all her young life. Without Callinda, we would not have this gift. I am not sure my old heart can take it." He held his pale hand to his chest and she reached over to kiss the back of it, feeling the veins with her lips.

And then Janine's gaze darted to the door. She struggled to breathe. Placing her fingers over her heart, her chest nearly too full to walk, she reached the door knob and turned to Michel. "My dear Michel, this is our François whispering hello and we will both forgive him as soon as we wrap our arms around this girl." She pulled open the front door as her stomach quaked and opened her arms to the young woman on the other side.

One week later, the grand opening of *Hybrid Designs* was splashed across the newspaper's front page in Pertuis. When Veronique's grandfather stared at the smiling photo of the young woman with dark blonde hair, he had wept.

The sidewalk was littered with potential business. Before she opened the doors, her extended family surrounded her inside for the first time. Aurore looked at Callie and nodded with an upraised eyebrow. Veronique was stunned to see them acknowledge one another. And she nearly fainted when her mother reached up, pulled the new banner off the *faux* wall, and crushed it between her fingers. .

Callie held up a hand to stop Veronique's rush toward her mother, surprising Veronique yet again. Unloosing a package beneath her own arm, Callie nodded toward Aurore, who wore a fragile smile on her face.

Jules watched in fascination as the women in his life each took hold of the ends of a new banner. The women stared at one another a moment before they lifted it upward, held it aloft and tacked it to the wall.

❧ VERONIQUE ARMAND BEAUVAIS ❧

❧ *HYBRID DESIGNS* ❧

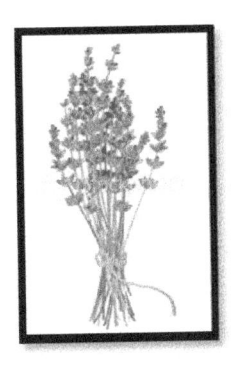

❧ Decidedly French ❧
With a Touch of America

Veronique's eyes leaked and she covered her face with her hands to stop the flow. Disbelieving, she whipped her face around toward her new grandparent's for approval. She was allowed to be a Beauvais in print?

Michel was leaning on a wooden cane. Janine held his arm. Both nodded firmly as tears rolled down their faces. Michel raised his free arm and lifted his wife's hand in the air. "Pour your cousin's pink sparkling rosé, *ma petite*, we will toast to your success…Your father would have been very proud of you. We know this." Janine leaned into his chest and sighed.

Aurore put her arm around her daughter and looked at Callie steadily. Not quite believing what had just happened, Veronique blinked moisture from her eyes.

Callie reached for Veronique's hand. "Remember, I told you I had a surprise for you? It wasn't the banner. That was your mother's and my surprise together. This is from me and I'm sure, your father would have agreed, regardless of the crazy choices he made. Callie pulled the small white box from her pocket and pinned a filigreed, gemstone bar to Veronique's scarf, anchoring its loops into place. Three large gold initials were woven through an intricate lace of shimmering grapevines, *V-A-B*.

Veronique's fingers lifted to touch the beautiful initial pin as Callie continued, "After a long discussion, your mother approved my new title." Callie and Aurore exchanged cautious smiles. "I am now officially your stepmother. It will not be easy for any of us to forgive your father, *ma chérie*, but we all agree that you are the sweetest gift he left behind."

Before Veronique could do any more than roll her fingertips over her new pin again and hug the women, it was time. Olivier got the nod and he opened the wooden framed, glass etched door with *Hybrid Designs* boldly painted in gold leaf.

Everyone stormed into Veronique's new shop, eager for a flute of Beauvais Cellars' wine and to meet the new owner of *Hybrid Designs*. Veronique caressed the pin again. With a peculiar, flippy jolt in her heart, she stood up straight as her mother had told her a hundred times, and smiled at Aurore's approving nod.

Jules looked at the women and closed his eyes, shaking his head in disbelief. When Callie and Aurore turned toward him, he thought his chest would explode. Would he never understand women? Did they change moods like flipping a light switch on and off? Could he possibly live without either of them? When his cell phone vibrated in his pocket, he ignored it. No business today. This was all about family.

Aurore walked toward him and kissed each cheek. "Thank you, Jules. You woke me up. I *have* been a real bitch. Callinda and I decided joining forces was better than killing each other. And I want you to like me again," she whispered. Having apologized, she walked regally toward the reception table, lifted a flute of pink sparkling rosé and let the silence filter in. Her crumpled dignity no longer seemed important.

Callie's eyes lifted to the new banner. Laughing as she relived the memory of François lifting the banner above her own shop, she sighed. As quickly as the laugh came, it went, and her face clouded.

In the short time she'd lived with her mother after her husband's death, mother and daughter had connected in a way that only the shared experience of pain and loss could produce. She'd gained wisdom and strength from their long conversations and the intimacy she felt with her mother before cancer snatched her away, was a treasure she still held close. She'd hoped for a child of her own, to feel that mother-love she saw in Millie Augustine's eyes. But it was not to be.

    She glanced at Veronique. Imagining her mother's soft stroke on her arm, the memory touched her, soft as a feather. Tears blurred her vision and a lump gathered in her throat. Overwhelmed with nostalgia for her mother, she found comfort in knowing that the daughter she would share with Aurore would have made her mother smile. She turned to swipe the tears away with her fingers and a movement, out of the corner of her eye, brought her head up. A reflection in the shop window wavered and the ghost of François looked at her through the glass. She nodded her head toward his daughter. When her eyes swung back to his image, she smiled a final good bye and walked across the shop toward Jules.

    Tracking little Bernadette and François with her eyes and watching *Maman* and *Papa* try to corral them made her laugh. And then she saw Cendrine, who was bursting at the seams with baby, draw her lips into a brilliant smile as she stared at her new cousin. Callie was wrapped in a silken envelope of exhilaration. She wasn't sure which list to begin first; learning to speak Spanish, pulling out her interior design hat or buying diapers for her new great nephew. Of course it would be a boy... And emptying both houses, meeting with a realtor, training someone for her job back in America, and then there was the lovely Jules. She raised her eyes to find him watching her.

    Jules pulled her toward him and said softly, "What is going on in that beautiful head of yours?" His gentle nudge brought her back from her daydreams. "You have made me very happy today. Seeing you with Veronique made me smile, but watching you with my sister was a miracle." When Jules saw the delicious smile spread across her face, he leaned down and whispered, "You said once, that if your lover's smile bent the wind that your love was real, remember?" His silver eyes softened and fixed on her unwaveringly.

    A tingling of excitement raced through her as his fingers trailed sensuously down her arm. Before she could say a word in response, he continued, "Well, the wind just bent for me, *ma chérie. Je t'aime.* I love you." He grinned and pulled her toward him with one arm, breathing in the lavender scent of her hair. "I cannot hold you close enough."

Callie's heart hammered, feeling Jules' body pinned to her side, as she reached her hand to caress his arm. "Jules…" She leaned her head back and gazed up into the faint light twinkling in his eyes, blushing at her own excitement. And then she sighed. With a pulse-pounding certainty, she whispered, "I love you too, Jules." There were no longer any shadows across her heart.

The End

Enjoyed this book? When you have a moment or two, and are so inclined, please jot down your thoughts and reactions in an honest review. Reviews are always welcome and really important to authors. The more reviews an independently published book has, the easier it is to market it and find new readers. Just go to the internet site where you purchased the book, click on the cover image and scroll down to "leave a customer review."

About the Author

Genealogist, family historian and fiction author Patricia Steele was born in Woodland, California and moved to Oregon when her mother remarried nine years later. Then she became a nomad as an adult, living in eight cities, five states and eleven houses before settling in Arizona closer to her roots. She speaks English and a touch of Spanish (which she learned from childhood and later through a visit to Spain with her brother and classes) and French which she learned before a trip to France. Her hobbies are gardening in pots of every color, traveling, being a grandmother to her six grandchildren and drinking wine as attested to in her cookbook, Cooking DRUNK.

Want some more of Patricia Steele's work for free?
Send an email with "Free Book" in the subject line

You can find out more about Patricia Steele and her other books at www.patriciabbsteele.com or you can email her at patricia@patriciabbsteele.com to receive notice of Patricia's newest releases by joining her mailing list.

Stop by and say hello at www.facebook.com/patriciabbsteele

Find other books by Patricia Steele at www.amazon.com/author/patriciasteele

CPSIA information can be obtained
at www.ICGtesting.com
Printed in the USA
FSHW020425200220
67194FS